PE

Bhisham Sahni was born _____ _____ ajist family in Rawalpindi (now _____ _____ school there, then went to Government College, Lahore, from where he took a Master's degree in English Literature. He returned to Rawalpindi to join his father's import business but finding the job too taxing, decided to teach at a local college. At the same time he also became involved in the activities of the Indian National Congress.

After Partition in 1947—his family settled in India and Bhisham Sahni took the last train to India—he settled down in Delhi and began to teach at a Delhi University college. His first collection of short stories, *Bhagya Rekha* (Line of Fate) was published in 1953. In 1957, Bhisham Sahni moved to Moscow to work as a translator at the Foreign Languages Publishing House. He worked in the USSR for nearly seven years during which time he translated several Russian books into Hindi. He returned to India in 1963 and resumed teaching in Delhi. He edited a literary journal, *Nai Kahaniyan* from 1965-67 and began working on *Tamas*, a novel based on his experiences as a young man, in 1971.

Bhisham Sahni won the Sahitya Akademi Award for *Tamas* in 1976. He also won the Distinguished Writer Award of the Punjab Government, the Lotus Award of the Afro Asian Writers' Association and the Sovietland Nehru Award. So far he has published seven novels, nine collections of short stories, six plays and a biography of his late brother, the actor and writer Balraj Sahni. Many of his books have been translated into various foreign and Indian languages. In 1998 he was conferred the Padma Bhushan by the President of India.

Bhisham Sahni lives in New Delhi.

Tamas

Bhisham Sahni

Translated from the Hindi by the author

PENGUIN BOOKS

Penguin Books India (P) Ltd., 11 Community Centre, Panchsheel Park, New Delhi 110 017, India
Penguin Books Ltd., 80 Strand, London WC2R 0RL, UK
Penguin Group Inc., 375 Hudson Street, New York, NY 10014, USA
Penguin Books Australia Ltd., 250 Camberwell Road, Camberwell, Victoria 3124, Australia
Penguin Books Canada Ltd., 10 Alcorn Avenue, Suite 300, Toronto, Ontario, M4V 3B2, Canada
Penguin Books (NZ) Ltd., Cnr Rosedale & Airborne Roads, Albany, Auckland, New Zealand
Penguin Books (South Africa) (Pty) Ltd., 24 Sturdee Avenue, Rosebank 2196, South Africa

First published by Penguin Books India 2001

Copyright © Bhisham Sahni 2001

10 9 8 7 6 5 3 2

Typeset in Aldine 401 by Abha Graphics, New Delhi
Printed at Chaman Offset Printers, New Delhi

This is a work of fiction, Names, characters, places and incidents either are the product of the author's imagination or are used fictitiously, and any resemblance to actual persons, living or dead, events or locales is entirely coincidental.

To Balraj, my brother

1

The clay lamp in the alcove flickered. Close to it, where the wall joined the ceiling, two bricks had been removed from the wall, leaving behind a gaping hole. With every gust of wind, the flame in the clay lamp quivered violently and long shadows flitted across the walls. But as soon as the flame steadied again, a thin line of smoke would rise from it in a straight line, licking, as it went, the side of the alcove.

Nathu was already breathless. He thought, perhaps it was his heavy breathing which caused the flame to quiver so violently. He slumped on the floor, his back resting against the wall. His eyes again fell on the pig. The pig grunted and put its snout to some sticky peel or rind in the garbage which littered the entire floor. With its pinkish snout, it had already licked Nathu thrice on his shins, causing him searing pain. At times the pig would begin walking along a wall, its eyes on the floor as though looking for something. It would then suddenly squeal and start running, its little tail curling and uncurling. Rheum, oozing from its left eye had trickled down its snout. Its bulging belly swayed from side to side as it walked or ran. By constantly trampling over the garbage, the pig had scattered it all over the floor and now a foul stench from the garbage, the pig's heavy breathing and from the pungent smoke of the linseed oil burning in the clay lamp pervaded the room making it unbearably stuffy.

Though drops of blood lay spattered on the floor, the pig did not seem to have received a scratch on its body. It was as if for the last two hours Nathu had been plunging his knife into water or a heap of sand. He had struck the pig several times on its belly and shoulders, but on pulling out the knife, only a few drops of blood would ooze out and trickle down to the floor. There was no trace of any wound or stab. A thin, red line of a scratch or a tiny blot were the only visible signs of his efforts. Every now and then, with an angry grunt, the pig would either rush towards Nathu's legs or begin running along a wall. Nathu's blade had not gone beyond the thick layers of fat to reach the pig's intestines.

Why of all the creatures, Nathu thought, had this despicable brute with its fat, bulging body, a snout covered with thick white hair like that of a rabbit's, thorny bristles on its back, fallen to his lot to tackle?

Nathu had once heard someone say that in order to kill a pig, one should, first of all, pour boiling water on it. But where was he to get boiling water from? On another occasion, one of his fellow-chamars, while cleaning a hide, had casually remarked, 'The best way to kill a pig is to catch it by its hind legs, twist them hard and turn the pig over on its back. While it is struggling to rise, one should cut open its jugular vein. That will finish off the pig.' Nathu had tried all the devices but not one had worked. Instead, his shins and ankles were badly bruised. It is one thing to clean a hide, it is quite another to slaughter a pig. He cursed the evil moment he had agreed to do the job. Even now, had he not accepted the money in advance, he would have pushed the damned creature out of the hut and gone home.

'The veterinary surgeon needs a pig for his experiments,' Murad Ali had said, as Nathu stood washing his hands and feet at the municipal water tap after cleaning a hide.

'A pig?' Nathu had exclaimed, surprised. 'What am I to do with it?'

'Get one and slaughter it,' Murad Ali had said, 'There are many pigs roaming around the nearby piggery, push one into your hut and kill it.'

Nathu had looked askance at Murad Ali's face.

'But I have never killed a pig, Master. If it were flaying an animal, or cleaning a hide, I would have been glad to do it for you. But killing a pig, I am sorry, I have never done it. It is only the people in the piggery who know how to do it.'

'Why should I come to you then knowing that the piggery people can do it? You and you alone shall do this job.' And Murad Ali had shoved a rustling five-rupee note into his pocket.

'It is not much of a job for you. I couldn't say no to the vet sahib, could I?' said Murad Ali, then added rather casually, 'There are any number of pigs roaming about on the other side of the cremation ground. Just catch one of them. The vet sahib will himself do the explaining to the piggery people.'

And before Nathu could so much as open his mouth, Murad Ali had turned round to leave. Then, stroking his legs softly with his thin cane stick, he had added:

'The job must be done this very night. At dawn the jamadar will come with his pushcart and take the carcass away. Don't forget. I shall tell the fellow myself to take it to the vet sahib's residence. Understand?'

Nathu had stood with folded hands. The rustling five-rupee note that had gone into his pocket had made it impossible for him to open his mouth.

'People living in this area are mostly Muslims. If anyone sees it, there can be trouble. So be careful. I too don't like getting such jobs done. But what to do? I couldn't say no to the vet sahib.' And flapping the cane against his legs, Murad Ali had left.

Nathu could not refuse either. How could he? He dealt with Murad Ali almost every day. Whenever a horse or a cow or a buffalo died anywhere in the town, Murad Ali would get it for him to skin. It meant giving an eight-anna piece or a rupee to Murad Ali but Nathu would get the hide. Besides, Murad Ali was a man of contacts. There was hardly a person, connected with the Municipal Committee, with whom he did not have dealings.

Waving his thin cane stick and walking jauntily along the road, Murad Ali was a common sight in the town. He would suddenly appear in one or another of the lanes or by-lanes. Everything about him, his swarthy face, his bristling, black moustaches, his small, ferrety eyes, the knee-length khaki coat he wore over a white salwar, even the turban on his head, all combined to make him look distinctive. Without any of these, even without his thin cane stick, or the well-bound turban, he would not be what he was.

Murad Ali had left after issuing his instructions, leaving Nathu in a tight spot. How was he to catch hold of a pig? At one time he had even thought of going straight to the piggery which stood on the outskirts of the town and telling the folks there to get a pig slaughtered and have it sent to the veterinary surgeon. But he could not so much as lift his foot in the direction of the piggery.

It had not been easy to draw the pig into the hut. The pigs were there, roaming about and sniffing at the rubbish that lay around. But it was a different matter altogether to lure one into the hut. All that Nathu could think of was to carry armfuls of wet hay and put it in piles outside his dilapidated hut.

Three straying pigs, wandering along dung-heaps and pools of stagnant water, chanced to come towards his hut. One of them sauntered into the courtyard and began sniffing at the pile. Nathu promptly shut the gate behind him. He then ran across the courtyard, opened the door of the hut, and picking up his lathi, drove the pig inside. Fearing that someone from the piggery might come that way and become suspicious on hearing the grunts of the pig, Nathu carried an armful of wilted hay into the hut and made small piles of it on the floor. The pig was soon absorbed in picking at the piles and Nathu, greatly relieved, came out and sat in the courtyard to have a quiet smoke. He smoked one bidi after another and waited for night to fall. When, at last, he went inside it was already dark. But what he saw in the unsteady light of the clay lamp, made his heart sink. The entire floor was littered with rubbish and a foul smell filled the room. As his eyes fell on the ugly, bloated pig, Nathu cursed himself for having taken on so repulsive and hazardous a task. He was half-inclined to throw open the door and drive the despicable creature out.

And now it was past midnight. The pig was still strutting about leisurely in the midst of the rubbish littered on the floor. All that Nathu had achieved was a few drops of blood on the floor, a couple of scratches on the pig's belly, and a few nasty bruises on his own shins where he had been butted by the pig's snout. Panting for breath and sweating profusely, Nathu could see no way out of the mess into which he had landed.

Far away, the tower-clock in the Sheikh's garden struck two. Nathu stood up, nervous and perplexed. His eyes fell on the pig standing in the middle of the room. It urinated, and as though irritated by what it had done, began running along the right-hand wall of the hut. The wick in the clay lamp spluttered and long shadows swayed eerily across the walls. Nathu's situation had not changed a whit. The pig, its head bent, would now and then stop to sniff at some bit of rubbish, then resume walking along a wall, or grunt and start running, its thin little tail curling and uncurling itself like an insect.

'This won't do,' muttered Nathu, grinding his teeth. 'It is beyond me to kill a pig. This damned pig will be my undoing.'

It occurred to him to try turning the pig over on its back by twisting its hind leg. He slowly moved towards the middle of the room, his left hand aloft, holding a dagger. The pig, which was walking along the left-hand wall, on seeing Nathu, stopped in its tracks and instead of breaking into a trot, turned and started walking towards Nathu. It grunted menacingly. Nathu slowly stepped back, his eyes on the pig's snout. Both confronted each other. The pig advanced towards Nathu, making it impossible for the latter to catch hold of its hind legs. The pig's eyes looked red with rage. Who could tell what the pig was up to? Nathu was losing his nerve. It was already past two in the morning. There was little chance that the job over which he had been straining so hard since last evening would be done before daybreak. The sweeper would be there with his push-cart, and Murad Ali would turn from a friend into a bitter enemy. Anything could be expected of him if the job was not done. It could mean the end of getting hides to clean; the fellow could have him evicted from the premises he was occupying, get him thrashed by a goonda and harass him no end. Nathu felt extremely nervous. He feared that even if he succeeded in catching the hind legs of the pig, the pig might kick him and free itself.

Suddenly a wave of anger rose within him and he felt furious. 'It is now or never for me,' he muttered and turning around picked up a slab of stone lying on the floor below the alcove. Holding it high over his head, he came and stood in the middle of the room. The pig was sniffing at the rind of a watermelon close to its forelegs, its bloodshot eyes blinking and its little tail swishing. 'If it does not move,' thought Nathu, 'and the slab falls pat on it, it may break a bone or two or maybe one of its legs. That too will be something. At least the damned creature will not be able to walk.'

Balancing the slab in his hands Nathu threw it down with all his might. The flame in the clay lamp trembled and shadows flitted across the walls. The slab fell on the pig with a loud thud. Nathu stepped back and looked hard at the pig. It was still blinking its small eyes and its snout still rested on its forelegs. Nathu could not say whether the slab had caused any injury.

The pig grunted and began to move, its bulky frame swaying. Nathu stepped aside and crept close to the door opening into the courtyard. In the quivering light of the clay lamp, the pig appeared to be moving like a dark shadow. The slab had hit it on the forehead, due to which, it seemed to Nathu, its vision had been affected. The pig was heading towards Nathu, and fearing that he might be attacked, Nathu opened the door and rushed out of the hut.

'What a nasty trap I am caught in,' moaned Nathu as he came and stood by the low wall of the courtyard.

The cool fresh air brought him some relief. It caressed his sweating body and rejuvenated him. 'To hell with all this! I care a damn whether the vet gets the pig or not. I am through with the whole business. Tomorrow I shall hand back the five-rupee note to Murad Ali and with folded hands tell him that I couldn't do the job, that it was too much for me. The fellow will be cross for a few days but I shall manage to bring him round.'

He stood by the low wall and waited. The moon had risen and the entire area around bore a mysterious and unfamiliar look. The mud-track in front of the hut which, during the day, resounded with the creaking of bullock-carts and the jingle of bells round the bullocks' necks was now silent and deserted. Deep fissures had been cut into the road by the rolling wheels which had ground the soil into powdery dust so deep that if an unwary person walked into it he would find himself knee-deep in fine dust. On the other side of the road was a sharp slope that descended to the flat ground. It was strewn with dust-laden thorny bushes which, under the light of the moon, looked washed and clean. At some distance was the cremation ground with two mud huts, one of which was occupied by the caretaker. There was no light burning in them. The caretaker had got drunk the previous evening and had babbled away till late in the night, but now all was silent. Nathu suddenly thought of his wife, who would be sleeping peacefully at this moment in the colony of the chamars. Had he not got into this mess, he too would have been in bed beside her, her buxom body in his arms. Suddenly he felt an intense longing to hold her in his arms. She must have waited for him, God knows for how long. He had come away without telling her anything. And now he missed her terribly, even though he had been away from her for hardly a few hours.

The dusty track, after some distance, turned towards the right and sloped downward. A little removed from the track stood a country well, which too, with its wheel and string of pots looked quite picturesque in the light of the moon. At some distance, the track joined the metalled road going towards the city, turning its back, as it were, on the lonely, flat, deserted area.

Far away, towards the left, stood the piggery, while all around was a vast, barren tract of land, with thorny bushes and stunted trees growing here and there. Far into the distance, hours of walking distance away, stood rows of military barracks, one long row behind the other.

Nathu felt weak and limp. How he would have loved to rest his head against the low wall and gone to sleep.

Coming out of the hut had been like stepping into a different world, bathed in moonlight, with a cool breeze blowing. He felt like crying over his nightmarish situation. The dagger in his hand looked odd and irrelevant. He felt like running away from it all. The next day the purbia would come looking for the pig and, on seeing the scattered hay, would locate the pig inside the hut and drive it back to the piggery.

Nathu thought of his wife again. His troubled mind would find comfort only when he lay by her side and conversed with her in soft, confiding tones. He longed for the torture to end and to go back to the haven of his tenement in the chamars' colony.

The tower-clock struck three causing Nathu to tremble from head to foot. His eyes turned to the dagger in his hand. The thought of his predicament and the fate that awaited him was like a stab of pain. What was he doing here when the pig was still alive? The sweeper would be here any minute. What would he tell him? A faint, yellowish tint had already streaked the inky darkness of the sky. Dawn was breaking and his task was far from over.

In desperation he turned towards the hut. He opened the door softly and peeped in. In the dim light of the clay lamp, the pig lay motionless in the middle of the room. It looked tired and exhausted. 'It should not be difficult now to kill the beast,' thought Nathu. He shut the door behind him and came and stood under the alcove, his eyes on the pig.

The pig lifted its snout which had turned red. Its eyes appeared to have shrunk. Behind it, at some distance, lay the stone slab which had been thrown upon it. The flame in the clay lamp flickered again and in its unsteady light Nathu thought the pig had stirred. He stared hard at it. The pig had actually moved. It walked ponderously towards Nathu. It had hardly taken a couple of steps when it staggered and emitted a strange sound. Nathu, with his dagger raised high, sat down on the floor. The pig took another couple of steps when its snout drooped to its feet, and before it could move further, it suddenly fell down on its side. There was a violent tremor in its legs and they soon stiffened in midair. The pig was dead.

Nathu put the dagger down. Just then, far away, in some house, a cock fluttered its wings and crowed. Soon after, a jolting pushcart came creaking on the dusty track. Nathu heaved a sigh of relief.

2

At the start of the prabhat pheri, before daybreak, only a handful of Congress activists would be present. But as it advanced and passed through lanes and by-lanes, whosoever lived en route would step out of his house yawning and scratching his belly, and join in.

It was the fag-end of winter: the air was dry and people still slept inside, swathed in blankets. Quite a few elderly people in the prabhat pheri were wearing woollen caps.

The clock-tower in the Sheikh's garden struck four. In front of the Congress office, three or four people stood waiting for their compatriots. Two constables from the Intelligence Department were already there standing on one side at some distance.

Just then a glimpse of light was seen far away. A man with a hurricane lamp had turned the corner of the Bara Bazaar and was coming towards the Congress office. The light of the lamp fell only on the man's legs so it seemed as though only a pair of pajamas was walking along.

'Here comes Bakshiji,' exclaimed Aziz recognizing the pajamas.

Bakshiji was a stickler for punctuality. 'Four o'clock means four o'clock,' he used to say. 'Not a minute past nor a minute to.' But on that day he was late.

Yes, it was Bakshiji, the thickset secretary of the District Congress Committee. His presence was essential to the programme.

As he drew near, Aziz greeted him by reciting a satirical couplet:

> The mullah, the preacher and the
> torch-bearer—all have one thing in
> common—they show light to others while
> themselves walk in darkness.

'I got up late because I slept late last night,' Bakshiji explained apologetically. Then, after the usual exchange of courtesies, suddenly remarked, 'But where is Master Ram Das? Hasn't he arrived?'

To this too Aziz answered, 'He will come after he has milked his cow. He can't come earlier.'

'He used to come running even at midnight when he wanted a raise in his salary. Now that he has got it, why should he bother about coming on time?'

In the surrounding darkness, a tall man, dressed in white, was seen coming up the slope from the side of the Naya Mohalla.

'Here comes piety personified,' remarked Aziz. 'Doesn't Mehtaji look every inch a leader?'

As he arrived, Mehtaji looked around and on noticing the absence of Ajit Singh, Shankar and Master Ram Das, turned to Bakshiji and said, 'Didn't I tell you not to fix so early an hour for the prabhat pheri? Four o'clock is too early.'

'It is only when you call the members at four o'clock can you expect the prabhat pheri to start at five o'clock,'

Bakshiji answered. 'Had I fixed five o'clock as the time, they wouldn't have been here even after sunrise. And how does it matter to you, Mehtaji, when you yourself are so late?' Bakshiji said and put his hand under his shawl to take out a packet of cigarettes from his waistcoat pocket.

'From a distance you look every inch a leader, Mehtaji.'

A condescending smile flickered on Mehtaji's lips. Putting his hand on Aziz's shoulder, he said, 'The other day I was standing at the taxi stand when I overheard someone ask another person, "Is that Jawaharalal Nehru standing there?"' Giving a little tilt to the Gandhi cap on his head, he added, 'Many people make this mistake.'

'You are in no way less great Mehtaji. You have a personality all your own.'

'I am slightly taller than Jawaharlal,' Mehtaji said.

'Did you take a bath before coming here, Mehtaji?' put in Kashmiri Lal.

'What a question to ask! As a rule I always take a bath before coming out, summer or winter. And it is a must so far as the prabhat pheri is concerned. Tell us about yourself, Kashmiri Lal, did you even wash your face?'

Just then someone's voice was heard from the direction of the slope: 'Left...left...right, left...left...'

Everyone laughed.

'Here comes the Jarnail,' said Bakshiji.

As the Jarnail (colloquial for General) arrived, the light from the hurricane lamp fell on his tattered shoes. It was difficult to make out whether what he was wearing was a pair of slippers or shoes. Nearly six inches above his shoes, appeared the lower end of his khaki trousers.

A crumpled khaki coat hung over his emaciated body. It was covered with innumerable medallions and badges of Gandhi and Nehru along with ribbons and strings of diverse colours. He had a sparse greying beard and wore a dark-green turban on his head.

The Jarnail was the only one among the Congress activists who courted imprisonment irrespective of whether a movement was on or not. He went about making speeches all over town and took a roughing-up every other day. But that did not deter him. A thin cane stick under his arm, he would be seen 'marching' in one street or another. Whenever an announcement regarding a public meeting was to be made, and a tonga went round the town for the purpose, he would be the one sitting in the back seat, beating the drum. And when a meeting took place, he would be the first to jump on to the dais to address the gathering in his hoarse, husky voice, hardly audible even to the first row of listeners.

As the Jarnail drew near, Kashmiri Lal made a dig at him, 'Jarnail, why did you run away from the public meeting yesterday?'

The Jarnail peered hard into the darkness and on recognizing Kashmiri Lal by his voice, tucked his cane stick under his arm and shouted, 'I don't want to have any truck with fellows like you early in the morning. You'd better keep out of my way.'

Bakshiji turned to Kashmiri Lal, 'This is no time for your tomfoolery, you had better keep quiet.'

But the Jarnail was already furious, 'I shall expose you and your doings. You keep the company of communists. I saw you with my own eyes, eating sweets at the hunchbacked sweetmeat-seller's shop, in the company of that communist—Dev Datt.'

'Enough, enough, Jarnail. Don't expose him further,' said Bakshiji, trying to pacify him.

Just then Shankarlal arrived, his loose wide pajamas flapping.

Dawn was breaking. Tints of yellow and orange coloured the sky. From the high wall of the bank building another layer of darkness had been peeled off. Across the road, smoke was already rising from the open furnace of the sweetmeat-seller's shop located in the Arya School building. Now and then, men emerged for their morning walk, coughing and pattering the ground with their walking sticks. Here and there a woman, her head and shoulders heavily covered, made her way to a temple or a gurudwara.

Bakshiji, lifting the hurricane lamp close to his face blew into it and put out the light.

'Why has the lamp been extinguished? And that too on my arrival, Bakshiji?'said, Shankar, the man who made announcements regarding public meetings.

'Why, do you want to look at my face or Mehtaji's?' Bakshi said, 'I cannot afford to waste oil. The lamp does not belong to the Congress Committee, it is my personal property. Get the oil sanctioned by the Congress Committee and I shall keep the lamp burning day and night.'

At this Shankar, who was standing behind Kashmiri Lal, commented in a low voice, 'When no sanction is needed for your cigarettes, why should one be required for kerosene oil?'

Bakshiji had heard Shankar but swallowed the bitter pill. It was demeaning to talk to such 'loafers'.

'You are the boss, Bakshiji. Even a sparrow cannot flap its wings without your permission. What do you need a sanction for?' said Shankar, then turning towards Mehtaji said, 'Jai Hind, Mehtaji. Forgive me. I did not see you.'

'Why should you take notice of us poor folks, Shankar? You are fortune's favourite these days.'

'Where is your bag, Mehtaji, by the way? You are not carrying it today.'

'Who needs a handbag on a prabhat pheri, Shankar?'

'Why, it is a handy thing. A client can be trapped at any time.'

Mehta kept quiet. Besides Congress work Mehtaji did insurance business.

'Why can't you keep your mouth shut sometimes, Shankar? Mehtaji is thrice your age. You must have regard for age.'

'I didn't say anything offensive. I didn't ask him whether he had succeeded in bagging the fifty-thousand-rupee insurance policy from Sethi.'

Shankar had shot the arrow. Generally the fellow was not given to talking in oblique, insinuating terms. He was a blunt, outspoken person. The reference to the fifty-thousand-rupee policy, however, was hitting below the belt.

Mehta squirmed. He had spent sixteen years of his life in jail and was the President of the District Congress Committee. He was always dressed in spotless white khadi. To level such an accusation was unmannerly, to say the least. But a rumour had been gaining ground that he was about to secure a fifty-thousand-rupee insurance policy from Sethi, a contractor, in lieu of which, Mehta would help him secure the Congress ticket for the next General Elections.

'He is a wag, Mehtaji, don't listen to what he says.'

'I never said that Mehtaji has promised to get him the ticket. Only the Provincial Committee has the authority to do that. The District Congress Committee can only make recommendations. Of course, if the president and the Secretary of the District Committee come to a secret understanding, it is a different matter. And both are present here, listening to what I am saying. If big contractors succeed in getting tickets in this manner, it will spell doom for the Congress.'

Mehtaji moved away and struck up a conversation with Kashmiri Lal. Bakshiji lit another cigarette. The fact of the matter was that Shankar and Mehta did not get along with each other. They had fallen apart ever since Mehtaji had struck off Shankar's name from the list of district representatives for a conference to be addressed by Pandit Nehru in Lahore. Ever since then Shankar had looked upon Mehtaji as his sworn enemy. Shankar had, nonetheless, gone to Lahore on his own and attended the conference. He had also attended the lunch meant exclusively for the delegates. The District Committee, on behalf of its members, was required to pay a nominal subscription for lunch, but Mehtaji had declined to pay for Shankar. At the lunch party, Shankar had made it a point to sit right opposite Mehtaji. He had gobbled the food like a hungry wolf, shouted at the volunteers serving the guests and, in general, caused much embarrassment to Mehtaji. When asked by Mehtaji to mind his manners and not bring disgrace on the District Committee, Shankar had retorted, 'Keep your advice to yourself, Mehtaji, I am eating from my own pocket. I shall settle scores with you when we go back home.'

'What will you do to me when we are back home? You are nothing but a babbler.' Mehtaji had asked.

On their return from Lahore, Shankar had succeeded in playing his master-stroke. The elections to the Provincial Congress Committee were at hand and every District Committee was required to send four representatives. Mehtaji had proposed Kohli's name as the fourth representative. He would certainly have been elected had Shankar not spoken out. The meeting of the Scrutiny Committee was on, when Shankar suddenly stood up.

'Excuse me, I have a question to ask.' Mehta felt alarmed. He realized that Shankar was spoiling for trouble and said, 'This is the meeting of the Scrutiny Committee. You can put your question to me later.'

'It is to the Scrutiny Committee that I want to address my question,' Shankar said, standing in a theatrical pose waiting for the Chairman's ruling.

'What is your question?' asked the Chairman.

'I wish to know the rules for the nomination of candidates.'

'Come to the point. This is not the time to discuss irrelevant things.' Mehtaji had retorted, only to be snubbed by Shankar's, 'Please keep quiet, Mehatji, I am not talking to you.'

'Let him speak,' said the Chairman. 'Son, you want to know the rules of the Congress membership? Well, a member is required to pay an annual subscription of four annas, ply the spinning wheel daily and wear clothes made from handspun, handwoven cloth...'

'That is so,' said Shankar, adding, 'Now may I ask Mr Kohli to stand up for a minute?'

There was silence on all sides.

'Excuse me, but everyone has the right to seek clarification from the Scrutiny Committee.'

At which Mehtaji grunted.

'Mehtaji, you do not have to play the high and mighty here. My queries are addressed to the Chairman of the Scrutiny Committee.' Then turning to Kohli, 'Yes, Mr Kohli, will you stand up for a minute?'

Kohli stood up.

'You wear khadi, don't you?'

'What's all this? Get to the point. What is it you want to know?'

'Can I see the cord with which you have tied your pajamas?'

'The fellow is being rude to an honourable member. What nonsense is this?'

'Please keep out of this, Mehtaji. You have no right to speak without the Chairman's permission. Now, Mr Kohli, I would ask you again to show me your pajama cord.'

'What if I don't?'

'You have to. The cord must be shown so that I can prove my point.'

'Show it, Kohli yaar. This good-for-nothing will not let us get any work done, otherwise. All kinds of riff-raff have come into the Congress.'

'What did you say, Mehtaji? That I am riff-raff and you are a gentleman? Don't force me to speak. I know black from white well enough. Yes, Mr Kohli... I don't want you to untie your pajamas. Only show us the cord with which you have tied them.'

'Show it, Kohli. Get it over, otherwise this man will...'

Kohli lifted his khadi kurta. Below it, a yellow cord was hanging.

Shankar leapt forward and caught the cord. 'See gentlemen. The cord is made of artificial silk. It is not handspun cotton.'

'So what? What if it isn't? It is only a cord.'

'It is incumbent on a Congress member to wear khadi. That he should be wearing an artificial silk cord compromises the principles the Congress stands for. And you propose to send his name as candidate for the Provincial Committee?'

Members of the Scrutiny Committee looked at one another. They were forced to strike out Kohli's name. Since that day, Mehtaji could not bear the sight of Shankar.

Bakshiji was becoming restless. Neither Ram Das nor Desraj had turned up. Who would lead the singing? There had to be at least one person who sang well. If neither came, then Bakshiji would manage it himself somehow, but then, those who were paid for the job were expected to be more responsible.

'I can tell you what will happen, Mehtaji,' Bakshiji said. 'When we have already covered three lanes, Master Ram Das will come running. "The calf had sucked all the cow's milk." That's the excuse he will make. That is how these people work.' Then, turning to the other members, he added, 'We can't go on waiting indefinitely. Let's start. Kashmiri Lal, you lead the song.'

Kashmiri Lal, who enjoyed pulling people's legs turned to Jarnail and said, 'We must have a speech, Jarnail. Come on, give us a speech.'

Nothing suited the Jarnail better. Waving his cane and marching military-style, he went and climbed up a stone by the roadside.

'What nonsense is this, Kashmiri? What are you up to?' shouted Bakshiji. 'There is a time for everything. If you don't want the prabhat pheri, tell us so.' Then he turned towards the Jarnail, but the latter had already begun his speech, 'Sahiban...'

'No Sahiban business. Come down!' shouted Bakshiji. 'Get him down, someone. Why are you out to make a tamasha of the whole thing? Making a public exhibition of ourselves early in the morning.'

'No one in the world can silence me,' the Jarnail said, commencing his speech. 'Sahiban...' he again said, in his grating, hoarse voice.

The Jarnail was a middle-aged man of fifty years or so, with a worn-out, emaciated body—the result of long spells of imprisonment as a political prisoner. Whereas other Congress activists would invariably be given 'B' class cells, he would be huddled into 'C' class cells, which meant, among other things, eating food mixed with sand. But the Jarnail neither relented, nor took off his self-designed 'military' uniform. During his younger days, he had attended the Congress session in Lahore as a volunteer. There the famous resolution calling for full Independence had been proclaimed. The national flag had been unfurled on the banks of the Ravi and Pandit Nehru had danced with joy along with other activists. The Jarnail too had been one of them. Ever since then, he had always worn his volunteer's uniform. As and when he had money, additions would be made to the uniform, a whistle, or a few more badges or a new string the colours of the national flag. But, in general, the uniform was crumpled and unwashed. The Jarnail never did any work, nor could he have secured one. He received a sum of fifteen rupees every month from the Congress office as propagandist's fee. If Bakshiji was not prompt in making the payment, the Jarnail would then and there, come out with a long speech. A passion had gripped his soul, and on the strength of that passion he was able to bear the troubles and tribulations of life. He had neither a home, nor a wife or child, neither a regular job, nor a regular roof over his head. Two or three times a week he would be roughed-up somewhere or the other in the town. Every time there was a lathi-charge by the police, while other activists would manage to get away to safer places, he would bare his narrow, shrivelled chest and get his ribs broken.

'Get him down, Kashmiri Lal; why are you out to create a scene?'

It was Mehtaji who had shouted this time. But the Jarnail became all the more adamant.

'Sahiban, I am sorry to say that the President of the District Congress Committee has betrayed the country. We shall live up to the pledge we took on the banks of the Ravi in 1929 to our last breath. Without taking much of your time, all I would say is, no man is born yet who can flout the rules of the Congress. Mehtaji is a nobody. We shall deal with him and his sycophants, namely Kishori Lal, Shankar Lal, Jit Singh and such other traitors.'

There was a guffaw of laughter.

'He won't come down like this,' whispered Kashmiri Lal, who had started this mischief, to Bakshiji. 'The more we try to stop him, the more adamant he'll get.' And Kashmiri Lal stepped forward and clapped his hands. Others followed suit.

'Fine, well said, Jarnail! Wonderful!'

'Sahiban, I am thankful to you for giving a patient ear to my stray thoughts. Not taking much of your valuable time, I would like to assure you that the day is not far when Hindustan will be free. The Congress shall achieve its goal and the pledge I had taken on the banks of the Ravi...'

There was a loud applause.

'Fine. Well said.'

'Sahiban, I thank you from the bottom of my heart. I shall address you again one of these days. Now, I would request you to repeat with me...' and raising his voice, shouted, 'Inquilab!' Inquilab... Zindabad!'

In response to which a few faint voices were heard saying 'Zindabad!'

'Can't you shout loudly?' said the Jarnail. 'Don't you eat two meals a day?'

A loud answer came from somewhere:

'Zindabad!'

And the Jarnail, putting his cane stick under his arm stepped down from the stone slab.

'Zindabad!' The voice had come from the side of

the slope; it was Master Ram Das who came, panting for breath.

'Is this the time to come?' Bakshiji asked him sharply.

To which the answer came from Kashmiri Lal: 'He got late because the calf sucked up all the cow's milk.'

Everyone burst out laughing. But Master Ram Das said soberly, 'There will be no prabhat pheri today.'

'Why not?'

'Today's been set aside for community work. That's what was decided.'

'Who took the decision?'

'It was Gosainji who told me that the drains in the locality behind Imam Din street would be cleaned this morning.'

'You are making excuses for coming late.'

'Why do you say that? I have even left brooms and shovels in that locality. I left some last night and some more were deposited there this morning. In all there are five shovels, twelve brooms and five iron pans. They are all kept in Sher Khan's house.'

'Why were we not told about it?'

'That's why I have come running. When I came earlier, there was no one here.'

'But there are no drains in that locality. What are you going to clean? Are you in your senses?' said Kashmiri Lal.

'There may be no regular drains there, but there are certainly kuchcha ones.'

'There must be years of filth in those drains. Who's going to clean them?'

'We shall!' shouted the Jarnail. 'You are a coward and a traitor!' He was suddenly peeved.

'Programmes are changed without any prior intimation. If Gosainji had already decided, why were we not informed?'

It was getting brighter. Those who had come prepared for prabhat pheri felt odd and uncomfortable at the sudden change in the programme.

'Let's at least get out of here,' said Bakshiji, picking up his lantern. 'We shall go singing from here. Start off, Ram Das,' he added and stepped forward.

Kashmiri Lal picked up the tricolour. 'Left, right, left,' shouted the Jarnail, marching right ahead. Ram Das cleared his throat and began singing the old, time-honoured song with which prabhat pheris invariably began and which was also invariably sung out of tune:

Those wedded to the cause of freedom
Are like the legendary lover, Majnu
Deserts and forests are their home...

Master Ram Das sang the first line and the group of activists, keeping time with their feet as they walked, repeated the lines, one after the other and headed towards Dhok Qutab-ud-Din.

3

Nathu heaved a sigh of relief as he stepped into the lane. It was still dark there, although on the roads, it was already daylight. He was eager to reach home as quickly as possible, and he hurried through the maze of lanes. Coming out of that stuffy, stinking hut into open air had refreshed him somewhat. After the hectic business of the night his mind was finally at rest in the half-awake dark lanes.

In the distance, he saw two or three women with their earthen pitchers beside them, sitting by the municipal water tap, chatting in low tones, their glass bangles making a soft, jingling sound. They were waiting for the water to be turned on by the municipality. The familiar morning scene gladdened his heart.

He had hardly covered some distance when suddenly his foot struck against something, and he felt as though the thing had got scattered. It did not take long for Nathu to understand what it was, and the thought sent a shiver down his spine. Some unfortunate woman had placed a 'spell' right opposite someone's house—a few pebbles tied in a rag, along with an image made from kneaded dough and pierced through with wooden needles—intended to transfer her misfortunes on to someone else. Nathu regarded it as a bad omen. After having spent such an awful night, the incident shook him in the extreme, but soon enough he regained his composure. Such a practice was generally carried out to protect a child from an evil eye. The thought gave Nathu some consolation, since he was himself childless.

He was quite familiar with the area through which he was passing. The entire row of houses in this lane was inhabited by Muslim families. Some were washermen while some others butchers who had their meatshops at the corner of the lane. Mahamdu, the hamam-keeper too lived in that lane. Further down, there were houses in which Hindus and Sikhs lived. Beyond which again there were some Muslim houses. The houses at the far end of the lane were inhabited by Sikh families.

As he passed by one of the houses, he heard someone praying: 'Ya Allah, Kul Ki Khair, Kul Ka Bhala'. It was some old man arising uttering his little prayer, followed by yawning and coughing. People were waking up to greet the new day.

At one place his foot fell into something sticky and slimy with a strong, pungent smell like that of cow dung. He steadied himself, extricated his foot from the half-broken pitcher. A swear-word was about to escape his lips when he suddenly understood what it was and a broad smile came to his lips. The ill effect of the 'spell' had been neutralized by this collision. Whenever the weather became hot and sultry, it was customary among young fellows in the town to fili a pitcher with cow dung and horse urine, and fling it into the entrance of some tight-fisted miser of the locality. It was commonly believed that the act would induce a shower.

Opposite another house in the lane, a man was mixing fodder for his cow. From another house close by came the sound of cups and saucers and the jingle of glass bangles. Tea was being prepared. Just then, a woman, her head and shoulders covered, stepped out of a house with a katori in her hand, mumbling words of prayer. She was obviously going to a temple or a gurudwara to offer her morning prayers. How calm and peaceful were the beginnings of the day's business. To cap it all came the sound of an ektaara from somewhere. It was some fakir on his morning round. Nathu was familiar with the voice but had never set eyes on the fakir. He had heard him singing softly, particularly during the Ramadan. As he drew near, Nathu saw that the fakir was a tall, elderly person, with a benign countenance like that of a dervish. Frail in body, with a sparse white beard, he was wearing a long cloak. A cloth bag was slung on one shoulder and he had on a skull cap. Nathu stopped to listen to the words of the fakir's song.

> The birds are chirping merrily,
> while you, ignorant one,
> are still fast asleep...

Nathu had often heard this song to the accompaniment of the fakir's ektaara. Nathu took out a paisa from his shirt-pocket and gave it to the fakir.

'May God be with you! May you be blessed with plenty!' said the fakir.

Nathu moved on.

As he stepped out of the lane he found that it was

much brighter outside. He was now in the street of the tongawallahs. Two or three tongas, with their shafts raised towards the sky, as though in prayer, stood by the roadside. One of the tongawallahs was brushing his horse; close by two women sat on the ground making flat dung-cakes and sticking them on the wall behind them; a horse with a harness still on its back walked leisurely up and down the road, all by itself. Here too the day's business was starting in a calm, peaceful atmosphere.

Nathu felt as though he had come out to have a stroll. He did not want to be seen by anyone. His mind at peace, he strolled from one street to another.

Where would the pushcart be at this time, the thought suddenly crossed Nathu's mind. In which direction would it be going? It was a pointless question, but the thought impelled Nathu to walk faster. It might have already entered the cantonment, it might be at that very moment standing right at the gate of the veterinary hospital. To hell with it—Nathu uttered a swear-word. What did the veterinary surgeon need a pig for? It must have been to sell its meat somewhere. The thought of what he had gone through made him shiver, what with the stench in that stuffy room, the sweat, the grunts of the wretched creature which had licked his shins so hard that the skin had come off. To hell with Murad Ali. Nathu would wander wherever he liked. He put his hand on his pocket and felt the rustle of the five-rupee note. 'What do I care? It is my well-earned money.'

At the corner of the street stood the horses' trough, Nathu turned to the right. Far away, he heard the chiming of the Sheikh's tower-clock. Perhaps it was striking the hour of four. How clear the chimes were at that hour! During the day it was muffled by street noises. It appeared as though the sound was coming from the sky. Soon after came the sound of temple-bells, from the temple on top of a mound in the centre of the city. City sounds were increasing every minute—of doors opening, of men going out on their morning walk, coughing, pattering of sticks on the ground. A goatherd with his three goats was already on his round to sell goats' milk. Nathu slowed his pace. He was enjoying his stroll in the cool morning air.

The tongawallahs' street had been left behind. Nathu walked along the railing of the spacious municipal grounds opposite the Imam Din Street. On the other side of the railing was the slope that joined the municipal grounds—the hub of activities in the town. In winter there were dog fights every Sunday morning with people betting heavily. If a badly-mauled dog tried to escape the field, those who had betted on it would block its way. The grounds were also the venue for pegging contests, drawing huge crowds; circus shows from touring circus companies such as Miss Tarabai's Circus or Parshuram's Circus. Baisakhi was celebrated here with drumbeats and wrestling-bouts. Of late, it had become the centre for political meetings primarily of the Muslim League and of the Belcha Party—meetings of the Congress took place in the Grain Market at a considerable distance from there.

Nathu took out a bidi from his pocket and sat down on the railing to have a leisurely puff.

Just then the sound of the Azan rang out from the mosque behind the Imam Din Street. It had became brighter by now and things looked clearer in the morning light. Nathu got down from the railing and putting out the bidi, headed towards the Imam Din Street. He had suddenly remembered that Murad Ali lived somewhere nearby, on the other side of the municipal grounds. He had seen Murad Ali coming from that direction once or twice. But then, Murad Ali was seen everywhere in the town—walking in the middle of the road, swinging his cane, his thick, bushy moustache almost covering his lips, so that even when he smiled or laughed his teeth could not be seen. Only his chubby cheeks bulged prominently and his small, penetrating eyes would blink. Maybe Murad Ali was strolling somewhere nearby even at that time. He had better leave the place, thought Nathu and quickened his pace. The fellow would be cross if he saw him loitering there. Murad Ali had given clear instructions that after delivering the carcass of the pig, Nathu should wait for him in the hut. But Nathu had run away from there. 'Why the hell should I have stuck in that filthy hole? Besides, I have got my remuneration.' Nathu again mumbled to himself.

Nathu turned into a narrow lane and after walking a short distance, turned into another lane to the right which zigzaged towards the north. The sound of a song, sung by a group fell on his ears. As he walked further, the sound became louder and clearer. Nathu understood that the group was out on a prabhat pheri. In those days public meetings, processions, demonstrations, and prabhat pheris were a frequent sight. Nathu did not have a clear grasp of developments that were taking place around him. The air was thick with slogans of all sorts. Soon enough he saw a group of persons coming from the other side. It appeared to be a group of Congressmen because the man walking in front was carrying the tricolour flag of the Congress. As the group drew near, Nathu stepped to one side, and it passed him by, singing. There were eight or ten persons in all, a couple of them had Gandhi caps on their heads, while some wore fez caps. A couple of Sikhs too were among them. Both young and old comprised the group.

As they passed by him, one of them raised a slogan: 'Quomi Nara!'

And the others answered, 'Bande Mataram!'

Hardly had they finished, when from a distance, the sound of another slogan was heard:

'Pakistan Zindabad!'

'Qaid-e-Azam Zindabad!' (referring to Mr Jinnah).

Nathu turned round. Three persons had suddenly appeared at the turn of the lane shouting slogans. It appeared to Nathu that they were standing in the middle of the lane trying to block the other group from proceeding further. One of them with gold-rimmed spectacles and a Turkish cap on his head, said challengingly: 'Congress is the body of the Hindus. The Musalmans have nothing to do with it.'

To which an elderly person from the other group replied: 'Congress is everyone's organization, of Hindus, Sikhs, Muslims. You know this well enough, Mahmud Sahib. There was a time when you too were with us.' Saying so the elderly man stepped forward and put his arms around the man with the Turkish cap. Some persons laughed. Disengaging himself from the elderly man's embrace, the man with the Turkish cap said, 'It is the chicanery of the Hindus. We know this well enough, Bakshiji. You may say whatever you like but the incontrovertible truth is that the Congress is the body of the Hindus, and the Muslim League of the Muslims. The Congress cannot speak for the Muslims.'

Both groups stood facing each other. They talked like friends, and they also exchanged diatribes.

'See for yourself,' Bakshiji said. 'In our group there are Sikhs, Hindus and Muslims. There stands Aziz. Here is Hakimji.'

'Aziz and Hakim are the dogs of the Hindus. We do not hate the Hindus, but we detest their dogs.'

He said it with such vehemence that both the Muslim members of the Congress looked crestfallen.

'Is Maulana Azad a Hindu or a Muslim?'

'Maulana Azad is the biggest dog of the Hindus who goes wagging his tail before you.'

The elderly man continued to talk patiently.

'Freedom of Hindustan will be for the Hindus. It is in sovereign Pakistan alone that Muslims will be really free.'

Just then, a thin emaciated Sardar, in soiled, crumpled clothes stepped forward, shouting: 'Pakistan over my dead body!'

Some members of the Congress laughed.

'Silence, Jarnail!' someone shouted.

To Nathu too the Sardar's loud exclamation had sounded odd. Seeing his friends laugh, Nathu concluded that the man must be crazy.

But the man kept on shouting: 'Gandhiji has said

that Pakistan can only be formed over his dead body. I too say the same.'

'Spit out your anger, Jarnail.'

'Enough, Jarnail. Learn to keep quiet sometimes.'

The Jarnail became furious.

'No one can silence me. I am a soldier of Netaji Subhash Bose's army. I know each one of you well enough...'

There was much laughter.

But when the group of Congressmen moved forward, resuming their prabhat pheri, the man with the Turkish cap blocked their way: 'Muslims reside in this street. You can't go there.'

'Why can't we go there? You go raising slogans for Pakistan all over the town without let or hindrance, while here we are only singing patriotic songs.'

The man with the Turkish cap softened somewhat.

'You can go if you wish, but we shall not allow these dogs of yours to enter our street.'

And he stretched his arms sideways so as to block the way.

Just then Nathu's eyes fell on Murad Ali. He was standing at the street-corner, at some distance from the man with the Turkish cap. Nathu trembled from head to foot.

What is the man doing here? Nathu slowly crept to one side so as to hide behind the singing group. 'Has the fellow seen me?' When he felt that he was completely covered, and from where he stood he himself could not see Murad Ali, he tilted his head a little to see if Murad Ali was still there. The fellow was very much there, listening intently to what those people were saying.

Nathu stepped back and slowly began to withdraw from the place. So long as those people kept arguing, he thought, Murad Ali would continue to stand there. 'I had better get away from here.' He said to himself. 'If Murad Ali sees me, he will surely come to my tenement and demand an explanation.' He continued to step backward for some distance, then turned round, and taking long strides turned a corner in the lane and then took to his heels.

4

They reined in their horses on reaching the top of the hill. Before them lay a vast plain stretching far into the distance, interspersed with mounds and small hillocks. A blue haze hung over the horizon. High above in the cerulean sky, kites glided with outstretched wings. Beyond the valley, the hill on their left tapered sharply down while the eastern flank, covered in a shimmering haze, barely revealed a range of low, reddish hills stretching far into the distance.

Richard had succeeded in persuading Liza, his wife, to accompany him on his morning ride that day. He had long been eager to show her the spectacle of a sunrise over the valley, to present it to her as a kind of gift.

The cool morning breeze gently ruffled Liza's golden hair. Her blue eyes looked clear and bright though tiny lines had begun to appear under her eyes, a result of boredom, long hours of sleep and excessive consumption of beer.

It was to provide Liza with some diversion that Richard had brought her here. She had returned from England after a long absence of six months, and Richard could not risk a repetition of what had transpired earlier. If Liza did not take kindly to the new place and resolved to return to England, life for both of them would inevitably turn into a veritable hell. When he returned home from his office after the day's work, the exchange of courtesies between them would often turn into a heated argument which soon degenerated to shouting, yelling and cursing. Richard now made a firm resolve to spend the mornings with her. Ever since she had arrived, hardly a week ago, he had been taking her out every morning to different place—the Mall, the Topi Park or horse riding. Liza too, on her part had been trying hard to take interest in her new surroundings and in Richard's work in order to keep herself occupied. Sometimes she would venture out alone to the cantonment where, being the wife of the Deputy Commissioner of the district, the natives would fawn on her, bow low to offer their salutations and would eagerly want to be of service to her. But for how long can a person go about alone, and the Deputy Commissioner is not the master of his own time. Therefore, neither was sure whether the new arrangement, despite earnest efforts on both sides, would work and, if it did, for how long.

'Very nice!' Liza exclaimed. 'What mountain is that, Richard? Is it part of the Himalayan range?'

'Yes, one might say so,' replied Richard, greatly encouraged by her interest. 'The valley down below extends far into the mountains for hundreds of miles.'

'What a desolate valley!' Liza muttered under her breath.

'But Liza, the valley has great historical significance. All the invaders that attacked India came through this valley, whether they came from Central Asia or Mongolia.' Richard was warming up to the subject. 'Alexander too came through here. Farther away, the valley gets divided into two routes, one leading to Tibet, the other to Afghanistan. Traders, monks, dervishes for centuries used these routes, covering long distances. It is truly a historic area. I have been exploring these parts for the last one month. For a historian no area could be more fascinating. At numerous places you find ruins of ancient buildings, Buddhist monasteries, fortresses, caravanserais...'

'Richard, you talk as though this was your own country.'

'It is not my country, Liza, but its history is certainly of great interest to me.' Richard replied smiling. Then, pointing his whip towards the high hill, said, 'On the other side of that hill, nearly seventeen miles from here are the ruins of Taxila. You know about Taxila, don't you?'

'Yes, I have heard the name.'

There was a time when it used to be renowned for its university.

Liza smiled. She knew that now Richard would narrate the entire history of that region. She liked Richard's enthusiasm. He could talk with so much zest even about rugged rocks. There was something childlike about him, despite his being the Deputy Commissioner. How she wished she too could take interest in such things.

'There is a museum there too. I am sure you will like it. Recently, I brought a sculpted head of the Buddha from there.'

'Why, you already have a huge collection of the Buddha heads. Why did you need another?'

'Excavations are going on nearby. They found quite

a large number of such heads. The curator presented one to me.'

Liza saw before her mind's eye their large living room which housed Richard's collection of statuettes and specimens of Indian folk art. The almirahs were crammed with books on the subject. Richard had had a similar obsession in Kenya too, while serving there. He had amassed a collection of African folk art—bows and arrows, all kinds of beads, feathers of birds, totems and the like. And here, in India, it was the Buddha heads.

Liza again turned her eyes towards the surrounding view. Down below, towards the left was a cluster of low, stunted trees through which they had come. The vista before them opened on crossing that patch of trees.

'The colour of the soil is red,' observed Liza, looking at the hills in front of her. 'There is no road to be seen down below. Shall we go back the way we came, through the shrubbery?' Then, turning to Richard, added half in jest, 'Where is the road by which Alexander came to India, Richard?'

'There were no pucca roads in those days, Liza, but there is surely a route, thousands of years old which lies on the other side of that hill.'

Liza looked at Richard. Below his thick-rimmed glasses, the lower part of his face looked very sensitive. Liza wished he would stop talking about ancient routes and ruins and talk to her about love. But Richard's attention was focused on his subject.

'The inhabitants of this area too have been living here since times immemorial. Have you noticed their features? A broad forehead, brownish tint in the colour of their eyes. They all belong to the same racial stock.'

'How can they be of the same racial stock, Richard, when invaders from all over, as you say, have been here?'

'This is precisely the mistake some people make,' Richard said vehemently, as though trying to prove some pet theory of his. 'The first wave of migrants who came from Central Asia three or four thousand year ago and the bands of invaders who came two thousand years or so later, both belonged to the same racial stock. The former were known as Aryans and the latter Muslims. But both had the same roots.'

'The people here too must know all this.'

'These people know only what we tell them.' After a little pause he added, 'Most people have no knowledge of their history. They only live it.'

Liza was getting bored. Once he got started on the subject there was no getting off it, she thought. At such moments, Liza felt relegated to the background. Though he was very fond of her, he had little time for her. Standing in front of a bookshelf, while leafing through a book he would get so absorbed in it that he would become oblivious of everything else. Inevitably, once again Liza would begin to have fits of boredom, everything around her would become insufferable, the natives would look abhorrent, and ultimately she would either have a nervous breakdown or leave for England for another six months or a year.

'Is there a picnic spot nearby?' Liza asked, interrupting Richard.

Richard was taken aback, but the query was not so irrelevant.

'Oh, there are many.' Pointing his whip towards the hill to the left, added, 'There are lovely water springs at the foot of that hill under the shade of the tall banyan trees. Water has spurted out from the inner recesses of the hill. The Hindus have turned them into bathing pools and named them after their mythological characters, like Rama and Sita.' Richard smiled as he said this, thinking that these names must sound very odd to Liza's ears, odd and unfamiliar. 'There are many such spots around,' he went on, then, pointing his whip towards another cluster of trees, said, 'Not far from it, there is another lovely place. A fair is held there, once a year, for a full fortnight, during the month of March. Singing girls come from all over India to participate in it. The fair has some religious sanctity to it because there is the tomb of a Muslim pir there. Devotees light clay lamps on it.' Then smiling, added, 'There is singing and dancing during the night, and gambling during the day. I shall take you there one evening.'

'Is the fair on, these days?'

'Yes, it is. But it is not advisable to go there now.'

'Why not?'

'There is some tension between the Hindus and Muslims. We fear a riot might break out.'

Liza had vaguely heard about the tension but she knew very little about it.

'I still cannot make out a Hindu from a Muslim. Can you, Richard? Can you immediately know whether a person is Hindu or Muslim?'

'Yes, I can.'

'What about our cook? Is he Hindu or Muslim?'

'He is Muslim.'

'How do you know?'

'From his name, the cut of his beard; he offers namaz. Even his eating habits are different.'

'You are so clever, Richard. Do you really know all this?'

'Yes, I do. Quite a bit.'

'You know so much. You must teach me, Richard, I too want to understand things. And that fellow, your stenographer, the man who came to the railway station, the fellow with glistening white teeth. Is he a Hindu or Muslim?'

'He is Hindu.'

'How do you know?'

'From his name.'

'From his name alone?'

'It is quite simple, Liza. The names of Muslims end with such suffixes as Ali, Din, Ahmed, whereas the names of Hindus end with Lal, Chand or Ram. If the name is Roshanlal the man is Hindu, but if it is Roshan Din, he is Muslim. If it is Iqbal Chand, he is Hindu, if Iqbal Ahmed, he is Muslim.'

'I will never be able to understand all this,' Liza said, discouraged. 'And what about the fellow who wears a turban, your chauffeur who has a long beard?'

'He is a Sardar, a Sikh,' Richard said, laughing.

'It is not difficult to make out such a person,' Liza said, laughing.

'Every Sikh's name ends with the word "Singh",' Richard said.

They began to go down the slope. The day was

warming up. The sun had risen and the thin curtain of haze which had lent an aura of mystery to the atmosphere was dispersing.

'It is great fun roaming in these parts. You will like it. We'll come out every weekend.'

As they were crossing the bed of a dry stream strewn with round pebbles and stones, Richard leading the way, Liza said, 'Where will you take me this weekend, Richard? To Taxila?'

Richard did not miss the touch of sarcasm in Liza's voice. Taxila drew Richard like magnet, he could wander there for hours. But what about Liza? Would she like to wander about in the midst of ruins?

'No, not to Taxila for a few days, Liza dear. There is some tension in the town as I told you. We shall go there when the situation improves somewhat. As for this weekend...'

Richard did not know what to say. He couldn't tell what sort of a weekend it was going to be.

'We'll go somewhere,' he said, as they reached the bottom of the slope and spurred the horses homewards.

Before sitting down to breakfast, Liza and Richard, passing through the numerous rooms of their bungalow, came and stood in the spacious living room. With the approach of April, curtains would be drawn over doors and windows immediately after sunrise to keep out the heat and harsh daylight. One needed to use electric light even during daytime. Along all the walls stood shelves sagging with books. In between them, on wooden stands, rested heads of the Buddha or the busts of Bodhisattvas. Each statuette had been provided with a separate electric light which illuminated the face or a profile from a well-studied, favourable angle. The walls were covered with Indian paintings. On the mantelpiece stood a colourful doll beside which lay an ancient manuscript on copper plates. On a wooden pedestal by the side of the fireplace stood a rock-edict, while in front of the fireplace were placed three cane stools with a long, low, mahogany teapoy. Richard often sat there, his pipe in hand and browsed through his books and ancient manuscripts. The cook had been instructed to put the kettle on a stove close by with the necessary tea-service as Richard was fond of making his own tea. On the long teapoy lay half-open books and periodicals. At one end of it stood a pipe stand with half a dozen pipes of different shapes and sizes hanging in it. The round lampshade over the teapoy had been so arranged that, switched on, the light fell only on the three cane stools and the teapoy, leaving rest of the room in semi-darkness.

His arm round Liza's waist, Richard was showing her the busts and statuettes that he had collected in her absence.

'When I step out of my bungalow, I find myself in some part of India; but when I am back in my bungalow, I return to the whole of India.'

Wearing an old tweed coat with leather-patches on its elbows, loose corduroy trousers, a pair of thick, black-framed spectacles, Richard looked very much like the curator of a museum.

They stopped in front of a Buddha.

'The most beautiful thing about a Buddha is the serene smile. The light should so fall on the face that it highlights that smile. Let me show you,' Richard said turning the Buddha head slightly to the right and switching on the light above the statuette.

'See? See the difference?' Richard exclaimed. To Liza too it appeared that the smile on Buddha's face had become more pronounced—calm, soft, yet slightly ironical.

'The smile always rests in the corners of the lips. If you shift the angle even slightly, the smile will become faint.'

Liza turned round and looked at Richard's face. Men are such odd creatures, she thought. A woman would notice all these things and yet not be so childishly excited about them. She pressed Richard's arm, resting her cheek on his shoulder.

'This is the most significant thing about a Buddha head—the soft mysterious smile,' Richard said bending down to kiss Liza on the head.

Every room in the bungalow had been fitted with all sorts of electrical devices. Wherever they chose to sit, a call-bell was available close by, linking them to the kitchen as also to the veranda outside.

Looking at Richard, going from one room to another, nobody could tell that the man was the highest executive officer of the district. He looked more like a connoisseur of Indian art and a scholar of history. But when he sat in his administrator's chair, he was the representative of the British Empire carrying out the behests and policies laid down in England. He was a pastmaster at keeping the two identities distinctly separate from each other as also the emotions involved with either. That was the hallmark of his mental make-up. He would, with the greatest ease, shift from one kind of activity into another, even though each might be diametrically different from the other. He could draw the line between private interests and official concerns. His life moved, impelled by a peculiar kind of discipline. Three days in a week he held court in his capacity as the District Magistrate. Sitting in the judge's chair he would forget that he was the rulers' representative and dispense justice in strict conformity with the rules of the Indian Penal Code. It was difficult to say what his own beliefs were, if at all he had any. Perhaps Richard had never put this question to himself. As a matter of fact, there was no room for personal beliefs in his life. The thought that one's actions should conform to one's beliefs was considered juvenile idealism to be dispensed with the day a person joined the Civil Service. As a Civil Servant, Richard was required to implement policies, grasp the essentials of a situation, take quick decisions and enforce them without the least fuss or noise. Personal beliefs or convictions had no place in such a role. Besides, who has ever bothered to consider the moral or ethical aspects of the profession he or she was in?

Arm in arm, they proceeded towards the dining room. It was Liza's favourite room. In its centre stood a big, circular dining table, of black mahogany. A lampshade hanging low from the ceiling right above the table shed its light on a copper vase filled with red roses. The room spoke of Richard's taste and Liza was well aware that if she was to live with Richard she would have to adapt herself to his idiosyncrasies.

Richard paused a little before stepping into the room.

'What's on your mind?' asked Liza, her head resting on his shoulder.

'Well, what exactly was I thinking? Where should I begin...?'

'Begin what, Richard?'

'You wish to know about the situation in the town, isn't it?'

'I don't want to know anything. All I want to know is when you'll be back from your office?' said Liza caressing Richard's chest. Richard bent down and kissed her on her lips.

'Getting bored already?'

Richard felt as though a small cloud had appeared on the horizon which could only grow bigger and darker till it covered the entire sky.

He drew Liza closer but his heart was not in it. Behind his affection lurked the fear that things might not turn out well again this time between them. Though his lips passed over her hair, her forehead, her eyes and her lips, he felt strangely removed from her. The ardour and passion of the night had now been replaced with indifference. He was only playing at love, observing a formality.

The khansama, who had been standing in a corner of the room, stepped forward, the red waistband over his white uniform shining brightly in the light. Walking softly, he began laying the table for breakfast.

Liza and Richard continued to hold each other in their arms. Earlier, if a servant would suddenly appear, Liza would try to extricate herself from Richard's arms.

Richard would continue to hold her close, and the servant would go on doing his work. Embarrassed, Liza would close her eyes to forget the servant's presence. But gradually, she came to realize that the servant was a mere native and that his presence was beneath notice.

'You had better start taking interest in some activity. A Deputy Commissioner's wife is looked upon as the first lady of the district. The officers' wives will be only too willing to help you in whatever you take up.'

'I know. I know. Collect donations for the Red Cross, hold flower shows; children's fêtes; collect shoes and clothes for disabled soldiers' wives...'

'There is another association which we propose to set up for the care and protection of animals. The stray dogs roaming freely on the cantonment roads may be rabid and bite people. Then some people make lame horses to pull carriages...'

'What do you propose to do with such animals?'

'Have them put to sleep. It is cruel to harness a lame horse to a vehicle, and stray dogs spread disease. You can choose any activity that may be of interest to you.'

'No, thank you. That I should go about killing stray dogs while you go ruling over the district... You are always pulling my leg, you never take me seriously.'

'I am not joking, Liza. I really want you to take interest in something.'

'I do take interest in your work. Tell me more of what you were telling me this morning. About the Indians.'

Richard smiled.

'Well, all Indians are quick-tempered. They flare up over trivial things. They fly at one another's throat in the name of religion. They are all terribly self-centred. And they all adore white women.'

His last words again made her feel as though he was pulling her leg. She regarded Richard as a very capable, erudite person and suspected that he considered her an ignoramus and would not miss any opportunity of making a dig at her. His conversations with her were often laced with sarcasm directed at her.

'You never take me seriously, Richard.'

'Why should anything be taken seriously, Liza?' Richard said in a tone of disenchantment. 'Listen, darling, we may have some trouble here.'

Liza looked up.

'What sort of trouble, Richard? Will there be a war again?'

'No. A riot may break out in the city. Tension is mounting between the Hindus and the Muslims.'

'Will they fight one another? In London you used to tell me that they were fighting against you.'

'They are fighting both against us and against one another.'

'You are again joking, Richard. Aren't you?'

'In the name of religion they fight one another; in the name of freedom they fight against us.'

'Don't try to be too clever, Richard. I also know a thing or two. In the name of freedom they fight against you, but in the name of religion you make them fight one another. Isn't that right?'

'It is not we who make them fight. They fight of their own accord.'

'You can stop them from fighting, Richard. After all

they are from the same racial stock. Didn't you say so?'

Richard was charmed by his wife's simplicity. He bent down and kissed her on the cheek.

'Darling, rulers have their eyes only on differences that divide their subjects, not on what unites them.'

Just then the khansama came in with a tray. On seeing him, Liza said, 'Is he a Hindu or a Musalman?'

'What do you think?' asked Richard.

Liza stared at the khansama for a while who, after putting down the tray, had stepped aside and was standing motionless like a statue.

'He is a Hindu.'

Richard laughed. 'Wrong.'

'How is it wrong?'

'Have a good look at him again.'

Liza looked hard at the man.

'He is a Sikh. He has a beard. He is wearing a turban on his head.'

Richard laughed even more loudly. The khansama continued to stand motionless, without a muscle of his face moving.

'The Sikhs do not trim beards. It is against their religion.'

'You did not tell me that.'

'There is a lot else that I did not tell you.'

'For example?'

'That the Sikhs, besides keeping their hair long, adhere to four other commandments; that many Hindus keep a tuft of hair on their heads; that the Muslims too have their dos and don'ts, they do not eat pork while the Hindus do not eat beef; that the Sikhs eat jhatka meat while the Muslims eat halal...'

'Which means, you do not want me to learn anything. Who can remember all this?' She looked at the khansama. 'When I have mastered all these details, shall I be able to tell, just by looking at a person, whether he is Hindu or Muslim? How can one tell without looking at those particular signs?' Liza said, and, laughing, added, 'I bet these people themselves cannot tell one from the other, who among them is Hindu or Muslim. I bet you too cannot tell.'

And turning towards the khansama she said, 'Khansama, are you Muslim?'

'Yes, Memsahib.'

'Will you kill a Hindu?'

The khansama was taken aback at the question. He looked at Liza. Then smiling, turned his eyes towards the Sahib. He came forward and placing a plate in front of Richard, stepped back into the semi-darkness. Richard picked up the paper on the plate, glanced through it and put it back on the plate.

'What is it, Richard?'

'Just a report, Liza.' Richard replied softly and was soon lost in his thoughts.

'What sort of report, Richard?'

'About the situation in the town, Liza. Every morning I receive reports from the heads of three or four departments—from the superintendent of police, from the health officer, the civil supplies officer... Excuse me, Liza...' Richard said abruptly and went out of the dining room.

Liza felt confused at Richard's abrupt departure. He had not even finished his coffee. She didn't know whether she should wait for him or drink her coffee. But Richard came back soon enough.

'Where was that report from, Richard?'

'From the superintendent of police,' he said, then added in a reassuring voice, 'Only a routine report.'

But Liza felt as though Richard was hiding something from her.

'There is something you are keeping from me, Richard.'

'Why should I keep anything from you? We have nothing to do with what happens in the town.'

'Still, there seems to be something urgent in the report. What has the superintendent of police written?'

'That there is some tension in the town between the Hindus and the Muslims. Nothing new. This kind of tension prevails in many parts of India these days.'

'What do you propose to do?'

'You tell me what I should do. I think I shall carry on the administration. What else?'

Liza looked up.

'You are again joking.'

'I am not joking, Liza. What can I do if there is tension between the Hindus and the Muslims?'

'You can resolve their differences.'

Richard smiled and taking a sip of his coffee said in a calm voice, 'All I can say to them is that their religious disputes are their affairs and should be resolved by them. The administration can only render any help that they may want.'

'Also tell them that they belong to the same racial stock and therefore should not fight one another. That is what you told me, Richard. Didn't you?'

'I shall certainly tell them, Liza,' Richard replied, with an ironic smile playing on his lips.

They sipped their coffee. Suddenly Liza grew anxious and her face looked bleak.

'I hope there is no danger to you, Richard.'

'No, Liza. If the subjects fight among themselves, the ruler is safe.'

She felt greatly relieved and an expression of profound respect for Richard shone in her eyes, as the implication of what he had said sank into her.

'Right you are, Richard. You know so much, I suddenly felt so frightened. Jackson's wife had once told me that on one occasion, Jackson, holding a revolver in his hand ran after a crowd of natives, trying to disperse them. And his wife, who stood watching from the balcony, got terribly scared. Just think, Richard, Jackson, all alone, revolver in hand, running after a huge crowd. Anything could have happened.'

'Don't be alarmed, Liza,' said Richard, getting up from his chair, he patted Liza on the cheek, got up, and left the room.

5

By the time the group of prabhat pheri activists, making their way through the maze of lanes, reached the Imam Din Mohalla, dawn was giving way to bright morning. Along the way they had picked up brooms, shovels and taslas from Sher Khan's house. In the early morning light, the exhaustion on their pale, wrinkled faces was clearly visible. Barring Mehtaji, they were all in crumpled, home-washed clothes. The Gandhi cap on Bakshiji's head was askew looking as though a heavy load had been lifted off it. Shankar, Master Ram Das and Aziz carried brooms on their shoulders while Des Raj and Sher Khan had taslas in their hands. The Jarnail carried a big bamboo pole. As the day broke, Master Ram Das, a Brahmin by caste, was acutely embarrassed at the thought of being seen with a broom in his hand.

'Oh Gandhi Baba, you have put a scavenger's broom in a Brahmin's hand. You are capable of anything. Isn't that so, friends?' and he tittered, putting the broom behind his back. Unable to catch anyone's attention, he turned to Bakshiji.

'I am telling you now, Bakshiji, I will not clean drains.'

'Why not? Are you from a royal family or what?'

'I can't be expected to clean drains at my age, surely?'

'If Gandhiji can clean his lavatory, why can't you clean a drain?'

'The fact is, I cannot bend. Honest to God, each time I bend I get a shooting pain in my back. Apparently, there is a stone in my kidney.'

'How is it that the stone in your bladder does not act up when you're milking your cow or mixing fodder for it? It only pops up when you have to do community work.'

At this Shankar turned round and said, 'We have come here to spread a message, not to actually clean the drains. But if you feel so awkward, Masterji, I shall do the cleaning and you carry the refuse in the tasla.'

They had hardly gone a few yards and turned into a lane when Gosainji, who was at the back of the group, shouted, 'Why are we going by this route today?'

Des Raj, walking in front, had taken a turn to the right and the others had merely followed suit.

'Tell him to stop,' shouted Bakshiji. He too had realized that they were not on the right route. 'This is their time for offering namaz. We should avoid going by the masjid. O Kashmiri! Have you gone out of your mind? Why have you taken this route? Are you listening?'

Kashmiri Lal stoppped and turned round.

'Sher Khan and Des Raj turned in here by mistake,' he said, 'But don't worry. We'll stop the singing when we pass by the mosque.'

'Why go in that direction at all? You know the times we are living in. Turn back and take the lane that leads straight to the crossing. We shall enter the Imam Din Mohalla from that side.'

They turned back and took the new route which was unfamiliar to the prabhat pheris. Generally, the Congress activists did not go to far-flung colonies located outside the town. Even otherwise the route was long, for it involved crossing the sprawling municipal grounds.

They stopped as they reached a cattle water-trough and Kashmiri Lal, who held the tricolour in his hand, raised a full-throated slogan: 'Inquilab!'

To which the others replied in a spirited voice: 'Zindabad!'

'Bharat Mata ki'

'Jai!!'

At the sound of the slogans, little children came running out of their houses, and women peeped through curtains. A cock with a red crest climbed up a mud wall and flapping its wings crowed loudly, as though in answer to the slogans.

'The cock did a lot better than you, Kashmiri. See how proudly it crowed!' commented Sher Khan.

'Kashmiri is no less than any cock! Kashmiri is the cock of the Congress.'

Shankar added, 'Put a red cap on his head and Kashmiri will have a red crest too. Get him a red cap, Bakshiji.'

'Why, Kashmiri doesn't need any crest. He is the female of the species, a hen. Kashmiri hen!'

Such leg pulling and broad humour were an integral part of the activities of fellow activists.

'Enough, enough! Let's get to work,' said Bakshiji as he put the lantern on the low wall of the trough.

Most of the houses in the locality were small, single-storeyed houses, built in two paralled lanes on either side of a spacious courtyard. Gunny-cloth curtains hung over the front doors of most of them. The lanes were not paved. Only one of the lanes had a kachcha drain, the other one had no drain at all. In some lanes, cattle was tied. From the houses, now and then, women emerged with earthen pitchers balanced on their heads to fetch water. A small boy was collecting dung from under a buffalo. Near the trough, two little boys sat on the ground, opposite each other, relieving themselves and chatting away merrily.

'Why is your shit so thin?' one asked the other.

'I drink goats' milk. That's why. What do you drink?'

In one corner of the open ground, stood a tandoor.

Entering the locality one felt as though one was in a village.

'Pick up your shovels and start working!' shouted Bakshiji.

Mehtaji and Master Ram Das picked a tasla each and went to work in the yard. Shankar and Kashmiri Lal, armed with shovels headed for the drain, while Sher Khan, Des Raj and Bakshiji began sweeping the courtyard with brooms.

The residents of the locality watched them, puzzled. A tonga-driver came out of his house, and squatting on the ground, watched the goings-on. As his eyes fell on Bakshiji, sweeping the ground, he went over to him and tried to stop him.

'Why do you put us to shame, Babuji? It is highly improper that you should sweep the ground of our locality. Pray, hand over the broom to me.'

'No, no don't worry. That's what we have come here for,' Bakshiji answered.

'No, good sir, I won't let you. You are well-educated men from good families. How can we let you sweep our floors? Heaven forbid! Please hand over your broom to me. Why must you push us into the fires of hell?'

Bakshiji was deeply touched by the man's warm sympathy. 'The community work is having its effect. This is precisely what constructive work stands for,' Bakshiji muttered to himself.

Kashmiri Lal and Shankar were shovelling out the mud from the kachcha drain which ran alongside the row of houses. Ever since the drain had been dug, dirty water had been accumulating in it and now it had turned into slimy mud of dark colour. So long as the mud had been inside the drain, foul smell did not emanate from it, but when Kashmiri Lal and Shankar took out shovelfuls of it and piled it by the side of the drain at different places, an unbearable smell filled the air attracting a horde of mosquitoes. The drain was about a foot deep and it was filled with mud right up to the top.

'O good fellow! What are you up to?'

It was the voice of an elderly man with a henna-dyed beard standing behind the low parapet wall on the roof of one of the houses. 'Have you come to spread disease here? Why can't you leave the filth where it is, inside the drain? By taking it out and leaving it to scatter all over the place you are making it a potential source of disease. Who will clean it when you are gone? You'll leave the place a lot dirtier than before.'

Bakshiji who was sweeping the lane close by, straightened his back and stood up. He felt angry with Shankar and Kashmiri Lal. 'These young fellows will never understand anything,' he muttered under his breath. 'Constructive work does not mean that you should actually clean the drains. It is only a symbolic gesture to make the residents aware of the need for civic sanitation and gradually earn their trust and participation in the struggle for Independence.'

The old man, having made his comments withdrew from the parapet wall and Bakshiji resumed sweeping the lane with his broom.

Just then another elderly man, with a flowing white beard and a rosary in his hand, emerged from the lane opposite. Obviously, he was on his way to the mosque for his morning prayer. In his white salwar and kurta, an open waistcoat embroidered with a fancy design, a mushaddi lungi on his head, he looked a very pious man. He stood watching the 'constructive' programme for some time, then turning to Master Ram Das, who was covered with dust from sweeping the yard, said in a voice trembling with emotion: 'We shall remain indebted to you for all this.' His eyes turned towards the other activists. 'God bless you! What goodness of heart! What nobility of purpose!' He muttered again and again.

Bakshiji walked over to the old patriarch. 'It is nothing,' he said in a self-effacing tone. 'We are contributing in our small way to social welfare.'

'It is not the work, it is the lofty sentiment behind it that is so inspiring! Congratulations! Wah, Wah! Wonderful!' and smiling, walked out of the locality at a leisurely pace. Hearing words of such high praise, Bakshiji felt gratified. 'Today's work has yielded rich dividends,' he muttered to himself.

'Look at Mehtaji and Aziz,' Sher Khan said, laughing. Neither of them has even touched his broom. Mehtaji can't risk soiling his clothes.'

Careful, lest his fingers should become dirty, Mehta was picking up a stone at a time from the ground, very daintily with his forefinger and thumb and dropping it into the pan. Master Ram Das already had a thick coating of dust on his hair and thick moustaches.

By then, besides children, quite a few residents of the locality had gathered. Women and young girls stood behind curtains while men stood on roof-tops, interestedly observing the goings-on.

The Jarnail, who had been standing with his long bamboo pole near the trough, moved slowly to where the drain was being cleaned.

'Is the drain blocked? Do you want me to open it with the bamboo pole?' People standing around burst out laughing at his military abruptness.

'This constructive programme is really worthless, if you ask me,' said Shankar to Kashmiri Lal as he straightened his back. 'Shovelling mud out of drains will not bring freedom.'

Sweating profusely, both Shankar and Kashmiri Lal had by then made three piles of slimy mud along the drain.

'Don't go blurting whatever comes into your head, Shankar.' Bakshi had overhead Shankar's remark. He stood in the middle of the lane, broom in hand.

'I credited you with more intelligence than that. Is Bapu a fool to want us to ply the charkha and do constructive work?'

'What else am I doing if not that? Still, it makes no sense to me.'

Bakshi was in no mood to get into an argument with a fellow like Shankar who was unerringly blunt and outspoken. Even so, he couldn't help adding, 'Try to understand, Shankar, what we are doing is only the symbolic expression of our patriotism; it brings us close to our people, to the poor. When we come, clad in khadi, brooms and shovels in our hands to their locality, they regard us as their own; it inspires confidence in them, which it won't if we came to them in the Western attire of coat and pant.'

'Ever since you got involved in this constructive work the freedom struggle has come to a standstill,' retorted Shankar. 'Go on plying the charkha and sweeping lanes with brooms,' he said angrily as he threw a shovelful of mud on the pile.

'You are a traitor,' the Jarnail shouted. 'I know you well enough. You hobnob with the communists.'

'Enough, Jarnail,' Bakshiji intervened. To let the Jarnail continue would only aggravate matters. Turning to Shankar, he said, 'Can't you hold your tongue, Shankar? Must you go on babbling all the time? Is this the place for an argument?'

Just then, a man came running from the direction of the municipal grounds, past the lane where Sher Khan lived and went straight to where the knot of local residents stood. He had on a black waistcoat and looked very agitated. He spoke to the residents in low whispers, all the while gesticulating furiously. The manner of his arrival seemed very odd. Suddenly the local residents began to disperse. Only a few children continued to stand in the lane. Soon enough, the women standing behind gunny-cloth curtains also withdrew and doors began to shut. One of the women hurriedly came out of her house, caught hold of one of the two children who had been easing themselves near the trough, and pulling him by the arm, took him inside the house.

An uncanny silence fell on all sides. The Congress workers were bewildered by the turn of events.

They saw the white-haired man, who a little while earlier had praised the Congress workers so effusively, coming towards them. Mehta and Bakshi were standing together trying to understand the situation and what had caused the sudden commotion. They wondered whether they should ask the old man about it, when the latter, swinging his rosary stopped in front of them.

'Clear out of here at once if you don't want to be skinned alive!' he shouted in his high-pitched voice. His chin trembled and his cheeks turned pale. 'Enough of your nonsense! Just get out of here. Aren't you listening? Rascals, clear out of here.' And turning round, he strode away.

The singing party was stunned. They looked at one another. It was Bakshi's surmise that perhaps, Shankar and Kashmiri Lal, who were given to loose talk, had said something offensive to the local residents. But did it warrant the scathing outburst of the old man?

Just then a stone came flying from somewhere and fell near Bakshiji. Shankar and Kashmiri Lal, confused and bewildered, looked at Bakshiji.

'There is something amiss. What do you think could have happened?' asked Master Ram Das, coming closer.

'There is something wrong somewhere. Let's get away from here,' said Bakshiji, 'it was a mistake to have come here in the first place. Where is Des Raj who had been so insistent that we should come to this locality?'

But Des Raj was nowhere to be seen. Nobody knew when he had slunk away.

'Some mischief is afoot.'

Two or three stones came flying, one after the other and one of them hit Master Ram Das on the shoulder.

'Let's get away at once. Let's not linger here, even for a minute.'

The group rushed towards the end of the lane.

Holding the bamboo pole in his hand, the Jarnail shouted, 'You are all cowards! I know each one of you well enough! I shall leave only after I have completed my job.'

At this Bakshiji shouted to the Jarnail like a military commander, 'Jarnail, pick up the flag! At once!'

The Jarnail at once stood to attention and marched in step towards the trough, against which stood the national flag.

Two more stones came flying, hurled from somewhere. At the same time three men came out of a lane and stood at its entrance.

Kashmiri Lal took the flag from the Jarnail's hand and the party of Congress workers started on their way out of the locality. Mehta overturned the tasla in which he had been collecting pebbles, and carrying it in his hand joined the others who were leaving the locality. The hurricane lamp once again swung from Bakshiji's hand, but Bakshiji's head was bowed as he walked out.

'Shall we put back the shovels and taslas in Sher Khan's house?' Master Ram Das asked Bakshiji.

'Keep walking. Don't stop anywhere.'

Kashmiri Lal turned round to look back. Instead of three, five men were now standing at the entrance to the lane. Across the yard too, some men had gathered and were staring at them. As the party entered the Qutab Din street the scene that confronted them was similar to the one they had left behind. Here too, opposite the Nanbai's shop, stood three men, silently watching them.

'Something is amiss,' Bakshi said to Mehta.

'For all we know, Shankar or Kashmiri might have misbehaved with someone in the locality. You have let in all kinds of riff-raff into the Congress.'

'What are you saying, Mehtaji? Kashmiri was busy cleaning the drain the whole time. Something else seems to be the matter.'

On entering the Mohyals' lane, they again saw a knot of men standing ominously at the far end of the lane.

They were suddenly stopped by a tall resident of the Mohyal street.

'Don't go to that side, Bakshiji,' he said, stepping forward.

'Why, what's the matter?'

'Don't go that way.'

'Why not?'

By then, Kashmiri, Jarnail and Master Ram Das had come to where Bakshi and Mehta were standing.

'Can you see anything lying at the end of the lane?' Bakshiji strained his eyes to look. Outside the farther end of the lane, across the road stood a mosque, known in the locality as the Khailon ki Masjid.

'What is it?'

'Look towards the steps, at the entrance of the mosque.'

'Something blackish, like a bundle seems to be lying there.'

'It is the carcass of a pig, Bakshiji. Someone has left a dead pig there.'

Bakshiji looked at Mehta's face, as though to say, 'See? Didn't I tell you something unusual has happened?'

Everyone was looking hard in that direction. On the steps of the mosque, lay a black bag from which two legs were sticking out. The green door of the mosque was closed.

'Let's turn back from here,' whispered Master Ram Das.

Kashmiri Lal spat on the ground when he saw the pig and turned his face away.

'Bakshiji, let's turn back. Beyond the lane is a Muslim locality,' Ram Das said again.

'A foul mischief has been played by someone,' Mehta muttered under his breath. 'But are you sure it is the carcass of a pig lying there? It may be some other animal.'

'Had it been some other animal, the Muslims would not have reacted so sharply,' Bakshiji said, somewhat peeved.

The Jarnail with his small eyes under his bushy eyebrows stared hard at the pig and exclaimed in a loud voice, 'It is the Englishman's doing.'

His nostrils were quivering as he said again at the top of his voice, 'It is the Englishman's mischief. I know it for sure.'

'Yes, yes, Jarnail, it is the Englishman's mischief. But

right now you had better keep quiet,' Bakshiji said to
him persuasively.

'Let's return by the back lane,' suggested Master Ram
Das once again. But the Jarnail pulled him up sharply,
'You are a coward. It is the Englishman's doing. I shall
not spare him. I shall expose him.'

Mehtaji whispered into Bakshiji's ear: 'Why do you
bring this lunatic with you wherever you go? He will
be our undoing one day. Why don't you expel him from
the Congress?'

Whenever the eye of a Muslim pedestrian walking along
the road fell on the steps of the mosque, he would at first
stare hard in that direction, then abruptly turn his face away
and quicken his pace, muttering something under his breath.

Suddenly a tonga dashed along the road. Soon after,
sounds of running footsteps were heard from the side
of the mosque. A few paces away, a butcher hurriedly
covered the carcasses of four goats hanging in his shop
with cloth and pulled down the shutters. Doors began
to shut in the Mohyals' lane too.

Bakshiji turned round. Master Ram Das, walking fast,
had reached almost the end of the lane. Behind him, at
some distance were Shankar and Aziz. Here and there
in the lane, stood small groups of local residents.

Bakshiji's Mohyal friend advised, 'You too should
leave the place, Bakshiji, your presence here will add to
the tension.'

Bakshiji looked at the man and turning to Kashmiri
Lal said, 'Fold up the flag, Kashmiri. Take it off the staff.'
Turning to his Mohyal friend, said, 'We must remove the
carcass of the pig from the steps of the mosque. Tension

will keep mounting so long as the carcass is there.'

'What? Are you suggesting that you will remove the carcass from the steps of the mosque? I think you should not even go near the place.'

'He is right,' said Mehtaji. 'We should keep away from it all. The situation can get worse.'

'Won't it be worse if we walk away from it? Do you think the Muslims will remove the pig's carcass from the steps of the mosque?'

'They can get it done by a scavenger or a sweeper. Anyway, under no circumstance should we get involved in it.'

Bakshiji put down the lamp on the steps of a nearby house, and turning to Mehtaji said, 'What did you say, Mehtaji? That we should slink away and allow the tension to aggravate? It would have been a different matter if we had not seen the carcass.' Then, turning to the Jarnail and Kashmiri Lal, added, 'Come with me,' and went out of the lane towards the mosque.

Kashmiri was nonplussed. He couldn't decide whether to follow Bakshiji or not. Stones had been hurled at them in the Imam Din Mohalla. God alone knew what lay in store for them here. Drops of perspiration appeared on his forehead. He put the flagpole alongside a wall and for a while stood wavering. But then, with a sudden resolve followed Bakshiji out of the lane.

On reaching the road, he turned round. The Mohyal too had left. Only Mehtaji was still standing in the deserted lane. The three or four shops standing in a row were all closed. Shops down the road near the well too were closed. Only four or five persons, stood in a knot there. They were all looking towards the mosque. People stood on their balconies or on rooftops with the doors of their houses shut tight.

'We must first remove the carcass from the steps of the mosque,' Bakshiji was saying.

The carcass was that of a pig with jet-black bristles. It was covered with a gunny bag from under which the pig's legs, its snout and a part of its belly peeped out.

Mehtaji, still undecided, stood inside the lane, close to a wall. Removing the carcass was not only risky it was a dirty business too, for it meant soiling his clothes of pure white khadi. The Jarnail and Bakshiji had, in the meantime, caught the pig by its legs and pulled it off the steps of the mosque. Dragging it across the road they had pushed it behind a pile of bricks, thereby concealing it from view.

'Let it be here for the present. The doors of the mosque can now be opened. Let us now wash the steps of the mosque.' Bakshiji said and turning to Kashmiri, added, 'The municipal corporation scavengers live in the lane at the back. Tell one of them to bring his pushcart and we'll get the carcass removed from here.'

Just then, sounds of commotion were heard from the direction of the well. A cow came running towards them, followed at some distance by a young man whose face was half-covered and who carried a big stick in his hand. His chest was bare and on it dangled a talisman. The cow was young, with an almond-coloured hide and big startled eyes. Its tail was raised from sheer terror. It looked as though it had lost its way. All three of them stood perplexed, their minds filled with apprehensions.

The youth with the half-covered face drove the cow and took it into a side-lane towards the right.

Bakshiji stood transfixed as it were, anxiety writ large on his face. He slowly nodded his head and muttered: 'It seems kites and vultures will hover over the town for a long time.'

His face had turned pale and gloomy.

6

Before the dispersal of the weekly congregation, the vanaprasthi led the chanting of sacred hymns. He believed that such chanting of hymns and sacred verses was like the last oblation offered at a sacred rite and that the weekly congregation was in the nature of such a rite. He considered the hymns, carefully chosen by him, the very essence of Indian thought and culture. After years of persuasion, the vanaprasthi had succeeded in making the members of the congregation memorize them. Sitting cross-legged on the platform, his eyes closed and head bowed, with folded hands resting in his lap, he began chanting the holy verses:

'Sarve Bhavantu Sukhina...' (May every living being in the world be happy and live a contented life...)

The vanaprasthi was the only one in the congregation well-versed in Vedic lore and recited the mantras in chaste Sanskrit. Every word uttered by him seemed to emerge from the depths of his soul. The members of the congregation hummed or recited the verse after him. Some of them could not keep pace with the vanaprasthi, and invariably, their humming would continue long after the verse had been fully chanted.

Shanti Path was recited last. It was a prayer for

universal peace. The entire congregation stood up and chanted it in a full-throated voice, since this was a mantra they were all familiar with. The invocation filled the hall with an atmosphere of serenity. It seemed as though this prayer for peace expressed so resonantly was reaching out to every home. It filled every heart with deep satisfaction. After the chanting of hymns, a prayer seeking the well-being of every living being was sung. The vanaprasthi kept the rhythm by softly clapping his hands.

'Grant mercy O Lord, to everyone
Grant every living creature your blessing...'

On his insistence the practice of chanting the traditional aarati had almost been given up, because it contained such mortifying expressions as 'I am a fool, a lout, O Lord,' which, the vanaprasthi thought, had a demoralizing effect on the singer. Similarly a song composed by some Khanna rhymester which comprised the line, 'We, your sons, O Lord, are utterly worthless,' had been discarded.

The prayers over, the congregation would normally have dispersed, but the members continued sitting because the secretary was expected to make an important announcement. The secretary stood up and requested the members comprising the core group to stay back to deliberate over an important matter. The members already had a hunch of what it was about, for in his discourse, the vanaprasthi had hined at it. Not only that, while making references to it he had got excited and agitated, and even recited, in a deeply anguished voice, the lines of a couplet:

Much blighted has this land been by
the sins of the Muslims, even the
Divine has refused us this grace,
and the earth its bounty.

After the announcement, the congregation dispersed.
Members exited from the seven big doors of the hall
into a long veranda and began putting on their shoes.
Some members, at the time of entering the hall, had
deliberately left one shoe outside one door and the other
outside another to ensure that no one pinched the pair.
This caused some confusion and crowding in the veranda.
Even otherwise, after congregational meetings, members
would hang around in the veranda, chatting and
exchanging views. It was even more so on that particular
day when the situation in the town was on everyone's
mind. The vanaprasthi, after his impassioned discourse,
continued to sit on the raised platform. His face was
flushed and he still appeared to be agitated.

Just then some people were seen coming towards the
hall from outside. They were important functionaries of
another Hindu organization in town. They were soon
followed by a group of six or seven Sikhs, representatives
of the local Gurdwara Committee. They too had been
invited to participate in the deliberations of the core group.

The secretary, a gaunt, wiry and very fiery person,
gave a telling account of the deteriorating situation in
the town, of the rumours that were rampant; he even
spoke about the carcass of a pig found on the steps of a
mosque and made a special mention of the fact that for
the last several days, lathis, lances and other weapons

were being stored in large quantities in the Jama Masjid. He then made a fervent appeal to give serious thought to the gravity of the situation and devise ways and means to combat it effectively.

'This place is not suitable for such deliberations' said the vanaprasthi, raising his hand. 'Let us move to some other place. It is only proper that the subject is discussed in a more suitable place.'

So saying, he got down from the chowki and proceeded towards the back of the hall. The members of the core group followed suit. Climbing up a winding satircase, the vanaprasthi led them into a small room on the first floor in which lay a few benches and some chairs.

After they had all sat down, the vanaprasthi continued in his sombre voice, 'Our primary concern is self-defence and safety. Everything must be done to ensure this. Every householder must immediately store in his house, a canister of linseed oil and a bag of coke and charcoal. Boiling oil can be poured over the enemy from the roof-top, red-hot coals can be flung...'

It was straight talk, members listened with close attention, but to some ears the suggestions, coming as they did from the mouth of a vanaprasthi, sounded rather odd. Most of the members present were elderly businessmen, a couple of them were lawyers or men in service. They were all anxious and concerned, no doubt, but not so agitated as the vanaprasthi. They were still not convinced that the situation had deteriorated to such an extent that people should store canisters of oil in their houses. They were largely of the view that even if a few untoward incidents did take place, the situation would eventually be brought under control by the administration.

One of the members, turning towards the secretary, said, 'How is it that our youth wing has gone into hibernation? You have put Shri Dev Vrat to all sorts of other jobs. It is absolutely necessary that our young men are activized. They must be given training in lathi-wielding. I would suggest that two hundred lathis be purchased today and distributed among them.'

At this, the chairman of the core group, a well-known merchant of the town and philanthropist, nodded his head and said, 'I shall pay for these two hundred lathis.'

'Oh how generous!' some voices were heard saying. The gesture of the chairman was received with high acclaim.

A voice was heard saying, 'This is the biggest shortcoming of the Hindu character. We think of digging a well only when we are thirsty. The situation is fast deteriorating; the Muslims have already stocked weapons in the Jama Masjid, whereas we are thinking now of buying lathis.'

To which the secretary was quick to retort, 'Our Youth Wing is fully active and alert. The matter has received our full attention. Vanaprasthiji himself is taking keen, personal interest in the activities. Besides the study of scriptures and performance of rites and rituals, vanaprasthiji is devoting heart and soul to the sacred task of Hindu unity. I, however, welcome the generous offer of our esteemed chairman. His generosity always helps us tide over many a difficult situation. But I assure you, no stone will be left unturned in our preparations.'

Just then an elderly gentleman, who had been listening with his chin resting on his walking stick, and both legs drawn up under him on the seat of the chair, said in his thin, squeaking voice, 'Brothers, all this is very fine. But I would say, first go and meet the Deputy Commissioner. Don't wait even to drink a glass of water. Just go and meet him. This nuisance is not going to end soon. Meet him and tell him that the life and property of the Hindus is in grave danger.'

'It is necessary to go to the Deputy Commissioner, no doubt, but Lalaji,' said the vanaprasthi, intervening, 'we have to depend on our own resources for our defence.'

'O Maharaj, give training to your young men in lathi-wielding. Teach them to handle lances and swords also. But first go and meet the Deputy Commissioner. He is the man in authority. Not a sparrow can flutter its wings without his consent.'

'But we cannot meet him today, it is Sunday.'

'I say, go to his bungalow and meet him there. This is just the right time to do so.'

At this a Sikh gentleman raised his hand and said, 'I am told that a deputation has already gone to meet the Deputy Commissioner.'

'What sort of deputation? Who are the members of the deputation?'

'It consists of some Congressmen and some members of the Muslim League.'

Silence fell on all sides.

'Of what use is such a delegation? A separate delegation of Hindus and Sikhs must wait upon the

Deputy Commissioner and tell him of the doings of the Muslims. If you go arm in arm with the Muslims what can you tell the Deputy Commissioner? The whole thing has been spoiled by the Congressmen. They keep pampering the Muslims.'

'The mischief is spreading fast. I have heard that a cow too has been slaughtered and its limbs thrown outside the dharmashala of Mai Satto. I do not know if it is true, but it is strongly rumoured.' The face of the vanaprasthi grew red with anger and his eyes became bloodshot. But he restrained himself and did not utter a word.

'Streams of blood shall flow if a cow has been slaughtered,' said the secretary, greatly agitated.

Everyone was silent. They all felt that some big mischief was afoot and that the Muslims would not stop at committing any outrage.

Thereupon they began considering seriously how best to unite the Hindus and the Sikhs on a large scale and draw up plans for joint defence. 'What is the position of the Mohalla Committees?' someone asked. 'It is not easy to set up Mohalla Committees here. Muslims have infiltrated every mohalla. After the riots in 1926, two or three such mohallas did come up which had exclusive Hindu and Sikh population such as the Naya Mohalla, Rajpura, but in other mohallas the Muslims and Hindus are present in a mixed population. How can you form Mohalla Committees there?'

The question of mohalla committees received serious attention and was discussed for a long time. A sub-committee was formed to forge links with the Mohalla Committees wherever they existed forthwith and devise ways by which they could be activized at short notice, and quick contact established among them. A plan was drawn up to this effect.

'What about the alarm-bell that was installed in the Shivala temple?' An elderly gentleman said, 'I think it should be checked too.'

'Why, is there anything amiss?'

'We should assure ourselves that it is in working order. It shouldn't happen that when we need to ring the bell, we pull the rope and the rope snaps. We shouldn't leave things to chance.'

Shivala temple stood on a high mound right in the heart of the city. It was surrounded by a cluster of shops.

'Many years have passed since the bell was installed. It is time we got it overhauled.' The old gentleman was saying. 'It was way back in 1927 if I am not mistaken.'

'God forbid that it should have to ring again.' One of the persons suddenly exclaimed.

The remark infuriated the vanaprasthi.

'It is such thinking that has made cowards of Hindus,' he said. 'To be afraid of danger at every step. That is why we are given the derogatory nickname of karars and baniyas by the mlecchas.'

They all fell silent again. Everyone present held the same views, though they were agitated to a lesser degree than the vanaprasthi. They too believed that the Muslims were at the root of all mischief, but at the same time they did not want a riot to break out, for that would pose a serious danger to the life and property of both Hindus and Sikhs.

The deliberations went on for a long time. Matters

concerning self-defence and measures for the prevention of a riot were discussed. Several suggestions were put forward concerning mohalla committees, formation of a Volunteer Corps to maintain contact with the Hindu and Sikh organizations of the town, provision for canisters of linseed oil, bags of sand, storage of water. During all these deliberations, like the refrain of a song, the elderly gentleman kept repeating his suggestion:

'O Brothers, first of all, wait upon the Deputy Commissioner; don't wait even to drink a glass of water, go and meet the Deputy Commissioner; as soon as this meeting ends, go straight to meet him. I too am willing to accompany you...'

It was finally decided that after the meeting, the secretary would stay back and through a peon circulate to all the members of the congregation the decisions concerning the storage of oil and coal. The secretary would establish contact with like-minded organizations, engage Gurkhas to serve as watchmen, speak to the secretary of the Sanatan Dharm Sabha to get the alarm-bell repaired and alert the Youth Wing. The other members of the core group except the vanasprasthi, would forthwith get into tongas and proceed to the bungalow of the Deputy Commissioner. The vanaprasthi, however, being a spiritual man, could not be expected to concern himself with mundane matters of the worldly householders.

On reaching home, the philanthropic chairman learnt that his son was not at home. It was a disturbing piece of information. He had a lurking fear that his young son might have been caught in the whirl of developments that were taking place in the town.

At the time when the chairman was returning home, Ranvir, his son, was somewhere in the narrow dingy lanes of the town, walking with bowed head behind his preceptor, Master Dev Vrat, the organizer of the Youth Wing's akhara. The clatter of Master Dev Vrat's heavy boots resounded in the lanes, while in the heart of the fifteen-year-old Ranvir, eager aspirations rose like ripples as he walked behind him. Every pore in his body throbbed with expectations. He was to be examined today and if he came out successful, he would receive his initiation.

It seemed that the town consisted of only crooked lanes; there was hardly a straight lane anywhere. For some distance a lane would appear to be moving straight, but then, from somewhere, a slanting lane, bent, as it were, under the weight of single-storeyed houses on either side, would join it and the lane would lose its sense of direction. Sometimes it would appear to them as though they were walking in a blind alley and that they would soon face a wall, but just as they would reach the end they would find a narrow slit and the lane would open out in a different direction. Dev Vrat's heavy boots were familiar with all the lanes.

Ranvir was as yet only a boy, his eyes shone with simple trust and eager curiosity. He lacked that sobriety which was so necessary for the initiation test. But the lack of sobriety was amply made up for by his enthusiasm, his sense of dedication to the cause, and by a strong determination to lay down his life at Masterji's command.

When he was small, Master Dev Vrat used to tell Ranvir stories of valour. There was one of how Rana Pratap, for the first time, became conscious of his helpless situation when the only piece of bread left with him was eaten up by a cat. Ranvir would imagine Chetak, Rana Pratap's horse, galloping away on the hills on the town's outskirts. He would see Shivaji on horseback, poised on a high rock looking toward the Turkish hordes in the distance, or holding in his iron embrace the mleccha chief. It was Masterji who had taught him to tie different kinds of knots, to scale a wall with the help of a rope, about arrows that produced fire or rain on striking against their target.

'The fire-arrow, when shot, goes piercing through the air, sparks flying from its head. Such fire-arrows were shot during the great Mahabharata war. The arrow would go flying at top-speed and eventually strike against the shield of a Kaurava warrior causing it to erupt in flames. It would continue coursing through the air—the arrow never fell to the ground, instead it flew round and round the entire battlefield and flames of fire leapt up from all sides. Its point had only to strike against the head-gear of a warrior, or merely grate against the canopy of a chariot and flames of fire would erupt. The fire-arrow turned back only after setting fire to the enemy's entire camp like a victorious warrior, with dazzling light shooting out of it as though it had set the whole firmament on fire.'

It was Masteriji who had told him that the technique to make a bomb or an aeroplane was inscribed in the Vedas. It was from his mouth too that Ranvir had heard about the powers of Yoga-Shakti. 'A man who has Yoga-Shakti can accomplish anything. Once, on the slopes of the Himalayas, a Yogiraj, already at the peak of his yogic powers, was in deep meditation when a mleccha tried to distract him. Mlecchas are unclean people, they don't bathe, don't even wash their hands after toilet, eat from one another's plate, they have no regular hour of going to toilet, so, the mleccha came and stood right in front of the yogi and stared hard at him. His abominable shadow had hardly fallen on the yogi when the yogi opened his eyes. The next moment, a ray of light shot out of the yogi's eyes, and the mleccha was reduced to a heap of ashes.'

The mleccha would appear before Ranvir's eyes again and again—in his neighbourhood, the cobbler who sat by the roadside was a mleccha, the tonga-driver who lived right opposite his house was a mleccha; Hamid, his classmate, was a mleccha too; the fakir who came to beg for alms was a mleccha; the family that lived in his immediate neighbourhood was also a mleccha family. It must have been one such mleccha who had gone to interfere with the samadhi of the Yogiraj, on the Himalayas.

Ranvir was the only one, from among the eight aspirants who had been chosen for the initiation test. Everyone was scared stiff of Master Dev Vrat who, in his heavy black boots, his khaki shorts, his loud thunderous voice and his menacing demeanour would strike terror in every heart. He could thrash anyone at any time. But this test was an undercover affair; only those young men knew anything about it who had passed the test and they would never divulge its contents to anyone.

The lanes looked deserted. It would sometimes appear to Ranvir as though the lane, at some distance was plunged in darkness, but on drawing near he would find that it was only a gaping dark hole in a wall, caused by the partial collapse of another wall.

Master Dev Vrat came to a halt opposite a discoloured, drab-looking door in a long wall. He pushed the door open. Ranvir's heart pounded with expectations, although when they had entered the dark lane, he had felt somewhat nervous. They stepped into a spacious courtyard on the other side of which stood a kothari with a tarpaulin curtain hanging over the door. A pile of bricks and stones lay on one side towards the left of the courtyard. The place sent shivers down Ranvir's spine. Masterji crossed the courtyard to the other side and knocked at the door. Someone inside coughed and the shuffling of feet was heard. 'It is I, Dev Vrat', Masterji called out. The door opened. In front of them stood an elderly Gurkha chowkidar, who folded his hands immediately on seeing Dev Vrat. It was dark inside the room. A charpai lay on one side. Against the right-hand wall stood a lathi. On the floor lay an upturned hookah. From a peg in the wall hung the chowkidar's khaki woollen overcoat and a bayonet.

Just then they heard the clucking of hens. Ranvir turned round and saw five or six white hens in a big basket.

Masterji put his arms round Ranvir's shoulders and led him into the backyard, a narrow slit of a place, across which stood the high wall of the adjoining house. The Gurkha followed, carrying a cackling hen in one hand and a big knife in the other.

'Ranvir, you slaughter this hen. This is your initiation test. You have to prove how mentally tough you are.' So saying, Dev Vrat guided Ranvir to the middle of the yard.

'An Arya youth must possess strength of mind, speech and action. Here, take this knife and get down to work.'

Ranvir felt as though an eerie silence had fallen on all sides. A pile of broken bricks and blood-stained feathers lay scattered about. Close by was a stone slab blackened with the blood of slaughtered hens.

'Sit down and put one foot of the hen tightly under your right foot.' Dev Vrat twisted the hen's wings together and after a while the hen lay still. All it could do was croak fiercely.

'Hold it tight,' he shouted and sat down by Ranvir's side, 'Now get going.'

Ranvir's forehead was covered with cold sweat and his face turned deathly pale. Masterji saw that the boy was feeling sick.

'Ranvir!' he shouted and gave the boy a stinging slap. Ranvir bent double and fell on the floor. His head was reeling. The Gurkha stood where he was. Ranvir looked as though he was about to burst into tears but his nausea abated.

'Get up, Ranvir,' said Masterji in a stern voice. Ranvir slowly rose and looked at Masterji's with scared eyes.

'There is nothing difficult about it. Let me show you.'

He put the hen's foot under the heel of his heavy boot. The hen's eyes became glazed and then closed. Masterji held the neck of the hen in his left hand and moved the blade of the knife on it just once. Blood spurted out, some spilling on Masterji's hand. The hen's head fell on the floor, near his heavy boot, but Dev Vrat continued to press the hen's artery, a white little thing which struggled as if to free itself. The bird's body heaved and trembled, and became motionless. Feathers soaked in blood, lay on the floor close to Ranvir. Masterji flung the dead hen to one side and stood up. 'Go, fetch another one from inside,' he ordered the Gurkha.

Master Dev Vrat saw that Ranvir had vomited and was sitting with his head in both his hands, breathing hard. He felt like giving him another slap but restrained himself. A little later, he said, somewhat persuasively, 'You are being given another chance. How will a young man who cannot slaughter a hen, kill an enemy? You are being given another five minutes to prove your mettle. If you fail again you will not be inducted.' So saying Masterji turned round and went into the room.

Five minutes later when he came out, the hen lay convulsing on the floor near the wall, its blood, splashed all over the place. Ranvir was sitting on the ground with his right hand pressed tightly between his thighs. Masterji immediately guessed that the hen had pecked at his hand which meant that Ranvir had succeeded only in wounding the bird, not in beheading it. Unable to control the bird, he had used the knife on its wriggling head, and at the sight of blood spurting out of its neck, had forthwith, released the bird.

The wounded hen leapt up again and again in agony, splattering blood as it flew about. Blood spurted from its neck.

But Ranvir had passed the test.

'Stand up, Ranvir!' Masterji said, patting him on the back. 'You have the necessary strength of will, you have determination too, even though your hand is still not very steady. You have passed the initiation test.' He bent down, dipped his finger in the blood on the stone slab and put a teeka with it on Ranvir's forehead, thus inducting him into the category of the initiates.

Ranvir still stood in a daze, his head reeling. But on hearing Masterji's words, though vaguely, he felt gratified.

They had managed to procure all the necessary things except çauldrons that were needed for boiling oil. Everything had been arranged neatly on the window-sill —three knives, a dagger, and a kirpan. Ten lathis had been stacked in one corner of the room, each had a brass-head with spikes at the other end. On the wall hung three bows and arrows. Bodhraj could shoot an arrow lying down. He could take aim at a target by listening to a sound, or by looking at its reflection in a mirror. He could even cut a hanging thread into two with his arrow. He had pointed metal-heads fixed to his arrows, and expatiated on their special features to his fellow 'warriors'.

'If you rub arsenic on the arrow tip, it will become a poison-arrow; if you rub camphor on it, it will become a fire-arrow, that is, it will produce fire wherever it strikes; if you put blue vitriol on it, it will produce poison gas on striking its target.'

Dharam Vir had managed to filch his uncle's leather-belt which had empty cartridges fitted into it. That too was hanging on the wall. The room looked like an arsenal store, and in acknowledgement to that, Ranvir had put up a sign-board saying 'Arsenal' in bold letters right above the door.

But the most important of vanaprasthiji's instructions concerning the boiling of linseed oil had not yet been implemented. None of the young men had been able to secure a cauldron big enough to boil a canful of oil. A can of oil however had been obtained and it was lying against a wall on one side. Each representative of the youth committee had contributed four annas from his pocket money to meet part of its cost, the balance was to be paid to the provision store later. Now, the cauldron was the only hitch. Even the temple, where every other day congregational lunches took place, did not have one.

Suddenly Bodhraj thought of a way out. Why not get a cauldron from the halwai's shop?

'His shop is closed.'

'Where does he live?'

'He lives in Naya Mohalla.'

'Has anyone seen his house?'

Bodhraj had, but at that time, being the group leader, could not take upon himself so petty a job.

Ranvir suggested breaking into his shop.

Though the others did not feel comfortable with the idea, it was the only option in the present situation.

For a while the group leader stood looking at the roof, pondering over the situation. To be a group leader was no joke, it was a highly responsible job. The youngsters must not be seen breaking open a lock. The group leader was the son of a clerk who worked in the commissariat and was a first-year student in a local college. He was the only one in the group wearing an army shirt with two pockets, much to the envy of others.

'Yes, you may break open the lock, but the work must be done on the sly. No one must see you doing it. Who will volunteer himself for this work?'

'I shall do it,' said Ranvir stepping forward.

The group leader glanced at Ranvir from head to toe and shook his head.

'No. You are too short for the job. Your hand will not reach the lock if it is high up on the door.'

'The lock is in the middle of the door. I have seen it several times,' Ranvir replied somewhat boastfully, as was his habit, which often irritated the group leader. Nevertheless, he was a smart boy, ran very fast too, but he lacked discipline.

The group leader believed that Ranvir would procure the cauldron, come what may, but the boy could be lackadaisical in his approach, make some mistake, and thereby land the group into trouble.

'You have my permission. But you will not go alone. Dharamdev will go with you,' said the group leader in a decisive voice. 'No one must see you breaking the lock. Go at a time when there is no one around. And don't go together. Go separately, one by one.'

The halwai's shop stood at the road-crossing, on the other side of the ditch. As they approached the shop, Ranvir saw something moving behind the shop, something white, like a turban. Perhaps the halwai had come to open his shop. But what was he doing, standing at the back of his shop? Maybe it was not the halwai but someone else. Who could it be? Maybe a mleccha had come to loot the shop. Ranvir looked closely. It was none other than the halwai opening the backdoor of his shop.

There was no one around. Even otherwise, at that time of the day, except for an occasional hawker or a plying tonga, the road was empty. It was only in the evening that the road was frequented.

Both the boys went over to the shop. The plan was that while one would engage him in conversation the other would go in and pick up the cauldron.

'It won't be necessary to steal the cauldron. He will give it to us on his own. He is our Hindu brother,' said Ranvir's companion.

'What nonsense. Who do you think you are, you midget?'

Both boys moved towards the back of the shop. The door was open. The halwai seemed to have gone in.

It was dark inside the shop. A swarm of flies buzzed over the greasy shelves. The place smelt of stale samosas. Ranvir peeped in.

'Who is it?' A voice came from inside the shop. 'The shop is closed today.'

The two boys went in. The halwai was standing in a corner of the shop pouring a tin of fine wheat-flour into a bag. He was taken aback on seeing someone standing at the door.

'Come in. Please come in,' he said smiling. 'No sweetmeats have been made today. I thought I would take some of the provisions home. The situation in the town is not good. Sons, you too should not stir out on a day like this. It is better to stay indoors.'

'Pick up the cauldron,' Ranvir ordered Dharamdev.

Dharamdev moved towards the row of utensils lying against the wall.

'The cauldron is being taken away for the defence of the nation. You will get it back at the right time.'

The halwai did not understand what the boy was talking about.

'What is the matter? Who are you? What do you need the cauldron for? Is it for some wedding?'

Neither of the boys answered.

'Pick up the one in the middle. It is lying right in front of you,' Ranvir said in a commanding voice.

'Wait! What is all this?' shouted the bewildered halwai. 'Why are you taking my cauldron?'

'You will know at the right time.'

'That's no way of doing things,' exclaimed the halwai.

'You can't just pick up a thing and take it away. You have to take my permission for it. Who are you, anyway?'

Just then Ranvir put his hand in his shirt pocket and shouted fiercely. 'Are you refusing us?' He advanced threateningly towards him and struck him.

Before the halwai could open his mouth to say something, blood was streaming down his right cheek. Ranvir put his hand back into his shirt pocket. The halwai sat down on the floor, both hands covering his face, moaning in pain, drops of blood falling on the floor.

'No one should know about it or you will be finished off.'

Dharamdev had meanwhile carried the cauldron across the ditch towards the other side of the road. After a short pause, Ranvir too left the shop and walked a few paces behind Dharamdev. 'Killing is not difficult,' Ranvir thought, 'I could have killed this man easily. One has only to raise one's hand and it is done. It is fighting that is difficult, particularly when the other person stands up against you. To stab a man to death is far easier. It poses no problem, killing poses no problem.'

On entering the house, Dharamdev paused in the

doorway 'Why did you hit him?'

'Why did he not carry out my order immediately? Why was he dilli-dallying?'

But Dharamdev's throat had gone dry and he stammered as he spoke. 'What if anyone had seen? What if the halwai had cried out for help?'

'We are not afraid of anyone. Let the fellow do his worst. You too may do your worst,' Ranvir said in a menacing voice and went towards the staircase.

7

'There must be something important, gentlemen, that has brought you to my residence, and that too on a Sunday,' Richard said smiling.

The peon lifted the bamboo curtain and members of the deputation entered the room one by one. Richard stood at the door, his eyes taking in each member as he went in. Then he too entered and sat at his table. Four of the men wore turbans while one had a Turkish cap on, and two were wearing Gandhi caps. The very composition of the deputation convinced him that it would not be difficult to handle them.

'What can I do for you, gentlemen?'

Members were pleased with the courtesy shown to them by the Deputy Commissioner. His predecessor was an insolent man who didn't believe in meeting anyone or discussing anything.

Richard had previously, with the help of police diaries, conducted an investigation on each member of the delegation. The unkempt, carelessly dressed man with the Gandhian cap must be Bakshi who had spent sixteen years in jail. The fellow sitting in a corner with a Turkish cap must be Hayat Baksh, a prominent member of the Muslim League. Mr Herbert, the American principal of a local college had also come along as a member of the deputation. And there was Professor Raghu Nath too, a lecturer in literature. He must have been included because he was on friendly terms with the Deputy Commissioner. The rest belonged to different organizations.

Looking towards Bakshi, Richard said, 'I am told there is some tension in the town.'

'It is precisely because of that that we have come to meet you,' Bakshi said. Bakshi looked anxious and agitated. Every occurrence since morning had been upsetting him. He had, on his own, called on the President of the Muslim League, but finding him indifferent, had decided to form a deputation and take it to the Deputy Commissioner. That too had not been easy. He had gone from house to house to get some local leaders together.

'Immediate action must be taken by the government to control the situation. Otherwise, my fear is that kites and vultures will hover for a long time over the town,' he said, repeating the expression which had been going round in his head.

The others were worried but not so agitated as Bakshi was.

Just then Richard and Raghu Nath's eyes met. The professor was the only Indian among them with whom Richard socialized, since he regarded him as a knowledgeable, well-cultivated person and since both were keenly interested in literature and ancient Indian history. Their eyes lit up, as if to say, 'We have been willy-nilly drawn by these people into mundane matters, otherwise we belong to a different world.'

Richard nodded his head and tapped the table with his pencil. 'The administration does not enjoy a good reputation with you gentlemen. I am a British officer, and you have little faith in the British government. You won't very much care to listen to what I have to say,' he said in an ironical vein and tapped the table with his pencil.

'But the reins of power are in the hands of the British government. And you represent British authority. To preserve law and order in the town is your direct responsibility,' Bakshi said, his chin trembling and his face turning pale in agitation.

'At this time, power rests in the hands of Pandit Nehru,' Richard said, in a low voice, a flicker of a smile playing on his lips. Then, turning to Bakshiji, he said, 'The British government is always to blame, whether you have differences with it or among yourselves.'

The smile still played on his lips. Then, restraining himself, as it were, he continued, 'But I believe, with our joint efforts we can tackle and resolve the situation.' He turned his eyes towards Hayat Baksh.

'If the police is alerted, the situation can be brought under control in no time,' said Hayat Baksh, 'despite the mischief played by the Hindus. You know what was found on the steps of the mosque?'

'How can you say that the Hindus had a hand in it?' shouted Lakshmi Narain, the philanthropist, jumping up in his seat.

For Richard the problem was resolving itself.

'Blaming one another will not serve any purpose,' he said persuasively. 'You gentlemen have obviously come to me with the intention of resolving the issue.'

'Of course we do not want rioting and bloodshed in the city,' said Hayat Baksh.

Lakshmi Narain felt isolated and angry. Had his colleagues been present, he wouldn't have had to face the Muslims all by himself. They would have supported him and told the Deputy Commissioner how weapons were being stored in the Jama Masjid, about the killing of the cow and a hundred other things. A deputation comprising exclusively of Hindus should have called on the Deputy Commissioner and apprised him of the real situation.

'If the police were to patrol the city and army pickets were set up at different places, there would be no rioting,' said Bakshiji.

Richard nodded his head, smiled and said, 'The army is not under my command, even though some army contingents are stationed in the cantonment.'

'The cantonment is as much under British rule as the city is,' said Bakshiji. 'If you will set up army pickets, the situation will come under control in no time.'

Richard shook his head, 'The Deputy Commissioner has no such authority.'

'If you cannot set up army pickets you can at least clamp curfew on the town. That might help bring the situation under control. Police pickets can be set up, too.'

'Don't you think clamping curfew will make the people more nervous?' Richard said. He picked up a piece of paper from the rack and jotted down something on it, and then looked at his watch.

'The administration will certainly do whatever it can, gentlemen,' he said in a reassuring tone. 'But you are the prominent leaders of the town, your word carries more weight with the people. I believe a joint appeal from you addressed to the people to keep peace will have a salutary effect.'

Two or three heads nodded.

'Leaders of both the Congress and the Muslim League are present here. A joint Peace Committee can be formed forthwith, with the inclusion of Sardarji and start its work. The administration will do all it can to help you,' said Richard.

'We shall of course do that,' said Bakshiji, still agitated. 'But the situation is critical and calls for immediate action. Once rioting starts, it will be difficult to control. If an aeroplane were to fly over the town, it will serve as a kind of warning to the people. They will know that the administration is alert. This small measure itself will prevent a riot from breaking out.'

Richard again nodded his head, and jotted down something on the piece of paper. 'I have no authority over aeroplanes either,' said Richard, smiling.

'Everything is under your authority, Sahib, only if you want to exercise it.'

The man was becoming over-assertive, thought Richard, he must be shown his place.

'It was wrong of you gentlemen, to have come to me with your complaint. You should have addressed it directly to Mr Nehru or the Minister of Defence, Mr Baldev Singh. It is they who are running the government now,' said Richard laughing.

On seeing the attitude of the Deputy Commissioner some people fell silent, but Bakshi's agitation increased.

'We have been told that hardly an hour ago, your police officer, Mr Robert forcibly ejected a family of Muslim tenants from a house, due to which tension has mounted in the entire area. The house belonged to a Hindu landlord. I believe, in the prevailing situation, such an action need not have been taken.'

Richard knew about the incident. As a matter of fact, the officer had consulted him before taking action. And Richard had asked him to go ahead, since implementation of a law-court judgement was a matter of daily routine and there was no point in postponing it. But before the deputation, he pretended not to know anything about it. He jotted down something on the piece of paper and said, 'I shall make the necessary enquiries,' and again looked at his watch.

At this Herbert, the elderly American pincipal of the local Mission College, said in a persuasive voice, 'Keeping peace in the city is not a political matter. It is above all political considerations; it concerns all the people. We are required to rise above our party affiliations. The administration too has a vital role to play. We should all join hands and bring the situation under control. Without losing another minute we should go round the entire city and make a fervent appeal to the people to desist from fighting one another.'

Richard at once supported the proposal, adding, further 'I would suggest that we engage a bus, duly fitted with a loudspeaker. All you gentlemen should sit in it and go round the town, making a fervent appeal to the people to keep peace.'

Hardly had these words been uttered by Richard when

strange, disturbing sounds were heard from the road outside.

'A Hindu has been done to death on the other side of the bridge,' someone was saying to the peon sitting outside. 'All the shops are closed.'

The members of the deputation sat up greatly perturbed. The Deputy Commissioner's bungalow was located far from the city. If the riot has actually broken out, it would be a problem reaching home. Then came the sound of a tonga rattling away at top speed on the road, followed by someone's running footsteps.

'It seems the trouble has started,' exclaimed Lakshmi Narain nervously and got up.

'Everything possible shall be done, gentlemen,' said Richard. 'Too bad if the trouble has started.'

One by one the members of the deputation stepped out of the room, lifting the bamboo curtain. The Deputy Commissioner accompanied them to the door.

'I can arrange for a police escort for you, gentlemen,' Richard said and turned towards the telephone lying on the table.

'You need not worry about us. It is more important that the trouble does not spread,' said Bakshji, stepping out. 'There is still time. I would say, clamp curfew on the town.'

The Sahib smiled, nodding his head.

On coming out of the bungalow all the members of the deputation felt confused. They exited from the gate and found themselves on the road without speaking to one another. They walked along, side by side, for some distance, then suddenly Lakshmi Narain and the Sardarji hurriedly crossed over to the other side of the road. Lakshmi

Narain had taken off his turban and tucked it under his arm. The road here sloped down and went straight up to the bridge which separated the city from the cantonment.

Herbert, the principal, had come on his bicycle. He went slowly down the slope. For a moment he paused, with the intention of asking them as to when or where the meeting of the proposed Peace Committee would take place, but, seeing them so nervous, desisted from saying anything. How can a meeting take place now, if a riot has actually broken out?

Hayat Baksh strode briskly looking over his shoulder from time to time. All of them, in fact turned to look back now and again.

'I need not walk fast. It is a Muslim locality,' Hayat Baksh mumbled reassuring himself.

On the other side of the road, the Sardarji was walking fast. The bulky Lakshmi Narain was trailing nearly two yards behind. He was breathless and had to slow down to wipe the perspiration from his neck again and again. Bakshiji and Mehta stood undecided for some time at the gate, but then they too walked down the slope.

'Let us take a tonga, that will be much quicker,' suggested Mehta. Bakshiji stopped. A tonga was approaching from the other side. Hearing the patter of the horse's hoofs, Mehta waved his hand to stop it.

'Where do you want to go?' asked the young, swarthy tonga driver, reining in his horse.

'Take us to the tonga stand.'

'It will be two rupees.'

'What? Two rupees? That is scandalous,' Bakshi said out of sheer habit. The tonga began to move on.

'Let us take it, Bakshiji.This is no time to bargain.' And Mehta jumped in and occupied the back seat. 'Take us to the city. Make it quick.'

Seeing them get into the tonga, Lakshmi Narain turned and went towards them. But the tonga was already moving away. Lakshmi Narain stood in the middle of the road staring at them.

'That is how a Hindu treats another Hindu. This has been so since times immemorial. Such is their character.'

Hurt and angry, he went stomping back to the pavement.

By now the others were walking down the slope, each on his own. A little ahead of Lakshmi Narain walked Hakim Abdul Ghani, an old Congress activist. At some distance ahead of him was Sardarji, while Hayat Baksh was walking ahead of all of them. He had taken off his coat and hung it over his right shoulder.

Sitting down in the tonga, Bakshi had said, 'Let us ask them if anyone wants a lift,' to which Mehta's reply had been categorical. 'No one need be asked. How many can you accommodate? Let us get away from here as soon as possible. You can't ask one and not ask the other. We can even take a turn to the left and get out of sight.'

Bakshiji felt uneasy sitting in the tonga. It had been a bad decision getting into it. He felt irritated, as much with Mehta as with himself. 'Why do I allow myself to be persuaded by fellows like Mehta. The members of the deputation had all come together. That is how we should have gone back too.' Nevertheless there was nothing much he could do about it now.

As the tonga drove past Hayat Baksh he remarked jokingly, 'Running away, Bakshi? The karars that you are! You first stoke the fires and then run away!'

They were on informal terms with each other, having grown up together in the same town. They could share a joke.

Seing the Sardarji coming at some distance, Hayat Baksh remarked, 'Bakshiji has decamped! Such is the character of these people!'

But the Sardar continued walking with his head bent, without uttering a word.

Walking at the tail-end of the line, Lakshmi Narain felt that he should increase his pace and join Hayat Baksh. They were passing through a Muslim locality and it would be safer to walk alongside Hayat Baksh.

'What's the big hurry? Let's walk slowly,' he shouted.

Hearing his voice all three stopped. But Lakshmi Narain, taking long strides, went straight ahead, pattering his stick and joined Hayat Baksh.

'It will be awful if a riot breaks out in the city,' he said, as he joined Hayat Baksh.

Hayat Baksh had sensed Lakshmi Narain's motive. In a way it served Hayat Baksh's interest too, because the locality on the other side of the bridge was predominantly Hindu and Hayat Baksh had to go through it in order to reach his house. The fear was largely baseless because all these gentlemen were well-known figures of the town, and it would not have been easy for anyone to raise his hand against any of them.

Sitting in the tonga, Bakshi felt uneasy and irritated. Whenever he was overwhelmed by events or circumstances he would lose his equilibrium and clarity of mind.

'Kites and vultures shall hover over the town, Mehtaji,'

he repeated peeping out of the tonga. 'Take it from me, kites and vultures...'

'We shall see what happens. The first thing is to reach the town.'

'What difference will that make?' said Bakshi irritably. 'We are already in deep trouble.'

Mehta was anxious but not as worked up as Bakshi.

'The Deputy Commissioner at least gave us a patient hearing. The previous DC was such a haughty fellow, he would not even talk decently with us.'

'What does he care? He doesn't give a damn,' Bakshi said irritably. 'What patient hearing has he given us?'

Bakshi's thoughts then turned towards something else.

'No one can be trusted,' said Mehta.

That further irritated Bakshi. 'If Muslims cannot be trusted, can Hindus be trusted?'

'Look Bakshiji, I shall tell you something. It may be a trivial thing, but for an intelligent person it is like a straw in the wind. This fellow, Mubarak Ali, who is a member of the District Congress Committee wears a khadi kurta and salwar, but his cap is not a Gandhi cap, it is a Peshawari fur cap. Muzaffar is the only Muslim Congressman who wears a Gandhi cap.'

Bakshi took his handkerchief and wiped the perspiration off his face.

'The Hindu Sabha people have formed Mohalla Committees but we have not done anything of the kind. We should at least have formed Peace Committees in every mohalla,' said Mehta, wiping his neck.

'You should be ashamed of yourself, Mehta,' Bakshi said, quivering with rage.

'Why? Why should I be ashamed of myself? What sin have I committed?'

'It is never good to try to ride in two boats at the same time. And that is exactly what you have been doing all along—one foot in the Congress and the other foot in the Hindu Sabha. You think nobody knows about it; well, everyone does.'

'Will you come to save my life when a riot breaks out?' said Mehta. 'The entire area on the other side of the ditch is inhabited by Muslims, and my house is on the edge of it. In the event of a riot, will you come to protect me? Will Bapu come to save my life? In a situation like this, I can only rely on the Hindus of the locality. The fellow who comes with a big knife to attack me will not ask me whether I was a member of the Congress or of the Hindu Sabha... Why have you gone dumb now? Why don't you speak?'

'You should be ashamed of yourself, Mehta. It is in such times that a man's integrity is put to test. You have gathered a lot of wealth and your brain is covered with thick layers of fat. If your house is located near the mohalla of the Muslims, is mine located in that of the Hindus?'

'It makes no difference to you. You are a sadhu, without a wife or family. What will a fellow gain by killing you?' Mehta said, getting excited. 'I told you to throw out Latif from the Congress organization. I can give you in writing that he has links with the CID. He gives information to the police about each one of us. You know this as well as I do. But you would not do a thing. You would go on feeding the snake in the grass. Then there is Mubarak Ali. He is always hobnobbing

with the League fellows. Gets money out of us and out
of the Muslim League. He has had a house built of pucca
bricks. And yet you choose to turn a blind eye to it.'

'There are only a handful of Muslims in the
organization. Shall we throw them out? Are you in your
senses? If Latif is undesirable, does that mean everyone
else is undesirable too? Is Hakimji who joined the
Congress long before you did undesirable? Is Aziz Ahmed
undesirable?'

The tonga had by then reached the end of the slope
and turned towards the bridge.

Across the bridge, on the right, the Islamia school,
was closed. Very few persons or vehicles were to be seen
on the road. A few persons stood in a knot in the school
compound.

The other four members of the deputation were still
walking down the slope. As Hayat Baksh passed by the
offices of the Electric Supply Company, he met Maula
Dad, standing by the roadside. Maula Dad worked as a
clerk in the Electric Supply Company and was also a
Muslim League activist.

'What have you achieved by going to the Deputy
Commissioner? You had gone to meet him, hadn't you?'

'Hardly had we sat down when there was some noise
outside and the meeting dispersed. Everyone got up and
left. What news of the town?'

'Tension is mounting, they say. There has been some
disturbance near Ratta. How is the situation there, at the
back, from where you are coming?'

By that time Hakim Abdul Ghani and the Sardar also
had arrived. After having walked separately for some

distance, they had begun to walk together. Since Hakimji was a Congress Muslim, the Sardar had little hesitation in walking alongside him.

'A riot must not break out. It is an awful thing,' said Lakshmi Narain.

Maula Dad looked searchingly at Lakshmi Narain. 'If it were left to the Hindus, a riot would certainly break out. It is we Muslims who are putting up with all kinds of provocations.' His eyes fell on Hakimji and his temper rose. 'This dog of the Hindus too had accompanied you? Whom does he represent?'

Both fell silent. Pretending not to hear what Maula Dad had said, Hakimji, with his head turned, kept looking towards the bridge. But Maula Dad was exasperated. 'It is not the Hindu who is the enemy of the Muslims, it is the tail-wagging Musalman who goes after the Hindus and lives on the crumbs thrown to him.'

'Listen, Maula Dad Sahib,' Hakimji said patiently. 'You can call me by any names you like, but the most important question is that of the freedom of India, of freeing the country from the British yoke. Hindu-Muslim differences are not the primary question.'

'Shut up, you despicable dog,' shouted Maula Dad, his eyes turning red and his lips trembling.

'No, no, no, this is no time for an argument.'

Lakshmi Narain suddenly felt weak in the legs, but the elderly Hayat Baksh was there to control the situation.

'Move on, Hakimji, but your patrons have already gone in a tonga, leaving you in the lurch.'

Hakimji slowly moved away. The Sardar went along with him. But Lakshmi Narain kept standing where he was.

'Are you going home?' Maula Dad asked Hayat Baksh.
'Won't you come to the League Office?'

'I shall be there later. You go along.'

Maula Dad understood why Hayat Baksh had tagged
Lakshmi Narain to himself. Putting his hand on his heart
he said respectfully to Lakshmi Narain: 'Rest assured,
Lalaji, as long as we are there, nobody dare touch even
a hair on your head.'

Hayat Baksh and Lakshmi Narain too moved on.

By twelve noon, Liza leisurely walked towards the
door opening in the veranda outside. Pushing aside the
curtain, she looked out. Dazzling hot sun, like a
shimmering sheet of glass covered the garden. Trembling
vapour seemed to rise from the ground. It was already
scorching hot. Liza pulled back the curtain.

As she passed by the fireplace, her eyes fell on a
statuette in the middle of the mantelpiece. Some Hindu
god, with a big paunch, red and white lines drawn across
his forehead, sat there laughing. Liza felt sick. It looked
so awfully ugly. Wherefrom had Richard picked it up?

She came into the large drawing room. With idols
and statuettes all over the place, she felt as though
everything around her had become lifeless, as though
they were not statuettes but heads of the dead Buddha.
It gave her the creeps. She felt suffocated in a house so
stacked with books and statuettes. Wherever she went,
she felt as though the Buddha heads were peeping at her
through the corner of their eyes. Richard had only to go
out of the house when these objects became dead-wood

for her. And yet she had to spend the endlessly long day, in the company of these statuettes and piles of books. She couldn't take her eyes off them, even if she wanted to, as she went from one room to another. Inadvertently, she came and stood in front of a Buddha statue. Out of idle curiosity she pressed an electric button. Truly enough, Buddha's face lit up with a soft smile. She switched off the light. The smile vanished. She pressed the button again. The smile returned. But it also appeared as though the Buddha was eyeing her through the corner of his eyes. She immediately switched off the light.

Liza returned to her room. As she entered, she was greeted by a soft, tinkling sound. Right in front of the window, above the bedstead, hung a tiny brass bell. With every whiff of air, the tiny bell tinkled softly, as though wafting from far away. This sweet, musical sound could be heard throughout the day. It was a new addition to the house, brought by Richard from somewhere before Liza's arrival, to welcome her with.

Just then, a sharp sound suddenly fell on Liza's ears. She looked around but for some time could not see anything. Then her eyes fell on a lizard lying on her dressing table. It had apparently fallen from the wall, close to the electric lamp. It was in convulsions, gasping for breath. Then, suddenly, it stopped moving and lay still. It was dead. The hot summer caused lizards to die everyday. Despite its numerous spacious rooms, the bungalow in which they lived was an old one, built at a time when the British rule had just struck roots in the Punjab.

Two years earlier when they were living in a different bungalow, a snake, nearly a yard-and-a-half long, had once crawled out of the servants' quarter. It would sometimes get under the cots, or would be seen slithering along the wall in the veranda. Liza had got so scared that for several days after that, she would not open the window leading into the veranda. Nor would she open her wardrobe, fearing that a cobra might be lying curled in it. Within days after that incident, she had left for England.

Liza pressed the button of the call bell and came out into the veranda.

Before coming to India, Liza had made many plans. She would collect specimens of village handicrafts, travel extensively, practise photography, get herself photographed sitting on the back of a tiger, go about wearing a sari. But now it seemed to her that she was destined to endure the scorching heat, imprisonment in a big bungalow, never-ending days, Buddha statuettes, lizards and snakes. Life outside the bungalow was no less monotonous. There was the British officers' club no doubt, but in the hierarchical relationship that existed there—the overassertive commissioner's wife, about whom it was said that she exercised the commissioner's authority more than the commissioner himself, the Brigadier's wife who socialized with other officers' wives strictly on the basis of seniority, while Richard was comparatively a junior officer—Liza felt ignored. Though there were parties every other day and dance parties every Saturday night, the days seemed interminably long. It was then that she got into the habit of drinking beer. Getting bored with going from one room to another the whole day long, she found in beer the only way to keep off boredom.

'You must have German blood in your veins that

makes you so fond of beer,' Richard would say in jest. But Liza's addiction increased with time. Sometimes, when Richard would come home for lunch, he would find Liza sprawled on a sofa, her eyes swollen. Amidst hugs and kisses and hiccups, she would swear again and again that she would give up the habit. But the next day again she would find it impossible to pass time.

This time however, she had returned with a more positive frame of mind. She had come fully resolved to take interest in Richard's activities, both administrative and otherwise, as also in those relating to public welfare.

She tried to figure out for herself the kind of work the Association for Prevention of Cruelty to Animals was doing and how she could associate herself with it. 'What assignment should I take in it?' Liza was thus ruminating when the 'khansama' came into the room and Liza was strongly tempted to tell him to get her some beer, but she desisted. The khansama was a new recruit and did not know anything about her weakness. 'What sort of assignment will it be? Shall I be required to go from street to street, getting stray dogs and old horses shot one by one? Or, being the first lady of the district, be only a presiding officer and the actual work will be done by the underlings?'

Liza was in a queer state of mind. There was the horror of boredom, but there was also the consciousness of being the wife of the virtual ruler of the district with a huge bungalow to live in and a retinue of servants and waiters; there was insufferable boredom, but there was also the strong sense of personal importance as the mistress of the house.

'Memsahib!'

The khansama stood before her, waiting for her orders.

'There is a dead lizard on the dressing table in my room. Go and remove it.'

'Huzoor!' said the khansama, then bowed and left.

Liza walked over to the window opening into the veranda. On lifting the curtain she was again faced with the glaring light of the midday sun. But she also noticed Richard's office-clerk sitting behind a small table on one side of the veranda. He was sorting out letters—a dark-complexioned young clerk with glistening white teeth who would say 'Yes sir' twice to every sentence uttered by Richard, always shaking his head sideways. On seeing him Liza smiled. The babu knew English. It was always interesting to talk to him. Liza came over into the veranda by way of the dining room.

'Babu!' Liza shouted, in the same way as Richard did, and sat down in a chair near the door.

The babu shut his file and came running.

'Yes sir, yes madam!'

Besides his dark complexion and glistening white teeth it seemed as though every limb of his body had been screwed into his torso, because one or the other of his limbs would always hang down to one side with a jerk. Sometimes it would be his right shoulder that would bend down or the left knee while his mouth would always remain open.

'You Hindu, babu?' 'Yes, Madam,' the babu replied somewhat embarrassed. Liza was pleased with her discovery. 'I guessed right!' 'Yes, madam!'

Liza stared at him. But the longer she looked, the more

confused she became. On what basis had she surmised that he was a Hindu? Surely not on the basis of the clothes—coat, a pair of trousers and necktie that he was wearing. She became contemplative. What are those signs by which a Hindu can be recognized? She got up, and putting out her hand searched through his hair for that distinctive something that distinguished a Hindu from a Muslim.

The babu became nervous. A man of nearly thirty years of age, he had been working as stenographer in the Deputy Commissioner's office for the last ten years. Liza was the first woman, and that too the wife of a Deputy Commissioner, who spoke to him with such familiarity. The wives of other Deputy Commissioners had always been curt and indifferent towards him.

At the far end of the veranda, near the passage that led to the kitchen, stood the khansama, the gardener and the cook, all looking towards them.

'No, it isn't here!' Liza said.

The babu again became nervous. The faint smile that had appeared on his lips vanished.

'You are no Hindu. You told a lie.'

'No, madam, I am a Hindu, a Brahmin Hindu.'

'Oh, no. Where is your tuft, in that case?'

There was danger of a riot breaking out in the city and he had, with great difficulty, managed to reach the office. He had felt somewhat reassured by the way the lady was treating him, and a broad smile appeared on his swarthy face, showing his glistening white teeth.

'I have no tuft, madam.'

'Then you are no Hindu,' Liza said, laughing, shaking her forefinger at him. 'You told a lie!'

'No, madam, I am a Hindu.'

'Take off your coat, babu.' Liza commanded.

'Oh, madam!' said the babu acutely embarrassed.

'Take it off, take it off. Hurry!'

Smiling, the babu took off his coat.

'Good. Now unbutton your shirt.'

'What, madam?'

'Don't say "What madam!" Say, "I beg your pardon, madam". All right. Unbutton your shirt.'

The babu stood perplexed. Then putting his hand under his necktie, he undid all the three buttons.

'Show me your thread.'

'What, madam?'

'Your thread. "What madam?" Show me your Hindu thread.'

The babu understood what the lady meant. The Memsahib was asking about the sacred thread, the yagyopaveet. The babu was not wearing any. After passing his matriculation examination he had cut off the tuft on his head, and on joining the intermediate class, had cast off the sacred thread.

'I am not wearing any thread, madam.'

'No thread? Then you are no Hindu.'

'I am a Hindu, madam. I swear by God I am a Hindu.'

He was getting nervous again.

'No, you are no Hindu. You told a lie. I shall tell your boss about it.'

The babu's face suddenly turned pale.

'I tell you sincerely, madam, I am a Hindu. My name is Roshan Lal,' he said, as he buttoned his shirt and put on his coat.

'Roshan Lal? But the cook's name is Roshan Din and he is a Musalman.'

'Yes, madam,' the babu replied. It was difficult for him to explain the difference.

'He is Roshan Din, madam. I am Roshan Lal. I am a Hindu. He is a Muslim.'

'No. My husband told me you people have different names.'

Then, raising her forefinger, she said in a mock-angry voice, 'No, babu, you told a lie. I shall tell your boss.'

The babu's throat became parched and his heart started pounding. 'There is trouble brewing in the city. It may be that the lady's questions have something to do with it. What does the memsahib want?'

Suddenly Liza felt bored and sick at heart.

'Go babu. I shall tell your boss everything.'

The babu picked up his file from the floor and went towards his table.

'Babu!' Liza shouted again.

The babu turned round.

'Where is your boss?'

'He is in his office, madam. He is very busy.'

'Go. Get out of here... You and your boss!' she almost shrieked.

'Yes, madam!' and the babu turned away, trembling in every limb.

As the babu left, her playful mood had turned into intense disgust. An acute sense of loneliness and desolation came over her. The babu, walking away with his shoulders bent, looked to her a slimy creature. How can Richard work with such people day in and day out? She heaved a long, painful sigh and turned to go in.

8

Each community in the town pursued a trade that was exclusive to them. Textile business was mostly in the hands of Hindus, business in leather goods was owned by Muslims; transport was run by Muslims, and grain merchants were Hindus. Petty jobs and professions, however, were pursued by both Hindus and Muslims.

The Shivala market was doing brisk busines. Looking at it, no one could say that there was tension in the town. The goldsmiths' shops were crowded with village women in burqas buying or placing orders for silver jewellery. In front of Hakim Labh Ram's dispensary two Kashmiri Muslims, pestles in hand, were pounding away at medicinal herbs, their noses covered with pieces of cloth; the hunchbacked halwai had, as usual, a crowd of customers at his shop; Santram, the vendor had arrived with his pushcart, punctually at one o'clock, as was his wont, and was slowly moving through the goldsmiths' market towards the Shivala Bazaar, serving half a chhatank or more of halwa on a pipal leaf to every customer on the way. At the Shivala Bazaar, the tailor Khuda Baksh and his two brothers were Santram's daily customers, besides many others.

The general atmosphere was calm and stable. There was the usual traffic on the roads. The tension caused by the incident that morning had partly been diffused and partly submerged. Opposite Khuda Baksh's shop at the corner of the lane, a municipal worker was standing on a ladder cleaning the chimney of the oil lamp fixed in the wall and replenishing it with oil. Every activity in the business of life appeared to be moving as rhythmically as part of a symphony. When Ibrahim the pedlar selling scents and oils with the bag on his back full of bottles big and small and another bag hanging from his shoulder, went from lane to lane shouting about his wares, it appeared as though his movements too were in keeping with that rhythm. So were the movements of the women with their earthen pitchers going to the water-taps, tongas plying on the roads, children going to school. Every activity gave the impression of having combined to create an inner harmony to which the heart of the town throbbed. It was to the same rhythm that people were born, grew up and became old, that generations came and went. This rhythm or symphony was the creation of centuries of communal living, of the inhabitants having come together in harmony. One would think that every activity was like a chord in a musical instrument, and if even one string snapped the instrument would produce only jarring notes.

It cannot be said that the even tenor of the town's life was never disturbed. In recent years there had been the ebb and flow of many a current and cross-current. During the days of the freedom struggle, every now and then, the town would shake under the impact of surging emotions and movements. Then there were disturbing developments. Once every year, on the occasion of Guru

Nanak's birthday, a Sikh procession would be taken out and tension would grip the city. Will the procession pass in front of the Jama Masjid, with its band playing or will it take some other route? There was the fear that even a stray stone flung on the procession might lead to a communal riot. Similarly, on the occasion of Muharram, tension would mount when Muslims would take out tazias, beat their bare chests and shout 'Ya Hussein! Ya Hussein!', perspiration dripping from their bodies, and pass through the streets of the town. But soon after, the atmosphere would cool down and life would regain its even tenor, linking itself once again with the inner rhythm. Once again its innate cheerfulness would return.

At the shop of Khuda Baksh the tailor, Sardar Hukam Singh's wife was complaining loudly: '0 Bakshe, when will you ever learn to keep your word? Why aren't my clothes ready? Why must I have to come to your shop again and again?'

Khuda Baksh smiled. He was familiarly addressed as Bakshe by the women of Hindu and Sikh families of the town. His shelves were heavily stacked with bundles of unstitched cloth, meant primarily for wedding dresses.

'Bibi, you never bothered to send me the required cloth in time. Didn't I keep reminding you of it throughout winter? You never bothered. After all it takes time to stitch clothes. God has given me only two hands, Bibi, not sixteen.'

'What is the man saying? Throughout winter?'

'Why, wasn't your daughter betrothed fifteen days after the wedding of Shiv Ram's son? Isn't that so? Which month was it?'

Hukam Singh's wife laughed. 'He even remembers the dates. Now teH me clearly—when will my daughter's suit be ready?'

'Which is the auspicious day, Bibi, of the wedding?'

'Look at the fellow. He knows the day of the girl's betrothal but not her wedding day.'

'Don't I know? It is on the twenty-fifth of this month. Isn't that so? Today is fifth. Have no fear, the suit will be ready on time.'

'Nothing doing. Tell me the exact date. Don't I know you? On the wedding day itself you will make us run to your shop again and again. Didn't this happen on my Vidya's marriage? The wedding party was already on its way and I was sending my man again and again for her gold-embroidered suit. Tell me the exact date when the suit will be ready.'

She had not yet finished talking when someone standing behind her threw a packet of light-green silken cloth and a spool of gold-thread border into Bakshe's lap.

'Get the cloth measured, Bakshe, and if more cloth is required get it in my account from Budh Singh's shop.'

It was another lady customer. Bakshe wet a corner of the cloth with his tongue and, taking his pencil from behind his right ear, put a mark on it and threw the packet and the spool on to the shelf by his side. The whole almirah was full of bundles and packets meant for wedding dresses.

'Yes, yes, the suit will be ready. I shall deliver it at your house myself.'

'You only know how to talk. If this time you fail me I shall never set foot in your shop again.' And Hukam Singh's wife turned and left the shop.

As she turned away, Khuda Baksh's eyes fell on the wall of the Shivala opposite. He noticed some movement there. He looked intently. A man was standing on top of the wall doing something. It was the Gurkha watchman. What was he doing there? On the other side of the wall was the old temple whose shining dome could be seen from far and near. A bell had been installed on top of the wall and the Gurkha watchman appeared to be cleaning it.

'What is he doing that for?' Khuda Baksh said to one of his assistants, who sat working on a sewing machine close by.

'The bell is being repaired, it seems,' the shop assistant answered.

'God forbid that it should ring again,' Khuda Baksh exclaimed.

Both fell silent.

The bell had been put up after the communal riots of 1926. Its weather-beaten metal was no longer as bright as it used to be. Much of the plaster on the wall too had cracked and fallen off. Khuda Baksh was then a young man of twenty or so, madly interested in body-building exercises, and had just joined his father in the tailoring business. It was in those very days that the bell had been installed. Khuda Baksh was now an elderly man; there was hardly a wedding in the town for which his services as a tailor were not sought after. The man perched on the wall too was the same Gurkha chowkidar—Ram Bali by name—who had originally installed the bell. After the riots, his services had been retained because of his alertness, integrity and spirit of service. Wrinkles had since appeared on his face and his hair had greyed. But as a watchman he was still as alert as he used to be.

A low ringing sound emanated from the bell. Khuda Baksh's eyes again turned towards the wall. The Gurkha chowkidar was tying a new rope to the bell. The pulley had been oiled and the bell was once again shining and ringing as before.

'I tremble when I hear that sound,' Khuda Baksh said. 'The first time the alarm bell was rung when the Grain Market had been set on fire and half the sky was covered with the glow of its flames.'

Perched on the wall, the Gurkha was still rubbing the bell with a duster so as to bring out its shine, as though for some festival or an auspicious day. A new, white rope was now hanging by its side.

From the wall, Khuda Baksh's eyes turned towards the neighbouring goldsmith's shop where an elderly villager and his wife were persuading their young daughter to buy a pair of earrings.

'Why don't you take it if it has caught your fancy? Only hurry up. We have a lot else to do before going back to the village.'

The girl's eyes were shining. She would put the earrings to her ears again and again and show them to her mother.

'How do they look on me, Ma?'

She was unable to make up her mind.

Khuda Baksh's eyes again went back towards the wall of the temple. The old watchman was now getting down from the wall.

'Ya Allah!' muttered Khuda Baksh and turned his face away.

It was a common practice at Fazal-din, the nanbai's shop, in the afternoons, when the hot sun was on the decline and there was little work to do, for friends from here and there to gather for a leisurely chat. With the hookah going around, all subjects under the sun would be discussed.

To begin with, the discussion had centred round the morning incident that the whole town was talking about. But then it branched out to other topics. Old Karim Khan was rambling on how impossible it was for an ordinary man to fathom what was in the mind of the ruler. 'The man in authority takes a long view of things; each one of his actions reflects his far-sightedness. It is beyond the ken of an ordinary man to see what the man in authority can see.'

'Musa said to Khizr one day,' continued Karim Khan, "Please take me on as your pupil..." Listen Jilani, listen attentively. This is a very instructive story. . . Now Musa was much younger in age, but he was aspiring to become a seer, a prophet. Till then he had not become one. Khizr was already a prophet. You are following me, aren't you? And was older in age too. Everyone held him in very high esteem.' Karim Khan went on. There was a glint of a smile in his eyes. Whenever he laughed, he would slap his thigh and all those sitting around would smile too.

'So, one day, Musa said to Khizr, "Make me your pupil" and Khizr replied "All right, I shall make you my pupil, but on one condition."

"What is that?" asked Musa.

"That you will keep your mouth shut at whatever I do. You will not utter a word."

"I agree," replied Musa.

'And so Khizr took him on as his pupil. Now Khizr wanted to impart to him an important lesson. What was that lesson? The lesson was: It is God Almighty alone who sees everything. It is not given to us humans to see everything. We may rack our brains and go into cause and effect but to no purpose. It is God who is all-seeing; it is God the Merciful who alone is omnipotent. And Khizr said, "You will not utter a word. I may do anything, say anything, and you will keep your mouth shut."'

Karim Khan had passed on the hookah and Jilani was now puffing away at it. The afternoon was on the decline, the water-carrier had already sprinkled water on the ground in front of the shop, the odour of wet earth filled the air, the traffic on the road had eased, and only occasionally a man would be seen going towards the Jama Masjid for his afternoon prayer.

'So, God bless you,' continued Karim Khan. 'The next day, Khizr set out on a journey to the next village, and Musa went along with him. Later on Musa became a great seer, a great prophet, but at that time he was only a pupil of Khizr. Now listen, Jilani. Are you listening? It is a very instructive story. So, both set out. On the way they came to a river. They found a boat tied to the river-bank, it was used by people to cross the river. Both sat down in the boat and the boatman began to row them across. After a little while Musa saw that Khizr was making a hole in the bottom of the boat It was a brand new boat, probably bought only the day before, and here was

Khizr boring a hole in its bottom. He finished boring one hole and started drilling another. Musa cried out, "What in God's name are you doing? The boat will sink and we shall both be drowned."

'Khizr put his forefinger to his lips making a sign to him to keep quiet. Musa was extremely nervous, because the boat was getting flooded with water, but he kept his peace, since he had given his word to Khizr. After some time Khizr put stoppers in each one of the holes he had made, but by then the bottom of the boat had been badly damaged. Reaching the other side, both of them stepped out of the boat and, God be praised, resumed their journey.

'They had walked a little distance when they saw a little boy playing on the ground. As they passed by, Khizr picked up the boy and without a word, wrung his neck and strangled him to death. "What?" shrieked Musa. "You have put an innocent child to death!" But Khizr put his finger to his lips, ordering him to keep quite.

'"How can I keep quiet?" shouted Musa. "You have twisted the neck of a little child, and you want me to keep quiet! You did not even know him. Never before have you set foot in this village. How had this innocent child offended you?" Musa was deeply troubled. In reality he too was a prophet, only a prophet in the making.' Karim Khan said, shaking his head, 'Now, God be praised, both of them again resumed their journey. After covering some distance, they passed through a village. On reaching the other end of the village they came across a dilapidated boundary wall. Musa jumped over to the other side at one go, but as he turned round he saw Khizr standing by it, picking up the bricks lying on the ground, one by one, and putting them on the wall, as though repairing it.

'Musa turned back. "Sir, you put to death the little boy who had merely opened his eyes on the world, and here you are, repairing an old, dilapidated wall. What is the matter? I can't make head or tail of what you are doing." Khizr again put his forefinger to his lips to indicate to Musa to keep quiet. Musa again fell silent.

'They went further, on and on, till they came to a garden in which, under the shade of a big tree, bubbled a lovely spring. Both washed their hands and feet and sat down to rest. Khizr said:

'"Listen, my dear. You had strongly protested when I bore holes into the bottom of that boat. Well, the fact of the matter is that the ruler of that village is a tyrant. For his own merry-making he takes away the boats of poor people. I thought if I made holes in the bottom of the boat, his men will not carry it away and the boatman will not be deprived of his livelihood."

'Musa was listening with rapt attention. "But why did you kill that innocent child?" he asked.

'"Well," Khizr said "That boy was a bastard, born of sin, the progeny of a cruel and wicked man. I could foresee that when he would grow up, he too would be a heartless, vicious man, a torment for innocent people. Now tell me, was my conduct right or wrong?"

'Musa fell to thinking, his head bowed.

'"Why did you repair that broken-down wall? For whose benefit did you do that?"

'And Khizr's reply was:

'"There is an explanation to that also. Under that wall lies buried a treasure, a fabulous treasure. But the villagers know nothing about it. They are poor, needy people. I wanted to help them. While ploughing their fields when they will come upon the wall, they will find it an impediment, an obstacle in their way and will, one day, pull it down and throw the bricks out of their fields. They will then discover this treasure which will make them wealthy and prosperous. They will then have bread to eat and clothes to wear. Now tell me, how was I wrong in what I did?"'

Having narrated the parable, Karim Khan turned his eyes towards his listeners, one after the other and said, 'The moral of the story is: a ruler can see what you and I, ordinary folk, cannot see. The British ruler has all-seeing eyes, otherwise how can it be possible that a handful of firanghis coming from across the seven seas should rule over so big a country? The firanghis are very wise, very subtle, very far-sighted...'

'Of course, of course!' said many of the listeners, nodding their heads.

Nathu too was sitting at the nanbai's shop, a glass of tea before him and in his hand a piece of dry rusk, which he would dip into his tea and nibble at, bit by bit. He too had been listening to Karim Khan's story and it gave him a sense of reassurance. Ever since he had come out of that despicable hole, he had been wandering from one street to the other. He would prick up his ears every time he heard people talking about the pig. Sometimes he would think that people were talking about some other pig, and not the one he had killed. Nevertheless his heart would miss a beat. In the nanbai's shop too, they had earlier been talking about the pig. But the narration of the elderly gentleman had given him considerable relief. If a riot did not break out, the incident would begin to look trivial. Since the ruler was far-sighted and alert, nothing untoward would happen.

Nathu again put his hand on his pocket to feel the currency note lying in it. The crisp note rustled. That pleased him. It was nice of Murad Ali to have paid the entire amount in advance. Even if he had put an eight-anna piece on the palm of his hand, saying that the rest would be paid later, he couldn't have refused, the poor skinner that he was. Since Murad Ali had been a man of his word, he too was expected to stand by him. But he had run away from that filthy hole; unmindful of Murad Ali's clear instructions that he should wait for him there. But it was so suffocating in that room. On reaching the town, however, when he found everyone talking about the pig his heart sank.

Nathu had been feeling extremely restless. The more nervous he became, the more confused he felt. He could not talk to anyone. He had been tricked. Using the veterinary surgeon as an alibi, Murad Ali had got the pig slaughtered by him, and got it thrown outside the mosque. But who could tell if it was the same pig? He had not seen the carcass on the steps of the mosque. What if people came to know that he was the man who had killed the pig? At times he wanted to go home and shut himself in. At others he felt like just knocking about the streets, from one lane to the other. There were other thoughts too that oppressed him. No, he wouldn't go home. When night fell, he would go to Motia, the prostitute. If she asked for one rupee, he would pay her five. He would pass the whole night with her.

The whole day passed thus, wandering about the streets, but when evening fell he suddenly began to miss his wife. Had he been in his colony he would have been sitting and chatting with his fellow-skinners, smoking his hookah. 'No I shall go home' he suddenly said to himself. 'I'll bathe, change my shirt, make my wife sit by my side and talk to her. As soon as I reach home I shall take her in my arms, I won't even mention the name of Murad Ali; it is not necessary to tell her anything; no need to talk about that hateful business. It is only when I rest my head on her bosom that I shall have peace of mind. If I go to a prostitute, she will talk nastily, even abuse me. My wife is a quiet kind, she will give me comfort and courage. Instead of wasting money on the prostitute I will buy something for my wife. She will be pleased. She will say, "Why did you have to bring anything for me? I have everything." She never makes any demands.' He felt the warmth of her body in his close embrace, despite the distance that lay between them. He felt as though his mental anguish was ebbing out. It is only to one's wife that one turns in moments of pain; she alone can relieve him of his mental suffering. She is blessed with infinite patience, her bosom is brimming with love.

It was smoky inside the nanbai's shop. On the two benches lying outside, sat two load-carriers cross-legged on each bench eating their meal out of tin-plates. Dipping their morsels of naan into the plate of lentils they ate hungrily. The water-carrier was again sprinkling the road.

Suddenly the sound of a drum-beat was heard from

far away. The porters turned their heads towards the sound. The drum was heard closer now. People sitting inside the nanbai's shop fell silent; some of them came out.

'What is it?'

'Some announcement, it seems,' someone answered. Soon enough, a tonga appeared with the tricolour fluttering on its top. Someone sitting inside was beating away at the drum. The tonga came and stopped right in front of the nanbai's shop. A man, sitting by the side of the tonga-driver, stood up. He began to make the announcement by first reciting a couplet, the purport of which was:

'Pray, think for once of your country. Calamity is knocking at your door, and confabulations are going on high above, plotting to bring about your ruin.

'Fellow countrymen, this is to inform you that a public meeting, under the auspices of the District Congress Committee will take place this evening at six o'clock sharp, in Ganj Mandi, in which the efforts of the British rulers to disrupt India's struggle for freedom through their perfidious policy of divide and rule will be fully exposed, and a fervent appeal will be made to all the citizens to preserve peace and tranquillity in the city at all costs. Citizens are requested to attend the meeting in large numbers.'

On the back seat of the tonga sat the Jarnail with a big drum between his knees. It was Shankar who had stood up to make the announcement. He sat down in his seat. The drum-beat was resumed and the tonga moved away.

As the tonga left, one coolie said to the other, 'I was carrying a babu's load from the Ganj Mandi when the babu said, "Azadi is coming. India will soon be free." I laughed and said, "Babuji, what is that to me? I am carrying loads now and shall continue carrying them then.'" And he burst out laughing, revealing the bright-red gums over his teeth. 'Our lot is to carry loads,' he repeated laughing.

An elderly man with a beard, sitting inside the shop said, 'Has that rascal been arrested or not who defiled the mosque? The swine! May his body be eaten up by worms, limb by limb.'

'What happened was awful!'

At this Karim Khan, the jolly old man with a twinkle in his eyes, said solemnly, 'It is said in the Holy Book, "Man's crops are standing by my orders; all man's schemes work by my orders; without my command, standing crops shall wilt and perish, floods shall inundate the lands, causing havoc to city after city." Everything is in God's hands. Every task is accomplished by His divine will. His and His alone will be done.'

People sitting around nodded their heads. The hookah continued to do its rounds. Outside the shop, one of the two coolies burst into song:

O why are you bending so low.
To stare at the folds of my salwar!

It was the same coolie who, a little while earlier, had been laughing and reproducing the dialogue he had had with the babu.

Nathu envied the man for his carefree, happy-go-lucky temperament.

There were again some stirrings on the road. Pedestrians on their way stopped and stepped aside, their eyes turned towards the Jama Masjid nearby.

'The Pir of Golra Sharif is here!' Someone standing by the roadside said to the nanbai, and putting his hand on his heart waited for the Pir Sahib.

The nanbai too stood up. All those sitting inside the shop came out and devoutly stood waiting for the Pir Sahib's arrival.

A tall, bearded man appeared. He was dressed in a long, black robe and had numerous necklaces of large beads round his neck. His long, flowing hair fell on the nape of his neck from under his turban. He had a bright, pious face and in his hand was a rosary. He was surrounded by a band of devoted followers.

The nanbai went and stood in the middle of the road, his head bent and his hands on his thighs. As the Pir put out his left hand, the nanbai touched both his eyes to it one by one, and then putting his right hand on his heart continued to stand with his head bowed. The Pir raised his hand a little, and without uttering a word moved on. Almost everyone standing by the roadside went up to him, put the Pir's hand to his eyes and received his blessing.

'He is not a pir, he is a sage!' said the nanbai coming back into his shop. 'What radiance! What a glowing forehead!'

Among the customers, some came back into the shop, while some others left for their homes. The Pir Sahib was now the topic of discussion inside the shop.

'He is a pir with very high spiritual attainments. He can read a person's mind merely by looking at him,' the nanbai said. Then, turning towards those who were sitting inside the shop, said, 'I once went on a pilgrimage to

Golra Sharif. As I stood in his holy presence, he said to me, "Pick up some grains from that heap. What are you looking at me for?" From the heap of grains that lay on the ground in front of him, I bent down and picked up a handful, at which the Pir Sahib remarked, "Is that all? Only a hundred and seventy grains? You could have picked up more." Amazed, I sat down and counted them. Not a grain more, not a grain less than a hundred and seventy.'

'He can cure any disease,' remarked Karim Khan. 'My grandson, now a grown-up lad by God's grace, when only a small child, developed mumps. Both his cheeks were swollen. Someone advised me to take the child to Golra Sharif, and so I did. As I stood in his presence, the Pir Sahib asked me to put down the child before him. He picked up a big knife lying by his side and touched the child's cheeks twice with it. Then, putting his right hand to his mouth, he spat on it, and smeared the sputum on the child's cheeks. Just that, and asked me to take away the child. I made my obeisance and left. By the time we reached home the swelling had subsided and the child's fever was gone.'

'Holy men are blessed with healing powers. Near here, in Masiadi, there is a Baba Roda—the bald sadhu—he too has the healing touch.'

'But the Pir Sahib does not touch kafirs with his hands. He hates infidels. Earlier, it was different. Anyone could go to him. Only, if an infidel came for treatment, he would feel his pulse with a stick—putting one end of the stick on his pulse and the other to his ear, and thus diagnose the disease. But now he does not permit any kafir to come near him.'

'It is surprising how he has come to the town at this time of the year. Usually he comes in late summer.'

'What difference does it make to holy men whether it is summer or winter.'

'It may be that the news about the defiling of the mosque has reached him.'

'He needs no telling. He must have come to know of it, on his own, intuitively.'

'It is the holy man's goodwill that is of paramount importance. Otherwise a pir-fakir has only to pronounce a curse and a whole city will be in ruins, reduced to dust!'

'True! Very true!'

'Will he deliver a sermon while he is here?'

'He will certainly do so, if he stays on till Friday.'

'Now that he has come, he will not go back without purging the city clean.'

Shades of the afternoon were lengthening when Nathu left the nanbai's shop. He felt light at heart. The apprehensions that had been gnawing at his heart had almost subsided. There was a lot of bustle and gaiety on the roads. Why should he allow that petty incident to torment him so much? People would curse the fellow who had put the carcass on the steps of the mosque and then dismiss it from their minds, calling the fellow a mad man. Besides, no one seemed to know how the pig was killed and by whom. Murad Ali was the only one who knew about it, and he, being a Muslim, would not tell anyone that he had got the heinous deed done.

Nathu was intrigued by the surrounding scene. Outside a small shoe-shop, a man from a village was persuading his wife to buy a new pair of shoes for herself.

'Why don't you buy it? You don't have an extra pair and the one you are wearing is worn-out.'

'No, no, it is you who needs a good pair of shoes. You have to do so much of running about. Mine is serving me well still.'

Nathu moved on. He felt good. He crossed the road and turned towards the right, and began walking at a leisurely pace. He passed by another row of nanbais' shops. Spicy aromas arose from huge metal pots of cooked meat and the piles of naans heaped one on top of another. Nanbais' shops were bursting with customers most of them coolies or families from surrounding villages who would come to these eating shops, tired and hungry after the day's work. That particular bazaar was located at one end of the town, from where the villagers, after satisfying their hunger, would get on to their bullock-carts and set off on the long road towards their respective villages.

Behind the row of nanbais' shops, stood the imposing Jama Masjid. In the declining afternoon sun, it looked milky white as though newly washed. The mosque presented the familiar, everyday scene, with beggars sitting on the steps, labourers reclining or lying about and devotees going in or coming out. Suddenly Nathu saw a crowd of people coming out of its vaulted entrance. Everyone was picking up or puting on his pair of shoes and hurriedly coming down the steps. Nathu just stood and watched. It was only on rare occasions, such as Id, that people in such large numbers would be seen emerging from the mosque. Was there some sermon? Suddenly the Pir of Golra Sharif came to his mind. It may be that he had delivered the sermon and people were returning

from it. His heart missed a beat. Perhaps all these
hundreds of people had gathered to discuss the awful
deed committed by him. The Pir too must have come
to deliver a sermon concerning that deed.

Nathu walked past the Jama Masjid. At the farther
end of the building was a ditch. All the dirty water of
the town flowed into it and was carried out of the city.
Nathu came and stood against the railing of the ditch.
As he looked down, his eyes fell on a man of dark
complexion lying utterly naked on a narrow ledge below
the railing, with a talisman round his neck. A tin-box
was hanging by a nail driven into the wall above him.
The ledge was so narrow that if the man turned his side
while asleep, he would surely fall into the ditch. Nathu
thought that for all he knew, this man too might be a
fakir of high spiritual attainments. He gazed at him intently.

Suddenly the fakir sat up, stared at him and began
shaking his head violently, as a man who is crazy or in
a trance does.

Nathu turned away and began looking towards the
bazaar. After a while when he looked back, the man was
no longer shaking his head; instead, he was beckoning
him with his forefinger. Nathu felt confused. He was
afraid lest the fakir should cast a magic spell on him or
pronounce a curse. He took out a one-anna coin from
his pocket and threw it in front of the fakir. The latter
picked it up and threw it into the ditch, and staring hard
at Nathu, again beckoned him. Nathu trembled with fear
and left the place.

The Bara Bazaar, the main market of the town, bore
a festive look. At the two shops of aerated water, which

stood side by side and were decked with long rows of coloured bottles, sat the neatly dressed shopkeepers, filling glass after glass with lemon squash and passing them on to customers. Those who sold flower-garlands on the pavement, had already arrived. Close to the aerated water shops were stalls selling meat cutlets and kababs. Round the corner was the prostitutes' lane with a wine-shop in front. Nathu stood undecided by the roadside.

By the roadside, stood a few tongas with shining well-polished harnesses and feather-plumes fluttering on the heads of horses, lending a festive air to the atmosphere. Now and then a tonga would stop in the middle of the road, with some wealthy landlord sitting inside chatting with a couple of friends, all of them in their well-starched clothes and turbans.

Nathu again felt reassured and relaxed and continued strolling about. People had come out to have a good time. As evening fell, the fun and gaiety increased. And Nathu, elated, went straight to the stall of meat kababs and bought eight-annas worth of kababs. Then walking over to the wine-shop, he settled down on a bench outside. He ate the kababs with zest and then put the glass of country wine to his lips.

The street lights went up. The odour of wet earth from the sprinkling of water blended with the smell of flowers and Nathu felt inebriated. He did not remember when he had bought a garland of flowers and put it round his neck. He even did not remember that after getting up from the wine-shop he had crossed the wide Raja Bazaar Road and gone into the prostitutes' lane.

It was then that he saw Murad Ali coming towards him. It was Murad Ali, wasn't it?—In his long coat coming down to his knees, his thin cane-stick, his bristling black moustaches—the short, stoutish figure of Murad Ali. Or was he dreaming? Like an apparition Murad Ali moved from street to street, swinging his cane-stick. Did a man, with the name of Murad Ali really exist or was he a figment of his imagination? No, no, it was really Murad Ali, coming from the side of the Grain Market, by way of the lane. Had Nathu not been a little high, he would have hidden behind the projection of some house. But Nathu was in high spirits. He came and stood right in the middle of the street. He had not had much to drink. For a low-caste skinner, two tumblers of wine are like water. It was only that after having knocked about the whole day, he had seen someone he knew, to whom he could talk. Of a sudden, Nathu felt elated and confident. 'Whatever job we take up, we do it to perfection!' he mumbled to himself.

'Salaam huzoor!'

Nathu stepped forward and greeted him jovially.

'Salaam huzoor!' he said again, standing erect, with his chest out.

Murad Ali, taken aback, stopped in his steps, but only for a moment. Looking at Nathu with his sharp, piercing eyes, he grasped the situation and without acknowledging Nathu's greetings or uttering a word, moved on.

'Salaam huzoor! I am Nathu. Don't you recognize me?' Nathu said and laughed.

By then, Murad Ali had moved ahead.

Confused, Nathu stood in the middle of the street and again shouted: 'Huzoor! Murad Ali Sahib!'

But Murad Ali did not stop or turn round.

Suddenly a thought occurred to Nathu: 'Murad Ali must know that I have done the job. He must not be under any misapprehension. He must not think that I am loitering about without doing the job.'

Nathu moved forward on his unsteady legs. The lane became more dark as he went farther; but he had his eyes on the receding figure of Murad Ali. He followed him. 'The huzoor has to be told that the job was done.'

He felt as though he had overtaken Murad Ali. That part of the lane was lonely, and it had seemed to him that Murad Ali had slowed his pace.

'I forgot to tell you, huzoor, that the job was duly done! The thing was despatched on time! The fellow with the pushcart had duly arrived!'

Nathu saw that Murad Ali had stopped, and with his cane lifted, was looking at him.

Soon enough Murad Ali would move towards him, but why was he holding up his cane? And why didn't he speak? At one end of the dark lane, they stood staring at each other.

'The work was done, huzoor!' Nathu said again. 'The stuff was sent off to the right place!'

Hardly had he uttered these words when it seemed to him that Murad Ali had again turned round and moved away, taking long strides. At the dark end of the lane, there was a slope and Murad Ali was going up the slope.

Nathu looked up. Murad Ali had moved farther away. He was now going up the slope which led towards the

Shivala. He again looked like an apparition to Nathu, going farther and farther away, and yet not vanishing from sight!

When she opened the door and saw Nathu standing on the threshold, Nathu's wife felt so relieved that tears welled up in her eyes. 'I have been on tenterhooks waiting for you'.

She went in and sat down on the cot, crying. 'I was so anxious, my heart was sinking. I kept wondering where you could have gone? I was so miserable.'

Wiping her tears with a corner of her sari she looked at him and suddenly smiled.

'You are looking like a clown, a garland hanging from one ear. Whom have you been visiting?'

Nathu went in and without uttering a word sat down on the cot.

'Oh, you have been drinking. But then, why aren't you laughing and singing as you always do when you come home drunk?'

Nathu's wife was a woman blessed with infinite patience. Even when Nathu, in a fit of rage, abused her, she would not answer back. She would only say: 'Go on, say whatever is on your mind, you will feel lighter that way.' Or, she would stand quietly on one side and putting her finger to her lips say, 'Enough, enough, don't say anything more otherwise you will regret your outburst later on.' Now, you can drive a pin into a person's flesh, but what is the point in driving it into a lump of clay? Seeing her cool temperament, Nathu too would keep his temper under control. In the neighbouring row of huts, no fewer than twenty chamar families lived, and she was on good terms with all of them, sharing their joys and sorrows. A God-fearing woman, she was content with whatever little she had. There is a quality of character which some people possess, an inner balance which strikes an equation with any situation, and does not make any demands on life that are beyond their reach. Such people are always cheerful and are like flowers that have blossomed fully.

Nathu had still not uttered a word.

'Why don't you say something? You have been away for so long. I felt a like a fish out of water.'

Nathu lifted his eyes and looked at her. Something welled up within him. He shook his head. 'To hell with Murad Ali and his pig,' he muttered to himself. 'I am safely back home.'

'Did the people in the colony enquire after me?' he asked.

'Yes, they did. Once or twice.'

'What did you tell them?'

'I said that you had gone out on some work and would be back shortly.'

'Did they ask about me many times?'

'No. Don't people go to work? In the evening, the woman next door asked about you. I said you had gone to skin a horse.'

A faint smile appeared on Nathu's lips.

'But where were you? Where did you go?'

'I shall tell you some other time.' Nathu's wife looked at him. There had never been an occasion in the past when he had hidden anything from her. But it was better to remain silent.

'I won't insist. Don't tell me if you don't want to...
Would you like to eat something? I shall make chapatis
for you. You can have them with a glass of tea. Good,
hot chapatis.' And she got down from the cot. Impelled
by some inner urge, Nathu pulled her back and made
her sit by his side.

'No, no, just sit here.'

And she sat down.

'Have you eaten?'

'Yes, I have.'

Nathu's wife noticed that he was behaving oddly.

'Don't lie,' he said. 'Tell me the truth. Have you had
your meal?'

She again looked up at him and said, laughing: 'I
cooked the meal all right, but I couldn't eat anything.'

'Did you eat in the morning?'

'Yes, I did.'

'You are lying again. Tell the truth. Did you eat?'

She looked at her husband and laughed.

'No, I didn't. I was waiting for you. How could I
eat?'

'What if I had not come home even tonight?'

'You had to come. I knew you would come.'

A vague uneasiness still troubled him. It was this
uneasiness which had impelled him to wander about the
streets the whole day long and later to get drunk at the
wine-shop. Even as he sat by his wife, it was gnawing
at his heart. Suddenly he thought he heard something.
It seemed to him that Murad Ali was standing outside,
the point of his cane-stick resting on the door. Nathu's
heart missed a beat. He tried to reassure himself, 'But

Murad Ali might not have recognized me. He would have spoken to me otherwise. He just went away. He must have taken me for some drunken lout who was bothering him. After all it was Murad Ali who had put the five-rupee note in my hand.'

'I knew there was something bothering you. That's why I was so worried.'

Nathu turned to look at her. Her anxious eyes were staring at his face.

'People said there was some trouble brewing in the town. Someone had killed a pig and thrown it outside, a mosque. That also made me nervous. I said to myself "If some trouble broke out, where shall I look for you? How shall I find you?"'

Nathu was taken aback.

'Which pig? What sort of pig?'

'Don't you know what a pig is?' His wife laughed. She was relieved that Nathu had come back. She only wished that they would just keep sitting and chatting with each other.

'What colour was the pig? Black or white?' Nathu asked. He was all ears to hear his wife's answer.

'What difference does that make?'

'Did you see it?'

'Shall I go to see a pig? What have I to do with it?'

'Has anyone in our colony seen it?'

'What are you saying? Will people from the colony go to see a dead pig? They were only repeating what they had heard.'

The night was deepening. Voices from the neighbouring tenements had virtually ceased.

'Where would you like to sleep? Out in the open or inside?' she asked, looking sideways at her husband.

'Why do you ask?'

'How can I be sure about you? When we are sleeping outside, you sometimes lift me and carry me inside. I thought I might as well ask you beforehand. If you have any shady intentions we may as well stay indoors, even though it is rather stuffy inside.' Saying so she sat down and began untying her hair. 'You have not told me whether you would like to eat something. Shall I make you some tea? Why are you so glum? I felt so lonely when you were not here.'

Listening to his wife talk a wave of emotion, at once painful and ecstatic, welled up within him and he put his arms round her and his eager lips sought her cheeks, her lips, her hair, her eyes hungrily, over and over again. His frenzy increased with every passing moment and he felt as though every pore of his body was melting into her warm flesh and her excited breathing.

'I cried three times during the day. Standing in the veranda I waited for you for hours and hours and then came into the room to cry. I thought you would never come back.'

His craving for mental peace would take him to her lips, then to her breasts, from one part of her body to another, seeking solace and comfort.

Just then dogs began to bark fiercely in the yard outside, and muffled noises were heard from far away. Nathu was oblivious of everything. A little while later however, his wife noticed something on the wall of their room, near the ceiling. It was a trembling glow of light on the wall opposite the ventilator. From far away, muffled sounds continued to come.

'What is that?' said his wife pointing towards the wall. 'What light is that on the wall? Looks like a fire has broken out somewhere. Just listen.'

Nathu looked up and a low moan escaped his lips. The dogs were barking even more fiercely than before; the distant noises had become louder too, their echoes filling the atmosphere like the sound of approaching armies. The unsteady glow of light too had become brighter and looked more like the reflection of flames.

'Fire has broken out somewhere,' Nathu cried out and sat up.

Just then, as though floating over the muffled, indistinct sounds, came the ringing of an alarm bell. For both of them it was an unfamiliar sound. Normally, they used to hear the chimes of a tower-clock in the Sheikh's garden during the night. After winding up her kitchen work for the day, when both of them would be preparing to retire for the night, the tower-clock would strike the hour and Nathu's wife would invariably count the number of chimes. They would be ten, sometimes even eleven. But this was not the sound of the Sheikh's tower-clock. The bell was ringing insistently and continuously. Its sound would get lost in the midst of increasing noises, but after some time, it would again be heard in all its clarity above other sounds.

The noises from far away were getting louder and louder. Now voices began to be heard inside the colony too. Neighbours were getting up and coming out of their tenements.

'The Grain Market is on fire!' someone shouted. Soon enough, from far away, was heard a voice, loud and clear: 'Allah-o-Akbar!'

Nathu trembled in every limb of his body. With wide open eyes he stared at the ceiling, as though struck with paralysis.

'Let's go out and find out,' whispered his wife, 'I feel so frightened. Let's ask our people.'

But Nathu, stone-stiff, continued sitting on the cot, holding on to her.

A little while later, a unison of voice rose over all other sounds: 'Har... Har... Har... Mahadev!' The last word of the slogan was shouted loud and long.

In the midst of the increasing noises and the incessant ringing of the alarm-bell, the slogans began to be heard more and more loudly and frequently. It seemed as though celebrations of some big festival had begun!

Nathu's wife could not restrain herself any longer. Extricating herself from Nathu's arms she got up, opened the door and went out. Nathu was still looking at the ceiling with wide-open eyes.

This confused mixture of sounds, like notes from a cracked musical instrument, had begun to strike against the walls of Richard's distant bungalow too. Now and then, another sound, that of an alarm bell too would come floating in the air. Richard was fast asleep, but the sound had woken up Liza. At first, on hearing it she mistook it for the soft tinkle of the little bell that hung in their living room and chimed softly with every gust of air. But on waking up fully she realized that the sound was different. Sometimes it would be lost among other sounds, and then suddenly it would again come floating through the distant caverns of darkness. Liza's eyes were heavy with sleep. The sound seemed to her as though it was the alarm bell of some ship, lost in a storm, desperately trying to find its way.

She sat up on her elbows and looked at Richard. Richard was snoring softly. Richard had only to put his head on the pillow and he would be fast asleep. Such was his remarkable nature, unattached, untroubled by what was going on around him.

It was oppressively dark in the room for Liza. At the gate outside, the loud pattering of the watchman's heavy boots could be heard.

'What sound is that, Richard?' said Liza, nestling close to Richard.

'What? What is it?'

'What sound is that?'

'There's nothing. Go to sleep,' and Richard turned his side.

'Some sort of bell is ringing somewhere, Richard. It sounds like a church bell.'

Richard woke up. He raised himself on his elbows and listened attentively.

'A church bell has a deeper sound. This is more like the sound of a Hindu temple.'

'Why is it ringing at this time of the night, Richard? Is there some Hindu festival today? The sound makes one feel as though there was a storm on the sea and some ship was sounding the alarm bell.'

Richard remained silent.

The confused din from the side of the city grew louder. Now and then a voice would be heard above the din, as though someone was calling someone, but it would again sink into that din. Just then, another voice was heard, loud and clear, as though wafting on the waves of darkness.

'Allah-o-Akbar!'

Every muscle in Richard's body became taut. But soon enough, he relaxed also.

'What sound is that? What does it mean?'

'It means God is great!' said Richard.

'Why is this being raised at this time? Is it some religious occasion?'

Richard laughed. 'It is not a religious occasion, dear Liza, a riot has broken out in the city between the Hindus and the Muslims.'

'What? A riot while you are present in the town?'

Richard felt that Liza, who was fairly well-informed, was purposely putting such an embarrassing question to him.

'We do not interfere in their religious matters. You know that well enough, don't you?'

For a fleeting moment Liza felt as though she was in the midst of a thick jungle and that the sounds she heard were coming from its depths.

'Why don't you stop it, Richard? I am frightened.'

Richard was again silent. His mind was at work again, as to what should be his role in the new situation and how best he should implement the policy of the government.

Liza put her arm round Richard's neck.

'They may be fighting among themselves but it puts your life in danger too, Richard,' she said and a surge of sympathy rose in her heart for Richard. Richard was so frail and sensitive, and was surrounded by such ferocious people. It is not easy to rule over such subjects.

Now and then, the sound of the alarm-bell would be heard.

'But Richard, it is such a horrid thing that these people should fight among themselves.'

Richard laughed.

'Will it be less horrid if they stopped fighting among themselves and joined hands to attack me, to shed my blood?' Richard said and turning his side, began stroking Liza's hair. 'How would you feel if at this moment, slogans were raised in front of our house and people stood with axes and lances ready to attack me?'

Liza shuddered and snuggled close to Richard, trying to look at his face in the dark. It seemed to her that human values were of little consequence, that it was only values that related to governance that mattered. Meanwhile Richard had again sat up. 'There is trouble in the city, Liza. You go to sleep. I have to make some enquiries.' Just then, the telephone bell rang.

9

'It is such a disorderly family, one can never find anything even if one rummages the whole house for it,' grumbled Lala Lakshmi Narain standing in front of his cupboard. He was looking for a small woodchopper that he had put in the lower drawer of his cupboard under a pile of clothes. In the city, a riot had already broken out. He had come out of his room twice to ask his wife if she had seen it lying anywhere, and each time his wife had given two answers to his single question

'How should I know where the woodchopper is? I don't have to cut twigs with it to clean my teeth. Nor do I need your tiny woodchopper to cut firewood for the kitchen. Why do you ask me about it again and again, good sir?'

'Is it a crime to ask about it? If I can't find the woodchopper whom should I ask, if not you?'

'My good man, don't get panicky. Have faith in God and sit quietly. How many people will you be able to protect with that tiny woodchopper?'

The woodchopper was truly a small one. Its yellow wooden handle was painted with green and red creepers and flowers. Lalaji had once taken his children to a fair and there the woodchopper had caught his fancy. Thereafter, whenever he went for his morning walks, he took along, instead of his walking stick, the woodchopper since it came in handy for cutting twigs from keekar trees. With the result, within a short time, quite a pile of twigs had gathered in the house. His own need did not go beyond one small piece from a twig every day. Now if a whole branch is cut and while walking home, the person keeps filing it, he automatically gets a few twigs out of a single branch. Whenever his wife wanted to throw them into the garbage can, he would get annoyed.

'Who throws away fresh twigs from the tree?'

'Fresh or stale, they are of no use to anyone. What's the use of storing them?'

'You can use them for cleaning your teeth.'

'My teeth are no longer strong. It is thanks to your twigs that they have become shaky. Earlier they used to be as strong as steel.' Saying that she would carry them towards the staircase where the garbage tin stood.

'At least you could wait till they dried and withered.'

The woodchopper could not be traced. With the woodchopper near at hand, Lalaji felt a sense of security, with it missing, he felt exposed to all kinds of dangers. Apart from the woodchopper, there was nothing in the house which could serve as a weapon apart from a few sticks used to hold up the mosquito nets and some kitchen knives. As for oil and charcoal, there was one small bottle of linseed oil and a tiny quantity of charcoal barely sufficient for the needs of the kitchen. Despite the vanaprasthi's behest, he had not been able to procure more. Besides, he was inwardly convinced that the government would not allow a riot to break out, and even if it did, his family would not be immediately affected by it.

The small woodchopper at that time was adding lustre to the arsenal of the Youth League. It was lying on the window-sill along with the arrow-heads tidily arranged by Ranvir.

'It is such a disorderly house. Where shall I look for it now?' Lalaji grumbled again. He called over the servant and asked him: 'Have you seen the woodchopper?'

'It was somewhere in the house, Lalaji, but I have not seen it recently.'

'If it was in the house, then, has it suddenly sprouted wings and flown away? Are you trying to fool me? Where has it disappeared?'

'Honest to God, I do not know, Lalaji,' Nanku said, standing in the doorway.

That very morning, out of anxiety for the safety of the Hindus, Lalaji had made a strong exhortation at the meeting held to discuss the deteriorating situation in the town. 'It is imperative that we train our young men to wield a lathi. This cannot brook delay. And for this work I hereby donate five hundred rupees.' Encouraged by his sense of concern, other members too had come forth and within a few minutes no less than two-thousand-five-hundred rupees had been collected. At that time he was hell-bent on confronting the enemy and had no thought of his own safety.

In reality, he was quite safe too. He was a man of means and lived in a spacious house, and was, besides, a prominent citizen. Who would lift his hand against a man of means? Muslim families lived in his immediate neighbourhood, but most of them belonged to the lower strata of society. Besides, being a businessman he had dealings with many Muslim traders and was on cordial terms with them. What was there to be afraid of?

But now, with the fire raging in the Grain Market, the situation had radically changed and his heart sank within him as he thought of it.

'Are you listening? It seems our darling son has taken away the woodchopper and given it to the Youth League.'

'How does it concern me? It is between you and your son. You have always regarded me as a know-nothing. Why should I meddle in your affairs?'

'Did he tell you where he was going before he left?'

'Who?'

'What do you mean who? Ranvir, of course, who else?'

'He didn't say anything to me. It is to your speeches and sermons that he keeps listening, day in and day out. How should I know where he has gone? On a dreadful night like this, the boy is not at home.'

With an angry wave of his hand, Lalaji went back into the room. But what was the point—the woodchopper was not there. He picked up the four long sticks of the mosquito net standing in a corner of the room and came out. He gave one of the sticks to Nanku, the servant.

'Now go downstairs and sit by the front door, holding this stick in your hand.'

He put the second stick against the wall near the bedstead on which sat his wife and their grown-up daughter. He held the third one in his own hand. But soon enough he felt rather odd holding the stick and put it back against the wall. Thereafter he went towards the staircase which led up to the family lavatory on the roof.

In the earlier riot too, the Grain Market had been set on fire. But there had been no killing then. This time the atmosphere was more tense and full of hatred.

The fire was spreading. Nearly half the sky had already turned copper-red with its glow. Down below, near the horizon, it rose in whirls, flames leapt up, curling like tongues of monstrous snakes towards the sky. The fire was spreading north. The scene reminded one of the Dussehra festival when Lanka was in flames and the fire enveloped the effigy of Ravana. Now and then a cloud of red dust would rise upward, turn into red smoke and disperse in the sky. The stars had lost their lustre. A little above the horizon the sky was burnished red, but above it a certain pallor blending with it gave it a pale-red colour.

Coming out of the lavatory, Lalaji stood at the parapet of his double-storeyed house. Against the background of the glowing sky, the sprawling clusters of flat-roofed single-storeyed houses spread far into the distance, looked like a picture in relief. On the roofs of neighbouring houses and even beyond, stood men and women and children, looking towards the Grain Market. Lalaji's godown was located in a lane close to the Burra Bazaar, at some distance north-west of the Grain Market. He was somewhat relieved to find that the fire had not as yet spread in that direction.

From behind the parapet wall, as Lalaji viewed the scene his eyes fell on three men standing on the roof of the neighbouring house looking towards the raging fire. They were none other than Fateh Din, his younger brother and their elderly father. Fateh Din turned his head and saw Lalaji standing behind the parapet wall. 'Hell-fire has broken loose, Lalaji! How terrible!' Lalaji did not answer, and Fateh Din added in a reassuring tone: 'Have no fear, Lalaji. No one will dare look with an evil eye towards your house. He will have to settle with us before he raises his hand against you.'

'Of course, of course!' Lalaji said. 'A neighbour is like one's right hand. I am fortunate to have neighbours like you.'

'Have no fear! It is hooligans who create trouble and harass decent people. All of us have to live in the same town after all, so why should there be any conflict? What do you say, Lalaji?'

'Of course, of course!' said Lalaji.

Lalaji trusted Fateh Din's words and yet did not trust them. For the last twenty years that he had been living in that house, not once had he had any complaint. Yet the fact remained that they were Muslims. As things stood he had little reason to feel unsafe. If anyone set fire to his house, the fire would spread and engulf the entire mohalla of Muslim houses. Besides, that very morning a person no less than the president of the Muslim League, Hayat Baksh, had assured him that so long as he was around, none dare do any harm to him. As for his godown, there was little to worry either. The entire lot of goods was insured. Even so the situation could worsen any time and the Muslims could not be trusted.

It was primarily about Ranvir that Lalaji was worried. Ranvir had chosen to be away from home on such a dreadful night. Being of an impetuous nature the boy might land himself into trouble. Most likely, Master Dev Vrat would keep him back at his place. One of Ranvir's

friends too had told him that evening that all the boys
were with Masterji. Yet who could tell, the boy might
turn his steps towards the Grain Market.

It was then that the sound of the alarm bell fell on
his ears. It came as a reassuring sound for him. He had
strongly proposed at the meeting that the old bell should
be repaired and a new rope attached to it, and he was
happy that his proposal had been implemented. But at
the same time the sound of the alarm bell appeared to
be too feeble to be of much use against the raging fire.

'On one side the alarm bell is ringing and on the other,
the Grain Market is being gutted down. It will be the
undoing of the Hindus,' Lalaji muttered as he strolled up
and down, with his hands joined behind his back. Each
time he thought of his daughter in the house, his heart
would skip a beat. 'If the trouble worsens, how will I cope
with the situation? And Ranvir is loitering about God knows
where. An unruly boy who doesn't listen to anyone, always
harping on social service, service to the nation. What social
service can a fellow do who has no thought of his parents?'
At times he would imagine Ranvir heading towards the
Grain Market where the fires were raging and the thought
would send a shiver down his spine. 'Other people too
have sons who go to learn to wield a lathi. But they don't
loiter about the streets at a time like this. Thinks he is a
great hero, or something.' Lalaji was angry with himself
too. 'At the meetings while others keep their counsels to
themselves and do not utter a word, I go on babbling.
They made me part with no less than five hundred rupees,
whereas no one else donated more than a hundred rupees.
If any untoward thing happens to me, none of those good-

for-nothings will come to my help. And here I am, like a forsaken man doomed in a Muslim locality.'

Standing behind the parapet wall Lalaji looked below. It was very dark there. Near the railing, both mother and daughter were sitting on a cot, close to each other. His wife was asking their daughter to pray. 'Recite the Gayatri Mantra, child. Pray.' And their daughter putting her clasped hands in her lap had begun to recite the holy Gayatri Mantra.

From the roof Lalaji asked in a low voice: 'Are you listening, Ranvir's mother? Has Ranvir come?'

'No, he has not.'

'Speak in low tones. Can't you speak in low tones?'

Lalaji again began pacing the roof. He would try to reassure himself again and again, 'If they set fire to my house, the entire lane will be gutted.' But at last he could not hold out any longer and came down.

On coming down, however, he felt differently: 'Why are you sitting so glumly, Ranvir's mother? What is there to be nervous about? Have courage. Buck up!'

Lalaji's wife remained silent. She was of course anxious about Ranvir. 'He is telling me to buck up, whereas he himself has been to the lavatory three times.'

Lalaji moved away from the railing—and went towards his room.

A little later Lalaji's wife became somewhat suspicious. 'Vidya, go and see why your father has gone into his room.'

Vidya went and found Lalaji changing his clothes, he had taken off his small dhoti and was putting on his pajamas.

'He is getting ready to go out.' Vidya came back and told her mother.

'O Lord, no one can tell what your father may be up

to,' and getting down from the cot went straight to her husband's room: 'You will see me dead if you step out of the house.'

'What? Shall I keep sitting at home feeling helpless? I must find out where the boy is.'

'And you will leave your grown-up daughter in my care on a night like this?' she said nervously.

'My son has gone out of the house. Should I, like a woman, put on bangles and sit at home?'

'He is not your son alone, he is my son too. Where will you go looking for him? The school is long since closed. He is a sensible boy, he must have stayed back somewhere. One of his friends too had told us that all the boys were at Masterji's house. How many times did I tell you that you should not try to make a Hindu warrior out of your son; that he should devote his time to study, play games, eat well and become a strong boy. But you wouldn't listen. You insisted on his taking part in drills and exercises and lathi-wielding, knowing fully well that we were destined to live our whole life in a Muslim city. To live in the ocean and make an enemy of crocodiles, who will call it wise? You are seeing the result now...'

'Don't keep lecturing me all the time. What is wrong with him being in the Youth League? One must do some work for the country and society.'

'Then work for the country and society and face the consequences. But on a night like this, I won't let you go out, whatever you may say.'

Lalaji gave up the idea of going out of the house. He had not expected that the riot would take such a fierce turn. He hated the Muslims, and he was sure that the

British authority would keep them under control.

His wife was saying: 'Other people make it a point to be on the right side of government officers, they socialize with their neighbours, whether Hindus or Muslims. Look at your own in-laws, their Muslim friends keep walking in and out of their house all the time, whereas you have not cultivated anyone, neither officers nor neighbours.'

The fact of the matter was that he too had been thinking on these very lines. His wife had, as it were, taken the words out of his mouth. Their in-laws were certainly on very cordial terms with some Muslims, with Shah Nawaz, for instance, who was a very influential person, ran a transport company and a petrol pump. They even ate together. Why not get in touch with Shah Nawaz and with his help get away with our daughter to a safer place, even for a few days, say to the cantonment area? But how to go about it?

Somewhere far away slogans were being raised. The sound of 'Allah-O-Akbar!' came again and again. Soon the same slogan began to be raised in the near vicinity, and to Lalaji's consternation, began to be repeated from the roofs of neighbouring houses too! The whole atmosphere resounded with slogans. From the side of the Shivala temple the Hindu slogan: 'Har Har Mahadev!' was also heard occasionally, but it was not repeated anywhere in Lalaji's neighbourhood. It made Lalaji shiver with apprehension.

'Tell Nanku to come upstairs,' Lalaji said to his wife.

'Why, what's the matter?'

'Don't question everything I say. Just call him. I want him to carry a letter from me.'

Dumbfounded, she stared at her husband's face.

'At this time of the night? Where do you want to send him?' She thought that he wanted to send Nanku in search of Ranvir.

'Where will he go looking for Ranvir? We have had word that the boy is with Masterji. Why should you be so nervous? Have faith in God and wait patiently till morning.'

'I am not sending him to look for Ranvir; it is some other work.'

'Listen, my good sir, why do you want to send this poor man anywhere at this time of the night when hell has broken loose? He does not know anybody, nor does anyone know him.'

'Why must you oppose whatever I say? We have young Vidya on our hands. It is not advisable that we should continue to stay here. I want him to take a letter to the in-laws. I want them to ask their friend Shah Nawaz to take us out of here.'

The wife pondered for a while and then said, 'This work too can wait till morning. This is not the time for it. Do you think, on getting your letter, our in-laws will go running to Shah Nawaz's house to seek his help? What are you saying?'

But Lalaji would not budge.

'Once an idea gets stuck in his head, it's impossible to make him change his mind,' she muttered to herself.

'How do you know he will take your letter to the right place? He is such an idiot.'

'Why not, he has to. What are we keeping him for, otherwise? He has only to cross a few lanes and he will be at their house in no time.'

'Why must you be so adamant? Even if we have to move out of this place, it cannot be done before morning. Of what use is it to write to anyone at this time? You will only embarrass the in-laws.' Lalaji paused a little as though undecided. 'No,' he said in a low voice. 'We must leave this house this very night.'

'Why should you be so worried? Are you afraid of the neighbours? I am not. Pray to God and relax,' said his wife and thereafter did not utter a word.

At the thought of their grown-up daughter, the mother too lost her equanimity of mind. 'Maybe he is right, maybe we should get away from here without any loss of time. There must be some good reason why he has become so restless. If anything untoward happens, where shall we conceal our daughter?'

'Tell Nanku to take one of the sticks of the mosquito net with him,' said Lalaji, expressing his sense of concern for Nanku's safety.

Handing the letter to Nanku, Lalaji gave him detailed instructions: 'If you find that there is trouble anywhere along the way, avoid that route and get into some by-lane. Try to take the Gurkha chowkidar from the temple with you. But the letter must be delivered. Understand? Now, go.'

But before Nanku left, Lalaji's wife again protested, greatly perturbed: 'I would again beseech you, wait patiently till morning. Leave yourself in God's hands. We shall see what can be done tomorrow. Nanku too is the son of some mother. Don't push him into the jaws of death.'

'No, no, nothing will happen to him. He is not a weakling.'

Just then the sound of running footsteps was heard

from the sidelane. The sound became louder as the footsteps drew near. On that night every sound seemed abnormally loud. It struck the ears as well as the heart. Someone was running for his life.

Lalaji stopped in his steps. He suddenly felt weak in the legs. His heart began to throb violently. Are these Ranvir's footsteps? Is it Ranvir running back home?

But how can anyone make out by merely listening to the sound of running footsteps?

Suddenly, the sound of another pair of running feet was heard. It seemed someone, having turned the corner and coming into the lane, was chasing the person who was trying to run away.

Then suddenly, a cry was heard, piercing the darkness of the night, 'Bachao! Bachao!'

The sound of running feet, not of one but of two persons, coming from the back part of the lane was heard by both the mother and the daughter sitting on the cot. It was also heard by those standing on the roofs of nearby houses.

'Help! Help! Help!'

The terror-stricken voice was heard again. It was a shrill voice of some desperate, terribly frightened person. It was impossible to make out if it was Ranvir's voice. The voice of frightened people, running for their lives and crying for help has the same tenor.

Then came the sound of some object being thrown— either a stick or a stone, which hit the nearby wall and making a loud, pattering sound fell on the ground.

'Get him! Catch hold of him! Kill him!'

Then the person who had been shouting for help

seemed to have gone out of the lane for the patter of his running feet suddenly grew faint and distant while that of his pursuers grew louder.

Was the object thrown on Ranvir? Has he escaped unhurt? Has Ranvir reached home safe? Then, any moment, there should be a knock on the door.

The pursuing feet too had gone out of the lane. Lalaji's heart was pounding while his ears were glued to the door down below, opening into the street.

But there was no knock on the door.

Lalaji felt somewhat relieved and his limp feet came back to life. He walked over to the balcony to see if he could make out who the pursuers were and who the pursued. But the road was empty. Across the road, on the roof of the mud-house, stood men, women and children, motionless as statues. They too must have heard the sound of running feet.

Then three persons emerged from the lane opposite and crossed the road. Their faces were half-covered and they had lathis in their hands, and they were all breathless.

'The Sikh has escaped. If he had not started running, we wouldn't have chased him,' one of them was saying.

They re-entered the sidelane and the sound of their footsteps gradually receded into the distance.

Lalaji heaved a sigh of relief and once again, with his hand tied behind his back began strolling up and down the room. Nanku too picked up the mosquito-net stick, went downstairs and sat down behind the door opening into the street.

10

As the day dawned, the town, as though stung by a cobra, bore a half-dead, half-alive appearance. The Grain Market was still burning; the fire-brigades of the municipality had long since given up fighting the fire. The smoke billowing from it continued to darken the sky, although during the night the sky had looked glowing red. Seventeen shops had been reduced to ashes.

Shops all over the town were closed, except a shop here and there selling milk. Outside such shops stood small groups of people talking about the happenings of the previous night. Information about the killings was largely based on rumours. Residents of Gawalmandi said that many people had been killed in Ratta, while those in Ratta said that a lot of killing had taken place in the Committee Mohalla.

At a road-crossing in Naya Mohalla lay the dead body of a horse. On the outskirts of the city, by the side of a road that led to the villages, the dead body of a middle-aged man had been found. Another dead body had been found in a graveyard on the western edge of the town. It was the dead body of an elderly Hindu in whose pocket some loose coins and a list of clothes required for some wedding had been found. A shoe shop on College Road and a tailoring shop adjoining it had been looted.

Overnight, dividing lines had been drawn among the residential localities. No Muslim now dared go into a Hindu locality, nor a Hindu into a Muslim locality. Everyone was filled with fear and suspicion. At the entrance to the lanes and at road-crossings, small groups of people sat hidden from view, their faces half-covered, holding lances, knives and lathis in their hands. Wherever Hindu and Muslim neighbours stood together, their conversation contained one and only sentence repeated over and over again. 'Very bad! What is happening is very bad!' The conversation would come to a standstill there. The atmosphere had become heavy. Inwardly everyone knew that the crisis was not over, but no one knew what course the events would take.

Doors of houses were shut tight. All business had come to a halt. All schools, colleges, offices were closed. A man walking in a street had the eerie feeling all the time that he was being watched from behind half-shut windows, from the dark entrances of houses, from crevices and peep-holes. People had shut themselves in. The only contact was through rumours. Those belonging to well-off families were preoccupied only with the question of their safety. In one day all public activity—the prabhat pheris, the constructive programmes and the like—had come to an end. Only the Jarnail, as was his wont, acting under his own compulsions, went along diverse roads and lanes and managed to reach the Congress office at the break of day, but seeing a big lock on the door waited for his comrades for a while, then climbed up the stone slab over the drain and began his speech:

'Sahiban! I am sorry to say that since all the cowards are sitting in their houses like rats in their holes, we shall not be able to hold the prabhat pheri this morning. I would beg forgiveness of all of you and would appeal to you to maintain peace in the town at all costs. It is all the mischief of the British who make brother fight brother and shed his blood. Jai Hind!' and alighting from the stone slab, marching in military style went out of sight in the darkness of a nearby lane.

Ranvir did not return home that night, but Master Dev Vrat had managed to send word about his safety. That morning, Lalaji was still worried and did not know which way to turn when a blue-coloured Buick car stopped outside his house and the man who alighted from it was none other than Shah Nawaz himself. The tall, impressive-looking Shah Nawaz had come on his own. Though both of them knew each other well enough they were not on intimate terms. Within minutes of his arrival, the family—Lalaji, his wife and Vidya, their daughter—were seated in the car. Nanku alone had been left behind to guard the house.

'Don't go to sleep, Nanku. Be alert and guard the house. We are leaving the entire house in your charge,' Lalaji had said.

And the car sped away through the deserted streets in the direction of the cantonment. Here and there, stray individuals and groups standing by the roadside would turn round to look at them—Shah Nawaz, with his fair, shining face, a trusted friend among friends, a swanky tuft of his turban fluttering in the air, sat in the driver's seat and Lala Lakshmi Narain sat by his side while the ladies were in the back seat. It was an act of courage to come out like this. Wherever Lalaji would notice a knot of persons standing by the roadside he would turn his face and look in another direction. His wife, on the other hand, sitting on the back seat was all praise for Shah Nawaz, showering blessings on him incessantly. 'God lives in the hearts of people who help others in distress,' she would say again and again.

After dropping Lalaji and his family in the cantonment at a relative's house, the Buick car again sped along the roads of the city. Shah Nawaz was now on his way to the house of his bosom friend, Raghu Nath. Shah Nawaz was not in the least worried about his own safety.

The car went past the Jama Masjid in the direction of Mai Satto's water tank. Drab, single-storeyed houses lined either side of the road; small dingy shops, their canvas awnings supported by bamboo dotted the road. The area bore a dilapidated look. It was a Muslim locality. After crossing a ramshackle bridge the car proceeded towards Syed Mohalla. Here the scene changed radically. Pucca double-storeyed houses with balconies and terraces, and here and there window panes of tinted glass, stood on both sides of the road. Mostly Hindu lawyers, contractors and businessmen lived here. Shah Nawaz was on friendly terms with many of them. As he drove, Shah Nawaz was quite conscious of the fact that many a curious pair of eyes was looking at him from behind windows and half-shut doors. But he was also confident that all those who saw him knew well enough the kind of man he was. Despite this, he accelerated the speed of the car.

On reaching Mai Satto's tank, he turned towards the right. He was now passing through a mixed locality. All sorts of people lived or worked here—there was a long row of shoe-makers' shops who were all Sikhs hailing originally from Hoshiarpur and who specialized in making jooties. The shops were closed. A little beyond, stood a row of mud-houses, their walls covered with hundreds of dung-cakes. The locality wore a deserted look. A little farther, was the scavengers' colony. Shah Nawaz had by then considerably slowed the speed of the car. It did not look like a riot-affected area. Two little children were chasing each other round an electric pole. Nearby was a group of urchins standing in a circle. Shah Nawaz could not help looking at them. Inside the circle lay a little girl on the ground, her shirt uplifted, and on her bare thighs sat a little boy who too had lifted up his shirt. The children around them were roaring with laughter. 'Bastards!' muttered Shah Nawaz, and laughed. 'They couldn't think of another game.' This part of the town appeared to be free from tension.

Looking at Shah Nawaz, a man with an imposing personality, a firm physique, elegantly dressed with polished shoes and a fluttering turra, one could not imagine that he could harbour any mean or petty thoughts. It was said about him that if on seeing a girl he smiled at her, the girl would smile back. But that was years ago. Now he was a staid, worldly-wise person, owner of two petrol pumps and a transport company whose cars and trucks plied in all directions, a dependable friend and a sociable, cheerful fellow.

Loyalty to friends was an article of faith with him.

When the trouble started he had gone to Raghu Nath's house to find out how the family was faring. In close proximity to Raghu Nath's house was the shop of a nanbai, Fakira by name.

'Look Fakira,' Shah Nawaz had said to him 'Listen, with your ears open. If anyone dares look at my friend's house with an evil eye, I shall catch hold of you and skin you alive. Nobody must go near this house.'

The car was now speeding along one of the main roads. It was now a more open area, the road was broad and the houses on either side at a distance from the road. It was a Muslim locality and the speed of the car was slow. Maula Dad was standing at the turn of the road, which led to Bhabarkhana. Behind him, on the projection of a shop sat five or six persons with lathis and lances in their hands, their faces half-covered. Maula Dad was, as usual, dressed in a queer costume—khaki breeches and a green silken kerchief round his neck. He stepped forward when he saw Shah Nawaz's car approaching.

'What news?' Shah Nawaz asked applying brakes to his car.

'What news should I give you, Khanji? The kafirs have done to death a poor Musalman in the mohalla at the back,' Maula Dad said angrily, almost foaming at the mouth.

Maula Dad's eyes blazed with anger. 'You go about hugging kafirs,' he seemed to say, 'and socialize with them while the Muslims are being butchered,' but he did not say anything. Maula Dad knew well enough that he could not dream of having access to places which were within easy reach of Shah Nawaz. Shah Nawaz was on friendly terms even with the Deputy Commissioner of the town, whereas Maula Dad had not gone beyond the four walls of the Municipal Corporation.

'We too have slaughtered five kafirs. Sons of...!'

Shah Nawaz pretended not to have heard what Maula Dad said and started the car.

Hardly had the car moved, when from a side-lane emerged a crowd of people heading towards the road. They were all walking silently, with their heads bowed, as they crossed the road. It was a funeral procession. At the head of it walked Hayat Baksh in his white shirt and salwar with a kulla (a skull cap worn under a turban) on his head. The soft patter of their feet appeared to be stroking the air. It must be the funeral of the Musalman who had been killed, thought Shah Nawaz. Behind the coffin walked two small boys, who, he guessed were the sons of the deceased.

Passing through the gate, Shah Nawaz parked the car under a tree and swinging the key-ring in his hand, walked towards the bungalow. Raghu Nath's wife was the first to see him from behind a curtained window and was overjoyed.

Knocking at the door, Shah Nawaz shouted: 'O karar! do you hear? Open the door!'

Raghu Nath's wife ran towards the bathroom: 'Shah Nawaz is here! I shall attend to him. Don't take too long!' Shah Nawaz's voice was again heard: 'O Yabu (a jocular mode of address among friends), now that you have begun living in a bungalow, you don't even open the door!'

Raghu Nath's wife opened the door.

'Salaam Bhabhi, where is my yaar?' he said and walked into the sitting room.

'He is in the bathroom,' she said and sat down in a chair near him.

'How do you find it here, bhabhi? Any problem? You did the right thing, getting out of that place.'

'It is all right here, but no place can be as good as one's home. We don't know if we shall ever be able to go back to our own house,' she said and her eyes filled with tears.

Shah Nawaz felt deeply touched.

'If I am alive, I shall see you safely back into your house. Rest assured.'

Raghu Nath's wife did not observe purdah from Shah Nawaz. And Raghu Nath felt proud of the fact that his closest friend was a Muslim.

'How is it that you always come alone, never bring Fatima with you?'

'There is trouble in the city, bhabhi. You think I have come out on an excursion?'

'She had only to sit in the car. If you can come, why can't she?'

Just then Raghu Nath appeared.

'Come, yabu, here too you must go to the toilet every five minutes. You have come away to a safe place, kafir, and are still shitting all the time.'

Both embraced each other. Shah Nawaz became sentimental. 'I would rather lay down my life than see any harm come to him. If anyone dare so much as touch him, I shall skin him alive.'

As bhabhi got up to go, Shah Nawaz stopped her. 'Where are you going, bhabhi? I am not going to eat here.'

'Janaki,' said Raghu Nath to his wife. 'This man will keep saying no. But you go and prepare the meal.'

'You want me to eat bhindi, I don't eat bhindi. Bhabhi, don't cook anything for me.'

But Janaki had left. Shah Nawaz shouted after her: 'I am in a hurry, bhabhi. I have come only for a couple of minutes.'

Janaki came back: 'You may not take your lunch with us, but you can have some tea with snacks.'

'I knew you were not very serious about lunch. But OK, let it be tea. I shall have tea.'

As the friends sat down, Raghu Nath said in a sombre tone: 'Things have taken a bad turn. One feels so bad. Brother killing brother.'

But after saying this, Raghu Nath suddenly felt that his utterance had created some sort of a distance between them. Their mutual relationship had been on a different plane whereas the Hindu-Muslim relationship was a different matter. He had, by this utterance, unwittingly linked the two kinds of relationships, their personal relationship with that existing between the two communities, about which both of them had their own individual perceptions.

'I am told the trouble is spreading to the villages too,' Raghu Nath said.

There was little scope for further conversation on this issue. Both felt awkward and embarrassed. It cast a pall over their informal, friendly dialogue.

'Come off it, yabu, talk about yourself,' said Shah Nawaz, changing the subject. 'Do you know whom I met yesterday? I met Bhim, of all the people.'

'Which Bhim are you talking about?' Raghu Nath asked and both of them burst out laughing. Bhim had been their classmate during school days, the son of a very junior postal official but who would always introduce himself by his father's designation. That was why all his friends used to make fun of him.

'The rascal has been living in this very town for the last two years and hasn't even bothered to meet us,' Shah Nawaz said and again started laughing, clapping his hands. 'I recognized him at once from a distance and I shouted, Deputy Assistant Postmaster sahib!" The fellow stood stock-still! But when he recognized me he met me very warmly.'

Bhabhi had brought in tea.

'I have a favour to ask, Khanji,' she said, putting down the tray.

Both of them felt relieved on bhabhi's arrival. It was awkward for them to talk about the riots, yet in the kind of atmosphere that prevailed, to talk about childhood pranks and jokes also sounded hollow.

'Yes, bhabhi, what can I do for you?'

'If it is not inconvenient... if it is not going out of your way...'

'Why are you hesitating, bhabhi, tell me.'

'There is a box of jewellery lying in the house. It contains all our family ornaments. When we left the house, we couldn't bring anything except a few articles of use.'

'That is no problem. Where is the box lying?'

'It is in our small luggage room on the mezzanine floor.'

Shah Nawaz knew every nook and corner of their house.

'But the room must be locked.'

'I shall give you the keys and also explain to you where exactly the box is kept.'

'No problem. I can bring it to you even today.'

'Milkhi, our servant is there. He will open the lock for you.'

'Milkhi is very much there, I know. I went there this morning on my round. I keep pulling him up.'

'How is he?'

'He has the whole house to himself, bhabhi. He must be cooking for himself in the kitchen.'

'The provisions in the house are enough to last him a year,' Raghu Nath's wife said. 'Then, shall I get you the keys?'

Shah Nawaz felt elated at the thought that so much trust was reposed in him, that bhabhi was handing over keys for jewellery worth thousands of rupees, that she regarded him as one of their own.

Janaki came in, the bunch of keys jingling in her hand.

'What if I decamp with all the jewellery, bhabhi?'

'Even if you throw away the box, Khanji, I shall say, "Forget it!"'

She picked out the right key and explained at length the exact location of the box.

A little while later, Shah Nawaz got up to leave. Both the friends stepped out of the house together and stood by the car.

'I have no words to thank you, Shah Nawaz. You have done for me what no one else would have done.'

This was a spontaneous expression of gratitude straight from the heart.

'Shut up, karar!' Shah Nawaz retorted. 'Go back in and sit on the shit-pot,' and opening the door of the car, got in.

Raghu Nath stood where he was, overwhelmed and somewhat nonplussed.

'Go in, go back to the house, don't bore me.'

Deeply moved, Raghu Nath put out his hand for a handshake.

'Go in, go in, I can't dirty my hand! Talk to someone who knows you! Why are you eating up my brain? I have seen many like you,' he said, speaking in the bantering language of their boyhood days, and started the car.

It was late in the afternoon when Shah Nawaz arrived at Raghu Nath's ancestral house to get the jewellery box.

Milkhi took time to open the door.

'Who is it, kind sir?'

'Open the door. It is Shah Nawaz.'

'Who?'

'Open the door. It is Shah Nawaz.'

'Yes, sir, yes, Khanji! Just a minute, Khanji! The door is locked from inside, I shall run and get the key, Khanji. It is lying on top of the fireplace.'

As Shah Nawaz turned round, he saw, across the road, Feroz Khan, the hide-seller, standing like a statue, on the projection of his godown, staring hard at him. Shah Nawaz looked away. But it seemed to him that Feroz was still looking at him with intense hatred in his eyes, which seemed to say: 'Even today you are kneeling at the door of the kafirs.'

A tonga passed by. Maula Dad in his queer costume of khaki breeches and a fluttering green scarf was making a round of Muslim localities in an open tonga. He laughed as his eyes fell on Shah Nawaz and waving his right arm longer than necessary, shouted: 'Salaam-e-leiqum!'

Shah Nawaz felt embarrassed. He felt angry at the servant who was taking so long to open the door.

From inside came the sound of the lock being opened. Milkhi opened the door slightly, and on seeing Shah Nawaz smiled broadly, showing all his teeth. Shah Nawaz kicked the door open and entered.

'Shut the door behind you.'

'Yes, Khanji.'

As he crossed the long dark corridor, Shah Nawaz felt the warm cosiness of the house. It was after a long time that he had come into the house through this entrance. He liked the familiar odour. Years earlier when he would enter the house through the dark corridor, Raghu Nath's young daughter would stare at him, her forefinger between her teeth, and would then raise both her arms wanting to be picked up. Every time he came, she would go running to the end of the corridor, raise both her arms and start giggling. In those early days the young women of the household would run inside on seeing him. It was only when they recognized who it was would they come back laughing.

'Oh, it's you, Khanji. We thought God knows who had come in,' they would say.

Shah Nawaz felt deeply moved. He had spent many lovely evenings with Raghu Nath and his family. As soon as he would enter, the young wife of Raghu Nath's younger brother would go into the kitchen to prepare an comelette for him. Everyone knew that Shah Nawaz was fond of eating omelette. And gradually, one by one, all the members of the family would come and sit with him in the inner courtyard.

'I hope all is well at home, Khanji?' Milkhi said with folded hands.

It was then that Shah Nawaz became aware of Milkhi's presence. Milkhi stood there, with folded hands, a beseeching smile on his face. Shah Nawaz had never liked Milkhi for his beggarly way of talking, his muddy eyes and shrivelled body. Sometimes when a family member would poke fun at him, Milkhi would hide his face in his arm in embarrassment, which would set the whole family laughing. At such times Shah Nawaz did not dislike Milkhi. But generally, he always reminded him of a slimy lizard. No one knew from where he had descended on the household. He was neither a Punjabi nor a Garhwali. He would utter words of some hybrid dialect, squeezing them out, it seemed, from the stumps of his teeth.

Right in the middle of the inner courtyard stood an improvised choolha made from three bricks, the ashes from which lay scattered on the floor, as also butts of the bidis.

'Why don't you cook your meal inside the kitchen?' asked Shah Nawaz. Milkhi merely tilted his head to one side and grinned.

'I am all alone, Sahibji, I cook my daal here only.'

'You have enough provisions here. You don't need anything, do you?'

'There is plenty, Khanji. The nanbai outside also keeps asking me. You had spoken to him.'

'Which nanbai?'

'Khanji, the one who sits by the ditch. He also throws packets of bidis for me. He is a very good man.'

The staircase went up from the side of the kitchen. As he put his foot on the first step, Shah Nawaz looked around. The door of the living room was shut tight. Shah Nawaz knew every article that lay in that room— the big bedstead, the large portrait of Raghu Nath's mother on the mantelpiece. The sight of the closed door gave him a sense of desolation. Lying against the closed door was Milkhi's hookah, with a dirty rag nearby.

'What do you keep doing here? You don't even sweep the floor.'

'They have gone away, Khanji. What's the use of sweeping the floor?' said Milkhi, grinning.

To Shah Nawaz it seemed as though their voices were like echoes coming from a vaulted dome, and when they ceased talking an eerie silence descended on the house.

'The store room is on the mezzanine, isn't it?'

'Yes, Khanji. Right opposite the staircase. All the big trunks are lying there,' said Milkhi as he followed Shah Nawaz up the staircase.

There were no fewer than fifteen keys, big and small, in the bunch. Bhabhi had singled out the key of the big lock hanging on the door outside and shown it to him and thereafter a small brass key to the cupboard in which the jewellery box lay, and had said, 'This is the key, Khanji. I hope you won't forget.'

But Shah Nawaz was finding it difficult to locate the right key.

'Which one is the key to the big lock? Do you know?'

'Yes, Sahibji, I shall show you.'

And Milkhi bent over the bunch, looking for the right key, like a clerk bending over his account book. The diminutive Milkhi barely came up to Shah Nawaz's waist, maybe a little higher. Shah Nawaz's eyes fell on the thin tuft of hair on Milkhi's head, his chutia falling over his left ear like a centipede, and it gave him a creepy feeling.

Milkhi opened the lock. It was dark and stuffy inside the small room. Milkhi stepped forward and unbolted one of the windows which opened towards the back of the house and overlooked the inner courtyard of a neighbouring mosque. Everything inside the room was now clearly visible.

It was stuffy inside but there was also the tantalizing odour of women's clothes. The wives of all the three brothers had hurriedly made bundles of their clothes and thrown them in. The room was chock-full of boxes and trunks.

Threading his way through the boxes, Shah Nawaz reached the cupboard which contained the jewellery box. As he looked casually out of the window he saw a large group of people sitting close to the water-tank where the devotees washed their hands and feet before offering the namaz. Then his eyes fell on a dead body, duly covered, in their midst. The scene of the funeral procession which he had seen that morning on his way to Raghu Nath's house also flitted across his mind. For a long time Shah Nawaz stood looking out of the window.

It did not take long to take out the jewellery box. Covered with blue velvet, it must have been given in dowry to one of the women of the house. He took it out carefully and locked the cupboard.

As they came down the staircase, Milkhi was in front holding the bunch of keys while Shah Nawaz followed with the jewellery box in both his hands, when suddenly something snapped in Shah Nawaz's mind. How and why this happened cannot be easily explained—whether it was the chutia on Milkhi's head, or the grieving crowd of people he had seen in the mosque or the funeral procession he had seen that morning on his way to Raghu Nath's house, or what he had been hearing during the last few days and— Shah Nawaz gave a sharp kick to Milkhi on his back. Milkhi stumbled and fell head downward. As he went tumbling down, his head struck against the wall at the turn in the staircase; his forehead split and his spine broke. When Shah Nawaz came down the staircase, Milkhi's head was hanging downward from one of the last steps in the staircase. Shah Nawaz was still in a rage, the spurt of anger had not subsided. Coming down the staircase, as he passed by Milkhi's body, he felt like lifting his foot and hitting Milkhi on the face so as to crush the centipede. But he desisted lest he should lose his own balance.

Coming down into the courtyard, he turned round to look at Milkhi. Milkhi's eyes were open and set on Shah Nawaz's face, as though wanting to know for which fault of his Khanji had done him to death. As Milkhi fell a muffled cry had escaped his lips out of sheer fright.

Shah Nawaz left him where he was, put the jewellery box under his arm and came out of the house. He put the lock which Milkhi used to put on the inside, on the door outside.

That very evening, handing the jewellery box to
bhabhi, Shah Nawaz was not perturbed. As bhabhi took
the box, her eyes filled with tears, she had no words to
express her sense of gratitude, and Raghu Nath was
overwhelmed by the nobility of his friend's character
and the loftiness of his thoughts—even in such
inflammatory times he could retain his balance of mind
and remain loyal and steadfast.

'But there is one bad news, bhabhi.'

'What is it? Has there been a theft? Has our house
been burgled?'

'No, bhabhi. Milkhi fell down from the staircase and
has perhaps fractured a bone or two. At first I thought
I should go for a doctor, but then, doctors are not so
easily available these days. But don't worry, I shall attend
to it tomorrow.'

'Poor Milkhi!'

'If you like I can bring him along and leave him here
and put one of my own men to guard your house. The
poor fellow is so utterly alone there.'

But both Bhabhi and Raghu Nath had their
reservations. They were strangers in the locality and could
not arrange for the injured man's treatment. If it was
difficult for Shah Nawaz to get a doctor, it would be
well-nigh impossible for them to get one.

'Don't worry. I shall look to it. There should be no
problem.'

For this too, the Bhabhi felt beholden to Shah Nawaz
and looking at his high forehead and beaming face she
felt as though she was standing before a saint.

11

After taking his morning bath, Dev Datt came and stood outside his house, rubbing his hands. Every time he rubbed his hands, or put his hand to his nose or gently stroked his cheeks and again rubbed his hands, it meant that he was busy preparing his work-schedule for the day. There lay a diary in his brain. By rubbing his hands and stroking his nose he was making one entry after another into that diary, another item of work to be attended to. 'There is trouble in Ratta, the comrade there will not be able to send his report, we must send another comrade there.' 'To put a stop to the riots, it is imperative that we bring together leaders of the Congress and the Muslim League, to arrange a meeting between Hayat Baksh and Bakshiji.'

On the previous day too, Dev Datt had somehow managed to call on some people. Raja Ram had straightaway shut the door in his face. Ram Nath had said derogatory things about the communists. Hayat Baksh had agreed to attend the meeting even though he had turned red in the face and, with his eyes burning, had started raising slogans and shouting, 'We shall not rest till we have achieved Pakistan... Pakistan will become a reality!' He had not given Dev Datt even the chance to speak. 'It will be necessary to go to him again today.'

Dev Datt again rubbed his hands and stroked his nose. 'Send Bakshiji to Hayat Baksh; take Atal along and go to Bakshiji, and take Amin along and go to Hayat Baksh.' But then he rejected the whole idea. 'Leave out the leaders. Let ten persons each from the Congress, the Muslim League and the Singh Sabha be brought together and have a joint meeting. No, this too will not work. This proposal will have to be discussed in the Party office with other comrades. Another problem. Every effort must be made to stop communal riots from spreading to the labourers' colony. To have only one comrade there is not enough. Ratta is a Muslim area. Comrade Jagdish is there, but he alone cannot be effective. Besides, two or three comrades must be sent to the villages; they must go from village to village, and try to stop the riots from spreading. We have so few comrades.' He again moved his hand over his face, then looked at his wrist-watch. 'There is a meeting in the commune at ten'clock, in which comrades will present reports about their respective areas. It is time to leave,' Dev Datt said to himself and quietly went back into the house to take out his bicycle from the veranda.

'Who is there? Is that you Dev Datt?'

Dev Datt left the cycle and went into the room.

'Are you going out again?' asked his father, a bulky, middle-aged man sitting on a cot. 'If you are bent upon getting killed, then first kill all of us, all your family members. Can't you see what is happening?'

Dev Datt stood in the doorway without uttering a word, rubbing his hands and stroking his nose. His mother came out of the kitchen, wiping her hands on her dupatta.

'Why must you torment us? Don't you know how we passed the night—that horrible fire raging and you not at home? Have you no thought for us? You were away the whole night.'

Dev Datt rubbed his hands and said, 'This entire area, right up to Murree Road on one side and the Company's Garden on the other side is inhabited by the Hindus, and well-to-do Hindus at that. There is no danger to you here.'

'Have you had a revelation that there is no danger to us?' growled the father.

'In this row of houses, ten families have licensed guns. The members of the Youth League of this area have already committed three murders.'

'You swine! Who is thinking of danger to us? It is you we are worried about.

'There is nothing to worry about,' Dev Datt said and came back into the veranda to take out his cycle.

His mother put the wrapper round her neck and tried to block his way. 'I passed the whole night tossing in bed. Don't you see the awful times we are living in?'

The problem was getting complicated, thought Dev Datt, his hand going back to his nose. He put his mouth close to his mother's ear and said, 'Don't worry, Ma. I shall come back soon.'

'You try to fool us all the time. Yesterday too you said the same thing. Put your hand on my body and swear that you will come back before nightfall.'

'I can't promise, Ma, but I shall come back.' And he began taking out his cycle.

From inside the house came the thundering voice of

his father. 'Why are you breaking your head against a wall? The swine won't agree. He must disgrace us. He has no thought for his parents! He thinks he will stop the riots. Bastard!'

His father's fulminations continued: 'No one has a good word to say about him! Good-for-nothing fellow, goes about gathering petty labourers, load-carriers, coolies and lectures to them. Hasn't even started shaving and has become a leader, swine!'

Dev Datt had already reached the road-crossing.

The situation had further deteriorated. Practically every road was now deserted. Not even a tonga plied anywhere. Shops were closed. If the panels of any shop were open, it meant that the shop had been looted. If some people carrying lathis were standing in a group somewhere, it meant that they were standing close to the dividing line between the mohalla of their community and that of the hated 'adversary'. But all the mohallas had not been so divided. The houses by the roadside, invariably pucca double-storeyed houses, were of the Hindus, whereas the single-storyed, mud-houses at the back were of the Muslims, or, to use Dev Datt's terminology, of the deprived classes.

'Dev Datt!' someone called.

The voice had come from the left side of the road-crossing. Applying the brakes and putting his foot on the ground, Dev Datt stopped.

'Don't go further. A man is lying dead there!'

A short-statured man with a lathi came up to him.

'Where?'

'Beyond the crossing. On the slope.'

'Who was he?'

'A Musla, who else? Where are you off to at this time?'

'To the Party office. I have work to do.'

'A Hindu is lying dead in the graveyard on the other side,' said the dwarfish fellow, adding angrily, 'Go and tell your Muslim patrons since you are always fawning on them, to take away their kinsman's body from the slope and deliver our dead body to us.'

From a balcony on the right came a voice: 'Don't go that way. The fellows there may cut you to pieces.'

'No one will kill him. He is always hobnobbing with the Muslims.'

'But he is a Hindu all the same.'

Those who had earlier been working under cover, had by then, come into the open.

'Go and tell them, if one of our men is killed we shall kill three of theirs.'

The man on the slope was perhaps not yet dead, and was struggling for breath, since his body had moved a little down the slope. He had a greyish beard but it looked red now, drenched in his own blood. His khaki coat had cheap nickel buttons on it—one could get eight such buttons for one pice—the shoe-laces had been loosened, as though he had loosened them himself in preparation for his journey to the next world. He appeared to be a Kashmiri. Dev Datt looked back towards the road. A group of men stood there, staring hard at him. When he again looked at the dead body, he recognized the person. He was a Kashmiri load-carrier who worked at the nearby timber-stall belonging to Fateh Chand, and carried firewood and charcoal to the customers' houses.

Dev Datt thought for a while, his hand stroking his nose. Then he shook his head. 'No. This is not the time to attend to this man, alive or dead. Nor is this the time to go and see the Hindu's dead body. I must proceed straight to the Party office.'

The Party office had any number of flags, but only three persons were sitting there. The commune consisted of eight comrades; five of them were on duty at that time. There was one bad news, though. A Muslim comrade had lost faith and was leaving the commune.

'Mischief of the British! You call this mischief of the British! They throw a dead pig at the door of the mosque? Are there any British to be seen here?' the erstwhile comrade said, his lips trembling with rage. 'Three poor Muslims have been hacked to death before my very eyes and you call this British machination. To hell with it all!'

All Dev Datt could say to him to cool his temper was: 'Don't take any step in haste, comrade. The class to which we belong—the middle class—is easily affected by traditional influences. Had you come from the working class, the question of Hindu and Muslim would not have bothered you so much.'

But the comrade picked up his handbag and left.

'The comrade's ideological understanding is weak. To view things emotionally can be very misleading for a communist. It is necessary to understand the evolutionary process of society.'

The meeting began. The situation in the town, particularly with reference to the working-class areas, was the first item on the agenda.

'In no working-class area has there been any rioting

so far. The information about Ratta is misleading. But tension remains. Comrade Jagdish's presence is effective— people still listen to him. There are twenty Sikh houses in the colony. Not a single incident has occurred so far. But Comrade Jagdish reports that the situation is worsening. There was a tiff between two workers yesterday. They abused each other. The rumours about what is happening elsewhere are affecting the morale of the workers. The decision is taken: Send Comrade Kurban Ali also to Ratta, so that Comrade Jagdish is not alone.' Dev Datt jotted down the decision.

'Dada has already left for the countryside. There has been no news from him so far. All traffic has come to a standstill—only one Buick car, of deep blue colour, has been seen going from village to village. Some people say that it is Shah Nawaz's car. Why is he going from village to village is not known.'

The meeting went on for a long time, with the three comrades deliberating over each item. And every item, on conclusion, was duly ticked on the notebook with a pencil by Dev Datt.

Then came the last item: to convene a joint meeting of the representatives of all parties.

'It will not be possible to hold such a meeting,' said one comrade. 'The Congress office is locked. If you talk to the members of the Muslim League, they start shouting slogans. Over every issue, their first demand is: Let the Congressmen first admit that the Congress is the party of the Hindus, then alone shall we sit with them. Besides, no one is stirring out of his mohalla. With whom will you hold the meeting?'

Dev Datt stroked his nose for some time and then dismissed the idea of having a joint meeting of ten representatives from each party. It wouldn't work. 'But we must bring together some select leaders. They may bring along some of their fellow-workers.'

'No one will come, Comrade,' said one comrade. 'If at all they do, there will only be accusations and counter-accusations. No positive result can be expected from such a meeting.'

'Comrades,' said Dev Datt, 'the very fact of their sitting together will exert a good influence on the people. We can then issue an appeal in their name asking the citizens to maintain peace. It can be put across through the loudspeakers in every mohalla.'

'What is the situation like at the moment? There is no large-scale killing but sniping continues.'

'It is of paramount importance to bring together leaders of political parties.'

A few other issues were also discussed. What should be the venue of this meeting? It was decided to hold it at Hayat Baksh's house.

'I shall bring Bakshiji there. As we enter the mohalla, Comrade Aziz will receive us at the entrance along with two or three other Muslim residents and we shall proceed to Hayat Baksh's house.'

'Have you spoken to Hayat Baksh?'

'I shall go now and talk to him.'

'Comrade, which dream-world are you living in? Who will let you reach his house?'

'You will accompany me,' Dev Datt said smilingly to Aziz.

'You are trying to put out a raging fire by merely sprinkling water on it. The fire will not be put out that way.'

But after the meeting, Dev Datt and Aziz went through lanes and by-lanes, hiding here and there, receiving threats and abuses and eventually succeeded in reaching Hayat Baksh's house.

And truly enough the meeting did take place that afternoon at Hayat Baksh's residence. Bakshiji was brought to the meeting by Dev Datt. Had he asked some other Congressman, he might have met with a refusal, but Dev Datt was sure that Bakshiji would not refuse. The man's thinking may not be very clear and he may not be good at solving political tangles, but he had spent a total of sixteen years of his life in jail and he abhorred bloodshed. During the last few days he had been speaking irritably with one and all because he felt both deeply disturbed and helpless. Even as he came with Dev Datt he kept talking ill of the communists all the way. But he did come, and also brought along two young Congress workers with him and the meeting did take place. At the meeting, there was angry exchange of words and accusations. For a full half hour Hayat Baksh kept insisting that Bakshiji must first declare that he had come as a representative of the Hindus and that the Congress was a party of the Hindus. At last Dev Datt had got up and said, 'Sahiban, this is not the time to go into such discussions. Outside, innocent people are being killed, houses are being burnt, and there is danger of the trouble spreading to the villages. Therefore it is our duty to stop this fire from spreading.'

Thereafter, Dev Datt read out the draft of the Appeal for Peace. Again a discussion started. 'The appeal cannot be issued in the name of the Congress and the Muslim League. It can only be issued in the personal names of Hayat Baksh and Bakshiji.' It was also suggested that some other persons too should be associated with it.

By then the people had grown tired. Hayat Baksh's son whispered into his father's ear that the appeal was an innocuous one since it was only an appeal for peace and that there was no harm in signing it. And so Hayat Baksh put his signature to it. Bakshiji too signed it. Thereafter slogans of Pakistan Zindabad were raised, and amidst these slogans, while Bakshiji was putting on his shoes, the news came that in the labour colony of Ratta too rioting had started and that two Sikh carpenters had been hacked to death.

Dev Datt refused to believe it. He thought it was a baseles rumour. Has anyone seen the rioting? With his own eyes? That was his first reaction. He kept repeating the question till the very end. Nevertheless, he was downcast, his head bowed and he felt that if the workers had started fighting one another, it meant that the poison had spread deep. Which also meant that the meeting had been a futile exercise.

Dev Datt decided that he would pick up his cycle from the Party office and forthwith proceed to Ratta. 'Come what may, I must reach Ratta. It will no longer be possible for Comrade Jagdish to face the situation alone. With my presence there the situation may improve and the workers may not lift their hands against one another.'

But when Dev Datt reached the Party office he found his father standing there, stick in hand. And when Dev Datt presented a Marxist analysis of the situation and said that every effort was being made to stop the riots, and began taking out his cycle, his father lost his temper. 'Swine, if you get killed, there will be no one even to pick up your dead body. Don't you see what is happening all around? You alone are going to stop the riots?' and the father stepped forward and shut the door opening into the lane. He would have given his son a thrashing, he even lifted his stick, but then burst out crying: 'Why are you tormenting us? You are our only son. Be sensible. Don't you see how miserable your mother is? If you want, I shall put my turban at your feet. Come home.'

Dev Datt's hand went to his nose, he rubbed his hands. The situation was getting out of hand. It was necessary to seek someone's help. Someone will have to escort father home.

'I must go to Ratta. I cannot stay back here. But I shall make arrangements to see you home. Comrade Ram Nath will go with you.'

That very afternoon another death took place. The Jarnail was killed. Whimsical as he had always been, he set out to quell the riots, marching military style, with the cane tucked under his arm. No one was any the wiser for his thoughts, but his heart certainly surged with emotions and also perhaps a crazy whim, that what was happening in the town was deplorable and that all those Congressmen who were sitting at home were traitors.

He set out on his mission, and at numerous places, sometimes from the projection of a shop or at a street-corner, he would stand and address the citizens:

'Sahiban, I wish to inform you that when Pandit Jawaharlal Nehru, on the bank of the Ravi took the pledge of full Independence, he danced round the national flag, and so had I. I too had danced with him. We had all taken the pledge on that day. Today all those who are sitting at home are traitors. Is this the day to sit at home? I say put on burqas and apply henna to your hands like women, if you have to sit at home.'

'Sahiban, Gandhiji has said that Hindus and Muslims are brothers, that they should not fight one another. I appeal to all of you, young and old, men and women, to stop fighting. It does great harm to the country. India's wealth is swallowed up by that fair-faced monkey who bosses over us...'

Through lanes and along streets he went making his appeal for peace till he entered the Committee Mohalla. The day was declining when, while he was delivering his speech quite a few bystanders gathered round him, and without knowing where he was, he went on in his usual vein:

'Sahiban, Hindus and Musalmans are brothers. There is rioting in the city; fires are raging and there is no one to stop it. The Deputy Commissioner is sitting in his bungalow, with his madam in his arms. I say, our real enemy is the Englishman. Gandhiji says that it is the Englishman who makes us fight one another. We should not be taken in by what the Englishman says. Gandhiji says, Pakistan shall be made over his dead body. I also say that Pakistan shall be made over my dead body. We are brothers, we shall live together, we shall live as one...'

'You, son of a...' shouted someone standing behind him, and with one swing of his lathi, hit the Jarnail on his head and broke his skull into two. Jarnail fell down in a heap, with his cane, his green 'military' uniform, his torn turban and his torn chappals, before he could finish his sentence.

12

'**O**ne of you will keep watch on the balcony,' Ranvir turned round and ordered. After passing the initiation test by slaughtering the hen, he had developed supreme self-confidence. There was now a ring of authority in his voice. And he was, without doubt, the smartest in his group of young 'warriors'.

The 'armoury', despite the sticks, the woodchopper, knives, daggers, bows and arrows, and the catapults, still looked rather bare. Outside the room, a little removed from the staircase stood an oven with a cauldron of oil on it, but the idea of boiling the oil had been given up due to shortage of firewood.

'Yes, Sardar!' Shambhu said and marched towards the balcony.

All the four 'warriors' were itching for action. Time had come to enter the battlefield and show one's feats of valour. Standing on the balcony they felt the same way as the Rajputs of yore did, who, taking cover behind rocks and dunes waited for the mleccha hordes to enter Haldi Ghati before they pounced upon them.

Ranvir was short of stature, that is why, he visualized himself in the role of Shivaji. With eyes screwed up he would survey the road below and the adjacent area. He had an intense longing to wear an angarakha and a yellow

turban with a steel ring covering it, and carry a sword
hanging from his broad waistband. A shapeless pair of
pajamas, an ordinary shirt and a worn-out pair of chappals
was no dress for a 'warrior', and that too on the verge
of a mighty conflict! But the impress of authority which
his dress lacked was more than made up for by the tenor
of his sharp commanding voice. He gave orders like a
seasoned army commander, and enforced strict discipline
on the members of the group. With his hands joined on
his back, and a slight stoop of his shoulders he would
stroll up and down the 'armoury' in much the same way
as Shivaji must have strolled, before taking on Aurangzeb.

'Sardar!'

Ranvir turned round. It was Manohar who had been
putting small piles of pebbles beside the catapult on the
window-sill.

'We have run short of firewood and therefore the oil
cannot be boiled.'

'Don't we have charcoal?'

'No, Sardar!'

Ranvir strolled up and down the room for some time.
War strategy demands that the commander assess the
situation in all its aspects and take a quick decision. That
was imperative for a leader.

'Get it from your house, coal or firewood, whichever
is available, in whatever quantity. Without delay!'

But Manohar continued to stand, somewhat
nonplussed.

'What is it?'

'What if mummy doesn't let me?'

Ranvir stared hard at Manohar's face and shouted

fiercely: 'What are you looking at my face for? Get firewood from wherever you can.'

'Yes, Sardar!' and Manohar stepped back.

'But wait. I can't send you home at this time.'

The idea of boiling oil was given up for the time being.

The 'armoury' had been set up on the upper floor of a double-storeyed house which was lying vacant. The ground floor was occupied by Shambhu's grandparents. The balcony on the upper storey faced the road. A stately banyan tree stood in front of the house. Its thick foliage provided a safe cover to anyone standing on the balcony. The entrance to the house was, however, from the side-lane—a dark, narrow lane with many turns and twists in it. A person entering it from the roadside would get lost in it in no time. While describing the locale to Ranvir, Shambhu had likened the entrance of the lane to the entrance to the Chakra Vyuh of Mahabharata and therefore eminently suitable as their base of operations. The lane, after some distance, turned to the left. At the turn stood a dilapidated grave of some pir, and right opposite the grave lived an old Musalman who had two wives. A little farther down was the municipal water-tap to which no one came till four in the afternoon. The houses beyond the tap were all inhabited by Hindus. Only at the end of the lane were there two or three mud houses in which Muslim families lived. In one of them lived Mahmud the washerman and in the other, Rahman who ran a hamam. Besides, there were many by-lanes which branched off from this lane and went in different directions. If a mleccha has to be attacked in this lane, then it must be done in the area between the water-tap and a little before the end of the lane. If anything goes amiss, one can immediately get into the entrance of a Hindu's house.

'What do you know about the mlecchas who live in this lane?' Ranvir had asked Shambhu.

'I know them well enough, Sardar. Mahmud, the washerman washes our family's clothes; and the Mianji who lives opposite the gate is on very cordial terms with my grandfather.'

'We shall not operate in this lane,' said Ranvir decisively.

Shambhu felt greatly discouraged.

The day had come to launch their operations, when they would attack their first victim. So far the 'warriors' had been preoccupied with preparations. The day had come to prove their mettle. The line of a war-song: 'Go into the battlefield like a whirlwind and vanquish the foe!' had been ringing in Dharam Dev's ears since long. Manohar was a little nervous. He had come away without telling his mother and it was nearing two in the afternoon. Manohar was afraid that his mother, after winding up her kitchen work, might come out looking for him and trace him out in that house.

Ranvir summoned the three 'warriors' into the armoury and reflecting over the strategy declared:

'Time has not yet come for the use of boiling oil. It is when the enemy attacks your fortress and other weapons become ineffective that you pour boiling oil on the enemy.'

Then, after thinking for a while he added: 'Here only a dagger will serve the purpose, a dagger with a spring.'

Turning to Inder, the Sardar said, 'We want to see your footwork. Give us a demonstration of how you will turn on your feet while attacking the enemy. Pick up a knife from the window-sill.'

Inder promptly brought the knife and came and stood in the middle of the room, his legs apart. Holding the knife in his right hand, its blade directed inward, he lifted his left foot, took a sudden leap in the air and making a semi-circular movement, came down on the floor, with his knife aimed at Ranvir's back.

Ranvir shook his head.

'Never aim at the enemy's chest or back. Always plunge the knife into his waist or stomach. And when the blade is inside, give it a twist; this will pull out his intestines. If you attack the enemy in a crowd, do not pull out the knife. Leave it there and get lost in the crowd.'

Ranvir was only repeating what he had heard from Master Dev Vrat's mouth.

A little later, the group was divided into two sections. It was decided that Inder would be the first one to attack. Hence, while Manohar stood watch on the balcony, Inder, Shambhu and the Sardar came downstairs into the entrance. Whereas Manohar would keep his eyes on the road, the other three would watch the lane. And when Ranvir gave his signal, Inder would step out of the house and pounce upon the enemy. On opening the door slightly one could see a part of the road and the front part of the lane. Beyond the thick trunk of the banyan tree the road was bathed in the afternoon sunlight.

A tonga stopped at the entrance to the lane. Through

a chink in the door, they all looked out. A man was alighting from the tonga.

'Who is he?' whispered Inder.

They all put their eyes to the chink.

'It is Jalal Khan, Nawabzada Jalal Khan,' whispered Shambhu. 'He lives across the road. A big landlord. Goes to meet the Deputy Commissioner twice a month.'

Through the chink the fluttering tuft of his white turban, his pointed moustaches and ruddy face could be seen. But he disappeared as quickly as he had become visible. As he passed through the lane, the rustling sound of his well-starched salwar and shoes was heard. But before any decision could be taken the man had already gone into some house. All the 'warriors' stood nonplussed. Otherwise too the man was tall and well-built, and on seeing him pass by, they felt overawed. He had given them so little time to think.

Masterji had said that one must never look closely at the enemy, because then, one begins to waver in one's resolve. Looking closely at any living being produces sympathy in one's heart, which must not be allowed to happen.

A door opened in the lane and was immediately shut with a bang. All the three 'warriors' pricked their ears. Ranvir adjusted the panels of the door in such a way that the chink between them revealed more of the lane.

'Who is there?' asked Inder in a low whisper.

'A mlecch, replied Ranvir.

Both the warriors glued their eyes to the chink, one below the other. An elderly man with a beard was coming through the lane towards the road.

'It is Mianji,' Shambhu said, on recognizing him. 'He lives in the house opposite the pir's grave. He goes everyday at this time to the mosque to offer his namaz.

'Shut up!'

The man went out of the lane and, near the banyan tree, turned left. He was wearing a black waistcoat, a salwar and a loose pair of chappals. A small rosary dangled from his right hand. Being an old man he walked slowly with a stoop.

'Shall I go?' Inder asked the Sardar.

'No, he is already on the road.'

'So what?'

'It is forbidden to attack a person on the road.' Shambhu had felt shaken by Inder's insistence, but felt greatly relieved when Ranvir said 'no' to him.

Some more time passed. At four o'clock, women would start going with their pitchers to the water-tap. And therefore, with the afternoon declining, more and more people would start stepping out of their houses.

Two persons, one behind the other, entered the lane from the roadside. One of them, wearing spectacles, was plying along a cycle.

'That is Babu Chunni Lal. He works in some office. He has a dog.'

The patter of their shoes was heard as they went through the lane.

The sound of footsteps was again heard. The 'warriors' put their eyes to the chink.

'Who is it?'

'It is some pedlar,' Inder whispered.

'No,' said Shambhu. 'He sells oils and scents. He

comes from far away everyday at this time. He is a mlecch a bulky person, his peaked beard and moustaches dyed in henna, with two or three bags hanging from his shoulders and one on his back, came in sight, entering the lane from the side of the banyan tree. Due to the heavy load he was carrying, drops of perspiration had gathered on his forehead. There were swabs of cotton in his ears and a couple of long needles stuck into his turban.

Ranvir felt as though something had moved behind his back. He turned round. Inder's hand had gone to his pocket in which lay the long knife with a spring.

Time was passing. The decisive moment had come. The man was a mleccha, loaded with bags so that he could neither run, nor defend himself, besides, he was tired—all these were favourable factors. Time was passing and the pedlar was moving farther and farther away into the lane. Ranvir made a sign, and the next moment, Inder had leapt into the lane. There was a flash of light as the door was opened, but Ranvir immediately shut the door.

Not a sound anywhere. Ranvir and Shambhu stood behind the door with bated breath. Ranvir became extremely tense. He couldn't control himself. He softly opened the door and looked out. The scent-seller, his back bent was walking unsteadily, swaying from side to side. And the tiny Inder followed him at some distance, his hand on his shirt-pocket.

Ranvir was in a fix. He was too curious to know what was happening and yet could not open the door, whereas Shambhu was scared stiff, his legs trembling. The last glimpse Ranvir had was of Inder walking alongside the bulky pedlar when both of them were turning the corner in the lane.

Shambhu bolted the door from inside.

Both of them stood facing each other in the dark, breathing hard. Ranvir was becoming increasingly impatient to go out and see what was happening; for Shambhu it was becoming impossible even to keep standing.

As they turned the corner, the scent-seller's eyes fell on the boy. Because of the sound made by his own shoes the pedlar had not heard him approaching.

The scent-seller smiled.

'Where are you going, son, at this time of the day?' and putting out his hand, patted him on his head.

Inder stopped short and stared hard at the man's face. His right hand was inside his pocket. Subconsciously he took note of the fact that the pedlar had bloated cheeks, and Masterji had once said that people with bloated cheeks were cowardly, that they had weak digestion and could not run, that they became breathless very soon. And the man was actually breathing hard.

Inder was balancing himself before pouncing upon his victim. His eyes were still riveted on the pedlar's face.

To the scent-seller the boy appeared to be young and tender, perhaps he was walking with him for protection. Perhaps the boy was frightened. Everyone in the city was frightened that day.

'Where do you live, child? Keep walking along with me. One should not stir out of the house on a day like this.'

But Inder was not shaken in his resolve. He still had his eyes on the pedlar's face.

'You can come with me up to Teli Mohalla. If you

have to go farther, I shall ask someone to accompany you. There is trouble in the city.'

And without waiting for the boy's reply, continued walking.

For a brief moment, Inder paused and stood where he was, but then stepped forward and continued walking.

There was silence all round. The houses around stood in utter darkness.

'I too should not have come out on my round today.' He said to Inder. 'The town is stricken by drought, as it were. This is not a day for selling one's wares. But then I thought, if I can make even a few annas, it will not be bad. If a pedlar sits at home, how will he eat?' And the man laughed.

They were getting close to the water tap, which was as yet dry. The stone slab under it had become hollow with time; a few wasps were hovering over it. Inder used to catch wasps here.

'Even if only four cotton swabs are sold in a day, we make four annas, which is good enough,' the scent-seller was saying, as though talking to himself. It seemed he wanted to talk, either to while away the time, or because it helped him somehow to walk through deserted streets.

'I know who my potential buyers are in every street of the town,' he said. 'A man with two wives is my potential client. He must buy scent; he will also buy henna and collyrium. An ageing man with a young wife will also buy scent. Shall I tell you more?' He said wanting to entertain the boy.

The scent-seller's continuous monologue succeeded in steadying Inder and he was able to walk more confidently, his hand firmly on the handle of the knife. He was all concentration now, and his eyes were set on the scent-seller's waist, as intently as Arjun's must have been on the bird on the branch of the tree. The bag hanging from the left shoulder of the scent-seller swayed to and fro like the pendulum of a clock, exposing his thick cotton shirt covering his waist.

The water-tap was left behind. Inder's attention now centred on his right hand. He was aware of every step he took. It appeared as though the pattering of the pedlar's shoes was marking time with the swaying bag.

'In the bazaar, the cotton swabs sell more, whereas in the lanes, oil and scent are more in demand.' The scent-seller was saying.

Suddenly, Inder took a leap and made a quick movement. The pedlar felt as though something had moved with a flash on his left side. But before he could turn round to see what it was, he felt as though something had pricked him badly under the bag. Inder had struck accurately, and as instructed by the Sardar, had given a twist to the handle too, while the blade was still inside, and thus entangled it with the intestines.

The scent-seller had hardly turned round when he saw the boy running away, with his back towards him. Even then he did not understand what had happened. He wanted to call the boy back, but then he noticed drops of blood falling on his shoes and felt as though something was tearing his waist. As yet the sensation was not so sharp, but it was soon followed by searing pain. The man became extremely nervous. Stricken with fear he shouted:

'O, I have been killed!'

He was so terribly frightened that he could hardly shout. He was dying, not so much from the wound inflicted on him, as from sheer fright. He still couldn't believe that an innocent-looking boy could have attacked him. The load on his back and shoulders became unbearable, and it was under its weight that he fell face downward.

Only a few seconds earlier he had clearly seen the boy's running feet, but there was now no sign of the boy in the lane.

'O, I have been killed!' he whispered.

A hoarse cry escaped his lips and his eyes rested on a patch of the deep-blue sky over and above the narrow lane, in which two or three kites were flying. Soon enough the number of kites seemed to increase and the patch of blue got blurred.

13

Nathu was deeply disturbed. Sitting outside his house he was puffing at his hookah incessantly. His heart would sink every time he heard about the killings. He would try again and again to console himself: 'I am not a know-all. How could I know for what purpose I was being asked to kill a pig?' For some time he would overcome his uneasiness and feel reassured. But he would again lose his peace of mind when he would hear about some other incident. 'It is all the result of my doing.' Since morning, his fellow-skinners in the colony had been sitting and chatting outside one another's houses. Time and again, Nathu would go and sit with them. He would try to join in the conversation, but each time he tried, his throat would go dry and his legs would tremble, and he would go back into his house. 'Should I speak out? Tell my wife everything? She is a sensible woman, she will understand and I shall feel relieved.' Sometimes he would wish he could gulp down a glassful of country-wine so that he could lie unconscious. 'To tell my wife can be risky. Suppose, in an unguarded moment, in a casual conversation, she blurts out what really happened. What then? No one will spare me. I may be put behind bars. The police can put me under arrest and take me away. What will happen then? No one will believe me if I said that I had done the job on Murad Ali's instructions. And Murad Ali is a Musalman. Will a Musalman get a pig killed so that it can be thrown outside a mosque?' He would again become extremely restless. He would again try to divert his mind by arguing with himself: 'It couldn't have been the same pig that was thrown outside the mosque. I have not seen it, but any pig can be of black colour. Can't there be two pigs of the same colour? I am worrying about it without any rhyme or reason. It was certainly some other pig.' Reassured by such thoughts he would begin to chat and laugh with his wife. He would even go to his neighbour's house and begin talking about the fire in the Grain Market. But such a state of mind would not last long. He had only to remember what had happened during the previous night—from the moment the pig was pushed into the filthy hut to the arrival of the pushcart under cover of darkness in that desolate area— the whole episode would be like a nightmare and he would relapse into the same jittery state of mind. 'Will a veterinary surgeon procure a slaughtered pig in this way? "The pigs go roaming about there, get hold of one... a pushcart will come to take the carcass; don't move out of the hut; wait for me." Is this the way jobs are done?' Nathu had a mind to go straight to Kalu, the scavenger and ask him where he had delivered the pig. Go straight to Murad Ali... 'But what will Murad Ali say? If there is evil in his heart, he will push me out of his house, hold me guilty and get me arrested. He is quite capable of doing this.'

He again picked up his hookah. 'To hell with Murad Ali and his pig! I have done nothing on purpose. Whatever I did, was done in ignorance. What about those who are setting fire and killing innocent pedestrians and committing such heinous crimes? Why are they indulging in such foul acts with wide open eyes? I have killed one pig. Of what consequence is the killing of one pig? If I am a criminal, aren't they worse criminals? If I am guilty, aren't they guilty too? What about those who have set fire to the Grain Market? I have not done anything deliberately. Whatever had to happen, has happened; I have nothing to do with it all...'

Nathu thought of his father. He was a God-fearing man who always used to say, 'Son, keep your hands clean. A man whose hands are clean, will never do an evil deed. Earn your bread with dignity and self-respect.' As Nathu remembered his father's words, tears came into his eyes. And his heart became heavy once again.

Across the yard, a man walking along the road, had stopped and was looking intently towards the skinners' colony. Nathu's heart missed a beat. It seemed to him that the man was looking for him; as though he had come to spot out the man who had killed the pig.

Nathu's wife came out wiping her hands with a corner of her dhoti. Nathu again felt uneasy. He felt like telling her everything. 'There should at least be someone to whom I can open my heart.' Nathu's eyes again turned towards the man standing across the yard.

'What are you looking at?' His wife said, then turning her eyes towards the road, asked, 'Who is he? Do you know him?'

'No. How should I know him?' Nathu replied with a bewildered look in his eyes. 'Why are you standing there? Go inside,' he said brusquely.

She promptly went into the room.

Nathu again looked towards the road through the corner of his eyes. The man was moving away. On reaching the end of the yard, he lighted a cigarette and went away puffing at it.

'I was mistaken,' Nathu said to himself. 'On a working day so many people come here on some business or the other.'

He felt relieved. 'It was wrong of me to have spoken so roughly with her.'

'Listen,' he said to her. 'Make some tea for me.'

His wife came and stood in the doorway. There was something about her which gave Nathu a sense of confidence. He felt more secure if she was by his side. Her presence in the house imparted a sense of stability. When she was not around, it was as though things were going haywire. Today too he was inwardly very keen that she sit close to him. She was never restless or tense or nervous; nothing ever seemed to gnaw at her heart. It was so, he thought, because she was physically buxom, not a dried-up stick as he was, with hollow cheeks and a perpetually worried mind. She was relaxed, with a steady, balanced mind and a warm presence.

She came and stood on the threshold, a soft smile on her lips.

'You generally don't ask for tea at this time of the day. You seem to be enjoying a holiday today. Is that why you want tea?'

'Am I enjoying a holiday? Do you think it is a holiday?' Nathu said peevishly, 'If you can't make it, I shall make it myself. Why are you making such a fuss about it?' So saying Nathu got up and went into the room.

'Why are you cross? I shall make it for you in a minute.'

'No, no, you needn't bother. I shall make it myself.'

'I would rather die than let you light the fire when I am around,' she said and pulled him by his arm.

Nathu stood up. He felt a stab of pain in his heart. For a second he stood undecided. Then, with all the eagerness of his heart, he clasped his wife to himself.

'What is the matter with you today?' His wife said, laughing. But in his ardent embraces she sensed his disquiet. There is something troubling him, otherwise he wouldn't behave in this queer manner.

'What has come over you? Since last night you have been behaving in a strange sort of way. Tell me what is on your mind. I feel frightened.'

'What have we to be afraid of? We have not set fire to anyone's house.' Nathu came out with this odd reply.

His wife's hand stopped stroking his back, but she did not disengage herself from him.

Nathu became all the more agitated. He was behaving like a crazy person.

Suddenly, the pig's carcass flitted across his mind. It lay, right in the middle of the floor, with its legs raised and a pool of blood under it. Nathu trembled and went limp and cold in every limb. His shoulders were covered with cold sweat. It appeared to his wife as though his mind had again wandered off to something else. Suddenly Nathu tried to suppress a sob, and disentangling himself from his wife's embrace, muttered, 'No, not today. I don't feel like it. See what is happening outside. People's houses are burning.'

And for a long time he stood where he was, as though in a daze. His wife grew anxious.

'What is on your mind? Why have you become so quiet? Swear by me that you will tell me the truth.'

Nathu stepped aside and quietly went and sat down on the cot.

'What is it?'

'Nothing.'

'There is something. You are hiding it from me.'

'There is nothing,' he said again.

Nathu's wife came over to him and stroking his hand said, 'Why don't you speak? Say something.'

'I would tell you if there was anything to tell.'

'Wait. I shall get you some tea.'

'I don't want tea.'

'A little while ago you were asking for it. You were going to make it yourself. And now you don't want it.'

'No, I don't want it.'

'All right then, come to bed,' she said laughing.

'No.'

'Are you angry with me? You are losing your temper over every little thing,' she said somewhat resentfully.

Nathu remained quiet. He was actually behaving like a sulky child.

'Where did you go last night? You have not told me anything,' Nathu's wife said, sitting down on the floor beside him.

Nathu looked at his wife, as though taken aback. 'She has sensed it. Soon enough, everyone will know about it,' Nathu trembled at the thought.

'If you won't tell me, I shall break my head against

the wall. You have never concealed anything from me. Why are you doing so today?'

Nathu's eyes rested on his wife's face. 'If she suspects anything, then God knows what she must be thinking.' His wife's trusting and beseeching eyes were still looking at him.

'Do you know why the Grain Market is burning?'

'I know someone killed a pig and threw it outside a mosque. And then the Musalmans set fire to the Grain Market.'

'I killed that pig.'

Nathu's wife turned pale.

'Did you? Why did you commit such a loathsome act?'

All the blood drained out of her face and she stared at her husband.

'Did you throw the pig outside the mosque too?'

'No. Kalu the scavenger took it on his pushcart.'

'Kalu is a Musalman. How could he carry it?'

'Kalu is not a Musalman. He is a Christian. He goes to church on Sundays.'

Her eyes were still on Nathu's face.

'What a horrible thing you have done. But you are not to blame. You were tricked into doing it,' she muttered, as though to herself. But she had trembled while listening to Nathu's account, and felt as though the shadow of some dreadful omen had fallen on their home which could not be eliminated even by fasts and prayers.

His mind felt weighed down by the confession. Nathu was deeply troubled at heart. His wife raised her eyes and looked at him. On seeing him so unhappy, a surge of warm feeling rose in her heart. She got up and sat down by his side, and taking his hand into hers, said, 'Now I know. I would say to myself, why is he so upset? But how could I know? Why didn't you tell me earlier? It is wrong to keep your grief to yourself.'

'Had I known what it involved, I wouldn't have done it,' Nathu muttered. 'I was told that the veterinary surgeon had asked for a pig,' said Nathu, sinking deeper into despondency. 'I saw Murad Ali last night. But he wouldn't talk to me. I ran after him, but he wouldn't stop. He quickened his pace and went farther and farther away. He didn't even care to talk to me.' Nathu's voice was again lost in doubt and uncertainty. He had once again begun to doubt whether he had actually seen Murad Ali or not.

'How much did you get for killing the pig?'

'Five rupees. He paid the money in advance.'

'Five rupees? So much money? What did you do with it?'

'Four rupees are still left with me. They are lying on the shelf.'

'Why didn't you tell me?'

'I thought I would buy a couple of dhotis for you.'

'Shall I get dhotis with tainted money? Shall I not throw this money into the fire?' Nathu's wife said angrily. But then she restrained herself and making a vain attempt to smile, added, 'But this is your hard-earned money. I shall buy with it whatever you say.'

She got up, went to the shelf, lifted herself on her toes, saw the coins lying on the shelf and turned round. Nathu sat with his head bowed, as though sunk deeper into despair.

'Did you notice the man who was standing on the other side of the yard?' Nathu asked, raising his head.

'Yes, I did. But how does it concern us?'

'I think it was his pig that I pushed into the room. He must have come to know of it.'

'What nonsense! If he has come to know of it, let him come and demand it from you,' Nathu's wife said somewhat loudly, then, shaking her head, added, 'Listen. We are chamars. To kill animals and skin hides is our profession. You killed a pig. Now, how does it concern us whether they sell it in the market or throw it on the steps of a mosque?' Then added, chirpily, 'I shall certainly buy dhotis with this money. You have earned it with your hard labour.' Then, going back to the shelf she picked up the money, but the next moment put it back.

'You are perfectly right,' exclaimed Nathu. 'How does it concern me? To hell with Murad Ali and his pig! Yesterday too I thought the same way,' he said, with a ring of self-assurance in his voice.

'I have full fifteen rupees with me now. You too can buy something for yourself.'

'I don't need anything,' said Nathu feeling elated. 'When you are by my side, I feel I have everything.'

Nathu's wife went straight to the fireplace and sat down to make tea.

'God is never angry with a person whose heart is clean. Our hearts are clean. Why should we be afraid of anyone?' she said and then added, 'You have told me about it but don't tell anyone else in the colony.'

'You too don't tell anyone,' said Nathu.

Nathu's wife was pouring tea into glasses, when she

heard the sound of running feet outside. Her hand shook. She raised her eyes and looked at Nathu, but did not say anything. Instead, she smiled.

A little later, they heard one skinner asking another, outside, in the colony. 'What's happened, uncle?'

'A riot has broken out in Ratta.'

'Where?'

'In Ratta. Two persons have been killed.'

'Who was the fellow running away?'

'I don't know. Must be some outsider.'

Silence fell again. The skinner had either gone into his house or towards the back of the colony.

Handing the glass of tea to Nathu, his wife said, 'You too should go and meet the fellow-skinners. It is not good to remain aloof from them. Let's go together; I too will come along.'

Nathu's wife got up, but then, without any explicable reason, picked up the broom and started sweeping the floor. She swept every nook and corner, picked up things and swept the floor under them. She herself did not know why she was doing it. It was as though, with the help of the broom she was trying to cast out some phantom or spectre from the room. After sweeping, she washed the floor clean, pouring as much water as she could. But when she sat down tired, on the cot, it seemed to her that the phantom was crawling back into the room through the chinks of the closed door and that the house was once again becoming dark with its presence.

14

Starting from Khanpur, the first bus would normally reach the village at eight o'clock in the morning. After every hour or two, buses would begin to arrive from the city or from Khanpur. It was already midday and as yet no bus had arrived. In the tea-shop, the water in the kettle for tea had been boiling since morning. Both the benches in front of the tea-shop lay vacant. Earlier, there used to be so many customers that the benches were always occupied. There was hardly a person who, passing by Harnam Singh's tea-shop would not sit down for a glass of tea. At the bus stop too, only a couple of stray dogs were to be seen moving about. A pall of silence lay over everything.

A woman has a keener insight into things. Since the previous evening, Banto had been insisting, 'Let us get away from this village and go to Khanpur where some of our relatives are living. In this entire village we are the only Sikh couple, all the others are Muslims.' But Harnam Singh would not agree. 'How can we shut down a running shop and go away? Riots and disturbances keep taking place but that is no reason why one should close down one's business. And where shall we go? Shall we go to the city which is already in flames? If we go to Khanpur, who will feed us there? What if our shop is looted when we turn our back on it? How shall we live? Shall we go to our

son? He is living twenty miles away in Mirpur. He is as
much alone there as we are here. Let us leave ourselves
in Guru Maharaj's hands and stick on where we are. If
we go to our son, won't we be a liability on him? Will he
try to protect us old people or try to save his own life?
For how long can we be fed by others? And for how long
can we live on our savings?' And sitting on his stool, Harnam
Singh would fold his hands and recite a couplet: 'Blessed
with your protecting hand, Lord, how can anyone suffer?'

Banto would listen and fall silent. But then, whenever
she felt nervous and anxious she would say, 'Let us go to
my sister's village, that is nearby. We shall not stay with
her, we shall stay in the gurdwara. Besides, there is a fairly
large community of Sikhs living there. They are our own
people. We shall feel safe living among them.' But Harnam
Singh would not agree to this either. He was somehow
convinced that while other people might have difficulties
to face, nothing untoward would happen to him.

'Listen, my good woman, we have never thought ill
of anyone; we have never harmed anyone. People in the
village too have been good to us. We do not owe anyone
anything. Right in your presence, Karim Khan has assured
me no less than ten times that we should continue to
live here with an easy mind, that no one would dare cast
an evil eye on us, and who in the village enjoys more
respect than Karim Khan? We are the only family of
Sikhs living in the village. Will they not feel ashamed of
attacking two defenceless old people?'

Banto again fell silent. Argument can counter
argument, but argument is helpless against faith. While
Banto's heart would, time and again, sink with anxiety,

Harnam Singh did not feel restless even once. He face glowed and God's name was ever on his lips, and this would impart courage to Banto too.

But on that day no bus had arrived and not a single customer had come to his shop. The road bore a deserted look. On the other hand, two or three persons whom he had never seen before, while going towards the village, had eyed him and his shop very closely.

When the afternoon sun was declining, he heard the sound of familiar footsteps coming from the side of the slope. Harnam Singh felt reassured on seeing Karim Khan coming towards his shop, pattering along with his stick. Karim Khan would give him the news besides good counsel. 'If it becomes unsafe, we can take shelter in Karim Khan's house,' thought Harnam Singh.

Karim Khan came over but did not stop at his shop. As he passed by, he merely turned his face once towards Harnam Singh, slowed down his pace, and muttered while pretending to cough: 'Things have taken a bad turn, Harnam Singh. Your welfare lies in leaving the place.'

Then after taking a couple of more steps added, 'Local people will not do you any harm but it is feared that marauders may come from outside. We will not be able to stop them.'

And coughing and pattering his stick, he moved on.

For the first time, his faith which had all along given him moral strength was badly shaken. Karim Khan did not stop at his shop, which meant that the danger was real. He must have come here at some risk to himself. The news did not scare him so much as it made him sad. He felt disenchanted, rather than angry or frightened.

About five minutes later Karim Khan was seen coming back. Climbing up the slope, his hand on his waist, coughing and breathing hard, he again slowed his pace and muttered: 'Don't delay, Harnam Singh. The situation is not good. There is fear of marauders attacking.'

And he continued climbing up, breathing hard, with his hand on his waist.

Where was Harnam Singh to go? For miles on end, on all sides, stretched roads and vast stretches of land. Karim Khan had of course advised him to leave, but leave for where? Where could he get shelter? At sixty and with a woman by his side, how far could he run for safety?

A voice again came from within him: 'Do not go anywhere, stay where you are. When the marauders come, offer them both your shop and your lives. It is better to die rather than to go knocking from pillar to post.' Harnam Singh still could not believe that anyone from the village would raise his hand against him or that the village folk would allow the outsiders to attack them.

Harnam Singh got up and went into the room at the back of the tea-shop where Banto was sitting.

'Karim Khan was here a moment ago. He said that we should leave the village immediately, that there was danger of marauders coming from outside.'

Banto's blood froze. She sat petrified. Night was approaching and there was nowhere to go. And there, in the middle of the room, stood her husband, a picture of despondency.

There was no time to think, nor could they linger here any longer.

'We must get away from here as soon as it gets dark.'

'I still maintain that we should stick on here,' said Harnam Singh. 'We shouldn't go anywhere.' Then, pointing to his double-barrelled gun hanging on the wall, he added, 'If it comes to killing or getting killed, I shall shoot you down with this gun first and then kill myself.'

Banto listened in silence. What could she say? What counsel could she give? They were left with no choice.

Harnam Singh came back to the shop. He collected his earnings from under the coir-matting on which he used to sit, separated the currency notes from the coins, put back the coins, and put the wad of notes in the inner pocket of his waistcoat. Thereafter he took down the gun from the wall and hung it from his shoulder. He was unable to decide what else to take with him. 'Shall I take the papers concerning the registration of the shop?' But there was no time to look for them or to take them out. Banto too was in a fix. 'Should I take my jewellery along? Shall I cook something for the way? Make a couple of chapatis? Nothing may be available on the way. Shall I change my clothes? One should wear clean and tidy clothes when going out.' Banto too was unable to decide what she should pick up, and what leave behind.

'What should I do with my ornaments?' she asked. 'Should I put them on?'

'Put them on,' Harnam Singh said, but then thought for a moment and said, 'No, don't put them on. Anyone seeing you with ornaments will be tempted to kill you. Go and bury them at the back of the house.'

Banto decided to put on some ornaments under her shirt, of some others she made a small bundle in a

handkerchief and put it in a trunk; the rest she took with
her to the backyard behind the shop and buried them
in the ground near the vegetable-beds.

The living room behind the tea-shop was full of boxes,
beddings and other household stuff. They had got so
many things made at the time of their daughter's wedding
yet nothing could be taken along.

'Shall I make a couple of chapatis? Who knows where
we may have to go knocking?'

'There is no time for making chapatis now, good
woman. Had we thought of leaving earlier, it could have
been done.'

Just then came the sound of beating drums from far
away. Both stood staring at each other.

'The marauders are here. They seem to be coming
from Khanpur.'

The sound of drums was soon followed by another
sound—of slogans being raised from the other side of
the mound in the village.

'Ya Ali!'

'Allah-o-Akbar!'

'It must be Ashraf and Latif who are shouting these
slogans,' murmured Harnam Singh. 'They are members of
the League in the village and keep shouting Pakistani slogans.'

The atmosphere became tense.

Evening had fallen but it wasn't dark yet. The sound
of the marauders appeared to be coming from the other
side of the ravine.

Just then Harnam Singh's eyes fell on the small cage
hanging from the roof in which sat their little pet-bird
myna.

'Banto, take the cage to the backyard, and let the myna fly away.'

Only a little while earlier Banto had put water and bird-feed in the two small cups lying in the cage. Now, as she took down the cage and carried it to the backyard, the little myna repeated by rote: 'God be with you, Banto! May God be with everyone.'

On hearing the words Banto's throat choked. In answer to the bird, Banto too repeated the words: 'Myna, may God be with you! May God be with everyone!'

The myna had learnt these words from Harnam Singh, who, while sitting in the shop, would often talk to Banto sitting in the back room about the Gurbani and other religious matters, and every time he would stand up or sit down he would utter such words as 'God is the Protector! God is everyone's protector!' Gradually, the myna had begun to repeat the words.

But the utterance of the myna gave a lot of strength to Banto. She regained courage and her steadiness, as though the little bird had taught her a lesson.

In the small backyard Harnam Singh had planted a few vegetables besides a mango tree. On reaching the middle of the backyard, Banto opened the cage and said softly:

'Go, fly away my little myna!

'May God be with you! May God be with everyone!'

But the myna continued to sit inside the cage.

'Fly away, my little one!

'Fly away!'

And Banto's throat again choked. Leaving the cage on the ground, she came back into the room.

The sound of beating drums was again heard. This

time it came from somewhere nearby. The hum of sounds from the village too had grown louder. A large number of people seemed to be advancing from somewhere. From within the village, the sound of slogans came intermittently.

Banto and Harnam Singh, locked the shop and came out. They left with a little cash, a gun and the clothes on their back. No sooner had they stepped out of the house that the entire place became alien to them. Which way were they to turn? To the left lay the sprawling village. In that very direction was the ravine, from the other side of which came the sound of beating drums. To their right was the pucca road that led towards Khanpur. To go in that direction was not without danger. Across the road, at some distance, flowed a streamlet with a wide bed and a high embankment. That was the only way of escape. They could cover a long distance without being noticed. To go along the road was risky. The streamlet had no water in it; its broad bed was dry and full of sand, pebbles and stones. Both of them crossed the road, and walking a few yards, went down the slope of the embankment. The marauders had already reached the outskirts of the village and seemed to be advancing in this very direction. The atmosphere resounded with the sound of drums and slogans.

Banto and Harnam Singh were going down the bed of the stream when they heard a thin, soft voice:

'Banto, May God be with you! May God be with everyone!'

The myna had come flying after them and had perched on a tree nearby.

The marauders had by then reached the top of the

mound, at the foot of which, to the right side Harnam Singh had his tea-shop. They came down the mound, shrieking and shouting and raising slogans, and beating their drums.

The moon had risen and its soft light spread all over. One felt as though an unknown enemy lurked behind every tree and rock. Under the light of the moon, the dry stream-bed looked like a white sheet of cloth. Both of them had come down the slope and, turning to the right, were walking slowly along the foot of the embankment. The edge of the stream-bed being strewn with stones and pebbles, they soon grew tired and breathless. Even as they walked they were all ears to every sound coming from the direction of the village.

The noise which had earlier risen to a high pitch had somewhat subsided. It appeared to Harnam Singh as though the marauders had stopped in front of his shop and were not able to decide their next move. Harnam Singh felt grateful to Karim Khan for his timely warning which had made it possible for them to escape. Suddenly they heard the sound of heavy blows falling on something. Harnam Singh understood that they were breaking down the door of his shop. Their legs trembled, making it difficult for them to continue walking. Holding each other's hand they slowly moved forward.

'Pray to God and walk on, Banto,' said Harnam Singh, pulling along his wife.

A dog suddenly barked somewhere. Both looked up. At the top of the embankment a fierce-looking black dog stood barking at them. Harnam Singh's face turned livid.

'For which sins of ours are we being punished so

severely by Guru Maharaj? The marauders have only to hear the barking of the dog and they will come running after us.'

'Keep walking, don't stop!'

The dog was still barking. It was the same dog which Harnam Singh had often seen in front of his shop, sniffing at things. After walking some distance, Banto turned round. The dog was still barking but it had neither moved down towards them nor along the top of the embankment.

They continued walking at a snail's pace.

'Let us somehow get away from the village. The rest is in God's hands.'

'The dog is not coming after us.'

'But it is still barking.'

Both of them took cover behind a boulder, and with bated breath listened to the barking of the dog.

The door of the shop had fallen, and the marauders, with a loud 'Ya Ali!' had rushed into the shop.

'They are looting our shop! Our house!'

The barking of the dog had gone unnoticed by the marauders. The husband and wife felt somewhat relieved. Even if the dog had attracted their attention they might not have cared to pursue the old couple, since there was so much in the shop for them to lift.

'Whose shop and whose house? It is no longer our shop, they stopped being ours the moment we walked out of the house.'

With the bed of the stream gleaming in the moonlight, a cluster of trees here and there, and the dog still standing on the top of the embankment, the entire scene seemed like a dream. How quickly had everything changed! They had lived at that place for twenty long years, yet within the twinkling of an eye, had been turned into homeless outsiders. Harnam Singh's hands were cold and wet with perspiration. The only sentence which he was repeating to himself over and over again, was 'Get away from here, by whatever means you can! Just get away from here!'

The village was left behind. The dog still stood there at the top of the slope; it had not come after them; very likely it would go back after a while. The shop had been looted. The marauders were no longer shouting; the noise had subsided. Perhaps they were satiated with the loot. But who knows, they may come looking for them now. Now, only the sound of pebbles under their staggering feet could be heard, in the surrounding silence. They walked on and covered some more distance. It seemed to Banto as if some light had spread in the sky. As she turned round she noticed that behind the top of the slope the sky was turning crimson. Banto stood transfixed.

'What is that? Do you see?'

'It is our shop burning, Banto!' said Harnam Singh.

He too was looking in the same direction. For some time they continued looking at the flames, as though under a spell. The flames rising from one's own house must be in some way different from the flames rising from someone else's house, otherwise why should they have stood like statues, watching them?

'Everything reduced to dust!' Harnam Singh said in a low whisper.

'Before our very eyes.'

'Guru Maharaj must have willed it so.' He heaved a deep sigh and they both resumed their trudge.

Walls keep men concealed, but here there were no walls, only mounds and rocks here and there, behind which a person could hide. But for how long? Within a few hours the darkness of the night would be dispelled and they would be rendered 'naked' as it were, once again shelterless; there would be no place for them to hide their heads.

Banto's throat was dry and Harnam Singh's legs would falter again and again. But at that time, not only them, but innumerable villagers were knocking about in search of shelter; the sound of crashing doors was falling on many ears. But they had no time either to think or to make any plans for the future. They barely had time to run for their lives. 'Keep walking so long as the shades of night provide you cover. Soon enough the day will break and terrors of the day, like hungry wolves, will stare you in the face.'

Within a short time they found themselves utterly exhausted.

But feeling relieved at having come out alive, the faces of their son and daughter began to appear before their eyes again. Where must Iqbal Singh be at this time? What must he be going through? And Jasbir? They were not so worried about Jasbir because the Sikh community in her village was fairly large. It may be that the entire community has moved into the gurdwara and found some way of protecting itself. But Iqbal Singh in a small village, running a cloth shop, was all alone. He might have left the village in good time, or he too may be knocking about for shelter. Every thought was acutely disturbing.

Harnam Singh shut his eyes, folded his hands, and

with the name of Guru Maharaj on his lips, repeated the
words of his prayer:

'With your protecting hand over his head, My Lord,
how can anyone suffer?'

When the day broke, they were sitting by the side
of a brook. Harnam Singh was well familiar with the
surrounding area. He knew that they were close to a
small village, Dhok Muridpur by name. They had passed
the whole night praying, brooding and dragging their
feet. But as the day dawned, their minds were at peace,
for no explicable reason. The sweet fragrance of the lukat
trees, wafted from far away filled the air. The moon
which was orange-red in colour a little while earlier had
turned pale yellow. The colour of the sky too changed
from muddy grey to pale yellow and soon to silvery white.
Soon enough it would be limpid blue. Birds were
chirping on all sides.

'We can have a wash in this brook, Banto, and then
say our prayers and leave.'

'But where shall we go?' asked Banto anxiously.

'We shall go to this village and knock at someone's
door. If he has mercy in his heart, he will open the door
to us and let us in; if not, then whatever is God's will.'

'Don't you know anyone in Muridpur?'

Harnam Singh smiled. 'No one gave us shelter where
I knew everyone, our shop was looted and our house set
on fire. Many of the villagers had been my childhood
playmates, we had grown up together.'

When the morning mist cleared, they set out for the
village. They first came to a grove of mulberry and
shisham trees, at the end of which was a graveyard with

broken-down graves, big and small. Near it stood, what appeared to be the grave of some pir for an earthen lamp had been lighted on it and green pennets hung over it. Then they came to the fields—the wheat crop was ready for harvesting. Beyond the fields stood the cluster of flat-roofed, mud-houses. Cows and buffaloes, tied to their pegs, stood outside. Hens with their chicks ran about looking for their feed.

'Banto, if we find them hostile, then I shall first finish you off with my gun and then kill myself. I won't let you fall into their hands so long as I am living.'

They stopped in front of the very first house to which they came, standing at the edge of the village. The door was closed. It was a discoloured door, made of thick timber. God alone knew whose house it was and who lived behind the closed door, and what fate awaited them when the door would open.

Harnam Singh raised his hand, for a second or two, his hand remained suspended in the air, and then he knocked at the door.

15

The gurdwara was packed to capacity. The entire congregation was swaying in ecstasy. It was a rare moment. The singers sang with their eyes closed, in frenzied exaltation: 'Who is there, beside you my Lord...'

Everyone sat with hands folded, eyes closed and heads swaying to the right and left. Here and there a devotee kept time with the tune by clapping his hands. The ecstatic rhapsody expressing sentiments of supreme self-sacrifice was once again being heard after a lapse of centuries. Three hundred years earlier, a similar 'war song' used to be sung by the Khalsa before taking on the enemy. Oblivious of everything they sang, imbued with the spirit of sacrifice. In this unique moment, their souls had merged, as it were, with the souls of their ancestors. Time had again come to cross swords with the Turks. The Khalsa was again facing a crisis created by the Turks. Their minds had been transported to those earlier times. The Khalsa did not know from which direction the enemy would launch his offensive, whether they would be outsiders or local residents. There was no trusting the enemy, but every 'Singh' in the congregation was ready for sacrifice.

The light in the gurdwara came from two stained-glass windows in the back walls set with green, red and yellow panes. The stool on which the Guru Granth Sahib lay, stood within four wooden pillars covered with a silken piece of cloth of red colour fringed with a gold braid. One end of this cloth stretched right down to the floor where sheets of white long-cloth had been spread. Coins and currency notes lay scattered on one end of it while on the other was a pile of wheat flour.

As one entered the gurdwara, the women members of the congregation sat on the left, their heads covered with dupattas, their faces aglow and their eyes lit up with the light of devotion and the spirit of sacrifice. Here and there a woman had a kirpan hanging by her side. Everyone in the congregation, man or woman, intensely felt that he or she was a link in the long chain of Sikh history, an integral part of it and, at that moment of crisis, like the ancestors, was ready to lay down his or her life.

Weapons were being stored in the long corridor at the back of the stool and in the Granthi's room. Seven members of the congregation possessed double-barrelled guns, with five boxes of cartridges. Jathedar Kishen Singh was organizing the defence. Kishen Singh was a war-veteran; he had taken part in the Second World War on the Burmese front and he was now hell-bent on trying the tactics of the Burmese front on the Muslims of his village. On acquiring the command for defence, the first thing he did was to go home and put on his khaki shirt which had been a part of his military uniform and on which dangled three medals received from the British government and a number of coloured strips. The shirt was crumpled but there was no time to get it ironed. Two pickets were set up, one at each end of the lane in front of the gurdwara, each provided with two guns. Later, the picket to the right of the gurdwara proved ineffective, since Hari Singh, in whose house the picket had been set up had been reluctant to open fire on his Muslim neighbours. With the remaining three guns a picket was set up at the roof of the gurdwara under the command of Kishen Singh. Kishen Singh had got himself a chair in which he sat all the time. That is how the seven guns had been utilized. The other weapons such as lances, swords, lathis, etc. had been placed against the back wall of the gurdwara. Swords in velvet scabbards of different colours stood side by side in a neat arrangement as though in an exhibition. The light of the sun through the windows fell straight on them, making them look very·impressive. The light also fell on the points of the lances making them glitter. There were a few shields too which had been provided by the Nihang Sikhs. Two Nihang Sikhs stood guard on the roof of the gurdwara, one at each end, facing the lane. Both-were in their typical attire, a long, blue robe, blue turban covered with an iron disc and yellow waistband. Lance in hand, each stood to attention with his eyes gazing far into the distance. No one knew from which direction the enemy might come raising clouds of dust.

'Lower your lance, Nihang Singhji, its tip glitters in the light of the sun; the enemy can see it from far off,' said Kishen Singh to the Nihang on guard duty. This annoyed the Nihang.

'A Nihang's lance can never be lowered.' He shot back and continued standing lance in hand as before, with his eyes on the horizon. Before Nihang Singh's eyes still

floated visions of old battles, of armies marching, naked
swords blazing in the sun, horses neighing and the air
resounding with the beat of drums. These visions would
instil in him new vigour and valour worthy of the Sikhs.

Two Nihangs had been posted below, at the entrance
to the gurdwara. Lances in their hands, both stood to
attention, their moustaches duly twirled and yellow
waistbands tied over their blue robes. In olden times it
was customary for the Khalsa to go to battle in yellow
robes, yellow being the colour of selfless sacrifice. In the
existing situation, everyone had made the effort to wear
something which was emblematic of the old tradition—
a yellow handkerchief, a yellow scarf or a yellow dupatta,
etc., which would link him or her emotionally with their
heroic past. Thus, Bishen Singh, a haberdasher by
profession, who had been made in-charge of the
community kitchen, had stuck into his turban a yellow
silk kerchief, which originally belonged to his son who
had donned it at the Basant Panchami fair. Bishen Singh
had practically snatched it out of his boy's hands to stick
it into his turban. In the congregation some people had
tied yellow waistbands. But most people were in their
everyday dress of salwar-kameez; even Kishen Singh was
wearing, below his crumpled, medal-studded shirt, a pair
of striped pajamas. For most of them this was no time
to bother about dress, since the heart was afire with the
spirit of do or die.

The atmosphere in the gurdwara was as solemn as
water-laden clouds. Heads swayed in the congregational
singing; the minds imbued with the past—engendered
by the spirit of sacrifice, the presence of the Muslim foe,

the Guru's 'prasad', the paraphernalia of past battles, the sword, the shield, the lance, and the bond that united them into one unbreakable entity. If anything was not there, it was the British presence. Hardly twenty-five miles away there was the sprawling British cantonment, the biggest in the country. But it was nowhere in their thoughts. Nor were the British officers, stationed in the city and in the entire province. They too did not exist in their consciousness. If anything did exist it was the Turk, the traditional enemy of the Khalsa, the advancing hordes of the Turks, the imminent combat which was to them like the great ritual into which they would plunge, ready to lay down their lives.

The danger of attack lay at the back of the gurdwara, where stood the house with the green balcony belonging to the Sheikhs. Inside that house, the Muslims of the village had been storing arms and ammunition. Inside the Sheikh's mansion too the atmosphere was very similar to the one prevailing in the gurdwara. Here too, all the Muslims of the village—farmers, oil-crushers, bakers, butchers—had assumed the role of mujahids, and preparations were going on to launch a Jihad against the kafirs. Here too, the eyes were bloodshot and hearts afire with the spirit of sacrifice.

Right in front of the gurdwara, across the lane, was a row of shops belonging to the Sikhs, behind which a slope went right down to the bank of a stream. Beyond the stream lay a big orchard of the lukat fruit. Therefore, there was little danger of an attack being mounted from the front. If anyone dared do so, the guns of Kishen Singh, stationed on the roof, would make mincemeat of them.

To the left of the gurdwara, some of the houses near the end of the lane belonged to the Muslims, behind which stood the Khalsa School. Beyond the Khalsa school, stretched the fields. To the right of the gurdwara, where the lane ended, there was a mohalla of Muslim houses. There too, in the last house in the lane a picket had been set up.

The Sheikh's house with the green balcony, however, was located at the back of the gurdwara, beyond two narrow lanes. It was Sheikh Ghulam Rasul's double-storeyed house and, according to the information brought by the informers, it had been turned into a fortress by the Musalmans. All the doors opening on the green balcony were shut tight. The room on the top floor too, with the green windows was closed. Not a soul was to be seen standing anywhere. But everyone feared that the first shot would be fired from that house.

The village otherwise was a lovely one, nestled in idyllic surroundings. Anyone visiting it in normal times would be enthralled by its picturesque beauty. As the saying went: 'God had made it with His own hands.' Overlooking the small stream the village stood in the form of a horse-shoe built on a small hillock. Across the bluish water of the stream there was the thick orchard of lukat trees where numerous brooks flowed. The fruit was ripening in those days, and the orchard resounded with the incessant chirping of birds, notably parrots. The colour of the stream was as blue as the colour of the sky while that of the earth was reddish brown. Outside the town, the fields stretched far into the distance, right up to the foot of the low hill. After every few hours, the colour of the hill would change.

Sometimes it would be covered with a blue haze, at another time its face would be flushed burnished copper. Fluffy white clouds played on its slopes almost all the time. Stretches of green foliage covered its lower parts. At the foot of the hill there were innumerable springs flowing under the shade of banyan and fig trees. It was in the lap of these idyllic surroundings that the inhabitants had been living from generation to generation.

Suddenly, something electrifying occurred in the gurdwara. All eyes turned towards the gate of the gurdwara through which Sardar Teja Singh, the chief of the congregation was entering. On stepping up to the raised projection of the gurdwara, Sardarji went down on his knees, and then bowing low touched the threshold with his eyes. The fingers of both his hands resting on the floor were trembling.

For a long time, Teja Singh kept his head bowed, his forehead touching the threshold. Teja Singhji was in an ecstatic state of mind. Tears streamed from his eyes. Every pore of his body throbbed with the spirit of sacrifice in defence of the Faith.

He stood up and with folded hands and bowed head, his flowing white beard covering his chest, he came and stood before the Guru Granth Sahib, the Holy Book. Here too, he stood with bowed head for a long time. His face was flushed and tears flowed from his eyes on to the white sheet of cloth spread on the floor.

The entire congregation watched with bated breath and rapt attention. They were deeply moved. When Teja Singhji stood up, a wave of emotion coursed through the entire congregation.

He slowly stepped up to a pillar against which stood an old sword in a red scabbard. With trembling hands he picked up the sword from its handle and came and stood in the middle of the hall. This was his maternal grandfather's sword, whose father had been a courtier in the royal court of Maharaja Ranjit Singh.

He had hardly raised the sword when a feeling of self-immolation surged through the entire congregation. Heads swayed. Young Pritam Singh, standing by the door, burst into a full-throated slogan:

'Jo Boley So Nihal!'

To which the entire congregation answered with one voice:

'Sat Sri Akal!'

The walls of the gurdwara shook under the resounding response to the slogan. Even though it was forbidden to raise slogans, lest the enemy should know that the entire Sikh community of the village had gathered in the gurdwara, the surge of emotions was such that it could not be contained. The pent-up emotions could only be released through a full-throated response to the slogan.

Sardar Teja Singh, now holding his sword in both trembling hands raised it and kissed it with both his eyes, at which the entire congregation sobbed uncontrollably. The head of the Nihang standing at the gate swayed to the right and left. Hundreds of heads swayed.

'Once again, today, the Khalsa Panth needs the blood of the Guru's Sikhs,' he began in a voice trembling with intense emotion. 'Time has come when our faith will be put to test. Time has come of our trial. The Maharaj has only one behest for this time: "Sacrifice! Sacrifice! Sacrifice!"'

(Die for the Panth! Die for the Panth! Die for the Panth!)

A kind of golden dust filled Teja Singh's mind. His ecstasy bordered on frenzy! All his emotions centred round the word 'Sacrifice!'

'Chant the Ardas, you Singhs of the Guru!'

The entire congregation stood up, and with heads bowed, hands folded began chanting the hymns of the Gurvani in full-throated voices. The gurdwara resounded. The entire prayer was recited, which took quite some time. At the concluding words the chant was at its loudest:

The Khalsa shall rule.

None shall remain in subjugation!

The chanting rose like waves, striking against the walls of the gurdwara.

No sooner had the prayer been chanted, than the Nihang standing at the gate raised his hand and with his eyes closed, shouted the slogan in a voice so piercing that the veins of his throat swelled:

'Jo Boley So Nihal!' (Redemption to the one who responds).

In answer to which the entire congregation, with hands raised responded with all the vocal strength at their command:

'Sat Sri Akal!'

There was a fresh upsurge of emotions. The raising of slogans added poignancy to the feelings of solidarity and sacrifice!

Just then, from a distance came a piercing sound: 'Nara-i-Takbir!' followed by the resounding answer:

'Allah-o-Akbar!'

The Nihang at the gate once again clenched his fist and, raising it above his shoulders, was about to raise a slogan when Teja Singh stopped him.

'Enough! The enemy has learnt about our presence!' But the answering slogan of the Muslims brought home to the congregation something relating to the prevailing situation.

'We do not want the enemy to know about our strength. We do not want them to know that the entire Sikh community has gathered in the gurdwara. It is a matter of strategy.' And giving an exposition of the prevailing situation, he said, 'We have tried to inform the highest authority of the district, the Deputy Commissioner Sahib Bahadur about the nefarious activities the Muslims have lately been indulging in. I know Richard Sahib personally. He is a gentleman, sagacious and justice-loving. This is the best that we could do, inform the highest authority about our situation. All sorts of news is reaching us. We have come to know that weapons are being stored in the house of Rahim, the oil-crusher, that a motor-car of blue colour came in the afternoon from the direction of the city and stopped outside the house of Fazal Din the school master, that some articles were taken out of the car and delivered to Master Fazal Din. This car has been going in different directions and stopping at different places. It has also come to our knowledge that the local Muslims have sent word to the Muslims of Muridpur that they should send men and weapons to them. We have tried hard to talk to Sheikh Ghulam Rasul and other Muslims of the village, but the fellows cannot be trusted.'

'You have made no efforts. It is a lie.'

Suddenly a voice was heard in the congregation. Silence fell on all sides. Who was this intruder? People in the gurdwara were enraged.

A frail young man stood up.

'We should not forget that we are being incited against the Muslims, and the Muslims against us. Due to rumours of all kinds tension is mounting and tempers are running high. On our part we should try our best to maintain contact with the Muslims and continue to interact with them, and see that violence does not break out.'

'Sit down! Shut up!'

Traitor! Who the hell is he?'

'I won't sit down. I must have my say. We must make every effort to meet Ghulam Rasul and other sober-minded Muslims of the village. If Ghulam Rasul is not amenable to reason there must be other peace-loving Muslims with whose cooperation we can maintain peace in the village. If they are getting weapons from Muridpur, aren't we trying to get weapons from Kahuta? No one wants bloodshed. The Sikhs and Muslims of the village should meet one another and maintain peace in the village. Only this morning I met Ghulam Rasul and some other Muslims...'

'What? What took you there? Is Ghulam Rasul your foster father?'

'Allow me to speak. It is the ruffians from another village who will do the mischief. We should try our best to see that no outsider comes into the village. That can be done only if the peace-loving Sikhs and Muslims jointly stop them from coming. They are collecting weapons out of fear of us and we are doing the same out of fear of them.'

'There is no trusting the Muslims. Sit down.'

'Those people say that Sikhs cannot be trusted.'

'Sit down!' an elderly man shouted, his lips trembling, 'Who are you to butt in? Your mother's milk has not yet dried on your lips and you have come to advise your elders?'

Three or four Sardars stood up at different places.

'Don't you know that they have set fire to the Grain Market in the city?'

'It is entirely the mischief of the British.' Sohan Singh's voice grew louder. 'It is in our interest that the riot does not break out. Listen, Brothers, roads are being blocked. No bus has come from the city today. The entire area is inhabited by Muslims. If people from outside attack the village, how will you defend yourselves? Just think. How much assistance can you expect from Kahuta? What are you so confident about?'

For some time there was silence in the hall.

Then, Teja Singhji came and stood in the middle of the hall and said, his voice trembling: 'It breaks my heart to see our misguided young men talk like this, and raise their voice against their own faith. Do we want bloodshed? I told Sheikh Ghulam Rasul myself and he put his hand on his heart and assured me that nothing untoward would happen in the village. But hardly had I turned my back when the Khalsa School was attacked, the school peon, a Brahmin, put to death and his wife carried away. I did not give this information earlier because I did not want that you should get worked up.'

A wave of shock and indignation swept through the entire congregation.

'You have been misinformed,' said Sohan Singh. 'The Khalsa School was attacked but it was not the Muslims from this village but gangsters coming from Dhok Ilahi Baksh who attacked it. Mir Dad, our comrade, who has come from the city, got there in time and he, along with two or three local boys intervened and saved the situation. The peon was only injured; he is not dead. And his wife was not carried away. She is very much present in the school premises.'

'Who is this Mir Dad?' one Sardar asked.

'I saw this fellow sitting with Mir Dad in a tea-shop. God knows what confabulations were going on between them. At a time when Muslims are molesting our women, our boys are socializing with them.' Then, turning to the same frail Sardar, he said, 'What are you trying to teach us? Why don't you go and teach the Muslims? Have the Sikhs, till now, killed anyone? Looted anyone's house? And here is a fellow teaching us what we should do.'

The atmosphere again became tense. The Nihang standing at the gate came over and gave the frail Sardar a blow on his neck.

'Enough, enough! Don't beat him.'

A few persons, sitting nearby stood up and intervened, pulling away the Nihang.

At the time when this flare-up was taking place in the gurdwara, in another part of the village, Mir Dad was being heckled by a few Muslims.

In the butchers' lane, though the shops were closed, three butchers sat on the projections of their shops, having a heated argument with Mir Dad.

'You shut up. The Englishman was nowhere around.

In the city so many Musalmans have been done to death; their bodies are still lying in the lanes. Were they killed by the Englishman? A pig was thrown outside a mosque; was that too done by the Englishman?'

'Try to understand,' said Mir Dad, with a wave of his hand, 'If Hindus, Sikhs and Muslims are united, the position of the Englishman becomes weak. If we keep fighting among ourselves, he remains strong.'

It was the same hackneyed argument which these people had heard before. In the prevailing situation, it would cut no ice with them.

'Go and massage your head with almond oil,' the fat butcher said. 'How has the firanghi harmed us? The Hindus and Muslims have been at daggers drawn all along. A kafir is a kafir and until he accepts the "faith" he is an enemy. To kill a kafir is a virtuous act.'

'Listen, uncle,' Mir Dad said. 'Who is the ruler?'

'Of course it is the Englishman, who else?'

'And whose is the army?'

'Of the Englishman.'

'Then, can't he stop us from fighting?'

'He can, but he does not want to interfere in our religious matters. The Englishman is justice-loving.'

"Which means that we should kill one another while he would call it a religious matter and keep watching it as a spectator. What sort of ruler is he?'

The fat butcher grew angry.

'Listen, you chit of a fellow, Mir Dad. The fight is between the Hindu and the Muslim. The Englishman has nothing to do with it. You stop jabbering. If you are your father's real son, go to the gurdwara and tell them

not to collect arms. If they agree let them leave all their
weapons in the gurdwara and go to their houses. We too
do not want bloodshed. We too shall go and sit in our
homes. If you are the son of a real man, go and talk to
them. Don't go on blabbering here.'

Ever since the communal trouble started, Mir Dad
would go and sit wherever he would find four or five
persons chatting—at the baker's shop, at Ganda Singh's
tea-shop, at the village-well, or at the Sheikh's courtyard
and converse with them. People would listen to him
because he had received some education, had travelled
to Bombay, Lahore, Madras, and so on, and had also
come from the city. He had originally come with the
intention of meeting his brother Allah Dad in the village,
and in due course of time to open a school here which
could serve as a meeting place for the villagers where
they could sit and talk about their affairs, where someone
could read a newspaper to them, which could develop
their understanding and widen their outlook and sphere
of interests. But he had not been able to cut much ice
with the people. The reason being that he had neither
a piece of land of his own nor a roof over his head. He
would sleep at night on a cot outside the baker's shop.
The village-folk thought that he had come to open a
school in order to eke out a living for himself, whereas
Mir Dad's objective was to provide and develop a
community centre in the village.

At that particular juncture Dev Datt had sent him to
the village to stay put there and try to prevent the riot
from breaking out. Sohan Singh too had been sent for
the same purpose. Both were activists of the same party,

both had relatives living in that village. But with the tension mounting and all sorts of news pouring in, both of them were getting more and more isolated.

It was while Mir Dad stood talking to the butcher that a small incident occurred nearby. In the dark part of the lane close by, sitting behind a sack-cloth curtain a man was listening to their conversation. He had been sent from the gurdwara to gather information about the plans of the enemy. Gopal Singh was his name. He had climbed over the back wall of an old widow's house and posted himself there. The adjoining houses on both sides were those of Muslims. While listening to the dialogue between Mir Dad and the butcher, he lifted a corner of the sack-cloth curtain and quietly stepped into the lane and sat down behind the chabutra of the adjoining house. From there the words of their dialogue were more clearly audible. Since the doors of houses were shut and it was dark in the lane, Gopal Singh had calculated that in the event of any sound coming from anywhere, he would rush back into the widow's house and hide behind the sack-cloth curtain. But he did not have the chance to do so. His ears were glued to the conversation when suddenly he heard an odd kind of sound behind him. He at once turned round. In the murky light of the lane, a man from the adjoining house had stepped out, and was advancing towards him. The man had stepped down from the projection, and was putting both his hands under his shirt-front, as though to pull out his dagger. Gopal Singh stood up, nervous in the extreme and a loud cry escaped his lips. Instead of turning to the sack-cloth curtain, he ran for his life and, in the confusion, collided against

BHISHAM SAHNI / 244

the man who, he thought, was taking out his dagger from under his shirt-front. In reality, before the collision took place, the man had untied the tape of his pajamas and had almost sat down by the drain to ease himself. In his nervousness Gopal Singh had not noticed that the man was old, bald and toothless, and almost blind. After the collision, the old man—Nur Din was his name—cried out loudly:

'O, I am slain! O, I am killed!'

All that had happened in the twinkling of an eye. As old Nuru's cries and the sound of running feet fell on the ears of the butchers, two men picked up their lances and went after them. Ashraf, the butcher, pursued the man who was running, and threw his stick at him. The lance did not hit the informer, but as it fell close to him, he lost his nerve and began shouting:

'O, save me! They are killing me!'

Those who stood inside the lane shouted to Ashraf: 'Come back! Don't go farther! Come back!'

Mir Dad, who too stood in the lane, went over to the old man and helped him stand up. Seeing this, the fat butcher shouted angrily at Mir Dad, 'Haven't you seen with your own eyes, rascal! Has Nur Din been attacked by an Englishman? Get out of my sight, this minute, or you shall have it from me! Leave at once. Go away' and almost pushed Mir Dad out of the lane.

'Homeless beggar! Has come here to bring about peace! Has neither a roof over his head nor anyone to call his own. Who the hell are you? Fellows whom even their mothers do not recognize come to show us the way! Bloody beggar, living on crumbs thrown by others.'

At the end of the lane, Mir Dad again turned round to say something but the butcher again shouted fiercely at him, 'Go! Get away from here! Bloody eunuch! I will give you one on the jaw and all your teeth will fall out! Go and lecture your father!'

Mir Dad, his shoulders bent, moved away. Earlier, some people would listen to him and would even nod their heads to what he said, but now such people were nowhere to be seen. Even this man, the fat butcher used to talk to him in a friendly way, laugh and chat with him, but now his eyes were bloodshot.

Gopal Singh, the spy, kept running and shouting for help, right up to the gate of the gurdwara. On hearing his cries a wave of anger surged through the congregation. People came out in great agitation. All discipline went haywire. Both the Nihangs on gate-duty rushed out; and the Nihangs posted on the roof came running down the staircase.

'What's the matter? What's happened?'

Those inside the gurdwara stood up.

No fewer than ten persons examined Gopal Singh's body limb by limb. There was no sign of any injury anywhere. He was breathless and his throat was dry. He tried hard but could not comprehend what had actually happened.

'He was coming straight to attack me.'

'Who was he?' asked Teja Singhji.

'Baba Nura,' he blurted out the name unwittingly. A split-second before running away, he had recognized Baba Nura.

'What? The blind Baba Nura?'

'How could I know who it was? He had come out of Baba Nura's house...'

'What happened then?'

'People came after me from the Butchers' Lane. They threw sticks at me.'

People in large numbers had come out into the lane, while one Sardar was persuading them to go back into the gurdwara:

'There is nothing to worry. The Singh Khalsa has come back from the enemy-lines safe and sound. He has had a narrow escape, though. Go in, please!'

When Gopal Singh was able to breathe more freely, Teja Singhji asked him in a whisper: 'What did you find out? What are their plans?'

'Mir Dad was blabbering away. I couldn't listen clearly. The fat butcher was telling him, "Tell the folks in the gurdwara to go back to their houses, and we too will go back to ours"... he was saying something like this.' The congregation again gathered in the gurdwara. Gopal Singh, by his shouting, had added considerably to the excitement. The kirtan was resumed. The sound of cymbals, tablas and harmonium grew louder.

'What do you have to say now, Sardar?' A man, standing in the middle of the hall was shouting at Sohan Singh, 'He has barely managed to come back alive. The Muslims tried their best to kill him. And here you are, trying to teach us what we should do.'

Another angry member of the congregation shouted, 'This man should be thrown into a dungeon, kept in solitary confinement! We cannot trust him. Who knows he may be spying for them.'

At this Nihang Singh stepped forward and gave another blow to Sohan Singh on his jaw.

'Enough, enough!'

'Go and give your sermons to your blood-relatives, in whose lap you are sitting all the time. Get out of here!'

The kirtan was resumed.

Shades of evening had begun to fall. Two large lamps, which resembled chandeliers, hanging from the roof, one to the right and the other to the left of the raised platform on which lay the Holy Book, were lighted. Under the blue turban of Sardar Teja Singh, his white beard and the white shawl over his shoulders, became all the more pronounced. Light also fell on the excited faces of women. Their eyes reflected apprehension as also boundless devotion. Here and there a young girl looked at the unusual scene with curious eyes. Among these young women was Jasbir too—the daughter of Harnam Singh, the tea-shop owner. She had been married in that very village. She had inherited from her father the intensely devotional frame of mind. At the time of the chanting of the Ardas, the only voice which did not harmonize with the voice of the rest of the congregation was that of Jasbir. A thin, somewhat shrill voice but she sang supremely unconscious of everything. A short kirpan tied with a black ribbon-band, hung from her waist. Everyone in the congregation was familiar with this voice and everyone called her 'the daughter of the Guru'. Her broad, beaming face was flushed most of all. Jasbir would wash the steps of the gurdwara with her own hands, she had embroidered the silken cloth-piece covering the Holy

Book. It was from her effusive heart that all sorts of initiatives would spring. She would stand up on her own and start fanning the congregation, would serve cool water, keep watch over the shoes of the congregation. In moments of ecstatic elation, would even wipe their shoes with a part of the dupatta with which she covered her head, and put them before the members to wear, nay, even help them put them on with her own hands. Ever since the crisis began, her eyes were riveted on Teja Singhji's face, as though she expected a divine message from his lips; and her ears were all too eager to hear it. A sentiment, very similar, coursed through the hearts and minds of all the members of the congregation.

Just then, one of the Nihangs posted on the roof, noticed a cloud of dust, far on the horizon. He looked intently. Yes, it was a cloud of dust and it was growing bigger. He came and told Kishen Singh about it, and Kishen Singh looked towards it through the peephole and kept his eyes on it for a long time. It was really a cloud of dust and it was surely advancing towards the village. At first he did not believe his eyes, but gradually as he looked, a deep, humming sound too became audible to him. He felt alarmed. Everyone had thought that the mischief would begin from within the village itself, that such people as Kalu, the loafer, Ashraf, the butcher and Nabi, the oil-crusher were dead set on creating trouble, but now, it was the marauders from outside, advancing towards the village. He was still watching when a deep muffled sound of drum-beat fell on his ears. What he saw and heard was alarming. The situation had taken a serious and dangerous turn. He decided to go down and inform Teja Singhji, but thinking that it was essential to keep constant watch on the movements of the enemy, he asked the Nihang to convey the information to Teja Singhji.

The Nihang went running down the staircase, and on reaching the last step, shouted at the top of his voice:

'Turks! The Turks are coming!'

The entire congregation was electrified. The drumbeat was now clearly audible.

For some time Teja Singhji stood bewildered. He had not expected that outsiders would attack them. As a matter of fact he had not thought that an attack would at all take place. He had thought that a stray incident or two might occur in the Teli Mohalla or on the outskirts of the village and if the Sikhs stood firm the Muslims of the village would not persist. The Sikhs were in larger numbers and most of the Muslims had dealings with them. Besides, the Sikhs were financially better off and were well provided with weapons. But the whole situation appeared to have changed radically.

The sound of drums drew nearer. The slogan 'Ya Ali!' was also heard close by. Just then, from behind the gurdwara came the slogan:

'Allah-o-Akbar!'

Eerie silence fell over the entire congregation in the hall. But it was soon followed by a powerful surge of excitement when, in answer to the slogans of the Muslims, the full-throated Sikh slogan 'Boley So Nihal—Sat Sri Akal' rent the air.

'No one shall leave the hall! Everyone to his or her post!'

Jasbir Kaur's hand immediately went to her kirpan. The Sardars, one after the other, picked up the swords. The entire congregation was on its feet.

'Turks! Turks have come! Turks are here!' was on the lips of everyone.

'Turks are coming!' repeated Jasbir Kaur, in a voice trembling with emotion. Taking the dupatta off her head she hung it round her neck, and clasped the woman standing next to her in a tight embrace exclaiming in a voice choking with emotion: 'The Turks are here!'

The women took off their dupattas, hung them round their necks, and embracing one another repeated in a frenzied voice: 'The Turks are here! The Turks have come!'

The men too, the 'Singhs of the Guru' were likewise doing the same.

Some of the 'Singhs' had taken off their turbans, loosened their hair, and taken the swords out of their scabbards.

'Everyone to his or her post!' reverberated the command.

Once again the slogan: 'Jo Bole So Nihal!' rose from the depths of their beings, as it were, and the gurdwara resounded with: 'Sat Sri Akal!'

All the three members of the War Council, Sardar Mangal Singh, goldsmith, Pritam Singh, cloth merchant, and Bhagat Singh, general merchant, went up to the roof to ponder over the changed situation in consultation with Sardar Teja Singh and Kishen Singh.

Beating their drums the Turks had arrived in the village. It was, very probably to give notice of their arrival that a gunshot was fired in the air.

The whole atmosphere reverberated with the shouting of slogans: 'Ya Ali!'

'Allah-o-Akbar!'

'Sat Sri Akal!'

Then someone said that the Turks were advancing from the side of the stream. This meant that climbing up the slope they would fall upon the houses of the Sikhs, loot and burn them.

At that time, besides some old people left behind by their sons in the excitement of protecting the Faith, there was no one to guard them.

It was not yet completely dark, and the water in the stream looked crimson under the light of the setting sun. The picket set up at the end of the lane, to the left of the gurdwara, was at considerable distance from the houses which were at that time exposed to the attack of the Turks.

Suddenly Baldev Singh was troubled by the thought of his mother. He had left her alone in the house and had not thought of her the whole day long. She must be in great danger. There were some other persons too in the congregation who became anxious about their aged relatives left behind.

In a state of frenzy, Baldev Singh loosened his hair, took off his pajamas, took the sword out of its scabbard and with only a vest and underwear on his body, he, waved the naked sword over his head and ran towards his house.

'Blood for blood!' he shouted.

Some people shouted to him to come back but he wouldn't listen.

'Blood for blood!' he shouted as he went running through the lane.

Baldev Singh was neither hefty nor strong. As he ran, his thin legs looked like the legs of a goat. People were unable to make out why he had taken to the lane on the left. It would have been understandable if he had gone down the slope, indicating that he had gone to settle scores with the marauders. Had he taken the lane to the right it would have meant that he was going to the Butchers' Lane. What was the point in taking the lane to the left?

A little while later however, he was seen coming back towards the gurdwara. He still held the sword in his hand but he was not waving it over his head. In the darkening light of the evening, the blade of the sword too looked dark. As he drew near, people noticed that blood was dripping from the sword. There were drops of blood on his vest and underwear too. He was no longer shouting, nor was he running. On the other hand he looked ghastly pale and frightened.

Some people had correctly surmised that he was returning after killing someone. Convinced that his mother could no longer be saved, that the Turks must have made short shrift of her, he had plunged his sword into the bosom of the old blacksmith Karim Baksh, the only person to whom he had access, thereby avenging his mother's murder.

Shades of night were falling over the village. But the noises had grown louder and sharper. Sound of slogans resounded with sounds of yelling and shrieking, of doors being battered and windows being pulled down.

The excitement inside the gurdwara was turning into a frenzy.

16

When Harnam Singh knocked at the door a second time, a female voice answered from the other side: 'Menfolk are not at home; they have gone out.'

Harnam Singh stood undecided, looking to the right and left and wondering if anyone had seen them. Then turning to his wife, said, 'Banto, you ask. It is a woman speaking from behind the door' and stepped aside.

Banto knocked at the door and said in a loud voice: 'Kind ones, open the door. We are in distress.'

Listening to his wife's entreaty, Harnam Singh felt stricken with remorse. Fate had willed it so that a time would come when his wife would be begging for shelter.

There was a sound of footsteps on the other side of the door followed by someone lifting the latch. The door opened. A tall, elderly village woman stood before them, both her hands covered with cow-dung and her head uncovered. Behind her stood a young woman with dishevelled hair; she too had her sleeves rolled up from which one could conclude that she was preparing fodder for the cattle.

'Who are you? What do you want?'

The elderly woman asked, although at the very first glance she had understood their predicament.

'We are ill-fated ones, coming from Dhok Ilahi

Baksh. The marauders came and looted our house and set fire to it. We have been walking the whole night.'

The woman paused. For a moment the woman stood undecided. It was that fateful moment when a person has to make up his or her mind, goaded by lifelong influences and beliefs. The woman kept looking at them, then, throwing the door open, said, 'Come. Come inside.'

Banto and Harnam Singh looked up, and stepping over the threshold came into the inner courtyard. As they came in, the woman peeped out to right and left and quickly bolted the door.

The young woman kept staring hard at them. There was suspicion and doubt lurking in her eyes.

'Spread the cot, Akran,' the woman said and herself sat down on the ground and resumed making dung-cakes.

Akran came out of the inner room covering her shoulders with a dupatta and spread the cot which was standing against the wall.

'May God bless you, sister. We have been rendered homeless in one night' and Banto's eyes filled with tears.

'We have spent our whole life in Dhok Ilahi Baksh,' said Harnam Singh. 'There we had our shop and our own house. At first everyone said, "Stay here, nothing untoward will happen to you." But yesterday Karim Khan advised us to leave immediately. He said it would be dangerous for us to continue living in the village. He was right. Hardly had we turned our back when the marauders came. They looted the shop and then set fire to it.'

The woman remained quiet. Meanwhile Banto got down from the cot and sat down on the ground beside her.

Akran came and picking up the tray full of dung-cakes,

went to one side and began sticking them on the wall one by one. The elderly woman went on making dung-cakes with her hands, from the heap of dung lying before her.

'Where have your menfolk gone?' asked Harnam Singh.

The woman turned round and looked at Harnam Singh but did not answer his question. Harnam Singh suddenly realized where the male members of the family must have gone and his whole body trembled.

'We came out in the clothes we were wearing,' Banto said, 'May God bless Karim Khan, he virtually saved our lives. And may God bless you, sister, for giving us shelter.'

An uncanny silence prevailed over the house, causing Harnam Singh to fall silent again and again. The younger woman had gone into the inner room and Harnam Singh felt that standing in the darkness of that room, she was staring at them.

The elderly woman got up, washed her hands with the water in the basin where the kitchen utensils lay. She then picked up an earthen bowl and filling it with buttermilk brought it over. Harnam Singh still had his gun hanging from his shoulder. The belt containing cartridges, drenched with his perspiration, clung to his shirt.

'Here, drink some buttermilk. You must be exhausted.'

Taking the bowl in his hand, Harnam Singh burst out crying. A whole night's fatigue, nervous agitation, and suppressed emotions, suddenly burst forth as it were, and he began to cry bitterly like a child. He had, after all, been a well-to-do shopkeeper, even now carried in his pocket a couple of hundred rupees, had never stretched his hand before anyone all his life, and now, hardly a day had passed when he was knocking from pillar to post.

'Don't cry so loudly, Sardarji, the neighbours will hear and come running. Sit quietly.'

Harnam Singh suppressed his sobs and became quiet, and wiped his tears with the tail-end of his turban.

'May God bless you, sister, what you have done for us we shall never be able to recompense.'

'God forbid that a person should become homeless. But with God's grace, everything will turn out all right for you.'

The bowl of buttermilk in her hand, the woman offered it to Banto, but Banto hesitated to take it, and looked towards her husband, who was himself looking at her. How could she take the bowl from the hand of a Muslim? At the same time she was dog-tired and her throat was dry. The woman understood her discomfiture.

'If you are carrying any of your own utensils, I can pour the buttermilk into it for you. We have a pundit's shop in the village. I could go and get a couple of utensils for you, but how do I know if the pundit will be there? You may not take it from my hand but how will you pass the day on an empty stomach?'

At that, Harnam Singh put out his hand and took the bowl from her.

'From your hand, sister, it is like nectar for us. We shall never be able to repay what you have done for us.'

The sun had risen and voices began to be heard from neighbouring houses. Harnam Singh drank a few mouthfuls from the bowl and passed the bowl on to his wife.

'Listen, Sardarji, I won't hide anything from you,' the mistress of the house said. 'Both my husband and my son have gone out with some men from the village. They may be back any time now. My husband is a God-fearing man, he won't say anything to you. But my son is a member of the League and I cannot say how he will behave towards you. He has some other people with him too. It is for you to decide what you should do.'

Harnam Singh's heart missed a beat. Only a little while earlier the woman was offering to get utensils for them, and now she was playing a different tune.

Harnam Singh folded his hands. 'It is broad daylight now. Where can we go?'

'What can I say? Had it been some other time, it would have been different. But nowadays everyone wants to go his own way. Nobody listens to others. I have told you that our men have gone out and that they must be about to return. I do not know how they will treat you. Don't blame me if anything goes wrong.'

Harnam Singh was lost in deep thoughts. After some time he raised his head and said in a weak voice: 'As you say, sister. Whatever is God's will, will happen. There was compassion in your heart, so you opened your door to us. Now if you tell us to go away, we shall do your bidding. Let us go, Banto.'

Harnam Singh picked up his gun and both husband and wife moved towards the door. He knew that the jaws of hell would open wide for them, the moment they stepped out. But there was no choice.

The woman continued to stand in the middle of the courtyard looking at them.

When Harnam Singh raised his hand to open the door, the woman said, 'Wait. Don't go. Put the latch back. You knocked at my door with some hope and expectation in your heart. We shall see what happens. Come back.'

Young Akran, who stood watching from the inner room, stared hard at her mother-in-law and came forward: 'Let them go, Ma. We have not even asked our menfolk. They may not like it.'

'I shall answer them myself. Go and get the ladder from inside. Hurry up. Shall I push out a person who has come seeking shelter? Everyone has to go into God's presence one day. What are you staring at my face for? Go and get the ladder.'

Harnam Singh and his wife turned back from the door. Harnam Singh again folded his hands:

'May Wahe Guru's protecting hand be over your head, sister. We shall do whatever you tell us to do.'

By then it was broad daylight. Women from neighbouring houses had started stepping into one another's house. Everyone talked about the riots. In that village too, the previous evening, many men had been raising slogans, waving lathis and lances and beating drums. They had been going about in the village and later they had left the village and gone out, towards the East. No one knew where they went and what they did during the night. But now it was daylight and they were expected back any time.

Akran brought the ladder. Her mother-in-law took the ladder from her and put it against the wall, just below the loft.

'Come here, both of you,' she said. 'Go up the ladder into that loft and sit there. Don't make any sound. No one should know that you are here. For the rest, leave it to God.'

Harnam Singh, being of a bulky frame, found it difficult to go up the ladder. Besides, the gun hanging from his shoulder kept getting between his legs. Breathless, he somehow managed to go into the loft. Banto followed. The loft was a small one with a low roof. One had to double up in order to be able to sit in it, and there was barely room to sit. At the back of the loft, all sorts of household stuff was stacked. When Harnam Singh shut the small door, it became utterly dark inside. Both sat staring into darkness. They could neither speak nor think of anything. Their fate hung by a thread.

It was not only dark, it was also very stuffy inside, and for a long time Harnam Singh could not breathe normally. After sitting there for some time, Harnam Singh, out of sheer desperation opened the door a little so that they could have some light inside. Out of that thin opening, he could see the door that opened outside as also a small part of the inner courtyard. It was silent below. It seemed to him that the girl and her mother-in-law had left the courtyard.

'If anything untoward happens, Banto, and our life is in danger, I shall first press the trigger of the gun on you; I would rather kill you with my own hand,' Harnam Singh said in a hoarse whisper, for the third time.

Banto remained silent. She was living by the seconds. Her mind could not think of anything.

Below, in the back room, the two women were talking in low tones.

'You are doing something very wrong, giving shelter to kafirs. What are they to us? Abba Jan will be terribly offended. They are sitting up there at a vantage point; the Sikhra has a gun with him. What if he fires the gun when our menfolk are here? You just took them at their word and sent them up there.'

The mother-in-law looked at Akran's face. There was sense in what she was saying. 'If the men fell out with one another, and Ramzan had almost been in a frenzy these several days what if the fellow sitting up there fires his gun? It will certainly kill the man standing below. It is one thing to give shelter to someone, it is quite another to jeopardize the lives of your son and husband. Nothing could be more foolish. Why did this not occur to me?'

She came and stood under the loft.

'Listen, Sardarji, listen to what I say,' she said in a low tone.

Harnam Singh opened the door a little wider.

'What is it, sister?'

'Give that gun to me. Hang it down, I shall take it.'

Harnam Singh was taken aback.

'How can I give away my gun, sister?'

'No, give me your gun. You cannot sit up there with a gun.'

Silence ensued between them. To surrender the gun meant surrendering one's life into their hands. If he declined, she would at once turn them out of the house, and once outside, even if he was carrying a gun, it would not be safe.

'Are you listening, Sardarji? Give over the gun. Why do you need a gun, sitting in my house?'

'I shall become totally unarmed, sister. With the gun I feel safe.'

'Hand over the gun. Hang it down. I shall give it back to you when you leave my house.'

Harnam Singh looked at his wife, and then quietly lowered the gun to her.

After handing over the gun, Harnam Singh suddenly realized that he had delivered a loaded gun to her, that he should have taken the cartridges out before giving it away. But then he shook his head. When life itself is hanging in uncertainty, what difference does it make whether one has taken out the cartridges or not. Had I taken them out, there would only be one chance less of death, and not taking them out meant one more chance added to the thousand other chances of likely death. Harnam Singh heaved a deep sigh, so deep that Banto thought the women standing below must have heard it.

It was once again dark inside the loft.

What a transformation! Only yesterday, at this time, Banto was tidying her box of clothes, whereas today, both she and her husband were like two rats shut in a hole! Yesterday, Harnam Singh and Karim Khan were condemning the riots, condemning those indulging in them as people who had lost all sense of decency, as though what was happening was something so remote that they could talk and comment on it in a detached way. And now, with one gust of the wind, as it were, they had been thrown overboard.

His heart sank within him as he suddenly realized that he was without a gun, that he might never get it back. 'What have I done? I have myself cut off my hands. The gun with me was like the blind man's staff. I shall never get it back now.' Harnam Singh felt as though he was drenched in cold sweat. By this act, his wife's situation had become all the more precarious. 'With what sense of confidence will I be able to take her along with me now? People can now stone us to death.' In one stroke of stark reality, Harnam Singh had lost all that he had earned through a lifetime of devotion, faith and love of humanity.

'I wish we had some news of Jasbir,' Banto muttered suddenly.

Harnam Singh did not say anything. Now and then, the mother in Banto would cry out. The previous night too, as they trudged along the dry bed of the stream, Banto had time and again thought of her children. Every time the shadow of danger lifted a little, her thoughts would turn to her children.

There was noise in the village outside and it was increasing. Men and women seemed to be talking animatedly. Then someone knocked at the door and a woman's voice was heard:

'Ai Akran, come out. Our menfolk are on their way.' It was one of Akran's girl-friends, shouting. Akran opened the door and ran out.

Harnam Singh's heart sank within him. Banto looked up at her husband's face. The face which had always looked radiant had turned pale, while his clothes were crumpled and dirty.

Through the slightly open window of the loft, Harnam Singh saw the mistress of the house. She was standing, both her hands on her waist in front of the open door of the courtyard. Looking at her tall figure and her graceful

bearing, his faith returned, as it were. He once again felt
like reposing all his confidence in her. So long as she is
there, there is still hope; everything is not lost.

'Through Guru Maharaj's kindness, we shall come
out unscathed. You are a devotee of God. Why should
you be afraid?' said Banto trying to instil confidence in
her husband. Harnam Singh remained silent.

Voices grew louder outside. Sounds of loud laughter,
jovialities as also of advancing footsteps increased.
Suddenly, Akran's voice was heard, talking and laughing
loudly. Harnam Singh understood that the male members
of the family had arrived after their night-long outing.

Akran and her father-in-law hauled in a big, black
trunk into the courtyard. The turban on the man's head
was sunk in indicating that he had carried the trunk on
his head all the way through.

Harnam Singh put out his hand and touched his wife
on her knee.

'Banto, it is our trunk, the big black trunk. They
have been looting our shop.'

Banto made no effort to look out.

'It is still locked. The lock on it is still there,' Harnam
Singh whispered.

Akran's father-in-law sat down on top of the trunk; he
took off his turban and wiped the perspiration off his forehead
with it. His wife stepped forward and shut the door.

'Why hasn't Ramzan come?'

'Ramzan has gone to participate in Tabligh.'

Harnam Singh again stretched out his hand and
touched his wife's knee: 'It is Ehsan Ali. I know him. I
have had dealings with him.'

'Abba, you have brought a locked trunk. Heaven knows if there is anything worthwhile in it.',

'Why, it was so heavy, my back bent double carrying it. It is bound to be full of many things.'

'And it is only one trunk you have brought. Hasn't Ramzan brought anything?'

'It was he who pulled it out. We have brought a full trunk. What more do you want?'

'Let's open it. Shall we break the lock?' Akran said and ran into the back room to bring a hammer.

In her eagerness to see what the trunk contained, she forgot to tell him about the kafirs sitting in the loft. Her mother-in-law still stood nearby without uttering a word.

'Get me some lassi, Rajo. I am dying of thirst,' said the father-in-law at which his wife went forthwith to fetch buttermilk.

Akran began hammering at the lock.

With the bowl in his hand Ehsan Ali drank buttermilk when Rajo, his wife, told him that she had given shelter to a Sardar and his wife in the house.

Just then, Harnam Singh opened the little door of the loft and putting out his head said, 'Child, why are you hammering at the lock? Here is the key. It is our trunk.' Then, turning to Ehsan Ali, said, 'Ehsan Ali, I am Harnam Singh. Your wife has been so kind as to give us shelter. May Guru Maharaj's blessings be on you both. This trunk is ours. But consider it your own. Good that it fell into your hands.'

Ehsan Ali looked up and felt embarrassed, as though he had been caught stealing.

Akran's hands too stopped moving, and she shouted, 'Ma has given them shelter. I told her that she should not let kafirs into the house but she wouldn't listen.'

Akran was saying all this to please her father-in-law, but Ehsan Ali still stood perplexed, feeling uneasy. Once upon a time they had had dealings with each other, and knew each other well enough. He had not anticipated such an encounter and therefore did not know how he should treat Harnam Singh. Besides, he was not so hot-headed either as to get enraged at the mere sight of a Hindu or a Sikh.

'Come down, Harnam Singh,' and as though covering his theft with the good turn done by his wife, said somewhat boldly, 'Thank your stars that you took shelter in my house. Had you gone elsewhere, you wouldn't have been alive by now.'

Akran was impatient to open the lock but Rajo had snatched the key from her hand and despite her repeated requests would not give it to her.

'I shall be considerate towards you, Harnam Singh, because you have come to my house, but you had better go away now. If my son comes to know that you are here, he will not treat you well. If the village folk come to know that we have given you shelter, they will be hard on us.'

'We shall do whatever you tell us, Ehsan Ali. We have no choice, no say. But who will leave us alive if we go out at this time, in broad daylight?'

Ehsan Ali fell silent and looked at his wife, so as to say, what a messy situation she had landed him in:

'People were looking for you last night,' Ehsan Ali said. 'If they come to know that you are hiding here, they won't spare us. It is as much in your interest as in ours that you leave this place.'

Akran brought the ladder of her own accord and put it below the loft. Both husband and wife quietly came down. Both looked like sacrificial goats.

Then the same drama was enacted as had been played in the morning. Both of them came down, resigned to their fate. Both of them were composed. Neither of them demeaned themselves by asking for consideration. As they stood in the yard, Harnam Singh was about to ask for his gun from Rajo, who stood in the middle of the yard, her hands on her waist, when Ehsan Ali suddenly said, 'Take them into the godown, Rajo, where we stack hay. Let them sit there and lock the door from outside. Here, take this very lock and put it on the door. Hurry up.' Then trying to show his magnanimity, he said to Harnam Singh, 'It is out of consideration for our past contacts, Harnam Singh, otherwise by God, what the kafirs have done in the city, makes one's blood boil.'

Rajo led the way and Harnam Singh and Banto followed her. They were taken to a godown at the back of the house. It smelled strongly of cow-dung, fodder and wet hay. It was stacked with hay, from top to bottom.

'Sit down here. My husband is a pious man. I did not know that you knew each other. Try to pass the time somehow.'

Here too, Harnam Singh and his wife accepted the situation as they had earlier when they had been asked to sit in the loft. Rajo shut the door and locked it from outside.

Time passed. Both felt that till nightfall they were assured of shelter. Some time during the day, Rajo came and gave them some chapatis and buttermilk. The food gave them much-needed respite. For a long time both sat staring into the darkness with wide open eyes. Banto again said to Harnam Singh: 'Where do you think Iqbal Singh must be at this time? I wonder if he is still in his village or has gone elsewhere.' 'Whatever is Wahe Guru's will. I hope some kindhearted person has come his way and saved his life. Thank God Jasbiro is not alone. Many of our people are there. I hope all of them have gathered in one place.'

At this Harnam Singh said, 'I hope these people give us back our gun. What do you think, Banto? I don't suppose they will.'

They talked in low whispers for a long time. Although the godown did not have a window or a ventilator, it was not so sultry as it had been in the loft. Sitting on a heap of sheaves, both felt sleepy. They had not had a wink of sleep during the previous night. A little later, both fell into deep slumber. They were suddenly woken up by someone battering the door with a pickaxe.

'Come out, bastards, come out, you...'

Harnam Singh and his wife woke up as though they had seen a nightmare.

'Where is the key? Give me the key. You kafirs, I'll show you...' and blow after blow fell on the door.

'Don't shout, Ramzan, don't shout.' A female voice was saying. Perhaps it was Akran, pressing her husband not to speak so loudly.

Blows from the pickaxe continued to fall and soon enough there was a crack in the upper part of the door. Through the crack some light entered the dark godown.

Thereupon the voice of another woman was heard, 'What has come over you, Ramzan? Stop shouting, and stop breaking the door. Where is this damned girl? Couldn't you keep your mouth shut? I shall pull out your tongue, haramzadi, I had told you not to tell Ramzan. Stop it, Ramzan. Will you kill those who have taken shelter in our house? This man is known to us. At one time we owed him money.'

'Stop chattering, Ma. In the city they have killed two hundred Musalmans.' And blows from the pickaxe began to fall on the door again. 'Come out, you kafirs, you bloody...'

Another two blows and the door fell open. The godown was suddenly filled with light. Pickaxe in hand, Ramzan stood outside, breathing hard. Close by him stood Akran, her face pale and frightened. On one side stood Rajo, her hands on her waist.

'Come out, you kafirs...' said Ramzan peeping in.

Harnam Singh and his wife sat close to each other, their eyes dazzled as they tried to look out. As the door was broken open, Harnam Singh stood up and slowly came out.

'Put me to death if you want to,' he said in a hoarse voice.

'You...' Ramzan shouted and putting out his left hand caught hold of Harnam Singh by the throat. The collar button on Harnam Singh's shirt broke and fell down on the floor, and the turban on his head became loose. With the swiftness with which he had caught hold of Harnam Singh's neck, he let go off it too. His fingers left reddish marks on Harnam Singh's neck.

He too had recognized Harnam Singh, for he had tea at his tea-shop a couple of times. Harnam Singh's beard had turned grey and he looked thinner.

Twice Ramzan raised his pickaxe to strike, but both times he let it fall. It is one thing to kill a kafir, it is quite another to kill someone you know and who has sought shelter in your house. A thin line was still there which was difficult to cross, despite the fact that the atmosphere was charged with religious frenzy and hatred. Ramzan stood there for some time, breathing hard and then, uttering abuses, went out of the house.

It was nearing midnight, when the tall, stately figure of Rajo, walking in front, led Harnam Singh and Banto out of the house and in the direction of the grove of trees. A bright moon shone above and bathed in its light the view on all sides looked ethereal and dreamlike. Patches of light and shade appeared to be playing hide and seek. The grove of trees and the vast valley beyond looked mysterious and almost frightening. Rajo, carrying the double-barrelled gun in her hand, looked sedate and very graceful.

They were again going towards the dry bed of the stream. Towards the left the sky was turning crimson. Harnam Singh softly pressed his wife's hand and said, 'Look towards the left, Banto! What do you see?'

'Yes, I have seen. Some village is burning.'

'Wahe Guru!'

They walked on. Harnam Singh again paused. Far into the distance, on the other side too, the horizon was turning red.

'Which village is that? That too is burning!'

Banto remained silent.

Harnam Singh turned round and looked towards the village that they had left behind. The flat-roofed mud-houses were bathed in the moonlight. Here and there, in some houses was the glimmer of light from the earthen lamps. Outside the houses, in the yards, stood haystacks, a bullock-cart here and there.

As they passed by the grove, their eyes fell on the pir's grave. No light was burning there. People had forgotten to light the earthen lamp on it that day..

Rajo walked along the edge of the grove. As they reached the end of the grove, they climbed up a small mound. It was from the top of this mound that Harnam Singh and Banto had gone down to the village that morning.

Rajo stopped. Handing the gun to Harnam Singh she said, 'Now go. May God be with you. Go along the edge of the stream. May Fate be kind to you.'

There was a slight tremor in her voice.

'We are deeply indebted to you, Rajo sister. We shall never be able to repay you for what you have done for us.'

'If we survive, we shall, one day...' and Harnam Singh's voice shook and he could not complete the sentence.

Rajo said, 'Everyone to his or her fate. I do not know whether I am saving your life or pushing you into the jaws of death. Fires are raging on all sides,' and so saying she put her hand into her shirt-pocket and took out a small bundle wrapped in a piece of cloth.

'Here, take this. It is yours.'

'What is it, Rajo sister?'

'I found this in your trunk and took it out. It is your jewellery. It will stand by you in difficulty.'

'We must have done some good deeds in our past life to have met you,' Banto said and burst into tears.

'It is getting late. Move on. May God be with you,' Rajo said. She could not tell them in which direction they should go, or towards which village or at whose door they should knock.

Husband and wife went down the slope. Rajo kept standing at the top of the mound. Once again it was the same stream-bed, strewn with pebbles and sand. Under the light of the moon the entire valley was divided into dark and bright patches.

After having covered some distance, they looked back. Rajo was still standing on top of the mound, as though watching their footsteps leading them towards the unknown. Then, as they looked, she turned and went back towards the village.

As she went out of sight a frightful desolation descended on all sides.

17

In the meantime, another drama was being enacted in the rugged countryside of this rural district. Ramzan and his fellow freebooters were returning from their exploits in Dhok Elahi Baksh and Muradpur. Chatting and laughing, and carrying their booty they suddenly noticed a young Sikh, at some distance running for his life, near a small mound. It is difficult to say whether he had started running on seeing the marauders, or had already been running frantically in search of shelter. When they set their eyes on him, they were greatly excited as though they had found a sport. 'Ya Ali!' Ramzan shouted and all the fellows—there must have been twenty or thirty of them—ran after him. The ground was uneven, with many small mounds, ravines, and hollows and deep recesses like tunnels inside the mounds. The young Sardar was heading towards some village but had left the road and chosen to go through the fields and the rugged area, thinking that in doing so he would escape the notice of those going by the main cart road.

The Sardar was soon lost from view.

'The Sikhra has gone into hiding,' said Ramzan and quickened his pace. When the pursuers had covered some distance—the Sardar must be about fifty yards away from them—they got another glimpse of him. He was running across a ravine towards a mound. But when they reached that spot he had again disappeared.

'He has gone into some hole,' Nur Din said. 'Let us get him out. Son of a...'

They went and stood on top of a mound. A little while earlier, these religious enthusiasts had picked up stones and clay-balls and hurled them at the Sardar, but now they began pelting stones into the holes and deep recesses inside the mounds, thinking that when a few stones would hit him, he would come out crying and whimpering. Had the Sardar continued running, he would certainly have been stoned to death like a rat under a volley of stones during the monsoons. But instead of running any farther, he had entered a deep, dark recess in one of the mounds, which looked deep enough and sat down in it, crouching to one side. All around were innumerable recesses or tunnels, so it was difficult for his pursuers to know in which particular recess the fellow was hiding.

'O Sikha! Vadi Trikha!' shouted Nur Din at which there was a guffaw of laughter. Nur Din belonged to the same village as Ramzan. His occupation was to carry donkey-loads of bricks and earth from place to place. He was conspicuous by his very red gums. Each time he laughed his red gums would be visible from a long distance.

Some persons ran down the mound.

'He must be hiding in this hole,' someone said. 'Come out, you son of a...'

No sound came. It was dark inside and the cave was deep.

Then many of them picked up stones and hurled them into the cave. But to no effect.

'We won't find him this way. Let someone go in and see,' Ramzan said.

'Be careful, Ramzan, the fellow must be carrying a kirpan.'

Ramzan laughed but to be on the safe side he took out his knife and flicked it open. As Ramzan went in, two others followed suit.

'Come out, you karar!'

They searched the hole thoroughly. The Sardar was not there.

'The bastard must be hiding in some other hole.'

Then another member of the gang who was standing on top of the mound, shouted: 'There he is! There he goes,' and pointing towards a mound which was located behind two or three mounds, said, 'He has gone in that direction.' He had caught a glimpse of the Sardar's white clothes.

All of them ran in that direction. Stones began to be hurled into two or three caves simultaneously. In one of the caves, a stone hit the Sardar on his right knee but he did not cry out; and crouched closer to the wall of the cave. This was followed by a volley of stones. Some stones hit the wall of the cave while others hit his knees or shoulders or forehead. The Sardar was in great pain but suppressed his sobs. Stones continued to be pelted in all the three caves. After some time the sound of low moaning and sobbing was heard from one of the caves. Detecting the exact cave in which the Sardar was hiding, the marauders increased instantly the volley of stones.

Then someone in the gang shouted: 'Stop! Stop pelting stones!' At this, the volley abated, but a stray stone now and then continued to be hurled.

The one who had shouted came and stood at the mouth of the cave and said: 'Sardar, we shall spare your life, if you accept the Faith.'

No answer came from the other side. Only the sound of low moaning continued to be heard.

'Speak Sardar, what do you say? Will you accept Islam or not? If you agree, then come out on your own. We shall not harm you. Otherwise we shall stone you to death.'

There was still no answer from inside. An occasional stone continued to be hurled to intimidate the Sardar into taking a decision quickly.

'Come out, you son of a..., otherwise only your dead body will be left there.'

No sound came from inside. The pelting of stones was resumed. Ramzan Ali picked up a big stone and went and stood at the mouth of the cave.

'Come out at once, otherwise with this stone I shall make mince-meat of you.'

Some fellows laughed. Pelting of stones continued.

Then, crawling on all fours, the Sardar came to the mouth of the cave. His turban was untied and hung loose round his head, his clothes torn in many places were smeared with mud and dust, his forehead and knees were bruised and swollen and blood oozed out of them.

The Sardar was still on all fours, gazing into vacancy. Because of pain his face was contorted.

'Tell us. Will you recite the Kalma or not?' Ramzan

said. He was still holding the big stone in his hands.

The frightened Sardar stared wide-eyed into vacancy and then nodded his head.

A man standing behind Nur Din recognized the Sardar. He was none other than Iqbal Singh, who ran a cloth-shop in Mirpur; his father Harnam Singh owned a tea-shop in Dhok Elahi Baksh. Very likely he was going towards Dhok Elahi Baksh to join his parents when he was waylaid. The moment he recognized him, the man stepped back a few steps so that their eyes did not meet. As a matter of fact, after this, he remained in the background, he neither spoke nor threw stones, but at the same time he did not stop others from tormenting the Sardar. He knew well enough that no one would listen to him, even if he tried to do so.

'Speak, you son of a—! Speak or this stone will crush your skull.'

'I shall recite the Kalma,' Iqbal Singh muttered between his sobs.

At this, a resounding slogan reverberated the air:

'Allah-o-Akbar!'

'Nara-e-Taqbir—Allah-o-Akbar!'

All joined in the full-throated response to the slogan.

Ramzan threw away the stone to one side. Everyone threw away the stones that he held in his hands. Ramzan put out his hand and said,

'Get up! You are now our brother!'

Iqbal Singh's body pained in every limb; he was still moaning piteously. Still fear-stricken and in great pain, he could not stand.

'Come, let's embrace each other!' Ramzan said and

put his arms round Iqbal Singh.

Thereafter, everyone by turns, embraced Iqbal Singh. The man embracing him would put his head on Iqbal's right shoulder, and then, by turn, on his left shoulder and back again on his right shoulder. This was the cordial Muslim embrace. Iqbal Singh's throat was parched and his legs shook under him, but after practising the embrace three or four times, he got the hang of it.

Iqbal Singh had not expected that the situation would change so radically and so soon for him, that people who were thirsting for his blood would begin to embrace him like a blood relation.

They came out into the open, leaving the area of the mounds behind. They were soon walking through green fields where the wheat-crop was ripening, driving Iqbal Singh along, as they would, a beast. They still did not know how they should look upon him, as a trophy of their victory, or as a hated foe who had tried to escape but had been caught, or as a fellow-Muslim whom they had clasped to their bosom. Iqbal Singh was unable to walk steadily. No fewer than five stones had hit his left knee, besides, his forehead was still bleeding. At one place, as they crossed one field and went into another, he staggered, Nur Din gave him a push and Iqbal Singh fell on his face.

'See Ramzanji, they are still pushing me,' he moaned, as he tried to stand up, like a boy who despite his assurance that he would behave better, was still being pushed around.

'Don't push, oi!' shouted Ramzan, and looking at his associates, smiled and winked.

'Don't push, oi!' someone else too repeated, imitating Ramzan and gave a shove to Iqbal Singh.

Hostility and hatred cannot turn into sympathy and love so suddenly, they can only turn into crude banter. Since they could not physically hit him, they could at least make him the butt of their vulgar jokes.

'See Ramzanji, someone has again pushed me.'

Iqbal Singh had, by then, touched the lowest level of demoralization. A person clinging to life can only grovel and cringe. If you tell him to laugh, he will laugh, if you tell him to cry, he will begin to cry.

Then Nur Din thought of a practical joke.

'Stop oi!' shouted Nur Din to Iqbal Singh.

Iqbal Singh, with a frightened look in his eyes turned to Nur Din.

'Take off his salwar. The bastard was trying to hoodwink us.'

And he put his hand into Iqbal Singh's salwar. Some fellows began to laugh.

'Do you see, Ramzanji?' wailed Iqbal Singh, looking at Ramzan.

'Don't! No one will take off his salwar.' Ramzan shouted.

'He has not yet recited the Kalma. Therefore he is still a kafir, not a Musalman. Take off his salwar.'

Iqbal Singh felt encouraged when he saw that Ramzan was sympathetic to him; so he too shouted, 'I won't let anyone take off my salwar. Come what may.'

Some people laughed at this.

Thus, bullying and humiliating him, they arrived in the village.

It was in the house of Imam Din the oil-crusher that the conversion ceremony took place. The village barber too arrived on the scene, so did the mullah from the mosque. A whole crowd gathered in the courtyard.

The barber's fingers began to ache as he cut off Iqbal Singh's hair. Surrounded by a big crowd Iqbal Singh's bewilderment intensified. In the beginning, the barber used only his scissors, but later, he tied his hair into tufts with the help of horse-dung and urine, and cut it tuft by tuft. In the end he brought along a pair of shears to help him out. As the shears worked, furrows appeared on Iqbal Singh's head. Thereafter, his head was shaved with a razor. It was only then that Iqbal Singh could lift his head. When the time came to cut his beard, many voices rose simultaneously:

'Give his beard a Muslim cut.'

'Trim the beard. Make it angular. Make the moustache thin.'

Iqbal Singh's shrivelled face, despite his frightened eyes, actually began to look like that of a Muslim.

Then came Nur Din, making his way through the crowd. When Iqbal Singh's hair was being cut, he had slipped out, unnoticed. But now, he was pushing people aside, in order to get in.

'Get out of the way. Let me go in.'

On entering, he went straight to Iqbal Singh, and sat down by his side. With his right hand he forced open Iqbal Singh's mouth and with his left hand, in which he held a big piece of raw meat, dripping with blood, forced it into his mouth. Iqbal Singh's eyes popped out; he was unable to breathe.

'Open your mouth wide, you son of a.... Suck it now. Bloody...'

And Nur Din, turning towards the crowd laughed, showing his red gums.

Just then the mullah of the mosque arrived, along with an elderly man of the village. The elderly man snubbed Nur Din for being flippant on a pious occasion:

'Get up. You are pestering someone who will soon be our co-religionist, one who is going to accept our faith.'

With the arrival of the elderly man the entire scene changed. People stepped back and became quiet. Iqbal Singh was given support to stand up. One man brought in a cot and Iqbal Singh was seated on it. The rest of the ceremony was conducted with care and attention. Rosary in hand the mullah made Iqbal Singh recite the Kalma: 'La Ilah Illallah! Muhammad ar Rasulallah!'

The Kalma was recited three times. People standing around touched their eyes with the tips of their fingers and then kissed them. Thereafter nearly everyone in the crowd embraced Iqbal Singh one by one.

He was then taken to the village-well in a procession. After the bath he was given new clothes to wear. As he emerged after the bath in his new clothes, Iqbal Singh actually looked like a Muslim. Once again the slogan went up: 'Nara-e-Takbir, Allah-o-Akbar!'

The procession again proceeded towards the house of Imam Din the oil-crusher. The atmosphere now was more solemn, full of religious ardour. Before the shades of evening fell, the circumcision ceremony had been performed. The pain involved had not been so unbearable for Iqbal Singh. The elderly man all the time beguiling his mind with temptations, whispering into his ears:

'We shall get you a buxom wife, the widow of Kalu, a peach of a woman... Now you are one of our own; you are now Iqbal Ahmed.'

By the time evening fell, all the marks of Sikhism on Iqbal Singh's person had been replaced by the marks of the Muslim faith. A mere change of marks had brought about the transformation. Now he was no longer an enemy but a friend, not a kafir but a believer; to whom the doors of all Muslim houses were open.

Lying on his cot, Iqbal Ahmed kept tossing and turning the whole night.

18

The Turks had come, but they had come only from one of the neighbouring villages. The Turks too mentally viewed their attack as an assault on the citadel of their age-old enemy, the Sikhs. In the minds of the Sikhs too they were the Turks of the bygone medieval times whom the Khalsa used to confront in battle. This confrontation too was looked upon as a link in the chain of earlier confrontations in history. The 'warriors' had their feet in the twentieth century while their minds were in medieval times.

A bitter fight took place. It went on for two days and two nights. Then the ammunition was exhausted and it became impossible to go on. At the back of the low platform on which the Sacred Book was placed, seven dead bodies covered with white sheets of cloth lay in a row. Five women sat with the heads of their husbands in their laps. For some time they would leave, when repeatedly persuaded to do so, but again, Sardar Teja Singh had only to turn his back that they would come back. Two dead bodies had no claimants. One of these was of a Nihang, who even under the hail of bullets stood on duty on the roof, with his moustaches twirled and his chest sticking out. The other one was that of Sohan Singh, who had come all the way from the city to prevent the riot from breaking out. His dead body was found lying at the end of the lane near the gurdwara. On the second day of the 'battle' he had been sent with a proposal for the 'cessation of hostilities' to Ghulam Rasul's house. His dead body was the adversary's answer to that proposal. His dead body would have continued to lie near the wall where he had been killed, had it not been picked up late in the night by some Muslims and left near the gurdwara to inform the Sikhs about the fate of their peace-proposal. His dead body lay to one side and no one put his head in his or her lap. Even otherwise, the status of both Sohan Singh and Mir Dad had been reduced from peace-makers to that of couriers.

Besides these, quite a few dead bodies lay scattered here and there in the village. The question of attending to them did not as yet arise. The dead body of the peon of Khalsa School lay in the courtyard of the school itself. On the day the attack took place, while the 'community' was gathering in the gurdwara, the peon was exhorted to stick to his duty of guarding the school. The peon's wife was alive and said to be safe and sound because she had been forcibly taken by the numberdar of the village to his house. Mai Bhagan's dead body was found lying in the inner yard of her own house. One stinging slap had been enough to finish her. Her jewellery, however, was saved because it lay concealed inside a wall, and her house escaped being set on fire because it stood adjacent to the house of Rahima teli. Saudagar Singh was another old man who lay dead and whose body due to oversight was not carried to the gurdwara.

There were some more dead bodies too that lay here and there. One of them lay face downward near a well.

The man had been killed by mistake. He was the water-carrier, Allah Rakha, who, despite the raging riot, had been sent to fetch water since they had run short of water in the Sheikh's house and children were howling for water. As he reached the well, under the light of the moon, a bullet accurately aimed from the roof of the Sheikh's house itself had made short shrift of him. Another dead body of a Sardar who had come from the city lay on the road. Two small children, working as shop-boys in Fateh Din the baker's shop were also found dead. The baker's shop was located at the end of the lane that led to the gurdwara. There was no stopping these boys from playing in the lane. Time and again they would rush out chasing each other.

Flames of fire still rose from the building of the Khalsa School. All the houses belonging to the Sikhs on the slope overlooking the stream had been gutted. Besides, all the three shops of the butchers, and the houses of three or four Muslims in the Teli Mohalla, had been set on fire.

The ammunition inside the gurdwara was almost exhausted. Kishen Singh, stationed on the roof, had begun to fire his gun sparingly. He would fire a shot after every few minutes, so that the enemy might know that the front was holding out. Inside the gurdwara however, the morale was pretty low. A sense of fatigue and helplessness had set in. Eyes would meet but lips would not open. No one knew who it was who had first uttered the words: 'Ammunition is finishing.' But it had left the listeners petrified. The ammunition was finishing even in the Sheikh's fortress. But to cover the reality, slogan-shouting on both sides had become all the more vociferous. 'Allah-o-Akbar!' had begun to be heard, not from one but from three directions. The slogan in reply, from the gurdwara was even louder. But the slogan-shouting too had begun to sound hollow.

The intelligence men had brought the news that the Muslims were getting succour from outside. The contact of Sikhs with the outside areas had virtually been cut off. Two men had been secretly sent to Kahuta for assistance, but they had not returned uptil then. The War Council was of the view that with the help of money peace might be bought; and so they had started negotiations through emissaries.

Inside the gurdwara, near the main door, members of the War Council sat discussing with Teja Singhji the possible terms and conditions for bringing about a truce.

'They are demanding two lakhs of rupees. This is an impossible amount,' Teja Singh said irritably.

'What offer did you make to them through the younger Granthi who was sent by you to them?'

After the death of Sohan Singh, Teja Singhji had tried to seek the help of Mir Dad for purposes of mediation, since before the riots, Mir Dad had been trying to bring about an understanding between the two communities, but when Mir Dad learnt that cessation of hostilities was being bargained for with money, he turned his back on it. Not knowing what to do, Teja Singhji had sent the younger brother of the Granthi, who was generally addressed as the 'younger Granthi', as an emissary.

'I told him to quote anything between twenty and thirty thousand rupees,' said Teja Singhji, 'but they are demanding two lakhs.'

'They must have come to know that our position is no longer strong.'

'How could they?' retorted Hira Singh, the general merchant. 'Our killings have in no way been fewer than theirs. It is our bad luck that we have run short of ammunition.'

From a distance was heard the slogan:

'Allah-o-Akbar!'

'How much of jewellery and ornaments have we been able to collect?'

Teja Singhji got up and went towards the box lying in front of the chowki of the Sacred Book and opening it, took the ornaments into his hand and tried to assess their value from their approximate weight.

'They can't fetch more than twenty to twenty-five thousand rupees. But they are demanding two lakhs!' Teja Singh repeated, like the refrain of a song.

'You alone can pay two lakhs, Teja Singhji, if you so desire. You have amassed quite a fortune.'

But Teja Singhji thought it fit to ignore the comment.

'Offer them a sum of fifty thousand.'

'Fifty thousand is too little. I don't think they will agree.'

'To begin with, we must quote a low figure. If you will start from a low figure, it will be possible to strike a bargain at a lakh of rupees.'

Teja Singh sent for the younger Granthi: 'Try to strike a bargain for any amount up to one lakh rupees, starting from a low figure. We shall make the payment only after the outsiders have gone to the other side of the stream. Make it clear to them. Thereafter, they can send three of their men for money, our representatives will be standing with the money bags.'

The younger Granthi folded his hands and said, 'Truth resides on your tongue, Good Sir, but what if they insist that money must be paid first and then alone will the outsiders go across the stream?'

At this the general merchant flared up: 'Why? Are we Lahorias or Amritsarias that our word cannot be trusted? We are citizens of Sayedpur, and our word is carved on stone.'

The Sikhs were as proud of being the inhabitants of Sayedpur as were the Muslims. Both took equal pride in the red soil of Sayedpur, its top-quality wheat, its orchards of lukat fruit, even in its severe winters and razor-sharp cold winds. Both took pride in the hospitality and liberality of the Sayedpur citizens, their sunny, hail-fellow-well-met temperaments. And ironically enough, while jumping into the fray against one another, both had boasted of their valour too, in the same vein, proudly striking their chests.

The moon had risen, presenting, a frightful view to those on guard. If there was firing again, anything could happen—arson, loot, murder. All earlier moves had proved disastrous. It was a big blunder to have gathered in the gurdwara; it was a big blunder to have snapped contact with Sheikh Ghulam Rasul. There was no end to such blunders. Had these moves brought success, they would have been viewed as examples of excellent strategy.

Some people sat chatting on the terrace of Sheikh Ghulam Rasul's house. They too had not had the time to attend to their dead. But whereas the position of the gurdwara was like that of a house under siege, the house of the Sheikh had no such duress; it could maintain contact even with far-flung villages.

The 'mujahids' sitting on the Sheikh's terrace had come from outside. They were narrating their exploits and experiences to one another.

'When we got into the lane, the karars began to run this way and that way. A Hindu girl went up to the roof of her house. As soon as we saw her, we ran after her. There were nearly ten of us. She was trying to jump over the low wall on the roof to go over to the adjoining house when she fell into our hands. Nabi, Lalu, Mira, Murtaza all had a go at her one by one.'

'Is that true? Swear by your faith.'

'By God it is true, every word of it. When my turn came there was no sound from her; she wouldn't move. I looked at her; she was dead. I had been doing it to a dead body,' he laughed a hollow kind of laughter, and turning his face to one side, spat on the floor.

'I swear that it is true. Ask Jalal, he was also there.'

Another mujahid had his own story to tell.

'It is all a matter of chance,' he was saying. 'We caught hold of a bagri woman in a lane. My hand was working so well, I would chop off a head at one go. The woman began crying and begging: "Don't kill me," she said, "All seven of you can have me as your keep."'

'Then?'

'Then what? Aziza plunged his dagger into her bosom and she was finished there and then.'

In the moonlit night, the younger Granthi was slowly going down the slope. The group of deputies from the

Muslim side sent to negotiate peace-terms stood at the edge of the stream. Through one of the windows of the gurdwara the slope was clearly visible, and many had their eyes on it, watching the young Granthi with bated breath. In the moonlight only a figure in silhouette could be seen moving down the slope. Suddenly from the roof above came the sound of running feet and a Nihang shouting:

'Turks are coming from the Western direction. The enemy has received succour from outside.'

And soon enough the familiar war-cries along with the beating of drums were heard.

'Allah-o-Akbar!'

Teja Singh's face fell. The elder Granthi who stood at the window watching his brother, suddenly called out to his brother: 'Don't go further, Mehar Singh! Come back!'

But the younger Granthi did not hear. He continued going down, walking unsteadily over the pebbles and stones which lay scattered by the side of the stream.

'Come back, Mehar Singh! Come back!' shouted the elder Granthi. Thereupon others too joined in. The younger Granthi looked back once but then continued going down. The drum-beat and war-cries of the advancing marauders grew louder every minute. The mujahids standing at the edge of the stream responded to their compatriots with full-throated 'Allah-o-Akbar!'

Under the light of the moon the figure of the younger Granthi would again and again be lost from view because of the patches of light and shade.

The view from the window was not so clear now. It appeared that some people had stepped forward to meet the younger Granthi; it also appeared as though the younger Granthi had been surrounded on all sides. It seemed to some as though a few lathis had been raised. Something glittered too in the light of the moon which was either a pick-axe or the naked sword of the younger Granthi.

'Allah-o-Akbar!' the slogan was again raised.

Blood drained from Teja Singh's face, and his heart sank within him. The elder Granthi, standing at the window, suddenly cried out:

'Killed! They have killed my brother!' and without a second thought rushed out of the gurdwara, and crossing the lane, ran barefoot down the slope.

'Stop! Somebody stop him!' someone shouted at the top of his voice at which the Nihang posted at the gate ran after the Granthi and by the time the latter had reached the middle of the slope, overtook him and putting his arm round his waist, lifted him up with both his arms and turned back.

The drum-beat of the marauders was now heard from inside the village. Slogans were being raised from all sides. Once again bullets began to be showered and people were seen running in all directions.

'Jo Boley So Nihal!
'Sat Sri Akal!'

The slogan pierced through the air.

A group of Sikhs—the elder Granthi was among them—brandishing their swords, and challenging the enemy, their hair loosened, ran down the slope, as though determined to do or die!

Inside the gurdwara, a large number of women and children sat huddled against the wall to the left. In the rising crescendo of shouting and shrieking, all the women had gathered in one place. The face of Jasbir Kaur was flushed as though she was in a state of frenzy. Her hand was on the handle of the kirpan, holding it tightly.

Women had started chanting the Japji Sahib; their murmuring voice gradually grew louder.

Flames of fire were seen rising from behind the houses standing at the end of the lane to the left, and the sky was turning crimson, even a deeper crimson than before.

'Fire is rising from the lane near the school...It is Kishen Singh's house burning!'

The words fell on Jasbir's ears too, but it seemed as though she had not heard them. A surge, a wave rose and fell within her, again and again. But she saw nothing clearly before her eyes, as though everything was floating, everything in a sort of twilight, everything going round and round, revolving round her. She was standing right under the light in the middle of the hall, and her face glowed as though with celestial light.

The picket on the left collapsed. Under the light of the moon, some men were seen crawling up the slope. The Nihang Singh posted on the roof was the first one to see them. He promptly informed Kishen Singh, but Kishen Singh was so despondent, he merely shook his head. The number of dark figures crawling up the slope was increasing every minute. They became clearly visible now because of the fire in the lane. But where was the ammunition to stop them, or even to arrest their advance? Kishen Singh pressed the trigger once or twice but then sat down, in despair.

The picket to the left having collapsed, another band of Sikhs, standing sword in hand outside the gurdwara, their hair hanging loose, rushed towards the end of the lane on the left. The Turks could attack the gurdwara only from that side, through that opening. A volley of fire followed by the shouts of 'Allah-o-Akbar!' rent the air.

The band of Sardars brandishing their swords were soon swallowed up by the darkness at the end of the lane. Just at that time a group of women, emerged in a row from the gurdwara. At their head was Jasbir Kaur, her eyes half-open, her face flushed. Almost all the women had taken their dupattas off their heads and tied them round their waists. They were all bare-footed, their faces too were flushed. As though under a spell, they came out of the gurdwara.

'The Turks are here! The Turks have come!' Some of the women shouted, while some others chanted the verses of the Gurbani and still some others, shouted in frenzied voices: 'I too shall go where my lion-brother has gone!'

Some of them had their children with them. Two or three women had little babies in their arms, while some, holding their children by their hands, were pulling them along.

Coming out of the gurdwara, the women turned to the right and after covering some distance, took to a narrow path from between two houses which went its zigzag way, down the slope right up to a well, at the bottom of the slope.

The atmosphere resounded with cries and wailing. Tongues of flame now rose from two places, their shadows danced on the walls of houses, on the slope, on the cobbled street, and were reflected in the water of the stream, turning the water red, as it were.

To the deafening noise was added the noise of doors being battered, and the shouts of plunderers. In front of the gurdwara, a Nihang Singh stood right in the middle of the lane, waving his lance and shouting: 'Come, Turks, come if you dare! I challenge you, come!'

The throng of women headed towards the well located at the foot of the slope. This was the well to which the women used to come every day to bathe, to wash their clothes, to gossip. They were now running fast towards it, as though under a spell. None knew why and wherefore they were heading towards it. Under the translucent light of the moon it appeared as though fairies were flying down to the well.

Jasbir Kaur was the first one to jump into the well. She raised no slogan, nor did she call anyone's name, she only uttered Wahe Guru and took the jump. After her, one by one, many women climbed up to the low wall of the well. Hari Singh's wife climbed up stood there for a moment, then pulled up her four-year-old son on to the wall and holding him by the hand, jumped too. Deva Singh's wife held the breast-fed child in her arms when she took the plunge. Prem Singh's wife jumped, down, but her son was left standing on the wall. The child was pushed into the well by Gyan Singh's wife, and thus sent back into the arms of his mother. Within a matter of minutes tens of women had gone into their watery grave, some of them along with their children.

By the time the Turks actually entered the lane which led to the gurdwara, after walking over a heap of dead bodies at the entrance to the lane, there was not a single woman left in the gurdwara. The air was filled with the heart-rending cries of women and children coming from inside the well and were mingled with the loud shouts of 'Allah-o-Akbar' and 'Sat Sri Akal.'

The light of the moon turned pale. Slowly the day broke. The nightmarish atmosphere of the night began to be dispelled. Despite the smoke from the smouldering fires, a cool fresh breeze was blowing as it did every morning. The fields outside the village in which the wheat-crop had ripened softly waved under the breeze. The air was laden with the scent of the bursting lukat fruit. It also carried the soft fragrance of the wild rose which grew on bushes in this weather. Now and then parrots sitting on the branches would flutter their wings and chirping noisily fly off towards another tree or grove of trees. The colour of the water in the stream had already turned blue. Every gust of breeze would produce ripples on the surface of the water.

It was difficult to say when, during the night, looting and arson had ceased. Not many houses had been set on fire, since in most localities Muslims and Sikhs lived in adjacent houses. The fire was still smouldering in the Khalsa School building and the flat-roofed houses located at the turn in the lane leading to the gurdwara, but the flames had largely subsided, and the colour of the dying flames had already turned pale.

Within the gurdwara, one light was still burning. The War Council was still in session, its four members waiting, as it were, for the final fall of the curtain. Teja Singhji, tired and exhausted, with his head bowed sat disconsolate on a bag of wheat-grains in the store-room of the gurdwara. Kishen Singh still sat in his chair on the roof. A Nihang Singh, lance in hand, still stood guard at the entrance to the gurdwara.

When it was broad daylight, kites, vultures and crows arrived in large numbers and hovered over the village, and particularly in the vicinity of the village well. Many a vulture was already perched on the surrounding trees; some vultures with their sharp yellow beaks had landed on the wall of the well, where the bloated corpses were slowly rising towards the surface, or the mouth of the well. The lanes bore a deserted look. Dead bodies lying here and there, added to the gloom and sense of desolation all round. Footsteps of a man walking in a lane would produce a deafening sound. The marauders had left the village, carrying all the booty they could. On the path leading to the 'well of death', lay scattered hair-clips, ribbons, dupattas, broken pieces of bangles and the like, while the lanes in the village were littered with empty boxes, trunks, canisters and cots. telling the story of the scourge that had befallen the village. The doors of houses were either open or battered.

But the rioting had not completely ceased. The young son of the fat butcher had stealthily gone to the backside of the gurdwara, carrying a can in his hand and was sprinkling kerosene oil on its windows.

Suddenly a strange deep and buzzing sound was heard. What was that? It was heard by Teja Singh, sitting in the store room; by Kishen Singh, on duty on the roof of the gurdwara; it fell on the ears of everyone in the Sheikh's house. They were all taken aback! The son of the fat butcher who was about to light the fire, stopped short not knowing what to do. What sort of sound was this? The low drone was getting louder. Some persons sitting inside houses, stepped out to find out what sound it was. Kishen Singh stood up from his chair and rushed to the parapet wall.

It was an aeroplane. Flying over hills and valleys, with its wings outspread, it was coming towards the village, making its hoarse, buzzing sound. Sometimes, its wings would turn black, at others, they would glitter like silver. Sometimes its right wing would bend downward, at others its left wing. The aeroplane was, it would seem, out on a joy-flight.

As it approached the village, people came out; they stood on raised platforms on roofs of houses and stared hard at the aeroplane with breathless curiosity. While flying over the village, it dropped height so that one could see the pilot sitting in the cockpit—he was a white man, waving his hand to the people standing below. Some people could even see the smile on his lips. He was wearing big goggles over his eyes.

'He smiled. I swear, I saw it with my own eyes,' one boy said to another, standing in a yard outside their house.

'He has white gloves on. He was waving his hand like this. Didn't you see?'

There would be no more disturbances. The news of the riots had reached the right ears, the ears of the firanghi; no shot would be fired now, nor a house set on fire. The fat butcher's son, who had already sprinkled oil on the windows of the gurdwara, and had only to light a matchstick, hastily withdrew his hand and stood standing wide-eyed at the aeroplane.

As he flew over the gurdwara, the white man sitting in the cockpit waved his hand. To Kishen Singh, standing on the roof, it appeared as though the white man had specially waved to him; that one soldier had saluted another fellow-soldier. Kishen Singh who till then had been feeling depressed, stood up to attention and clicking his heels gave a salute in return, and his heart leapt with joy. A soldier after all, was a soldier. During the war-days on the Burmese front, Kishen Singh would go every evening to meet Captain Jackson, his superior officer. And Captain Jackson would always lend an attentive ear to whatever he had to say. Not only that, he would always acknowledge his salute with a salute in return.

Excited beyond words, Kishen Singh waved his hand and shouted: 'God save the King, Sahib, God save the King!'

The aeroplane had by then moved ahead and was flying over the Sheikh's house. Kishen Singh stared wide-eyed towards it. People had run up to the roof of the Sheikh's house too and were waving excitedly at the white man. Kishen Singh was keen to know if the white man, the British soldier, acknowledged the salutations too; and it actually appeared to him as though the pilot had withdrawn his gloved hand into the cockpit. Kishen Singh was thrilled at this and shouted: 'Had you come a couple of days earlier, we would not have suffered so. But it is still OK Sahib!'

Thereupon, excited in the extreme, Kishen Singh clenched his fist towards the house of the Sheikh and shouted at the top of his voice: 'Why don't you fire your guns now? Here, fire at me, I am standing before you! You thought you were hellishly brave! Now fire! Why don't you?'

And the stocky, pot-bellied Kishen Singh, like a man in a frenzy, waving his hand and showing his clenched fist, danced behind the parapet wall.

At the back of the gurdwara, the fat butcher's son, emptied the can of kerosene oil in the drain and hid the empty can under a projection, threw the dry rags into the gurdwara through a window and lighting a cigarette with the match-stick in his hand, went merrily puffing back home.

The aeroplane circled twice over the village. Quite a crowd of people had by then come out and were waving to the white sahib! After the third round, the aeroplane flew away towards other villages.

The atmosphere in the village changed radically. People started coming out into the open. There was little apprehension of any trouble erupting. Corpses began to be removed. People went back to their houses to check on their jewellery and household goods. The sevadars and the Nihangs began to wash the floors and to tidy up the gurdwara. On the other side under Sheikh Ghulam Rasul's orders, the floors of the mosque were being washed. People of both communities were washing clean their respective holy places.

Over whichever village the aeroplane flew, hostilities ceased, drums stopped beating, slogan-shouting ceased, looting and burning stopped.

19

As you walked along the roads of the city, you sensed a change in the atmosphere. In front of the mosque in Qutab Din street, four soldiers in uniform sat in chairs. At every important crossing in the city, two or three armed soldiers were seen either sitting on terraces or standing by the roadside. Army pickets had been set up in the city. On the fourth day of the riots, an eighteen-hour curfew had been clamped on the city; on the fifth day, however, the curfew had been relaxed to twelve hours from 6 p.m. to 6 a.m. The news had gone round that the Deputy Commissioner was doing the rounds of the city in an armoured car. Here and there a shopkeeper had begun sitting in his shop, with only one panel of the shop door open. Mounted constabulary patrolled the streets led by two officers with pistols hanging by their sides. Offices, schools and colleges were still closed. In the dark corners of lanes or at street turnings, small groups of men sat with lances and lathis in their hands and their faces half-covered, but after the imposition of the curfew and the setting up of pickets, the situation was no longer that of a disturbed city. People had begun to stir out, they would go from one locality to another, although still looking apprehensively to the right and left. The tenor of the news too had changed. It was strongly rumoured that two refugee camps would soon be set up, each having the capacity of accommodating refugees from twenty villages. Two government hospitals—one in the city and the other in the cantonment—were already attending to the treatment of the wounded and the disposal of dead bodies. In every piece of news, the name of the Deputy Commissioner figured prominently. His pipe between his teeth, he was seen everywhere. It was said about him that once, on one of his rounds during curfew hours, when he found a young fellow standing outside a hospital, he gave him two warnings and then shot him dead. By this single act, the whole city had been alerted. People understood that rioting would not longer be tolerated. The National Congress had set up a Relief Office inside a school building which was crowded all the time since refugees were pouring in from the villages. The Deputy Commissioner had visited even this relief office no less than three times. The impression gaining ground was that the government was keen to resolve the situation with the cooperation of the public bodies. And so, leaders of public bodies had begun to work with alacrity. So much so that even in Congress circles, the opinion about the Deputy Commissioner had begun to be revised. 'A Deputy Commissioner may be only a cog in a machine but this particular Deputy Commissioner is different, he is sympathetic and capable.' It was said that the day he shot down the young man outside a hospital, he could not sleep the whole night. Prof. Raghu Nath was of the view that the man was not cut for administrative service, that the man was too sensitive, gifted with too warm a heart, that the British

Government had done grave injustice by appointing him to that administrative post. Even though some political activists sharply condemned him and held him directly responsible for all the mischief that had taken place.

On one of his rounds, the Deputy Commissioner's jeep stopped outside the Health Officer's residence. The Health Officer had been duly informed on the telephone that the Deputy Commissioner was on his way. Greatly excited, the Health Officer got ready, put on, instead of the usual workday clothes of coat, tie and trousers, his native Punjabi dress—a long silken kurta, a well-starched salwar and a pair of Peshawari chappals on his feet. His wife forthwith made arrangements for tea and coffee. The Deputy Commissioner came into the courtyard bringing with him the aroma of pipe tobacco. He did not take either tea or coffee. He merely stood in the courtyard and that too for a few minutes, and talked of business. As he shook hands with the Health Officer, he remarked, smilingly: 'Even in these days you can be so particular about the clothes you wear, Mr Kapur. Nice. Very nice. The Indian dress suits you.'

Then, shaking hands with the Health Officer's wife, who was in her dressing gown, he remarked, 'The day doesn't seem to have begun for you yet, Mrs Kapur.' and turning to the Health Officer began talking about the business at hand.

'It will be necessary to check up on the arrangements for the water-supply to the refugee camps,' he said, in a manner as though talking to himself. 'The drains have still not been dug for the outflow of the water.' He smiled, shaking his head.

The smile was meant as a reminder to the Health Officer that a task assigned two days earlier had not so far been attended to.

'All arrangements have been made, Sir, work will commence today.'

'Good,' said the Deputy Commissioner and smiled again.

'I would like you to visit the village where women jumped into the well. Some disinfectant must be sprayed over the well, otherwise there is great danger of a contagion spreading.'

'Yes, sir,' said the Health Officer, but he felt somewhat shaken. People were running away from that village, seeking shelter in the city. It would be unsafe going there, he thought.

But the Deputy Commissioner was well aware of the situation.

'It is the third day going,' he went on. 'The swollen dead bodies must have begun to decompose. A disinfectant must be sprayed. Do go there tomorrow morning.' And then, to allay his discomfiture, added, 'An armed police guard will go with you. There is nothing to fear.'

The Deputy Commissioner had his finger on the pulse, not only of the city but of the entire district.

The Health Officer's wife, in the meanwhile, had changed her clothes and tied her hair into a knot, and was pressing for tea and coffee.

'There will be time for tea, Mrs Kapur, but not now. Thank you,' said the Deputy Commissioner smiling. Then, in his typical persuasive manner, added, 'You too must lend a hand, Mrs Kapur. Two thousand cots will be delivered at the Refugee Camp today. We need to have beddings and clothes for them. I believe a small committee comprising of women can do a lot of good work. Do think it over, Mrs Kapur,' and Richard again smiled and nodded his head.

Richard had this great quality in his character. He would give instructions in a manner as though he was suggesting a proposal to the other person, and seeking his opinion. The Health Officer's wife felt flattered. The Deputy Commissioner was offering her the opportunity of her life. She would be working in close association with the Deputy Commissioner's wife, what more did she want? But before she could give a reply, the Deputy Commissioner, taking the Health Officer along, had already crossed the yard and was going out of the gate.

'What do you think about the disposal of dead bodies, Mr Kapur? I think the Municipal Committee can handle this work very well—the bodies can be disposed of quietly. To let all and sundry know about it might create unnecessary tension. What do you think?'

The Health Officer was a hundred per cent in agreement.

'That's the only way, Sir, throw the bodies into pits and bury them. There can't be a funeral for each deceased,' the Health Officer said, then warming up, added, 'At first they go and kill one another, and then expect the government to dispose of their dead too with proper ceremony.'

The Deputy Commissioner looked at the Health Officer through a corner of his eyes, paused for a moment, and then, smiling said, 'Well, let's get going. There's a lot to do,' and nodding his head got into his jeep.

Ten minutes later he was at the Relief Committee Office, giving a resume of the government plans concerning relief work, before a gathering of prominent citizens: 'The markets have opened. Four wagons containing charcoal are already in the railway yard. Ten more wagons will have arrived by Tuesday. Twelve hour night curfew will have to continue for some more time, the army pickets and police patrolling will also continue. Dead bodies have been removed and the administration is attending to them. The post offices will reopen this afternoon. A lot of mail has accumulated and cannot be taken in hand. Those heaps of letters have been put outside the General Post Office. But so far as registered letters and parcels are concerned, every effort will be made to sort out and distribute them.'

Sometimes, while speaking, Richard's face would get flushed and he would appear to be struggling for words like one who is not adept at speech making, but no word or phrase would be superfluous or out of place.

'We would like public bodies to assist the administration in running the refugee camps. Arrangements have been made for the supply of rations, tents have been pitched as you know. We shall need some doctors, and quite a number of volunteers who can assist us in looking after the refugees.'

As he spoke, Richard's penetrating eye recognized quite a few faces in the audience, and also sensed their likely reactions to what he was saying. Near the threshold stood the dark and fat Manohar Lal, his arms folded on his chest and a derisive, cynical smile on his lips. He was the very person who, before the commencement of the riots, had come with the delegation of citizens and had shouted all sorts of vituperative things against the government outside his office. He might again give vent to his spleen. There was also Dev Datt, the communist. Richard had twice sent him to jail for his inflammatory speeches among workers against the government, but of late, he had been working for peace in the town and had been trying to get the leaders of political parties together. He would not rake up any other issue. There was also Mr Bakshi, the elderly Congress leader and several others whom he knew, several lawyers whom he recognized. There was also one of 'our own' intelligence men, who was both a Congress activist and a functionary of the Socialist Party. This man might be vociferous in raising slogans, swear at the government and even use abusive language.

But Richard saw to it that he confined himself to simple statements and proposals and after giving his resume, promptly sat sown.

Hardly had Richard sat down, when Lala Lakshmi Narain stood up: 'We assure the Deputy Commissioner Sahib Bahadur that the citizens and all the institutions shall wholeheartedly cooperate with the government. It is our great good fortune that so capable and sympathetic an officer is the head of the administration in the district and is present in our midst.'

Richard got up, took leave of the members of the Relief Committee and left. Lala Lakshmi Narain and some lawyers went running to escort him to his jeep. Thereafter the meeting was over in fifteen minutes.

Suddenly someone was heard shouting near the door:

'All the toadies have gathered here. Flatterers, sycophants all! I am not in the habit of mincing matters. I tell a fellow to his face what I think of him. Where was the government when the tension in the city was mounting? Couldn't the curfew be clamped at that time? Where was the Sahib Bahadur then and what was he doing? We talk straight, at a fellow's face...' It was Manohar Lal, letting off steam.

But by then the jeep had left.

'Enough, enough, what do we get by raking up such issues now?'

The members of the Relief Committee were getting up when one of them said to Manohar Lal as he passed by him: 'What's the point in abusing the government all the time? What do you gain by it?'

'O Bakshiji, I am amazed at you, that you too should talk like this. Go home and ply the charkha, or sweep the lanes. You are not cut out for politics.'

'Why do you shout? Don't I know that riots are manoeuvred by the British? Hasn't Gandhiji said so umpteen times?'

'What were you doing then?'

'Why, what have we not done? Didn't we approach the Muslim League to work jointly with us to preserve peace in the city? Didn't we go to the Deputy Commissioner and ask him urgently to take preventive measures, to station troops and so on, so as to prevent the riot from breaking out? And now when homeless refugees are pouring into the town, what should we do? Should we help them or should we go on abusing the government? Tell us what we should do, the big revolutionary that you are!'

'I have seen many like you, Bakshiji, don't force me to speak. Members of the Congress are seeking contracts from the government for supplies to the Refugee Camps.'

'What am I to do if they are taking contracts?'

'You have made them honored members of your organization. That's what you have done. Put them on a pedestal.'

Just then, an activist went over to Manohar Lal and putting his hand round his waist took him out of the room.

'Let go of me, yaar, I have seen many such fellows. They are all Gandhi's parrots. Gandhi, sitting in Wardha makes statements, and they go on repeating them. They have no mind of their own. Why was the Deputy Commissioner invited? What business had he to come here?'

But his friend pulled him along right up to the gate. As they reached the gate, Manohar Lal stopped grumbling.

'Out with a cigarette,' Manohar Lal said to his friend. 'Let me have a puff at least.'

Both the friends sat down on a projection near the gate.

Inwardly, Bakshi too had been feeling uneasy.

'This is the role the British have all along played— they first bring about a riot and then quell it; they starve the people first and then give them bread; they render them homeless and then begin to provide shelter to them.'

Ever since the riots had broken out, Bakshi's mind had been in a sort of mist. He kept saying to himself again and again that the British had again had the last word, had again had the better of them while his own hold on the situation had been feeble all along.

While Richard was out on his rounds, Liza was in the throes of acute boredom. She left her bedroom and came into the big living room. The rows upon rows of books looked as oppressive as ever before. It appeared to her as though time had stopped and everything was in a state of paralysis. If there was anything alive, it was the wily eyes of the Buddhas and the Bodhisattvas, who, from the dark corners in which they stood, kept looking at her and laying traps for her. She was now scared of even entering the room in the evening. The heads of the statuettes, standing at numerous places, looked to her like so many heads of cobras!

She went into the dining room. The atmosphere here was less oppressive. Here, there were flowers and the light was soft, and the room was free from statuettes and the unbearable burden of books. It had some warmth too because of the soft light; in which a person could relax, and forget a lot, as also remember a lot, as he pleased. Soft light was meant for relaxing, for making love, for sweet hugs and kisses. Liza felt as though her throat was parched and there was a prickly sensation in her eyes. Something was welling up in her again. Her restlessness increased. The coziness of the room soon gave her an appalling sense of desolation, which made her feel all the more restless. She got up, suppressing her sobs and went to the veranda that led to the kitchen, and once there, shouted at the top of her voice: 'Waiter!'

From somewhere far away, making its way through innumerable doors, came the answer: 'Mem Saab!'

And soon enough, the waiter came running into the Mem Sahib's presence, a duster on his shoulder. It was nearing four o'clock in the afternoon and he could anticipate what the Mem Sahib's order would be. Mem Sahib gradually lost her patience and self-control any time between three and four-thirty in the afternoon and would shout for him, from wherever she happened to be, at the top of her voice: 'Get me some beer! Chilled beer!'

Liza, sighing deeply returned to the dining room. She was wearing her house-gown of which the belt had not been tied. In the wilderness in which she lived, beer was her only solace.

When Richard returned home by eight o'clock in the evening, he found Liza dead drunk, and asleep, sprawling on the sofa. There was still some beer left in the bottle standing on the tea-poy. Liza's head was hanging from the arm of the sofa, her hair covering half her face. The flaps of her house-gown having slipped, her knees lay bare.

'Damn this country! Damn this life!' muttered Richard, as he stood in front of the sofa.

On reaching home, Richard would find himself in a different world. It was his private world, his little England, with problems all its own, which were not even remotely related to the outside world. Within the home was his real life. In the outside world he pursued his profession, which was so extraneous to his 'real' life. Of course he had his books, his statuettes which belonged neither to one nor to the other world. He would bury himself in his books to forget both the worlds.

He sat down at the edge of the sofa and bending forward, kissed Liza on the cheek, as though performing a duty. Her body which he, at times, would clasp to himself with such intense ardour, felt coarse and fleshy and unalluring. Liza was again putting on weight, he thought, and crow's feet had appeared under her eyes. Boredom was making her obese. On coming home, whenever he would see Liza in that state, his mind would be filled with revulsion.

'Liza!' he almost shouted into her ear, and, putting out his hand, brushed aside the tuft of hair on her forehead.

Liza was too drowsy to open her eyes. Seeing that Liza was in no position to go to the dining table to have dinner with him, he thought it would be better to put her to bed; Richard put his right hand under her head and the left one under her knees, and lifted her up. As he did so, Richard felt that Liza's house-gown was wet under her, and his eyes fell on a roundish patch on the sofa. As he stood, his mind filled with repugnance, Richard shook. his head. 'The story is beginning to repeat itself,' he muttered.

Liza had only recently returned from home after spending nearly a year in London. Earlier, she had virtually run away from India out of boredom. 'She may again run away,' he was thinking, 'or I shall have to get myself transferred to some other station.'

Looking at the patch on the sofa, Richard was reminded of a strange coincidence that had occurred, and a smile flickered on his lips. That sofa had been taken by him from Mr Lawrence, the Commissioner when the latter was leaving for Lucknow under transfer orders. When he had removed the cover from the sofa he had noticed an ugly patch on it; the kind of patch that he was seeing then. And he had learnt that the Commissioner's wife too was a victim of boredom who would, when in her cups, wet the sofa either in a fit of laughter or of crying. The Commissioner too kept getting himself transferred to different stations, till at last his wife had left him and married a young army captain. Richard looked at his wife and again at the sofa. 'A similar fate awaits this marriage too, it seems,' he muttered to himself and lifting up Liza, carried her to the bedroom.

By the time they reached the bedroom, Liza had woken up, she had also sobered a little.

'What is it, Richard? Where are you taking me?'

'Your gown is wet under you, Liza, I am taking you to your room.'

But Liza did not catch the import of what Richard had said.

He put Liza down into an armchair by the bedside.

'Shall we have dinner, Liza? Would you like to eat something?'

'Eat? Eat what?'

Richard felt like holding her by her shoulders and giving her a big shake. That would wake her up at once. But he desisted from doing so. Instead, he kept looking at her, his hands on his waist.

Liza lifted her face, over which her hair had again tumbled.

'Richard, are you a Hindu or a Musalman?' she asked and laughed softly. 'I didn't know when you came. Have you come home to take lunch or dinner?'

For a moment Richard thought that Liza was being ironical, that she was not as drunk as she was pretending to be. He sat down on the bed in front of her and putting his hand on her arm, said, 'I have too much work on hand these days, Liza, you must understand. The Grain Market in the city has been burnt down, and no fewer than a hundred and three villages razed to the ground.'

'One hundred and three villages, and I know nothing about it? Did I sleep that long? Richard, you should have woken me up and told me. Such big events occurred and you did not tell me about them.'

'Go to sleep, Liza. Change your clothes and go to sleep.'

'Sit by me. I can't sleep alone.'

'Go to sleep, Liza. I have a lot of work to do.'

'So many villages burnt down, Richard, and you still have work to do? What more is there for you to do?'

Richard stopped short. Is Liza being ironical? Has she developed an aversion for me that she is talking in this vein?

Like any drunk person, Liza too was babbling away, saying whatever came into her head. She got up from the chair and staggered to the bed and sat down close to Richard. She put her arm round Richard's neck and her head on his chest. No, it cannot be aversion, he thought, she must have uttered these words unconsciously.

'You don't love me. I know you don't love me. I know everything.'

Then, stroking Richard's hair, said, 'How many Hindus died, Richard, and how many Muslims? You must be knowing everything. What is Anaj Mandi, Richard?

Richard kept looking at her. 'The more she drinks, the more unattractive she is becoming,' he thought to himself. 'A relationship of this kind cannot last long.' Richard's eyes rested on Liza's face. His feelings towards her were rather indefinable. 'Why not put an end to this relationship? Snap the marital tie. But this question needs to be viewed in the context of my career, my future prospects. This is a decisive moment in my career. So far I have done extremely well in implementing policies. But at this juncture, a delicate balance has to be maintained; it is extremely necessary to see that the discontent among the people does not explode against the government. People are impressed with my sincerity. They think I am a sagacious and efficient officer. At this time, therefore, it is extremely necessary to keep Liza by my side.'

He bent forward and kissed Liza on her cheek.

'Listen, Liza,' he said enthusiastically. 'I have to go to Sayedpur tomorrow, to get a disinfectant sprayed into a well in which many women and children jumped to their death. Why don't you come along too? It is a lovely drive. From there we can proceed to Taxila. We can have a look at the museum there—it is a unique museum. What do you say? The entire area is very lovely.'

Liza looked at Richard with drowsy eyes. 'Where do you want to take me for a drive, Richard? Will you take me for a drive through burning villages? I don't want to see anything. I don't want to go anywhere.'

'No, no, what's the point in sticking on at home? The situation is different now. No one can move about freely,' he said, trying to keep up the pretence of enthusiasm. 'Now we can go out together. You have not seen the rural area, in these parts, it is lovely. The other day, in Sayedpur itself, while on my rounds I saw a lark. I heard it singing in an orchard. It is true. I never thought a lark was to be found in India. There are several other kinds of birds too, which you couldn't have seen before.'

'Is it the same place where women had drowned themselves?'

'Yes, yes, the same. A stream flows near the well. It is a lovely stream. And across the stream is the fruit orchard.'

A fleeting smile appeared on Liza's lips; and she kept looking at Richard's face.

'What sort of a person are you, Richard that in such places too you can see new kinds of birds and listen to the warbling of the lark?'

'What is so strange about it, Liza? A person in the Civil Service develops the quality of mental detachment. If we were to get emotionally involved over every incident, administration would not go on for a single day.'

'Not even when a hundred and three villages are burnt down?'

Richard paused a little and then said, 'Not even then. This is not my country, Liza, nor are these people my countrymen.'

Liza kept looking at Richard's face.

'But you were planning to write a book about these people, Richard, about their racial origin. Isn't that so?'

'To write a book is something different, Liza. What has that to do with administration?'

Finding Liza unresponsive, Richard said, 'Two camps are being set up for the refugees. I told the wife of the Health Officer this morning to take up relief work with other women. I believe you too could lend a hand in that work, collect clothes and things for the refugees, toys, etc. for their children and so on. It will give you a chance to move about...'

Liza still remained silent. Richard again bent forward and kissed her on the cheek, and stroking her hair with his right hand, added, 'I must be going, Liza. There's a lot of work waiting for me. At this time I should have been in my office.'

And he got up.

'Shall see you later, Liza. Don't wait for me. And be ready to go to the villages tomorrow morning. We shall start at eight o'clock.' He left the room.

For a long time Liza sat looking towards the door. A shiver ran through her, and an oppressive silence again descended over the house.

20

'I want figures, only figures, nothing but figures. Why don't you understand? You start narrating an endless tale of woe and suffering. I am not here to listen to the whole "Ramayana." Give me figures—how many dead, how many wounded, how much loss of property and goods. That is all.'

The functionary of the Relief Committee (or the 'Statistics Babu' as he was called) with the register lying open before him, would get impatient with the refugees, would even shout irritably at them, but the refugees were such that they wouldn't understand. One may keep sitting the whole day long, scribbling in one's register, yet, at the end of the day, when the figures are summed up and the list finalized, not even two villages might have been covered. Who can make them understand—the Statistics Babu would say—one can't speak roughly to them, or turn them out of one's office—they would keep barging in, even if you did—nor do they observe any order, instead of one three refugees would start speaking at the same time—sometimes it would appear to the Statistics Babu as if hundreds of refugees were speaking at the same time, dinning their tales of woe into his ears. But what can one tell them? They have been rendered homeless, ruined and helpless, and have nowhere to go. They all keep bending over his table. If they didn't start narrating their experiences, it would not take more than a few minutes to collect figures for the entire village. 'Don't tell me all this, give me just figures, only numbers,' but Kartar Singh, the man sitting in front of him with his hands folded, would go on speaking.

'I told him again; I said, "Imdad Khan, we were once playmates, you seem to have forgotten me." It is morning time, babuji, I wouldn't tell an untruth. The fact is, Imdad Khan did not first raise his hand against me.'

The babu was at his wits' end. He asks for figures, whereas the refugees show him their wounds.

'The sickle hit me on my forehead and tore this eye of mine. What do you say, babuji, will my eye be cured? My grandfather said, "Ganda Singh, don't remove the bandage from your eye." And I have not removed it since.'

These were not figures, these were lamentations.

Another fellow had come and was sitting in the chair in front of him.

The babu, without lifting his eyes from his register, went on asking questions and putting down answers:

'Name?'

'Harnam Singh.'

'Father's name?'

'Sardar Gurdial Singh.'

'Village?'

'Dhok Elahi Baksh.'

'Tehsil?'

'Nurpur.'

'How many houses belonging to the Sikhs and Hindus?'

'Only one house. That was ours.'

The babu lifted his eyes. An elderly Sardar was answering his questions:

'How have you come out alive?'

'We had very good relations with Karim Khan. In the evening when...'

The babu raised his forefinger, asking him to keep quiet.

'Any life lost?'

'No, babuji, my wife and I have come out alive. But our son Iqbal Singh was in Nurpur; we have no news of him. And our daughter, Jasbir Kaur was in Sayedpur. She jumped into the well and is no more.'

The babu again raised his forefinger and the Sardar fell silent.

'Come straight to the point. Any life lost?'

'Our daughter died by drowning herself.'

'But she did not die in your village?'

'No, babuji.'

'Her death occurred in a different village. Talk only about your own village. Any material loss?'

'Our shop and house were looted and burnt down. There was one big trunk, it was taken away. There were two gold bracelets lying in it. But I gave away the trunk myself to Ehsan Ali. Rajo, his wife, a very God-fearing woman...'

The babu had again raised his forefinger, and Harnam Singh had become silent.

'The value of your shop?'

'Let me ask my wife,' and turning round he said, 'Banto, what must be the value of our shop?'

'Give me total value, including the goods. Hurry up. I have other work to do too.'

'About seven or eight thousand. There was a piece of land at the back, besides some...'

'Shall I put down ten thousand?'

'Yes, I think you may.'

'Do you want any goods to be recovered?'

'Yes. There is a gun, babuji, a double-barrelled gun, left with Jalal Din Subedar in Adhiro.'

'But you are not from Adhiro... You are from Dhok Elahi Baksh.'

'We had run away from Dhok Elahi Baksh. We walked the whole night. The whole of next day we were in Ehsan Ali's house. During the next night we again kept walking. In the morning, we were given shelter by Subedar Jalal Din at Adhiro. He is a noble soul. He gave us utensils to cook our own food...'

'Enough, enough... What is the name of the Subedar and his address.'

Harnam Singh wanted to narrate the whole story of what had transpired at Adhiro. He also wanted that enquiries should be made about the whereabouts of his son, Iqbal Singh. But the babu would have none of it. He kept putting his forefinger to his lips and then dismissed him.

'You can go now.'

The babu dealing with figures had got what he wanted. He had picked out the grains, the rest was all chaff. Just chaff. But sometimes, the babu could not help lending an ear to what the refugee was saying, the account would be so compelling that it would entice his mind and heart.

'Why, babuji, it may be that my Sukhwant did not jump into the well. Who knows, she may be still hiding in the village, along with her son. You see, Asa Singh was wounded and I had gone to fetch a charpai from my house. It was then that I saw a large number of women coming out of the gurdwara. Sukhwant was also among them. How could I know where they were going? Her hands were raised high and her wrapper was hanging round her neck. When I came back with the charpai, Sukhwant was standing in the middle of the lane. She had stayed back, she had not gone with the other women; our son, Gurmeet, was standing on the raised platform of the gurdwara. At that time the light in the lane would sometimes become dim. It was because of the flames from the school building which was on fire, which would sometimes flare up and sometimes subside. I noticed that Sukhwant was nervous. She had never been nervous before. She came back, came back to her son. Again when the flames of fire rose, I noticed that she was again standing in the middle of the lane, trembling all over. "Sukho, what are you doing?" I shouted. But then, where was the time to think or say anything. If at that time, Sukhwant's eyes had fallen on me, she wouldn't have taken Gurmeet with her. She went towards her son and again stopped short. How could I know what was on her mind? Just then, a loud noise was heard from the outskirts of the village. Slogans of "Ya Ali! Ya Ali!" were heard. And Sukhwant leapt back, picked up Gurmeet in her arms and began running towards the group of women. The last I saw of her, her green wrapper was fluttering in the air and she was turning the corner at the end of the lane. Then she vanished from sight. That is why I say, babuji, it may be my Sukhwant did not jump into the well. It may be she did not take little Gurmeet with her. Who knows, he may be loitering about near the well, babuji, can't you find out?'

But in the entire episode there were no statistics, no figures. The recovery of living beings was not his job. That was being looked after by Dev Raj—all the work relating to recovery, whether it was jewellery or household goods or living persons.

'Sardarji,' the babu said. 'It is the third time you have come to me, and you repeat the same story every time you come. It is not my job to listen to all this.'

But the Sardar continued sitting and looking hard at the babu's face. 'Clinging to what hope he comes running to me. How can I make him understand that I can do nothing for him in this regard?'

'Sardarji,' the babu said in low tones, 'Next Monday a bus will go to your village. I shall ask Dev Rajji to take you along too. But don't tell anyone about it; otherwise any number of people would want to go there.'

But to no effect. The Sardar was still going on with his story.

'If my son is hiding somewhere, on seeing me he will come running to me. Or will shout to me from wherever he is: "Search me out, papa, search me out!" as he used to do at home. Every time I came home, he would hide behind a door and shout, "Search me out! Search me out, papa!"...'

The babu quietly got up from the chair and went out of the office.

It was when one came out and stood on the balcony that one realized what a vast concourse of refugees had gathered in the compound of the Relief Office. The compound was teeming with refugees. They were sitting in groups everywhere, on the raised projection at the back from where the vanaprasthi used to deliver his sermons and expatiate on the grandeur of Vedic religion; refugees were sitting even on the steps.

'Don't cry, Ganda Singh,' the babu heard someone say. An elderly man was trying to console someone, 'Those that have gone are now in God's care, dear to the Lord. They have made supreme sacrifice for the Panth. They have become immortal.'

'Wahe Guru! Wahe Guru!'

'Sat Naam, Sache Padshah!' three or four Sardars sitting on the steps prayed.

The Statistics Babu was still standing on the balcony when another Sardar, with large eyes and a bulky frame, came over to him. He too had been 'pestering' him a good deal. He came and, as was his habit, put his mouth close to the babu's ear, and said, 'You said that a bus would leave. When will it leave? I hope it will surely go.'

'I shall let you know when it leaves, even though it is not part of my job...'

'I hope my work will be done.' Thereupon putting his mouth close to the babu's ear, said, 'You will have your share, I assure you.'

At this the babu said somewhat peevishly, 'Talk sense, Sardarji. No fewer than twenty-seven women jumped to their death in the well. How will you be able to make out who among them was your wife?'

'Leave that to me, Virji. I shall recognize her from her bracelets. She was wearing a gold chain round her neck. Of course, I am not the only sufferer, what happened to many others, happened to me also. But how can I give up my claim to the gold chain and the bracelets? What do you say, Virji?'

Then again putting his mouth to the babu's ear, said, 'I shall not be ungrateful if you will get me my ornaments, I shall duly repay you. The good woman should have at least thought of it and left the ornaments with someone before jumping to her death. Isn't that so, Virji? What do you say? I shall not be ungrateful. You get this work done for me.' Then, stepping aside, looked at the babu's face, 'No one else need know about it. Let it remain between you and me.'

'O, Sardarji, the corpses are swollen and have come up to the surface. Can you take a bracelet off the wrist of a swollen body? Talk sense. Will the authorities permit you to do that?'

'Why, it is my wife, it is my jewellery that I am claiming. I got the bracelets made with my own money. I have not stolen them. We have only to take along a hammer and chisel and the work will be done in a matter of minutes. If you like, we can take some goldsmith's boy with us. Where there is a will, there is a way.'

'Talk sense, Sardarji. The government will demand proper identification. Witnesses.'

'But, Virji, that is your job. If I have to give you your share, you will at least do this much. Won't you?'

'Sardar, understand once for all, this is not my job. I only collect statistics. In the Lost Property List, I have included your wife's bracelets and chain. Recovery is not part of my job.'

'Don't be annoyed, Virji. The affairs of the world do not come to a stop,' and taking the babu's right hand into his, separated his three fingers one by one, and whispered into the babu's ears 'Do you agree?' (To hold three fingers means three times twenty, i.e. sixty rupees.)

'Why are you wasting your time, Sardar? I cannot help you.' The Sardar let go of the babu's hand but kept staring at the babu's face for a long time. Then, adjusting the sheet of cloth over his shoulders turned towards the staircase. Getting close to the staircase he turned round again.

'O babu, what do you say?' and putting up his hand, showed four of his fingers. 'Do you agree?'

The babu turned his face away.

A little while later, the Sardar was heard saying, 'Have some pity on us. We have been ruined.'

When the babu turned round, he was going down the staircase.

After some time the babu himself felt tired and went down into the yard. To keep sitting at the table for long was impossible. By the time it was evening a resume would be prepared by adding up the figures collected during the day, one copy of which would be sent to the press, another to the Congress office, while the third one would go into the file. He had by then concluded that in the matter of deaths, the number of Hindus and Sikhs killed equalled more or less the number of Muslims killed. The material losses of Hindus and Sikhs were much higher.

Dev Datt had come the previous evening.

'What have been your figures for today?'

'Today I got the figures for Tehsil Nurpur. There is not much difference in the number of deaths. Almost the same number of deaths among Muslims as among Hindus and Sikhs.'

Dev Datt picked up the register, and kept turning its pages for some time, then, putting it down said, 'Add another column to your tabulations indicating the number of poor people killed as against well-to-do people.'

'What is the sense in that? You bring in the rich and the poor into everything.'

'It is an important aspect which will reveal to you quite a few things.'

As he went through the yard, the babu could recognize a good number of faces. At the foot of the staircase, a little to the right, the girl whose fiance's whereabouts were not known, still stood bewildered as on previous days, a vague look in her eyes. She had been to all the hospitals, but to no avail. A little farther down, sat Harnam Singh with his wife, the man who only talked about the recovery of his double-barrelled gun. The babu looked away. He knew that if their eyes met, the Sardar would again start bothering him about his gun.

On one side of the platform sat a few Congress workers, having a heated argument. Kashmiri Lal was saying: 'Give a straight answer. What should I do, if I am physically attacked by someone? Being a believer in non-violence should I fold my hands before the fellow who has come to kill me and say, "I shall not resist since I am a believer in non-violence. You can chop off my head?"'

'Who will care to kill a puny, little fellow like you?' Shankar said, in his usual bantering tone.

'Why, are only wrestlers attacked? It is always a weak person that is attacked.'

'It is not a trivial matter. I am not joking. I want to know what guidance non-violence has to give me at such a juncture,' he said to Bakshiji, but Bakshiji had not been very attentive to what was being said.

'Tell me, Bakshiji. Don't be evasive.'

'What is it? What do you want to know?'

'Bapu has advised us not to use violence. If, in the event of a riot, a man were to attack me, what should I do? Should I fold my hands and say, "Come, brother, kill me. Here is my neck?"'

Shankar, intervening, said, 'Gandhiji has said that a person himself should not indulge in violence. Nowhere has he said that if a person is subjected to violence he should not resist.'

'What should I do?'

'If anyone attacks you, Kashmiri,' said Jit Singh, 'You tell him, "Just wait brother, let me run up to the Congress office and ask them what my line of action should be. Whether I should defend myself or not."'

'Bapu has advised us not to use violence. If such an eventuality arises, my first duty is to tell the fellow patiently that what he is doing, is something very wrong, that he should desist from doing it.'

'I would say, fight the fellow tooth and nail,' said Master Ram Das.

'Fight him with what? All I have in my house is my charkha.'

'You are yourself a charkha that has taken up this issue after the riots, after all the killing has been done.'

'You fellows are making light of it, but the matter is serious,' said Jit Singh.

'Listen, son,' said Bakshiji, with a tremor of emotion in his voice. 'The Jarnail did not suffer from any such mental conflict. He was never bothered about his personal safety. Jarnail was eccentric, unlettered, crazy, but he was never worried as to what he should do in the event of his being attacked...'

All fell silent. Everyone had been deeply pained over Jarnail's death.

'But this is being oversentimental,' Kashmiri said, after some time.

'Listen,' Bakshiji said. 'You yourself should not indulge in violence. That is number one. You should persuade the fellow to desist from using violence. That is number two. And if he does not listen, fight him tooth and nail. That is number three.'

'That's it. That's what I call an answer. Are you satisfied, Kashmiri? Now keep your mouth shut.'

But Kashmiri Lal was still arguing: 'But with what weapons? With the charkha?'

'Why with the charkha? Fight him with a sword,' said Jit Singh.

'Then, am I allowed to keep a sword, Bakshiji? What do you say?'

Bakshiji made no answer.

'Or a pistol?'

'Pistol is too violent a weapon.'

'Is a sword any the less?'

'Yes. You have to use your own energy to wield a sword, whereas with a pistol you have only to press the trigger.'

'Then I should buy myself a sword. What do you say, Bakshiji?'

Bakshiji did not answer. Had he spoken, he would again have cited Jarnail's example.

The Statistics Babu moved away, shaking his head. To him a discussion of this nature, after the riots, sounded so pointless.

Like the receding tide of the sea, the tide of the riots had subsided, leaving behind all kinds of litter and junk and garbage.

By the side of the door that led to the veranda a group of refugees seemed to be having a good laugh over something. As the babu drew near, he saw an elderly, short-statured Sardar with a thick, greying beard, lying on the floor in their midst. The man, his eyes twinkling, was shaking his legs and striking the floor with his heels and laughing like a child, while those sitting around him appeared to be enjoying a dialogue with him.

'Will you go to your village, Natha Singh?'

At this, Natha Singh, who was lying on the floor, folded up his legs, turned on one side and joined both his hands between his thighs.

'No, I won't.'

'Why won't you go?'

'No, I won't,' he repeated, shaking his head from side to side like a child, and clasped his hands still more tightly between his thighs, and joined his knees together. It appeared to the babu that the question had so often been put to the man that the whole exercise had turned into a prank.

'Why won't you?'

'No, I won't,' he said and folded up his legs even tighter and again shook his head from side to side.

'But why won't you go?'

'There they will circumcise me.' And he began laughing as he folded his legs even more tightly and shook his head. All the Sardars burst out laughing.

At the other end of the veranda stood the room of the school peon. Outside the room, as on previous days, sat a Brahmin pundit and his wife, a picture of despondency with their heads bowed. On the first day of their arrival, the school peon had brought them to the babu. Their daughter was missing, and both husband and wife had cried bitterly and had beseeched the babu with folded hands to recover the girl. The Brahmin had also said that a tonga-driver of the village had kidnapped the girl. But thereafter they had not come to him.

The Statistics Babu walked over to them.

'A bus will leave for Nurpur tomorrow morning, with an armed police guard and a government officer. They will help you trace your daughter.'

The pundit looked at the babu with his rheumy eyes and shaking his head in despair, said, 'She can't be traced now, babuji; our Parkasho can't be traced now. She is lost for ever.'

'But you told me that a tonga-driver of the village had kidnapped her, and was keeping her in his house.'

The pundit again shook his head and said, 'God alone knows what has been her fate.'

There will be other people too going in the bus. What does your wife say?'

The pundit's wife raised her head and, as though looking into vacancy, said, 'What should I say, babuji? May our Parkasho live happily wherever she is.'

The babu was taken aback by the answer. He thought the parents of the girl were scared of going to the village.

'You explain to me the location and the address and I shall make enquiries through the police.'

'Of what use is her coming back to us?' said the woman peremptorily. 'They must have already put the forbidden thing into her mouth.'

To which the pundit added: 'It is hard for us to make both ends meet, babuji. There is not a pie in our pockets. How are we going to feed her as well?'

The Statistics Babu, well familiar with such experiences, stood there for a while and then moved on.

Parkasho had really been kidnapped by Allah Rakha and brought into his house. When the riot broke out mother and daughter were collecting faggots from the slope of the hill. Allah Rakha, along with two or three of his friends, was already on the prowl, waiting for an opportunity. They came running, Allah Rakha picked up Parkasho, who shouted and cried but to no avail, and brought her home, while her mother, dumbfounded, looked on and then came whimpering home. During the first night, Parkasho was left alone in a dark room. On the second day, Allah Rakha got some sort of nikah rites performed and married her, and brought a new pair of clothes for her to wear. For two days Parkasho lay crying without a morsel of food or a drop of water going into her, and kept staring at the walls of his house. But on the third day she accepted a glassful of lassi from his hand and also washed her face. The faces of her father and mother were constantly before her eyes but Parkasho was painfully conscious of the fact that as against Allah Rakha, they were too feeble to rescue her. Gradually her eyes began to turn towards the objects that lay around her in Allah Rakha's house. Outside his mud-house, stood a horse tied to a peg. Every time it flicked its tail, the flesh on its back rippled. Outside the house under a tree stood Allah Rakha's tonga. Earlier too Parkasho had seen the tonga several times. As a matter of fact, Allah Rakha had had his eyes on Parkasho for quite some time. Parkasho too had, time and again sensed it, while going about in the village drawing water from the spring or washing clothes. Allah Rakha would tease her, pass all sorts of remarks and, on the sly, throw pebbles at her. She knew it was him who threw them, but would not complain to her father because she knew that he would not be able to do anything. She was afraid of both Allah Rakha and her father.

And then, during the riots, Allah Rakha had succeeded in carrying away the hapless girl, crying and shouting, and brought her home. At the time when, in the Relief Office, Parkasho's mother was crying her eyes out remembering her daughter and could not muster enough courage to try to get her back, at that very time, Parkasho was sitting on a cot in Allah Rakha's house, having put on, under duress, the new suit of clothes brought for her by Allah Rakha. Then, Allah Rakha had come, opened a small box and holding it out to her had sat down on the cot beside her, saying: 'Eat! Here, Eat!'

Parkasho had her downcast eyes fixed on the strings of the cot. She did not lift her eyes either to look at Allah Rakha or at the packet, nor did she utter a word.

'Eat! It is mithai, haramzadi, eat! I have brought it for you.'

This time Parkasho cast a glance at the sweetmeats, but she still did not have the nerve to look at Allah Rakha.

'Eat!' Allah Rakha suddenly shouted at which Parkasho trembled from head to foot.

'It is mithai, not poison. Eat!'

Allah Rakha picked up a piece of milk-cake and bending forward pressed her cheeks with his left hand, and with his right hand thrust the sweetmeat into her mouth.

Parkasho sensed a certain eagerness in Allah Rakha's brusque manner but she still sat frightened and subdued. How could she eat a sweetmeat from the hand of a Musalman?

'It is from a Hindu sweet-shop, haramzadi, eat!'

Slowly, the frightened Parkasho began chewing the piece in her mouth. Allah Rakha laughed, 'Is it a sweetmeat or poison?'

Parkasho would, from time to time, move her jaws and then would stop masticating and shut her mouth tight.

'Eat!' Allah Rakha would shout and Parkasho's jaws would start working again.

The odour from Parkasho's body had begun to work as an intoxicant on Allah Rakha, making him increasingly restless.

'Now eat with your own hand.'

This time there was a touch of softness in Allah Rakha's voice.

'If you don't, I shall lay you down and force all the mithai down your throat. Eat.'

Parkasho raised her eyes and looked at him. She had seen Allah Rakha several times earlier too but never from such close quarters. She noticed his thin, black moustache. Allah Rakha had put collyrium in his eyes, combed his hair and was wearing clean clothes.

Parkasho's fear grew less somewhat, but she continued to look frightened and subdued.

'Will you eat or shall I force it down your throat?' and his left hand again rose to catch hold of Parkasho's chin.

Slowly Parkasho began to feel as though the fear of Allah Rakha was subsiding within her. Chewing the piece of milk-cake she again looked at him. This time her eyes fell on the black thread round his neck to which an amulet was tied. The collar button was open. Her eyes also fell on his striped shirt. Allah Rakha looked very clean and tidy.

Allah Rakha was holding another piece of sweetmeat in his hand waiting for Parkasho to finish chewing so that he could force another piece into her mouth. Parkasho's eyes also rested on his hand. Suddenly, Parkasho said in a low voice: 'You eat!'

The words had an electrifying effect on Allah Rakha.

'At last you spoke! Now, eat!'

'No.'

'Eat!'

Parkasho shook her head. It appeared to Allah Rakha as though a flicker of a smile had crossed Parkasho's lips. Parkasho raised her eyes to look at Allah Rakha.

'I shall eat if you will put it into my mouth,' he said.

For a few seconds Parkasho's eyes rested on Allah Rakha's face. Then she slowly picked up a piece. Even after picking it up, she was unable to lift her hand towards him. Parkasho's face had turned pale and her hand trembled as though with the sudden realization of how her parents would react were they to know what she was about to do. But just then she saw Allah Rakha's eyes full of eager desire and Parkasho's hand went up to Allah Rakha's mouth.

Both were opening up to each other. Allah Rakha moved closer to her and enveloped her in his arms. Even though frightened and subdued, she became receptive to his embraces. It seemed to her as though the past had drifted far away, while the present was waiting to receive her with open arms. The situation had so radically altered that Parkasho's parents had begun to appear irrelevant to it.

They remained wrapped up in each other's arms for a long time. For a long time too Parkasho did not speak. But when her back was turned towards Allah Rakha and her eyes rested on the wall opposite, she said softly: 'Why did you throw pebbles at me when I went to fetch water?'

In answer to this, Allah Rakha raised his hand and put it on Parkasho's waist.

'I would throw pebbles because you wouldn't speak to me.'

'Why should I have spoken to you?'

'Aren't you speaking to me now?'

Parkasho remained quiet for some time, then said softly: 'Where is my mother?'

'How should I know where your mother is. She is not in her house.'

A sigh rose from the inner depths of her being and her eyes brimmed with tears. She felt as though her parents had been left far behind and that she would never see them again.

'Did you set fire to our tenement?'

'No. People went to burn it down, but I stopped them. I put a lock there.'

His answer comforted her. She slowly lifted her hand and put it on Allah Rakha's hand which rested on her waist.

Every person coming to the Relief Office had, as it were, brought with him, his bag of experiences. But no one had the ability to assess these experiences or to draw inferences from them. They all stared into vacancy and listened, with their ears pricked to whatever anyone said. A rumour would spread and people in the yard would stand up on their toes, or gather into knots in order to listen to what was being said. No one knew in which direction to turn, or what lay in store for him or her, or the kind of future it would be. It appeared as though a remorseless whirl of events would occur into the vortex of which they would all be sucked, none having either the capacity or the option to stay out, that no one would be able to take into his own hands the reins of his life. They moved about like puppets, when hungry they would put into their mouths whatever they would get, they could cry when tormented by the memory of what had happened to them, and from morning till night would listen to whatever anyone would say.

21

People were gathering in the college hall for a meeting of the Peace Committee. The place chosen for the meeting was, for once, non-controversial—the college was neither of the Hindus, nor of Muslims, it was run by a Christian Mission. The Principal too was not an Indian, he was an American missionary, a very sociable, peace-loving man. There was still time before the meeting commenced; all the prominent citizens, of all shades of opinion and party affiliations had been invited. Quite a few had already arrived and strolled up and down the long veranda exchanging views or stood inside the hall, lost in discussions.

The short-statured property dealer was saying to Sheikh Nur Elahi: 'This is the right time to strike a bargain. Property prices are low. But soon they will begin to rise. I am the one who should know. If you have any intention of buying property, this is the time.'

'The prices may fall further,' the Sheikh commented.

'They have already touched rock-bottom. How much more can they fall?' the property dealer said. 'Earlier I had myself sold land at Rs 1500 per ahata. The same ahata, in the same locality is now available at Rs 750.' Then, putting his hand on the Sheikh's elbow, and standing on his toes, added, 'When conditions become peaceful, will the land-prices go up or come down?'

'I shall think it over.'

'Do. But do not keep thinking indefinitely. Earlier too you missed good bargains.'

After the riots a strong trend had set in—Muslims were keen to move out of Hindu localities, and likewise, Hindus and Sikhs from predominantly Muslim localities.

'I shall try to bring down the price by another hundred rupees. This is a good bargain. You were keen to buy a house on the main road in a Muslim locality. Weren't you?'

'Yes, yes. I shall let you know soon.'

Had Sheikh Nur Elahi continued to stand there for another two minutes, there was every danger that the deal might have been struck; but he had succeeded in shaking off Munshi Ram, the property dealer and gone and joined the group of Municipal Councillors. For a while Munshi Ram continued to stand where he was, then he moved slowly over to Babu Prithmi Chand.

'The house adjoining yours is on sale, Babuji.'

'You call that pigsty a house?'

'Even if it is a pigsty I would advise you to buy it. It is going darned cheap. You can pull it down and rebuild it as part of your house.'

'What if Pakistan is formed?'

'Oh, go on, Babuji, these are only gimmicks of the politicians.' Then lowering his voice, added, 'Even if it is formed, people are not going to run away from their homes.'

Munshi Ram did not want the day to pass without a bargain. It was not always that so many well-to-do people got together at one place.

Babu Prithmi Chand's reaction was different: 'When conditions become normal, no one would like to leave the locality he has been living in.'

'Get such thoughts out of your mind, Babuji,' said Munshi Ram.

'No Muslim wants to live in a Hindu mohalla any longer. This is as sure as daylight. Whether Pakistan comes into being or not, this is sure as daylight.'

As he saw Lakshmi Narain approaching from a distance, Sheikh Nur Elahi remarked jokingly: 'So you too have come, karar.'

As he drew closer, Sheikh Nur Elahi said more loudly, 'So, you saw to it that the riot broke out. You couldn't rest content otherwise.'

People standing around, laughed. Sheikh Nur Elahi and Lala Lakshmi Narain were on informal terms, both had studied together in the local Mission School, both were cloth merchants.

'There is no trusting a karar, I tell you.'

On seeing them talking so cordially to one another, Sardar Mohan Singh who was standing on one side, said to the person standing close to him: 'Come what may, ultimately we all have to live here. There may be ups and downs and fits of frenzy, but the reality is that all of us have to live here. Small tensions are of little consequence; even the utensils in a kitchen keep striking against one another. Neighbours too have quarrels, but the fact remains that all of us have to live here. To think of it, a neighbour is like one's right hand.'

Both embraced each other. Deep inside, both were fanatics, but since they had been playmates in their younger days they had retained an air of friendly relations with each other. In times of need they would be helpful to each other too. But it was difficult nonetheless to fathom whether Sheikh Nur Elahi's words were spoken in jest or were an expression of sheer hatred for the Hindus.

And then, added softly: 'I got your bales shifted from the godown.'

Lakshmi Narain smiled. Thereupon Nur Elahi added jocularly: 'At first, I said to myself, let the karar's bales be put to flames, but then, something within me said, "No, a friend is a friend after all."'

To people standing around such encounters among friends made a very pleasant and favourable impression.

Nur Elahi was saying, 'It was not easy to get coolies that night. My son did not know what to do. But I said to him, "By whatever means you can, get the bales shifted, otherwise the Lala will make life hell for me." Eventually, he managed to get two coolies from somewhere.'

Both of them laughed.

The jocularity, coupled with a measure of consideration for each other, was all very well, only it lacked sincerity. Within their hearts lurked aversion, even hatred. But both were elderly, worldly-wise businessmen, who knew well enough that they needed each other.

Standing on the steps facing a lawn, Hayat Baksh was describing the locality of some town to a Sardar: 'In the evening when the lights would go up, the whole town would be lit up, the seaside, the roads, all looked so resplendent like a newly-wed bride.'

'Whose panegyric are you singing, Hayat Baksh?'

'It is Rangoon I am talking about. What a city! I was

there during the war days. How can I describe it to you?'

Men from different communities were purposely avoiding any reference to the riots in their conversation. Otherwise who would talk about a town as pretty as a bride in the context of burning villages and the Grain Market in flames?'

At some distance from them, standing in the midst of a group, Babu Prithmi Chand was saying in his sharp, squeaky voice: 'I said to them, "Fools that you are, do you think, by putting up an iron gate at the entrance to your lane, you will become any the safer? Talk sense," I said to them, "If an outsider will be prevented from coming in, a resident of the locality too, out on an errand, will find it difficult to come in. By getting the iron-gate fixed, you will be putting up a prison wall for yourselves. Talk sense," I said.'

In another part of the veranda, Lala Shyam Lal had caught hold of the Statistics Babu and was taking him to one side: 'You have to listen attentively to what I tell you. Let us sit down on this bench and talk.'

Both sat down. The Lala put his mouth close to the babu's ear and said, 'Who will be the Congress candidate for the Municipal Elections from our ward?'

'I don't know, Lalaji, at present everyone is engaged in relief work.'

'Not everyone. Only you are engaged in relief work. But you must have heard something.'

'No, Lalaji, I have not heard anything so far. But I doubt very much if under the prevailing conditions the Municipal Elections will at all take place.'

'Affairs of the world do not come to a stop. I have

already met the Deputy Commissioner. Elections will be held after two months. June 15 is the date fixed for filing in nominations. Therefore there is not much time left.'

'I plead ignorance, Lalaji, I am sorry.'

'One should go about in the world with eyes and ears open, son. Men of my generation will not be here for long now; it is you who have to take over.' Then putting his mouth close to the babu's ear, added, 'I am standing for elections.'

The babu turned round and looked at the Lala's face.

'My information is that Mangal Sen will get the Congress ticket from our ward.'

'But Lalaji, what for should you need the Congress ticket?'

But hardly had he put the question, when the babu, as in a flash, understood the change that had occurred in the situation. If a Hindu stood for elections now, he would need the support of the Congress, likewise if a Muslim stood for elections, he would need the support of the Muslim League. Such a polarization had taken place. Lala Shyam Lal was not an activist of the Congress. He was close to the Congress only to the extent of wearing clothes made from material resembling khadi.

'What will be left of the Congress image if it gives tickets to such fellows?' and again putting his mouth close to the babu's ear he said, 'He runs a gambling den. He runs two such dens. He is hand in glove with the police in running those dens. He dances attendance on Gandhiji and Pandit Nehru when they visit the town, but that does not make him a genuine Congress worker. He does not even wear khadi.'

'He does,' said the Statistics Babu.

'It is only recently that he has started wearing khadi. He never wore it earlier. Nobody wears khadi in his house.'

Finding in the babu a patient listener, Lalaji went on: 'He drinks beer. If you don't believe me, go to the club in the Company's Garden any evening and see for yourself. His father too was an addict.' Thereupon, the Lala, twisting his facial muscles into a scowl, said venomously, 'His father had a carbuncle, and he died of that carbuncle. This fellow too will one day die of carbuncle.'

The Statistics Babu did not know what exactly a carbuncle was, but he was surprised why Lalaji felt so bitter about Mangal Sen.

'If I were to expose him, the fellow would be stark naked before the public in one day, but I say what's the point, it is his own business how he lives. But then, he should not cheat people, throw dust into their eyes.'

'But Lalaji, Mangal Sen is a member of the District Congress Committee, whereas you are not even a four-anna member of the Congress. How can you claim a ticket from the Congress?'

'Who is asking for a ticket? All that I want is that the Congress should not put up its own candidate from this ward. If anyone wants to stand for election, let him stand in his individual capacity.'

Close to where they sat, Lala Lakshmi Narain was enquiring about some herbal medicine from Hayat Baksh. Hayat Baksh knew about some medicinal herbs, as for instance, about the herb that cured stone in the bladder;

he would prepare the medicine himself and give it free of charge but would not disclose the prescription to anyone, since he was of the firm belief that a medicine lost its efficacy if the prescription was given out or if the person made money out of it.

Ranvir, Lala Lakshmi Narain's son had sprained his foot. While running, his foot had fallen into a gutter, his knees too had been badly bruised. Hayat Baksh listened patiently about the boy's ailment and then said, 'No, no, no oil massage. This oil has a cooling effect. I have got some oil which Ashraf had brought from Lahore. That will relax the boy's nerves. I shall send it on to you. Don't worry; the boy will get well soon.'

Then, lowering his voice, said confidentially, 'How did the boy sprain his foot?' Then, lowering his voice still further, added, 'I hear he has been taking part in some Youth Organization.' Then, without waiting for Lakshmi Narain's answer, said, 'Do as I tell you. Send him away for a few days. There is a danger of arrests being made.'

Lala Lakshmi Narain pricked his ears but did not betray any nervousness.

'He is only a child, barely fifteen years of age. What can a child do?...' he said, but he made a mental note of the suggestion that the boy should be whisked away somewhere for a few days.

Close to the college gate, two college peons sat on a bench talking to one another. One said to the other: 'We poor people are such ignorant fools, we go breaking one another's head. These well-to-do people are so wise and sensible. They are all here, Hindus, Muslims, Sikhs. See how cordially they are meeting one another.'

The representatives of almost all the political parties had arrived, except Bakshi who was being awaited. Dev Datt was happy at heart that at last, going from house to house, he had succeeded in getting all the leaders under one roof. His organizational skill was again manifest, in the way, at the very commencement of the meeting, he had proposed the name of Mr Herbert, the Principal of the Christian College, as the chairperson for the meeting. Mr Herbert, an elderly person, an American, had taught three generations of local students; he was not an Englishman, nor was he a Hindu, Sikh or Musalman. In the midst of loud applause, he came and sat down in the President's chair. People from the veranda sauntered into the hall one by one and took their seats. Just then a heated argument started between a young Muslim League Member and a Congress activist.

The Muslim League Member sprang up on his feet and shouted: 'No one can stop us from achieving the goal of Pakistan. Bakshiji, (who had in the meanwhile arrived) had better give up this farce, once and for all and admit that the Congress is the organization of the Hindus, and I shall hug him to my heart. The Congress cannot speak for the Muslims; the Congress does not represent the Muslims.'

Such an utterance used to be heard frequently enough even before the riots. Just then another raised the slogan: 'Pakistan Zindabad!' This was followed by many voices shouting: 'Silence! Silence!'

Mr Herbert stood up:

'Gentlemen, at this delicate juncture, we should all strive together to improve the atmosphere in the town. Eminent personalities of the town are present here. Their voices will be heard with respect by the people. I am of the view that a Peace Committee should be set up here and now and that the members of the Peace Committee should go into every mohalla, into every locality of the town and spread the message of peace. The Peace Committee should comprise of representatives of all the political parties. I believe a bus could be arranged, fitted with a microphone and loudspeaker, in which representatives of all political parties could go from place to place making a fervent appeal for peace. This will have a salutary effect.'

The proposal was greeted with loud applause.

Suddenly a person stood up. It was Shah Nawaz: 'I shall make the necessary arrangement for the bus.'

There was again a loud applause. Dev Datt came forward and said, 'We learn that the arrangement for the bus will be made by the government.'

Again, there was loud applause. Shah Nawaz was still standing: 'I shall pay for petrol,' he said.

'O Fine! Bravo! Wonderful!'

At this another person got up and said, 'Gentlemen, before drawing up the programme, won't it be better to set up a regular committee, elect the office-bearers and proceed in a systematic manner?'

That was a danger signal—the question of elections was being raised. Dev Datt immediately stepped forward and said, 'I propose there should be three vice presidents of this Peace Committee. I propose the names of Janab Hayat Baksh...'

'Please wait!' someone shouted. 'Let us first decide about the number of vice presidents we should have, whether three or more or less. I would propose that there should be five vice presidents. The more vice presidents we have, the more representative will the Peace Committee be.'

A Sardarji raised his hand: 'Let the number of vice presidents remain three: one Hindu, one Muslim and one Sikh. The Executive Committee may be expanded to accommodate as many persons as you like.'

'The question of Hindu and Muslim should not be raised here. This is a Peace Committee.' Dev Datt was again on his feet. 'Eminent leaders from all political parties should be included. My proposal is: Janab Hayat Baksh from Muslim League, Bakshiji from the Congress and Bhai Jodh Singhji from the Gurdwara Prabandhak Committee should be elected as vice presidents.

One person got up:

'If representation on the Peace Committee has to be on the basis of political parties, then I would propose that presidents of all the three political parties should ipso facto be on the Committee in their capacity as presidents. Their names should not be mentioned.'

Lala Lakshmi Narain was on his feet.

'I am deeply pained to see that you have named three political parties but forgotten the Hindu Sabha. Isn't it a political party too?'

'No. Hindu Sabha is not a political party.'

'If it is not a political party, then the Gurdwara Prabandhak Committee is also not a political party.'

Five or six persons got up, all together.

'It is an insult to the Sikh community. The Gurdwara Prabandhak Committee alone represents the Sikhs.'

Dev Datt leapt forward again:

'Gentlemen, this will not lead us anywhere; and we shall not be able to do any work. We have to fight against communal elements. It is not important who gets the representation. What is important is that the Peace Committee becomes the joint forum of all communities, so that all of us, Hindus, Muslims, Sikhs, Christians, can issue an appeal for peace from a joint platform. Keeping this in view I propose that Janab Hayat Baksh, Bakshiji and Bhai Jodh Singhji be elected as vice presidents of the Peace Committee.'

'Agreed! It is right. Now move to the next item.'

A voice was heard. Someone clapped. And then there was more clapping and thus no chance was given to anyone opposed to the proposal to raise his voice. The proposal was adopted unanimously.

Master Ram Das got up:

'For the post of general secretary I propose the name of Comrade Dev Datt. He is a tireless worker; it is thanks to his efforts that we have all assembled here today. The next few days are going to be rather challenging. The Peace Committee will have to be very alert and persevering. Comrade Dev Datt is eminently suited for this post.'

'Are all other young men dead in the town?' It was Manohar Lal, standing near the door with his arms folded on his chest.

'I want to know if this work can only be done by lackeys of the British government and traitors of the nation, the communists? Are there no suitable young men left in the town? As a mark of protest, I refuse to participate in the deliberations of the meeting.'

And he turned round to walk out of the hall.

'Wait, Manohar Lal. Don't behave like a child. Allow some work to be done.'

But Manohar Lal, still in his tantrums, shouted back: 'Let me be. I have seen many like him. Manohar Lal is not afraid of anyone. We talk straight at a fellow's face.'

But some young Congress members held him back. One of them put his arm around Manohar Lal's waist, lifted him up and lugged him back into the hall.

'All toadies of the government have gathered here. I know each one of them.'

'Silence! Silence!'

'I second the name of Comrade Dev Datt.'

'I support him.'

Loud applause. Once again the meeting appeared to proceed smoothly.

But when it came to the election of Working Committee members all sorts of names began to be thrown up—Lakshmi Narain, Mayyadas, Shah Nawaz. Suddenly some Muslim members got up all together and went towards the door. At their head was Maula Dad.

'Hindus are in a majority on this Committee. We cannot work on such a Committee. This meeting is nothing but a trickery of the Hindus.'

Ten persons, including Dev Datt ran after them to dissuade them from walking out of the meeting. There was quite a scene near the door for some time. Eventually, a formula was evolved for the election of members to the Working Committee, viz, that the Committee, consisting of a total of fifteen members will have on it, seven Muslims, five Hindus and three Sikhs. A discussion ensued which went on for a long time, so much so that people began to grow tired. In the end, the formula was accepted and Lala Lakshmi Narain, was also included, as also Mangal Sen, Shah Nawaz and quite a few others. Poor Lala Shyam Lal's name was not proposed by anyone. He kept pulling at the Statistics Babu's coat for a long time but the latter continued to waver and vacillate. At last Lala Shyam stood up:

'I would request that I too should be permitted to serve on this Committee.'

'All the seats have been filled. Please sit down,' said Mangal Sen.

Another gentleman got up.

'I see no harm if one more Hindu, one Sikh and one Muslim are added to the Committee.'

'This cannot be done.' Mangal Sen said again, 'How can you go on adding more and more names?'

The matter was still under discussion when the blaring sound of a loudspeaker was heard and Comrade Dev Datt went over to where the president sat, and addressing the audience, said, 'Gentlemen, the bus for Peace is here. We shall set out on our mission right from here and now. I would request that besides the president and the vice presidents all those who wish to come along are most welcome. Please get into the bus. As you know, a loudspeaker has been fitted into the bus. The bus will keep stopping at regular intervals on the way, and our eminent leaders, by turns, will address the citizens and appeal to them to maintain peace in the city.'

The meeting dispersed, people began stepping out.

The bus for Peace stood there in all its glory, pink and white stripes painted on it. On the roof of the bus, at both ends, facing the road, fluttered the flags of the

Congress and the Muslim League. Two amplifiers, one in front and the other at the back of the bus, had been fitted. 'Put up a Union Jack too on the bus,' shouted Manohar Lal sarcastically. As the members came out, the air resounded with slogans: 'Long Live Hindu Muslim Unity!'

'Peace Committee Zindabad!'

'Hindus and Muslims are one!'

The bystanders peered into the bus to see who it was that was raising the slogans. On the seat next to that of the driver sat a man, holding a microphone in his hand. Many did not recognize him, but some did. Nathu was dead, or he would have recognized him at once. It was Murad Ali, the dark-complexioned Murad Ali, with bristling moustaches, his thin cane lying between his legs, peering to the right and left with his small ferretty eyes and raising slogans with all the passion at his command.

There was a brief discussion before they set out on their Peace Mission—who should sit in which seat and who should be the first speaker, and which slogans were to be raised.

The Presidents of the Congress and the Muslim League sat, not one behind the other, but side by side, on the seats behind the driver.

For some time there was confusion. The bus had got heavily crowded partly because some people intended to get down on the way near their houses. Manohar Lal was still throwing tantrums.

'I refuse to sit in a bus in which a communist, a traitor to the country, is sitting.'

Dev Datt, who was standing on the footboard of the bus, said: 'Manohar Lal, we don't mince matters. We are not the tail of the Congress. We are professional revolutionaries. We are working to bring about peaceful conditions in the town and to that end it is necessary to bring together the leaders of all the parties, including your party of which you are the sole follower. We too know who is what; but the need of the hour is to bring all parties on one platform.'

'The peace you are talking about,' said Manohar Lal sardonically, 'has already been brought about by your British master. It was he who instigated the riots, now it is he who is working for peace.'

Standing in the veranda Lala Shyam Lal had begun canvassing for support for the forthcoming Municipal Elections for which he was standing from such and such a ward. In the meanwhile Mangal Sen had jumped into the bus and had gone and sat down in one of the front seats. On seeing him, Lala Shyam Lal, piqued in the extreme, whimpered. 'No one tells me to get into the bus, no one asks me,' and lunged forward, and pushing his way through the bystanders climbed into the bus, breathing hard.

Sitting beside the president of the Muslim League, Bakshiji was looking towards the road, but was feeling extremely sad.

'Kites shall hover, kites and vultures shall continue to hover for long...'

Just then, Murad Ali, sitting next to the driver, began raising slogans and in the midst of resounding slogans the Peace Bus set out on its Peace Mission.

Sitting opposite each other in the soft, mellow light of the dining room, Richard and Liza sat ruminating

over their future plans. Liza had regained her composure.
Richard too had little work to do that day. Life in the
town had begun to move, more or less, on an even keel.
Junior officers had assumed control of their departments.

'I had very much wanted to continue living here, do
a bit of work in the Taxila museum; study the genealogy
of the local inhabitants, but it doesn't seem likely that I
shall live here for long.'

Liza was inwardly pleased to hear the tidings.

'Will you be transferred? Will you be promoted,
Richard?'

Richard smiled. He did not say anything.

'Why don't you tell me? Are you really going to be
promoted?'

'It is not a question of promotion, Liza. If there are
disturbances in a place, the government usually effects
a change of personnel at the higher level, senior officers
are transferred and new officers sent in.'

'Shall we have to leave soon?'

'Perhaps. I do not know for certain.'

'But you said you wanted to live here, to work in
the Taxila museum, didn't you? To write your book...'

Richard shrugged his shoulders. He then lighted his
pipe and, stretching his legs under the table, said,
'Wherefrom should I begin?'

'Begin what, Richard?' said Liza, raising her eyebrows.

'You wanted to know about the developments that
had taken place here, didn't you?'

This time it was Liza who shrugged her shoulders,
as though to say, 'You may or may not, Richard. It makes
little difference.'